THE EUNUCH OF STAMBOUL

*

He had been sent to Istanbul to check rumours of a planned uprising.

But as a spy Destime was an amateur, alone in a city of intrigue and fear, a dark web in whose centre squatted the repulsive form of Kazdim Hari Bekar, formerly a Palace eunuch, now Chief of the Secret Police. A job which admirably suited his own depraved personal tastes.

BY DENNIS WHEATLEY

NOVELS

The Launching of Roger Brook
The Shadow of Tyburn Tree
The Rising Storm
The Man Who Killed the King
The Dark Secret of Josephine
The Rape of Venice
The Sultan's Daughter
The Wanton Princess
Evil in a Mask
The Ravishing of Lady Mary Ware

The Scarlet Impostor
Faked Passports
The Black Baroness
V for Vengeance
Come Into My Parlour
Traitors' Gate
They Used Dark Forces

The Prisoner in the Mask
The Second Seal
Vendetta in Spain
Three Inquisitive People
The Forbidden Territory
The Devil Rides Out
The Golden Spaniard
Strange Conflict
Codeword—Golden Fleece
Dangerous Inheritance

Gateway to Hell

The Quest of Julian Day
The Sword of Fate
Bill for the Use of a Body
Black August

Contraband
The Island Where Time Stands Still
The White Witch of the South Seas

To the Devil—a Daughter
The Satanist

The Eunuch of Stamboul
The Secret War
The Fabulous Valley
Sixty Days to Live
Such Power is Dangerous
Uncharted Seas
The Man Who Missed the War
The Haunting of Toby Jugg
Star of Ill-Omen
They Found Atlantis
The Ka of Gifford Hillary
Curtain of Fear
Mayhem in Greece
Unholy Crusade

SHORT STORIES

Mediterranean Nights

Gunmen, Gallants and Ghosts

HISTORICAL

A Private Life of Charles II (*Illustrated by Frank C. Papé*)
Red Eagle (*The Story of the Russian Revolution*)

AUTOBIOGRAPHICAL

Stranger than Fiction (*War Papers for the Joint Planning Staff*)
Saturdays with Bricks

IN PREPARATION

The Devil and all his Works (*Illustrated in colour*)

Dennis Wheatley

The Eunuch of Stamboul

ARROW BOOKS

ARROW BOOKS LTD

3 Fitzroy Square, London W1

AN IMPRINT OF THE HUTCHINSON GROUP

London Melbourne Sydney Auckland
Wellington Johannesburg Cape Town
and agencies throughout the world

*

First published by
Hutchinson & Co (*Publishers*) Ltd 1935
Arrow edition 1960
Second impression October 1960
Third impression 1963
Fourth impression 1965
This new edition 1972

*Made and printed in Great Britain
by The Anchor Press Ltd,
Tiptree, Essex*

ISBN 0 09 905790 5

CONTENTS

1	A Royal Invitation	9
2	The 'Incident' at Maidenhead	13
3	A Most Distressing Affair	22
4	The Man Without a Job	28
5	The Secret Mission	36
6	The Jealous Lover	47
7	The City of the Sultans	58
8	The Drudgery of the Quest	71
9	The Impulsive Student	80
10	The Tower of Marble	86
11	Old Lamps for New	98
12	The Gifted Amateur Bungles Badly	114
13	The Old, Old Story	124
14	'For Them There are Gardens Beneath which Rivers Flow' (*The Qur'ân*)	137
15	'For These are the Fellows of the Fire and They Shall Burn Therein for Aye' (*The Qur'ân*)	150
16	The Stopped Earth	164
17	Trapped	173
18	The Desolate City	187
19	The Lion's Mouth	199
20	Cocktails for Two	208
21	The Cat With Nine Lives	216
22	Love at the Sweet Waters	230

23   The Man Hunt   252

24   When the Heart is Young   268

25   The Plain Van   288

26   Two Go Home   303

I

A Royal Invitation

If the postman who served the southern side of Belgrave
Square that summer had not been a 'lewd fellow of the
baser sort', many things might have panned out differently.

It is doubtful if Diana Duncannon would have met a
certain distinguished foreigner who was then visiting
London. Swithin Destime might have terminated his
career, unusually brilliant to that date, as Chief of the
Imperial General Staff. The life of an elderly Russian lady,
then living in Constantinople as a refugee, might have
been considerably prolonged, and a number of other
people might not have had the misfortune to lose theirs in
the flower of their youth. The Turkish Government would
have found itself—but there, the postman *was* a 'lewd
fellow of the baser sort' and, strange as it may seem, it is
just upon such delicate matters as the glandular secretions
of postmen and their moral reactions to the same that the
destinies of human beings and the fate of nations hang.

During the early months of the summer this otherwise
estimable minor Civil Servant had felt the urge to toy in
gentle dalliance with the under housemaid at number 56.
The young woman had permitted what are legally termed
'certain familiarities' and then, one evening towards the end
of Ascot Week, learned that the postman possessed a wife
and seven sons. If she had wept out her heart upon the
broad bosom of the cook, all might have been well, but
instead, dry-eyed and silent, the poor girl went upstairs,
swallowed a quantity of disinfectant, and collapsed upon
the floor of Lady Duncannon's bathroom.

A doctor was sent for, restoratives applied, and the girl's
life pronounced out of danger. All might yet have ended
there but for the fact that Lady Duncannon, who was a dear
motherly soul, refused to leave her house that night with
one of her staff in such a sad condition.

Her husband, Sir George, knew her too well to argue
with her decision despite his annoyance; they were both

9

expected at a Foreign Office dinner in honour of His Serene Highness the Prince Ali, a nephew of the late Sultan, within the hour and, as Sir George was the head of a famous international Banking House and many of his most important interests were in the Near East, it was certain that his wife and he would be placed at the top table. It was unthinkable that any seat so near the illustrious visitor should be left unoccupied; there was no time to telephone to the Foreign Office and suggest a re-arrangement of the tables so a substitute for Lady Duncannon obviously had to be found. Sir George, his dress trousers bagging about his knees and such hair as remained to him feathering his polished skull, came out upon the landing in his shirt sleeves and called loudly for his daughter.

Had Diana Duncannon lived in Queen Anne's day she would have been a reigning toast. As it was she was just known as 'a pretty decent looking girl'. But when she ran downstairs from the floor above to answer her father's summons, she was hardly decent and, had they seen her, the beaux of the early eighteenth century would have been shaken to their buckled shoes.

She also had been dressing, since she was going that night to dine with a party at the Guards' Boat Club at Maidenhead and afterwards to participate in the Ascot Dance. A dressing-gown disguised her slender figure but failed to conceal certain portions of her delicious limbs. Her hair had been pushed up under an ugly net and her delicate complexion was smothered under a hideous coating of grease.

Her father stated the position briefly and after a momentary frown of annoyance she shrugged her slim shoulders, blinked through the shiny mask and said :

'All right, Daddy. I'll telephone to Peter and you'll have to send me down later in the car. I suppose I'll be able to get away about ten.'

And so the die was cast. Three quarters of an hour later Sir George was announced at the Foreign Office reception with a very different Diana on his arm. Tall, slim, sheathed in glittering satin, her auriol of pale gold hair swept back and curling upon her small fine head, she was presented by Mrs. Hazeltine, the wife of her father's friend, the Foreign

Office official who was responsible for the function, to a tall dark muscular gentleman in quite perfect evening dress, upon whose breast glittered a great diamond star and a constellation of miniature medals; General His Serene Highness the Prince Ali, Emir of Konia and Grand Commander of the Star and Crescent.

The dinner was the usual affair of its kind, brilliant to look down on from a balcony but dull for the majority of the guests. An English diplomat made a charming speech in which he said all sorts of nice meaningless things about Turkey, and Prince Ali responded in excellent English saying, with equal charm, all sorts of nice meaningless things about Britain.

After the banquet the Prince was escorted back to the reception rooms. Sir George and his daughter, having been seated near him, were among the first to follow, and Diana was just thinking that she would soon be able to slip away when the royal guest flashed a quick smile at the woman to whom he was talking, broke off the conversation, and strode over to her and her father.

He bowed to Sir George and murmured affably: 'Your name figures so frequently in our financial counsels that I am delighted to have the pleasure of meeting you now.' Then, adjusting his monocle, he turned immediately to Diana. 'Permit me to compliment you, Miss Duncannon. You are, I think, the loveliest woman I have seen during my visit to London.'

Diana was well aware that her dark eyes beneath long, narrow eyebrows gave her a distinctive beauty, contrasting as they did with her fair complexion and pale gold hair, but it was embarrassing to be told so quite so brazenly. Her glance fell from the haughty, well-marked olive features of the Turkish Prince to his waistline, so narrow that one might almost have suspected him of wearing corsets, and a long cigar that he was holding. Half unconsciously she noticed that for so tall a man his hand was surprisingly small—plump, sensitive, womanish—and that the index finger was distinctly crooked.

Without waiting for her to reply he turned back to Sir George and went on smoothly in his well-modulated voice which only held the faintest trace of foreign accent: 'The round of official engagements makes private arrangements

11

difficult during my short stay, but I should like to see more of you, and a little private party tonight would be a pleasant relaxation to me. Mr. Hazeltine!—Mustapha!'

The Foreign Office official and the Turkish Equerry hastened up, and although as the Prince addressed the Englishman his words were couched in a form of a request, his tone had all the imperiousness of a command.

'Would it not be possible for us to go on somewhere from here—to the Embassy or the Florida perhaps. Sir George Duncannon and his daughter will, I am sure, honour me by being our guests.'

Diana could not help feeling just a little flattered that the royal visitor should single her out for his special attention. It was obvious that he wanted to dance with her. He would never have selected a night-club if he were anxious to talk with her father on finance. But the blatant admiration in the Prince's dark, intelligent eyes warned her that she might be taking on a little more than she could handle and she had already caught an uneasy glance from Sir George so she said quickly:

'Your Highness is most kind, but I must ask you to excuse me. I already have a party expecting me at the Guards' Boat Club Dance, so I am leaving almost at once for Maidenhead.' The shadow of a frown darkened Prince Ali's rather heavy features for a second and he passed a plump hand over his thick, smooth, black hair. Then his face lightened and he turned again to Hazeltine.

'I heard this dance mentioned when I was entertained by the officers to lunch in the mess at Aldershot yesterday. The Club is a charming place with gardens by the river—is it not? Perhaps this evening they would extend their hospitality to myself and my suite?'

Hazeltine bowed slightly. 'I am sure sir, that the officers would be honoured to have you as their guest.'

'Would you be good enough to arrange the matter please.' Prince Ali gave a little wriggle of his neck above the stiff white collar and glanced again at Diana. He was smiling now and his smile said many things.

'We shall meet later then,' he announced affably. 'The night is fine, so there is every promise of a pleasant evening, and you will be so kind as to show me your beautiful Thames.'

2

The 'Incident' at Maidenhead

For once the English climate had really favoured Royal
Ascot and no more perfect setting could have been found
for a dance that night than the Guards' Boat Club at
Maidenhead.

The lawn and gardens were illuminated by the soft glow
of chains of fairy lamps strung from tree to tree. Here and
there shadowy patches, where couples might conveniently
linger, had been discreetly left unlit, and at the bottom of
the gardens the waters of the Thames, rippling only under
the prow of an occasional boat seeming to glide out of a
land of dreams, flowed gently on their way.

When Diana arrived, the dance was already in full swing.
A number had just ended, the crowd was streaming out of
the lighted windows on to the lawn or congregating in
little groups about the entrance of the ball-room.

Her father and Frank Hazeltine were with her. Both had
considered it their duty to put in an appearance as Prince
Ali was coming down and, since the banker and the Foreign
Office man were often confronted with similar problems
regarding policy in the Near East, neither was displeased
at the prospect of a talk over a brandy and soda in a quiet
corner while the younger people danced.

Peter Carew, with whom Diana had been going in the
first place, had judged the time of her arrival and was
waiting in the doorway to meet her. He was a tall fair young
man, an ensign still, having only been with his regiment a
little over a year. Not overburdened with brains, he possessed charming manners and a delightful personality.

Handing her a programme, he secured a few dances for
himself and led her inside, where she was soon surrounded
by a little group of men, most of whom she had met before.
Her programme was nearly full when Peter thrust his way
back through the press with a short wiry little man of about
thirty-five.

13

'Diana,' he said. 'May I introduce Captain Swithin Destime, the Adjutant of my Battalion? He saw us talking together in the enclosure on Gold Cup Day and when he heard you were coming tonight he was terribly keen to meet you.'

'That's perfectly true,' Swithin Destime admitted with a quick smile. 'And I've been on tenterhooks all the evening because it looked as if you weren't going to turn up after all. May I have a dance?'

As Diana handed him her programme she glanced at him again. He had a bluish chin which could obviously have sprouted a passable beard in a week if he had stopped shaving, a dark moustache brushed smartly upwards, a pair of the bluest eyes that she had ever seen, and a thin, hawk-like nose set below a wide forehead and curling black hair. There could be no doubt that he was English, but his quick restless movements and smiling dare-devil eyes, in addition to his name which was obviously a corruption from the French, made her certain that he had quite a bit of Latin blood in him.

'Number seven—that's the next,' he said swiftly. 'And may I take nine as well? There doesn't seem much else left does there?'

'That's because I happen to know so many people here,' she smiled. 'But you may have them both if you like.'

'Thanks.' His bluish chin tilted and his quick eyes laughed into hers. 'But your programme would be just as full if you'd arrived here with an ancient chaperone and knowing no one. There's the band starting now. Shall we dance?'

'Yes, let's.'

They were just about to move off when Diana saw Prince Ali being led into the room by General Lord Edward Bennington, the senior member of the Club Committee present.

Immediately the Prince caught sight of her he left Lord Edward with almost indecent haste and walked stiffly over to the corner where she was standing. Swithin Destime politely stood aside as the tall Turk took Diana's programme, screwed his monocle more firmly into his eye, and ran his glance over the heavily pencilled card.

He made no comment that it was already full, but calmly

struck a line through four sets of initials, then handed it back with a haughty little smile.

'I see that this is number seven,' he observed. 'But I should like a glass of wine before I dance, so I have taken numbers nine, ten, eleven and twelve. Had you had the kindness to remember that I came here especially to dance with you, it would not be necessary for you to apologise to these gentlemen whom I am compelled to rob of your company.'

Swithin Destime's blue eyes suddenly went hard and cold. 'Number nine . . .' he said icily, but Diana intervened before he had time to say more.

'Your Highness, may I present Captain Swithin Destime.'

For a second the two men stared at each other angrily. Then Swithin lowered his eyes. 'I'm sorry, sir,' he said. 'I had not realised . . .'

The Prince gave a curt nod and turned away.

As Swithin and Diana moved off across the floor, he smiled again. 'I nearly put my foot in it that time didn't I? Who is this dago Prince, or am I being rude about a friend of yours?'

'Not a bit, and I'm terribly sorry that I shall have to cut your second dance.' Diana proceeded to explain, and he nodded thoughtfully:

'Well, if he's a "Royal" I suppose he's entitled to ride rough-shod over all of us, especially as he is a guest of the Club. But if it were anyone else I'd see them damned before I let them rob me of that second dance you were good enough to give me. If there's a third extra perhaps you would let me have that instead.'

'Certainly I will,' she assured him. 'Really I've no wish to dance with Prince Ali. He's probably an awful bore, but in addition to being a prince he is such a big bug in Turkish affairs just now and so many of my father's business interests are in the Near East that it might make it awkward for him if I refused to dance with the man at all.'

'Have you ever been out there—to Constantinople I mean?'

'Yes, several times with father in the yacht.'

'How did you like it?'

'I loved the old palaces and mosques, but some of the slums are pretty grim.'

'I know,' he agreed. 'The East doesn't change much really although they say that Mustapha Kemal is making a big difference there now.'

'Do you know it then?' she asked with interest.

'Yes, I was in the country for some time just after the War, and five years ago I put in a few months there before I qualified as interpreter in Turkish, Arabic and Greek.'

'Dear me, you are a clever person!' She caught the swift glance of his quick intelligent eyes again.

'Not really,' he almost apologised. 'But these are so many things that can be useful to a soldier outside the ordinary training for his job, and it just happens that I am pretty keen.'

As the music stopped he led her through to another room where they found a comfortable corner and sat down.

'Tell me some more about this Turkish Prince,' he went on after a moment. 'I like to get all the dope I can about his part of the world.'

'I don't know much really,' she confessed: 'except what I heard my father and Mr. Hazeltine say about him in the car coming down from London tonight. He is a General of course, and I gather one of considerable ability. Mustapha Kemal is said to think very highly of him and looks on him as one of his right-hand men. That is what makes him so important to us in one way, but he has got a foot on the other side of the fence as well because he is a nephew of the ex-Sultan, and all the old Turkish party who hate Mustapha Kemal's innovations respect him on that account.'

'By jove! I should have been in a fine mess if you hadn't stopped me being downright rude to him then—if he's as big a bug as all that. How old is he I wonder?'

Diana shrugged. 'About forty, I should think. It is difficult to tell with Orientals. He may be a good bit more but he can't be much less because Frank Hazeltine was saying that he served with distinction in the War.'

At that moment, to Swithin's intense annoyance, the band struck up again. The dance to which he had looked forward so much ever since he had learned from Peter Carew that Diana was coming that evening was over all too soon. It seemed that they had hardly exchanged a dozen words, but as she stood up he made the most of his opportunity.

'Look here,' he said: 'say there isn't a third extra, I'm going to ask you for compensation. If I get Peter and another girl to make a four, would you dine one night and do a show? I'd look forward to it tremendously if you would.'

His vivid blue eyes held hers for a moment and she nodded. 'Yes, why not? If I have to dance four dances with Prince Ali it is I who shall need some compensation, and I should enjoy that.'

'Thank you most awfully.' They had reached the doorway of the ballroom and as he spoke she was carried away from him by an impatient partner.

Not being a keen dancer he had few other names on his card and for the next three he was free so he joined some other men at the buffet. Prince Ali was quite near him, punishing the champagne.

Three other Turks had accompanied the Prince down from London. One, a fat-faced, jolly-looking fellow was laughing with him and keeping his glass well supplied. The other two stood a little in the background watching him intently and Swithin happened to overhear a fragment of their conversation.

'If he drinks much more he is going to become troublesome,' said one morosely, and the other nodded.

'Yes, it's extraordinary how vicious he can be when he lets himself go on champagne. He becomes so damned unreasonable, and I'd rather be back at Brusa with my regiment than have the job of trying to coax him into behaving properly when he gets like that.'

Peter Carew came up to Swithin at that moment so he heard no more, but he observed a little later that General Lord Edward Bennington was beside the Prince asking if he would not like to dance. To which Prince Ali replied with the barest civility that he had no intention of doing so yet.

'Are you dancing the next one, Peter?' Swithin asked.

'No, worse luck. My leg's not fit yet from a fall I had last week so I've got to go easy on the dancing and limit myself to a couple each with a few young women that I like. Why?'

'Only that I'm not either and I thought we might stroll down to the river for a breath of air. What about it?'

'By all means if you like.' Peter finished his drink and the two men sauntered out into the garden.

Immediately the band broke into the opening bars of number nine Prince Ali abandoned the champagne at the buffet in search of other pleasures. He had ordered one of his aides-de-camp to keep Diana in sight. Directly her whereabouts were reported he joined her and, placing a strong right arm firmly round her waist, swept her away across the floor.

His height gave him an easy command of the passages which opened out among the kaleidoscopic throng and she admitted to herself at once that he danced divinely. She soon found too that he could throw off his abruptly haughty manner when he chose to do so.

After one turn round the floor he had her laughing at his description of an elderly General whom he had met at Aldershot the day before. A nice old gentleman whose mentality had not advanced since he had posted his last vedette as a cavalry subaltern in the South African War. Then to her surprise he told her that he was a hopeless sailor and had been terribly sick when crossing the channel. That he should confess to any weakness seemed to make him infinitely more human. For the rest of the dance he entertained her with shrewd, witty criticisms upon a number of people who had been present at the Foreign Office dinner that evening, and although she had at first disliked him, she had to admit to herself that he had both brains and charm.

As the music ceased he swung her in a last graceful pirouette, released her swiftly, made a semi-mocking bow and then, catching her arm again, led her with quick decisive steps out into the garden.

The two Turkish A.D.C.s whom Swithin had noticed near the buffet were standing together by the window. Seeing the Prince go out, one made a rueful little grimace to the other and then they both followed at a distance.

As Diana and Prince Ali crossed the lawn he took her hand and drew it through his arm. She tried half-heartedly to withdraw it but he gave it a gentle pat of protest and murmured:

'Now please; you are far too nice to be unkind. Think of all the hard work which I have to do here. These boring official receptions, the old women and the stupid men I have to talk to. Surely, you would not rob me of these few moments of charming relaxation?'

Her sympathy was aroused at once. He was quite a nice person really she decided, and she had often thought that it could not be much fun to be a royalty—passing one's days and nights in one long succession of dull duties. Why should she not treat him like a human being and let him hold her hand if he wanted to.

At the river bank he paused, looking down for a moment at the dark, smoothly flowing waters. Then he said suddenly: 'If only we had been in Istanbul I would have ordered a launch to be in readiness and carried you off to supper with me.'

Diana laughed a little nervously. His tone was bantering, but there was just the faintest timbre in his voice which suggested that he meant exactly what he said. She was exceedingly thankful that they were not in Turkey for, despite his admirable European attire, his eyes spoke the unmistakable language of the Oriental and she had no certainty as to what he meant to imply the generic term of 'supper'. She knew instinctively too that he would have cared nothing for her point of view or any scandal which might have resulted had they been standing on the edge of the Bosphorus instead of the Thames.

He took her arm again and turning, gently propelled her along the river bank, until they came to a little arbour which stood almost hidden in the shadow of a group of trees.

'We will sit here,' he said, 'and smoke a cigarette.'

To Diana's relief the music started again just then so she did not sit down but replied quickly: 'No, you dance so beautifully that I do not want to miss one moment of the band. I would much rather go back to the ballroom.'

'Thank you,' he smiled, obviously pleased by her flattery but not to be lured away from his purpose. 'We will dance again later if you wish. I prefer now that we should stay here.'

'Then I must get my coat,' she parried. 'By the river here it's quite cold.'

As she spoke she glanced back over her shoulder at the lighted windows of the Club. The lawn was almost empty and in the distance the guests were hurrying back into the ballroom. The heavy shadows of the trees hid the little arbour in which they stood from all but two men, the Prince's A.D.C.'s who were standing near some bushes about twenty yards away.

'Cold? But I will make you warm,' he laughed suddenly and his voice had a little guttural note which made her catch her breath in fear. Then before she could reply her slender body was gripped tightly in his powerful arms.

'Please!' she gasped, throwing back her head with a jerk. 'Please!' But he only laughed again and she felt his hot breath on her cheek. Then his mouth was pressed down firmly upon her own.

She beat her clenched fists on his shoulders and tried to force him away but he gave a grunting chuckle and buried his face gluttonously in the curve of her white neck.

'Stop!' she flared at him. 'Let me go—D'you hear? Let me go!' She tried to keep her voice low, dreading the scandal if someone came upon them with her struggling in his arms, but despite herself she had raised it to a higher pitch in her excitement and next moment everything seemed to happen at once.

She caught the sound of running feet on a nearby path that led further in among the bushes. Prince Ali was wrenched backwards and she fell against a tree. She heard his collar stud snap as his assailant hauled him from her by the neck.

The Prince swung round and lashed out at the man who had attacked him. Small, lithe, panther-like, only the greyish blob of his face and his white-front showing in the semi-darkness, the other sprang at him and they crashed to the ground together.

The two A.D.C.'s rushed forward and hauled the little man off. Then another figure entered the fray. A tall man who promptly laid out one of the A.D.C.'s. The other was yelling at the top of his voice for help.

Prince Ali was on his feet again. Diana caught one

glimpse of his face, distorted by furious rage as he staggered past her and launched himself at his original assailant.

For a moment the *mêlée* became general. Then the lawn was full of running figures. A dozen, two dozen, fifty newcomers seemed to throw themselves into a sort of rugby scrum.

There were shouts of 'Stop that! . . . Hi! Hang on to him! . . . Who is it! . . . For God's sake keep quiet can't you!' and the five combatants were dragged forcibly apart.

Diana, her dress badly torn where Prince Ali had caught at it as he was wrenched away from her, leaned panting against the tree. She was utterly horrified now at the thought of the scandal which was certain to result from this unseemly fracas. Then, with fresh distress, she recognised the two men who had attacked the Prince and his aides-de-camp as Peter Carew and Swithin Destime.

Prince Ali was still struggling with the men who had intervened. A little trickle of blood ran down his cheek from a cut which he had sustained in his fall. His eyes glared murder at the Englishman.

Swithin stood with tight-shut mouth eyeing him stonily a few feet away. He had heard a girl shouting and come to her assistance without the faintest idea as to the identity of the man he was attacking. Now in a flash he realised to the full the enormity of the thing that he had done. No matter what the justification for his act might be, he, a British officer, had knocked down a guest in his own Club, and that guest was no less a person than General His Highness Prince Ali, the Envoy Extraordinary of a foreign power who was receiving the hospitality of the country. Swithin knew only too well that there was going to be real trouble for him before he heard the end of this.

3

A Most Distressing Affair

General Lord Edward Bennington, tall, grey-haired and stooping a little, a worried frown on his lined face, walked slowly into the small card-room at the back of the Club. Frank Hazeltine followed and closed the door quietly behind him.

The five men who were already assembled there glanced at Lord Edward's face with carefully concealed anxiety. Peter Carew, a trifle white and rather sullen-looking, was leaning over the back of a chair; Swithin Destime, his legs spread wide apart, one hand thrust deep into his trouser pocket and the other toying with an unlit cigarette, stood near him; their Commanding Officer, Lieutenant-Colonel Kerr-Crighton, a little brown man whose upturned moustache and aquiline nose made him appear not unlike an older edition of Swithin, sat perched on the edge of the table. Sir George Duncannon and Major Faulkner Wilde, a tubby fellow with beetling eyebrows who was a member of the Club Committee, completed the party.

'Well, he's gone,' announced Lord Edward. 'And I don't think I've ever seen a man display a more evil temper.'

Sir George, his hands clasped behind his back, had been thoughtfully studying the pattern of the carpet. He looked swiftly at Hazeltine.

'So you failed to persuade him to come in here for a moment, Frank?'

The Foreign Office man shook his head gloomily. 'I did what I could, but he would not listen to any suggestion of an apology.'

Colonel Kerr-Crighton's hot little eyes nearly popped out of his head with indignation. 'Apology be damned!' he snorted. 'The fellow ought to be made to crawl himself.'

'Now, Toby,' Lord Edward protested quickly; 'we all know that he behaved like a cad, but he happened to be a guest of the Club and a visiting royalty to boot. Whatever the rights of the matter it would obviously have been to the best interests of the two officers concerned if the Prince had consented to accept the apology they were willing to make.'

'I cannot say how distressed I am that my daughter should have been the innocent cause of this unfortunate incident,' Sir George put in with evident feeling. Then turning to Peter and Swithin he added: 'I can only repeat that the manner in which the two of you went to her assistance was most chivalrous—most chivalrous.'

Lord Edward stared at Swithin through his monocle. 'I am a little in the dark as to what actually did take place. Would you mind giving me the facts as you know them.'

'Certainly, sir. Carew and I were walking round the garden for a breath of air between dances. As we came out of the bushes at the end of the lower path the lawn was practically deserted and just on our right in that little arbour I heard a girl fighting and struggling with a man. It was obvious from her voice that they weren't just fooling but that something pretty nasty was going on. I caught a glimpse of her dress and of the fellow's back. He was a tall chap, but all cats are grey in the dark and I had not the faintest idea that it was Prince Ali. Anyhow, I grabbed him by the neck and pulled him off. He turned and hit out at me, so I slogged him under the chin. Next moment two of his A.D.C.'s dashed up and then Carew entered the scrum as well. He laid one of them out and the other started to yell for help. The Prince was on his feet again by that time and had me round the body. Then a whole crowd of people came on the scene and we were pulled apart.'

'So you actually knocked him down,' said Lord Edward thoughtfully.

'Yes, sir, I knocked him down,' repeated Swithin, and the faintest suggestion of unholy glee flickered in his bright blue eyes for an instant.

Frank Hazeltine coughed discreetly. 'I do not think we need stress that point. In fact, the fewer details that are mentioned about this affair, even among ourselves, the better.'

'Among ourselves, Hazeltine, I sincerely trust we can say what we damn well please,' remarked Lord Edward with some asperity. 'As the senior member of the Club Committee present it is my duty to make myself acquainted with the facts.'

Major Faulkner Wilde drew slowly upon his cigar. 'I'm afraid, sir, that most of the details are pretty public already. Much as we should like to do so it is beyond our power to hush this wretched business up. At least fifty people must actually have seen them scrapping. Let's face it. The story still be all over London by midday tomorrow.'

'Well, if this damn dago refuses to accept an apology I don't see what more we can do about it,' declared the bellicose little Colonel.

'But will the matter be allowed to rest here?' inquired Lord Edward. 'What do you think, Hazeltine?'

The diplomat smoothed his long silky moustache. 'I take rather a grave view,' he said after a moment. 'You see, not only is Prince Ali of royal blood and a nephew of the ex-Sultan, but he is also a high official in the Turkish War Office. We might get round one of those points, but it is trying them rather high to expect them to overlook both. I cannot express any definite opinion at the moment, but it is only fair to say that Captain Destime and Mr. Carew may have to consider the advisability of resigning from their regiment.'

'What!' snapped the Colonel.

'Damn it all! that's bit hard.' Major Faulkner Wilde's bushy eyebrows shot up in astonished distress towards his bald forehead.

'No, no, Frank . . .' Sir George began in protest, but the choleric little fighting Colonel was off again in defence of his officers.

'It's preposterous! I've never heard of such a thing.' He thumped the table with a small, very hard, fist. 'D'you mean to tell me that because some garlic eating bounder comes down here and behaves like a rank outsider that I'm to be robbed of two of my officers who're well up to their jobs. I won't have it! By God I won't! Not if I have to go on the mat myself in front of the Army Council.'

Peter Carew forgot that he was endeavouring to appear natural and unconcerned by leaning on the chair back. At first he had been a little scared by this solemn meeting. It was as though he were back at Wellington, still a fourth form boy who had been called on to give an account of himself in some escapade at a prefect's meeting. He saw now that, whatever the outcome of the affair, the sympathy of the Olympians was with himself and Swithin. No horrid scene was therefore to be expected in which his father, his aunts and his grandmother would go into some awful family conference to reprove him for the error of his ways. He abandoned the chair back and stood upright.

Hazeltine endeavoured to pacify the Colonel by raising a deprecatory hand. 'No foreign power can demand the resignation of a British officer,' he said a trifle unctuously. 'It is unthinkable that we should allow ourselves to be dictated to in such a manner, but on the other hand, in view of our relations with the Turkish Government it might be considered expedient for the officers concerned voluntarily to send in their papers.'

'Damn the Turkish Government!' exclaimed the Colonel heatedly.

'My dear Frank,' Sir George broke in; 'the banking activities of my firm in the Near East enable me to appreciate the fact that Prince Ali is a most important figure in Turkish national life. But I cannot think that because of this disgraceful incident any question can arise of two promising young officers being ruined in order to give him a satisfaction to which he has not the faintest right. He should be the first desire to hush the whole thing up.'

Hazeltine shrugged. 'I sincerely trust that their resignation will not be considered necessary. But unfortunately Prince Ali has no more power to hush this matter up than we have. It has gone too far. An opinion was expressed a few moments ago that the story will be all over London by tomorrow and I associate myself entirely with that view. I have already given a guarded account of the affair to the Permanent Secretary for Foreign Affairs, over the telephone, and he, of course, will consult the Minister. It will depend on his decision whether we can afford to ignore the matter as though it had never taken place, or if he feels that some gesture should be made to placate the Turkish Government for what they may well assume to have been a deliberate assault on one of their most prominent men.'

'That is the devil of it,' Lord Edward growled. 'If this fellow proves vindictive, he will distort the whole story and spin some yarn of having endeavoured to intervene himself between Miss Duncannon and two drunken young officers who proceeded to knock him down.'

'Yes,' agreed Hazeltine quietly. 'That is more or less what I have in mind.'

'No, no. He'll come to his senses by the time he gets home,' Sir George protested reassuringly. 'His two A.D.C.'s witnessed the whole occurrence and they are probably gentlemen even if he is not. Most of the Turks I know are fine fellows. If they are any good at their job they will talk him into being thoroughly ashamed of himself and urge him to forget the whole affair.'

For a good quarter of an hour the elder men continued to discuss the situation, the argument swaying first one way and then another. Swithin watched them and listened to the debate with a certain sense of unreality. He had no father such as Peter's and very little family to be bothered about. Yet his future was a very important thing to him. He could hardly realise that it was *his* career which was hanging in the balance. It seemed rather as though he were witnessing again the Club scene in Galsworthy's play 'Loyalties', in which a few nice elderly English gentlemen, who are in reality profoundly distressed, conceal their emotions with the outward calm that generations of tradition have imposed upon them—and discuss the fate of a junior member of their order.

In this case Swithin knew that he had all their sympathy and understanding. But there were rules in this game of life; sometimes unfair perhaps, but not to be broken even accidentally without the payment of a penalty. As he thought of all the long years of work that he had put in, the routine of everyday service, the interesting courses, the leaves spent in acquiring special knowledge, all to make himself a pretty useful soldier who would one day be really fitted for command, his thin mouth tightened under the small upturned moustache.

A Club waiter entered and said: 'Mr. Hazeltine is wanted on the telephone.'

'You will excuse me.' Apparently unhurried but with his long legs covering the distance to the door quite swiftly

Hazeltine left them. The others stood there for a few moments in silence.

When the diplomat returned he said slowly: 'I am afraid the news is not very good. Prince Ali stopped his car in Slough and spoke to his Embassy on the telephone. Apparently they have been raising Cain already. The Foreign Secretary seems to think that some gesture must be made unless all the good work which we have put in during the Prince's visit is to go for nothing. Needless to say, I cannot sufficiently express my personal regret for the situation in which these gentlemen find themselves.'

4

The Man Without a Job

Swithin Destime sat up in bed and took fresh stock of
his unfamiliar surroundings. It was the first morning that
he had woken in the narrow bedroom of the rather dingy
hotel near the Adelphi which he felt, with his now uncer-
tain financial prospects, was the best accommodation anywhere in central London that he could afford.

His guns, rods, books, and a whole mass of miscellaneous
belongings, accumulated over a long period of years, lay
scattered in the corners and piled against the walls, just
as the porter had left them on his arrival the previous
afternoon after taking leave of his old quarters in Wellington Barracks.

The sympathy of his friends had been poured out in
abundance and he had been no less touched by his bat-
man's murmured expression of just what he would like to
do to 'that 'ere ruddy wop' than by his fiery Colonel's
blasphemous denunciation of 'these snivelling politicians
who kowtow to any damned foreigner'. But that was not
very helpful now.

Swithin was thirty-five and jobless. His father had
settled on him just sufficient funds to provide the few
pounds a week private income which an unwritten regula-
tion demands that every officer in the Brigade of Guards
should possess; then died, practically penniless, having
sunk the remainder of his capital in an annuity. Swithin
knew that his record as an Army officer must be considered
as a liability rather than an asset in seeking civilian employ-
ment. Yet if he could find nothing the appalling prospect
opened up of endless empty days, eking out his tiny income, cheese-paring in some ghastly boarding-house, and a
gradual decline to shabby gentility while he ate his heart
out for some active occupation.

However, despite his financial instability, it was charac-
teristic of the man that he had not hesitated to spend fifteen

pounds the night before. He had claimed Diana Duncannon's promise that in compensation for the loss of his second dance, she would dine and do a theatre with him, and had rung her up the day after the affair at Maidenhead to ask her to fix a date.

She had chosen one ten days ahead and by the merest chance it had turned out to be the day upon which Peter Carew and Swithin had said good-bye to their Regiment. That it should be so tickled the latter's sense of humour mightily. Peter had produced another girl and the four had deliberately gone out to cast dull care aside.

Peter, with the ease of youth, had taken the blow to his military ambitions better than Swithin had hoped. His father, a retired Major-General, had married the daughter of a Baronet whose forebears had supplied the worthies of three counties with beer for several generations, so there was no lack of money in the family. He talked now with considerable gusto of travelling the world and doing a dozen different things which had previously been impossible owing to his military duties.

The two girls had been a little silent at first. Knowing what had taken place that day they had been nervous of striking a false note by attempting any spurious gaiety, but Swithin's irrepressible vivacity had soon carried them over the line and turned what might have been a grim and funeral party into a hectic and uproarious evening.

Diana had sought to probe him as to his future plans but he was most desperately anxious that she should not blame herself in any way for what had happened and above all learn nothing of his true position, so he had spoken airily of a projected fishing expedition to Norway and, to set her mind at rest, had even fabricated the existence of an immensely rich uncle whose joy in life it would henceforth be to see that his nephew lacked for nothing.

He had planted the story of his imminent departure for Norway deliberately, in order that she should not think it strange if he did not ring her up again for, much as he would like to do so, he knew that he could not possibly afford to take her about in the manner to which she was accustomed, and that to see more of her under such difficult circumstances was only to court future misery for himself.

Swithin reached for a cigarette from the box on his bed-side table and, wrenching his thoughts from the charming subject of Diana, forced himself to face again the grim problem of what he was going to do.

He was too old to start in any of the ordinary professions even if his brain were still sufficiently plastic to absorb masses of new knowledge in arduous university courses. His commercial experience was absolutely nil so he would be lucky if he could even persuade a business magnate to entrust him with a bag of samples. He could go abroad of course but that did not offer the prospects that it had in the days before the War. Then, a fellow of his parts might have found a billet somewhere up country in the tropics, overseeing native labour, which carried sufficient pay to ensure a decent time during long leaves to England and a pension at the end of a term of years if one could survive the fever; but all that had been altered, modern sanitation minimised the risk of disease in such places and wireless enabled the big companies to control their subordinates from offices in London. They no longer needed men who were willing to shoulder responsibility and act on their own initiative now that every problem could be submitted day by day over the ether to headquarters. Young boys were sent out instead and the pay for most jobs in these outposts of Empire had dropped enormously in consequence.

He might work as a crammer perhaps, licking young cubs into shape before they went to Sandhurst, but he had nothing like enough capital to start a place of that kind on his own and to become a sort of under-usher did not seem to offer much of a life to a man of his temperament.

Suddenly the telephone shrilled beside his bed. He picked up the receiver and Diana's voice came, joyous with youth and life, over the line.

'Hullo,' she said. 'Is that Swithin Destime?'

'Yes,' he answered, his depression lifting in a moment. 'You are up early after last night.'

'Why—did I wake you?'

'No—I've been awake some time.'

'Listen,' she went on urgently; 'I want you to come to tea today—before you see father—about half-past four. Will that be all right?'

'But I'm not seeing your father,' he replied in some surprise.

'Aren't you?' Diana sounded doubtful. 'Perhaps you haven't had his letter yet—but it's in the post—he has just told me so. He has asked you to call here at five o'clock.'

Swithin hesitated for a second. To allow himself to become involved with her further, as things were at the moment, was sheer madness. Yet the temptation to accept was enormous—and if her father had asked to see him. . . .

'All right,' he said. 'In that case I'd like to—ever so much.'

'Good—four-thirty then,' she repeated and rang off.

Swithin sent down for his mail at once and among it there was a letter from Sir George Duncannon which read:

My dear Destime,

As you are doubtless aware Bankers have certain facilities for ascertaining the financial situation of their friends and I hope you will not consider it a gross impertinence that I have informed myself regarding yours. If excuse is needed believe mine to be a very real concern at the situation in which recent events have placed you.

I imagine that you will wish to secure some remunerative position at an early date and if you have not been fortunate enough to make your plans already I have an opening to offer which you might at least care to consider.

It is not a job which you need scruple to accept from any idea that I am offering it with a view to compensating you for the loss you have sustained through your service to my daughter since, although the pay is high, many people might hesitate before accepting it.

If you would care to hear more of the matter perhaps you could call at Belgrave Square tomorrow at five o'clock or, if that time is inconvenient to you, and you will telephone, we could arrange another appointment.
Yours, etc.

Recalling the fact that the Banker's firm had constant dealings with the Near East Swithin suddenly realised that they might well have a job for a man with his knowledge of Greek and Turkish. At the thought his mercurial spirits went up with a bound and he leapt out of bed. By the time he had shaved he was visualising himself as the traditional clerk who rises to a position of importance, saves his firm at a time of crisis, and marries the Chairman's daughter.

Overflowing with good spirits and vitality he presented himself at half-past four that afternoon at the house in Belgrave Square and was shown at once into the small sitting-room that was Diana's special sanctum.

She was busily tapping away at a typewriter but she rose at once to meet him and exclaimed, as her glance took in his neat lounge suit, 'How nice you look in grey. Do you realise that I've never seen you, except in evening dress, before today?'

His blue eyes twinkled. 'Nor I you, yet we seem to have known each other for ages—don't we?'

'Yes, I feel that way too,' she beckoned him over to the sofa and as he sat down he nodded towards the typewriter:

'What's the great work. Are you writing a novel? Everyone seems to these days.'

'No—just some private papers of father's. I help him now and then by typing out anything which is especially confidential.'

He took her hand and carefully examined the finger tips.

'If you're looking to see if typing has worn down my nails you needn't worry,' she laughed. 'I protect them with rubber thimbles.'

'No,' he declared earnestly. 'I was seeking inspiration in case I ever sit down to write a novel myself.'

'What—in my hands?'

'Yes, they say that the art of the game lies in accurate observation and one of the things to observe must surely be your heroine's hands. You know—"her tapering fingers strayed among his curling hair"—sort of thing. It would have been awful if yours had been short and fat but fortunately they look quite up to the heroine standard.'

'Swithin, you are an idiot!' As she pulled away her hand they burst into simultaneous laughter.

Tea arrived at that moment and Diana began to pour out, but paused with the teapot suspended in mid-air over the second cup: 'I'm so sorry I forgot to ask, but perhaps you'd prefer a whisky and soda?'

'No, really,' he protested and placing his hand dramatically upon his heart, he added:

> 'I'm only an old-fashioned soldier
> So beer means nothing to me
> And the sight of a whisky upsets me so much
> That the Sergeant revives me with tea.'

The pot tilted dangerously as Diana's sense of the absurd got the better of her. 'There!' she exclaimed in mock anger. 'Now you've made me upset the beastly thing. Do be sensible.'

'I can't,' he declared: 'unless . . .'

'Unless what?'

'Well, you know what Gladstone said when he dined with Queen Victoria in 1884.'

'No.'

'Love and laughter are the only two recreations suited to persons of our years. Madam—the choice lies with you.'

She set down the teapot, regarding his smooth brown face and vivid smiling blue eyes seriously for a moment. Then she shook her head. 'You know you're impossible! My ribs are still sore from the way we laughed last night and now you are trying to start me off again. Do you always behave like a rather wicked small boy?'

'I'm a devil on the parade ground,' he assured her solemnly.

'Have I to choose between the conversation of an imbecile and that of a martinet?'

'There is always the one suitable alternative which I have suggested.'

'No.' She shook her pale gold head. 'I don't want to be made love to—at least not at the moment. But how old are you really?'

'Old enough to be your father.'

'You're not!'

'Well—stepfather.'

'Or elder brother,' she smiled.

'Damn it! Let's settle it at lover—why not,' his blue eyes twinkled at her mischievously.

'No, court jester perhaps, but I bet you'd lose your job within a week.'

'Never so long as the Queen's countenance was inclined kindly towards me—take me on and see—but talking of jobs I have a special reason to be gay today since your good papa is about to offer me one.'

'I know. It was about that I wanted to see you.'

'Only for that,' his expression of dismay was quite comical.

'Well—not quite only,' she confessed. 'But particularly —because I want you to promise me that you won't take it.'

'What!' he exclaimed. 'Why in heaven not?'

'I can't go into details, but you don't need it. You have plenty of money and you are just off to Norway so you would have to cancel that.'

'True,' Swithin admitted, suddenly remembering all the tarradiddles he had told her the night before so that she should not worry about him. 'But I'm a glutton for work, so I could never be happy idle and this chance may never come again. I don't mind two hoots about cutting out Norway.'

'You don't even know what the job is yet.'

'No—do you?'

'Amongst other things you will have to take over a Tobacco Depot outside Constantinople.'

He nodded. 'I feared it might be something in the Near East and that's a pity because if it had been in London I could have continued to see you.'

'That does not affect the question as I am leaving with father on his yacht for Constantinople at the end of the week in any case, but I'd much rather you didn't take this job.'

'Why!—that's all the more reason that I should. I may be able to see something of you there.'

'Oh, you'll see me I dare say,' she said a little crossly, 'we may even travel out together, but don't expect me to devote any of my time to you if we do. My party is already made up.'

He placed his hand gently on her shoulder and turned her face towards him. 'What's bitten you all of a sudden, Diana,' he asked earnestly. 'I have been fool enough to think you rather liked me—isn't that true after all?'

34

'I do like you,' she looked away quickly, 'but I don't want you to come with us on the yacht and above all I don't want you to take this job.'

'But why? Surely you can give me some reason?'

'In the first place you don't really need it.'

'But suppose that I *do* really need it and that it is absolutely necessary for me to earn a spot of ready cash?'

'I should still ask you not to take it.'

'But why?' he persisted.

'I can't explain,' she said sullenly. 'But if you do really like me and I ask you to refuse it—surely that is enough.'

For a moment Swithin hovered in miserable indecision. If she had asked him to do any stupid, childish, reckless thing just for her amusement he would have done it without a second thought, but it seemed so utterly unfair that, for some absurd girlish whim, she should ask him to sacrifice the prospect of a decent job.

The butler came in to remove the tea things. 'Sir George is ready to see you in the Library, sir,' he announced as he picked up the tray.

Swithin stood up. 'I'm sorry,' he declared as the man left the room, 'but if it is a job that I can do I mean to take it.'

'Very well.' Diana's dark eyes clouded with angry tears which he could not see because her head was turned away. 'You'll think you can do it I've no doubt, but you've no experience so you'll make a muck of it before you've done. Anyhow don't expect any sympathy from me because I hate pig-headed people.'

The butler reappeared in the doorway. 'This way, sir. If you will follow me I will show you down to the Library.'

5

The Secret Mission

Sir George Duncannon held up a restraining hand. 'My dear fellow it is quite unnecessary for you to go on. Far from being a sinecure which I am about to offer you it is a job which requires courage, brains, and ability.'

'That's nice of you, sir.' Swithin wriggled a little uncomfortably in his chair. 'But I hope you are not ranking my mental capacity too highly.'

The banker smiled, 'I don't think so. Of course it requires other attributes and among them a sound knowledge of Greek and Turkish, but I understand that you have that, also that you have lived in Constantinople for a time—is that correct?'

'Yes, I know the city and I'm pretty fluent in both languages.'

'Good. Then unless I've completely misjudged you I should be hard put to it to find a man better suited to the work I have in mind. It is much more a question as to whether you would be willing to undertake it.'

Swithin's lips twitched into a smile beneath his short, dark, upturned moustache. 'If you really think that—go ahead, sir. I'm pretty well up against it at the moment so it would have to be a very queer business for me to turn it down.'

'It *is* a queer business and before we go any further I am sure you will understand that anything we say must not go outside these four walls.'

Swithin nodded and the banker went on quietly. 'First of all I should like you to accompany me when I leave England on Friday. We go overland to Marseilles, join my yacht, the *Golden Falcon,* there and proceed to Athens where I have a series of conferences which I must attend. From there you would go on independently to Constantinople and take over the management of a Tobacco Depot on the Bosphorus which, owing to certain financial difficulties, has now become the virtual property of my company.'

'You realise, sir, that I do not know the first thing about banking—or tobacco?'

'That is immaterial. You will have a score of technicians to advise you.'

Swithin's eyes narrowed a fraction. 'Then I can only assume this to be cover of some sort. Of what is my real work to consist?'

'There!' Sir George smiled quickly. 'I felt certain that I should not be disappointed in you. Your position at the Depot, as you have guessed, will be nothing but a blind. I only wish it was as easy for me to tell you what I really want you to do. Have you any knowledge of Turkish history?'

'I have never passed an exam. in it but I am familiar with its general outline from the time of the Crusades up to the Great War.'

'And that of the other Balkan States?'

'I know a little about them all.'

'I see. You will know then that there is good reason for that part of the world to have been termed the Plague-spot of Europe. The history of the Near East has been one long tale of wars and strife. Mohammedans massacring Christians one day and Greeks or Armenians slaughtering Turks the next.'

Sir George paused for a moment and then went on thoughtfully: 'Perhaps that was inevitable up to the period of the Great War. Although for three hundred years in a state of decay and bordering on collapse, the Ottoman Empire had still managed to maintain suzerainty over a great area of South-Eastern Europe containing many million Christians, while to the south and east they held Syria, Palestine, and the vast Arabian peninsula, all peopled by races alien to the Turks and constantly in rebellion against them. But the Great War changed all that.

'At its conclusion the Allies had practically driven the Turks out of Europe while Allenby had cleared Palestine and Syria. Liman Von Sanders had been facing Allenby and, as all German officers were recalled to their country immediately the Armistice was signed, he handed all that was left of his army over to Mustapha Kemal who had been fighting under his orders. The history of Turkey has been, for all practical purposes, the history of Mustapha Kemal—or Mr. Ata Turk as he calls himself now—from that date.

'He was not a person of any real importance at that time. From his youth he had been a revolutionary, a prominent member of the Vatan and, later, of the Committee of Union and Progress which was pledged to replace the despotism of the Sultan with constitutional government and to abolish the antiquated religious restrictions which stifled all progress. But he was such an aggressive, dictatorial and unsympathetic individual that his associates loathed him. In consequence, when the revolution actually came in 1908, Enver Pasha, Talat, Jemal and Javid took all the credit for freeing the country from the tyranny of the Sultan Abdul Hamid. They squeezed Kemal out and he remained practically a nonentity. Henceforth he was the lone wolf, hating and hated both by the Sultan's party whose power he had helped to break and by his old comrades who were the new masters.

'However, fate has been kind to Mustapha Kemal in giving him unique opportunities and his genius lies in his quickness to seize them. When the British were about to attack Gallipoli he was still very much an under-dog, suspect and unpopular with the powers of the day. Not wishing to give him any chance to get in the limelight they relegated him to the command of a reserve division at Maidos. The Turks knew of course that the Allies were about to make a landing in force but where it was to take place along the sixty miles of coast line they had no idea. Liman Von Sanders believed that the attempt would be made at Bulair, on the north end of the Peninsula, and had concentrated his forces there. Kemal was forty miles farther to the south and on the eastern coast, watching the Dardanelles.

'As it happened the British landed just opposite him on the west coast at Ari Burnu. They drove the Turkish pickets in at once. The news reached Kemal as he was exercising his troops. Immediately it became a race from opposite sides of the Peninsula as to which could reach the mountain crests of the Chunuk Bair first and thus dominate the whole position. Kemal won by a matter of minutes—no more—but he was hopelessly outnumbered, having only his reserve force, a couple of Arab regiments and a few police, against the flower of the Australian divisions. Yet somehow he managed to cling on.

'All that day, all night, and all the following day as well, he fought with magnificent tenacity and courage, forcing his utterly exhausted troops to maintain their position, until help arrived, by the sheer power of his personality. By ignoring the orders of his superiors and utilising the whole of the Army Reserves to the last man he saved Constantinople. That prompt action of his in the beginning, and his second almost equally brilliant performance when he repulsed the whole weight of the fresh British landing at Suvla Bay, under very similiar circumstances, were directly responsible for the enormous loss in lives and treasures sustained by the British Empire in that disastrous campaign.'

Swithin nodded quietly: 'I know, sir.'

'Of course,' Sir George smiled apologetically, 'I forgot for the moment that I was talking to a soldier. To return then to the political side. Kemal's victories did him little personal good. He was still cold shouldered by his superiors and increased his unpopularity by a display of open hatred towards their Allies. He had always proclaimed the doctrine of "Turkey for the Turks" and loathed the Germans only a fraction less than the British.

'After his brilliant exploits on Gallipoli he was too big to break, so his old enemy Enver Pasha, who was running the country under the direction of the Germans, fearing his acid-tongued interference at Constantinople, got him out of the way as much as possible by giving him various missions. One was to accompany the Prince Vaheddin, who afterwards became Sultan, on a tour of the Western Front. Then when he returned, to get rid of him again they packed him off to the distant Syrian Army where Liman Von Sanders was facing Allenby near Jaffa. That was where fate played into Kemal's hands again for, after the retreat when Allenby had forced the Turks back on Alexandretta and right up against the frontier of Turkey proper, the Armistice was signed. Von Sanders was recalled and Kemal Pasha left in supreme command.

'Enver, Talat, Jemal and the rest fled the country to

save their skins, and of the leading men Kemal, practically alone, remained. He refused to evacuate Alexandretta or lay down his arms in accordance with the terms of the Armistice.

'Instead, he dug himself in and prepared to resist the occupation of Turkey. Then he made the defiant declaration which he has stuck to ever since. In effect he said that the retention of her possessions in Egypt, Palestine, Syria, Arabia, Greece and Bulgaria had been the means of draining the life blood from Turkey for generations. The Allies had conquered them and they were welcome to keep them but *now* they meant to dismember Turkey herself and that he would not permit. The Victorious Allies might say that the War was over, but it was not for him and his men. Unless Turkey were left inviolate they meant to hold the mountain passes of the frontier and die there rather than give in.

'The Allies threatened him. His own Government ordered and begged him by turns to accede to the Allies' demands and trust the generosity of the British. He would not.

'He visited the Northern Army which had fought against the Russians, won them over to himself, and called a conference of Deputies from all Turkey at Erzerum. The Sultan repudiated him and then ordered his arrest. He replied by saying that the Sultan and the Constantinople Government were prisoners in the hands of the British and therefore no longer free to act in the country's best interests. The Deputies gave him the emergency powers of a Dictator.

'The Allies' troops were tired of fighting and clamouring to be taken home. Each week, as a few more regiments were withdrawn, Kemal's position became stronger; so that by the time the Great Men at Versailles had made up their minds how Turkey was to be cut up on paper they no longer had the troops in the Near East to enforce their orders.

'Venizelos, greedy for more territory, suggested that the Greek Army should be sent against Kemal. The offer was accepted and the Greeks landed large forces at Smyrna with all the munitions and resources of the Allies to assist them. Mustapha Kemal marched west with his tattered, ill-equipped, half-starved veterans. There was a terrible campaign which dragged on for many months. No quarter was given or prisoners taken by either side. It was sheer ferocious butchery. Despite the odds against them Kemal was victorious. He captured the Greek Commander-in-Chief and drove his army into the sea while the sailors of the Victorious Allies sat watching the rout from the great battleships, powerless to intervene.

'Kemal turned then to the problem of liberating Turkey in Europe. That also was held by the Greeks and, to add to his difficulty, the British still occupied Constantinople, barring his way across the straits. He was too sensible to force a war upon Britain by a direct attack so he ordered his men to reverse arms and walk peaceably through our lines at Chanak. It was a very awkward situation for our Commander, Sir Charles Harington. If his men had opened fire it might have dragged us into another war with Turkey and he knew that the Government at home would be very adverse to that. Moreover, he had nothing like sufficient troops under him to put up a serious opposition against Kemal. The French representative came to the rescue and hurriedly patched up an agreement. Kemal asked no more and no less than he had nearly four years earlier at the time of the Armistice. That Turkey proper should remain inviolate for Turks to run and Turks to rule without foreign interference. The Mighty Allied and Victorious Powers caved in, giving this ferocious but courageous soldier what he demanded. The foreign troops were withdrawn from Turkish soil and Mustapha Kemal had saved his nation.

'At what a price you can imagine. Since the outbreak of the first Balkan War in 1912 the manpower of his race had been decimated by ten years of slaughter, the country laid waste, thousands of towns and villages burnt to the ground. Besides which Kemal was by no means the master yet in this country of ruins that he had saved from final partition at the hands of the Allied Statesmen.

'He is said to be a licentious drunken brute, a cynic and a liar, whom no decent men could respect or trust. He was feared and hated even by the men who, from patriotic motives, had stood by him in his long struggle. It is said that in all his life he has only had one really intimate friend,

41

a Colonel Arif who used to be the companion of his de-
bauches, yet he hung him with a batch of others because he
played some small part in a political intrigue, without the
least compunction.

'Once Turkey was freed from the foreigner, all his associates turned against him. They had not risked their lives
in the early days to force a constitution on the Sultan in
order that Kemal should usurp his powers and become
dictator. They wanted a Republic, but in order to fight
Kemal, they rallied round Vaheddin, who was still nomin-
ally the head of the State and powerful in his dual capacity
of Sultan and Caliph of the Faithful.

'Kemal then forced a decree through the National Assem-
bly severing the Sultanate from the Caliphate. Vaheddin
fled from Constantinople, and his nephew Abdul Mejid
was created Caliph in his stead. A year later, Turkey was
declared a Republic, and six months after that Mustapha
Kemal abolished the Caliphate as well. Then in 1926 he
hung the entire opposition and at last became the sole
and absolute master of Turkey.

'From that time he has come out into the open, and with
an utter disregard of everybody's else's views proceeded to
smash all the antiquated religious taboos which have kept
the development of Turkey so far behind that of the Western
world. And that brings us to a new phase in Turkish history.'

Sir George Duncannon paused to light a cigarette and
then went on. 'At first, of course, we thought of Kemal
only as a dissipated and ruthless but brilliant general.
I have studied the problems of the Near East all my life,
so I may fairly say that I am something of an expert, and
I can honestly assure you that neither I nor others equally
well acquainted with the situation considered that there was
the least likelihood of Kemal succeeding in getting the
people genuinely to accept the reforms he advocated. Yet he
has succeeded and it is my belief that he has succeeded
beyond his wildest hopes.

'The Turks are almost entirely a peasant population.
Lazy, ignorant, hidebound with tradition, accepting
blindly as their rule of life on the smallest issue the deci-
sions laid down thirteen hundred years ago by a fanatical
soldier-preacher in the Koran. Their only good quality is

that they make loyal and courageous troops. All business in Turkey before the Kemal era was transacted by Greeks, Armenians, and Jews. The Turks despised such men and all their activities. The majority of these they have now butchered or deported, so how could one expect the country to carry on. Yet it does, and is slowly returning to prosperity.

'Kemal forcibly confiscated the fezzes of the entire population and made them wear peaked caps, which, being contrary to the holy word, had always previously been the distinguishing mark of the hated unbeliever. He has abolished the harems and torn away the veils of the women, giving them equal status with men. Their whole law consisted of the Koran and its commentaries. He has torn it up and instituted the German Commercial, the Italian Penal and the Swiss Civil Codes. He has done away with the religious ban upon images in the form of man or beast and set up statues of himself which one would have thought would rouse these people to a fenzy. He has banned the ancient script and introduced our Latin alphabet. He has even gutted the Turkish tongue of all its foreign Arabic sounds and altered the whole language so that grown men and women have had to go to school again in order to learn to talk to each other. It is almost past belief that the Turks should submit to such things, but there it is! In less than ten years this one man has utterly changed the life and outlook of his whole people.'

The banker stubbed out his cigarette and then resumed more slowly. 'Now to return to the problem which interests me personally. The forces which have actuated the foreign policies of these Near Eastern countries in the past were highly complicated, but now that the Turks have withdrawn within their own frontiers, the position is slightly simplified. However, the conditions which influence merchant banking in them are no less intricate than they were.

'In a fully civilised country the individual trader, and after all we merchant bankers are nothing but glorified traders, does not feel the immediate effects of an alteration in Government, or Government policy, on his trade. But out there, where every man's throat is dependent on such things, there is a far more sensitive appreciation of the part which such changes may play in each individual's problem.

'Now with Turkey rapidly recovering and adapting itself to Western methods under an apparently stable Government I feel that we should invest in the country. If the present policy is pursued, we should have what almost amounts to gilt-edged security. Yet I, who have studied the question all my life, still hesitate to do so.

'I cannot, and it annoys me, put my finger on the spot where the canker that my imagination suspects really is. Yet somehow, without the least evidence to support my view, I sense a strong movement which is about to sweep the country.

'If there is such a movement, I have not the least idea who is at its head or the object of it. It may be a new step which Kemal himself is contemplating. A *volte-face* to territorial ambitions perhaps, now that his country is getting on its feet again, or a complete reversal of his anti-religious policy.

'Ibn Saud holds all Arabia; for the first time in many hundred years the warring tribes have united under his leadership. Ben Djellone, the Mahommedan Hitler of Algeria, is causing the French appalling trouble. Even the native regiments are deserting to him. At the price of reinstating the Caliphate and the law of the Koran, Kemal could form an alliance with those two in order to drive every Christian out of Palestine, Egypt, and Northern Africa. That sounds fantastic, I suppose, but I cannot get any wholehearted confirmation from my people on the spot that Kemal's reforms are really being accepted as permanent, and the lust of massacring Christians is in the blood of every Turk. They gave him the title of "Gazi, The Destroyer of Christians", on that account, and he is such a dark horse that one can never tell what he means to do next.

'On the other hand, this movement that I suspect may not come from Kemal at all, but from the people. Perhaps his day is almost done and the religious reactionaries are about to rise against him. But if that happened, it would be almost equally dangerous for us. The revival of religious fanaticism would mean certain trouble for Great Britain in Transjordania and the Arab Kingdoms which were part of the Turkish Empire before the war, over which we now have Mandated Powers.

'Well, there it is!' Sir George sighed a little wearily and leaned back in his chair. 'My co-directors are pressing me, they have been for months past, to seize this apparently golden opportunity of investing heavily in the new westernised Turkey that Mustapha Kemal is creating. I have opposed them, almost entirely on instinct, with the argument that, if Kemal is hatching something, or his Government is likely to fall, we are almost certain to lose our money. I want someone like yourself to go out at once and investigate the situation at first hand. It will be a dangerous undertaking, mind you, for if anything *is* going on, and they catch you trying to find out their plans, they'll kill you without a second thought.

'The remuneration, of course, if you take this job on, will be handsome, you may leave that to me, and you would have the additional satisfaction of knowing that you are also serving your country, since any information you may secure will be passed on to the Foreign Office and might enable them to avert serious trouble by acting in time if there are any grounds for the sort of thing I fear. Now, how do you feel about it?'

Swithin's blue eyes twinkled. 'I'm your man, sir. I was afraid that you were going to offer me a job in an office, but this looks the very thing for me.'

'Good—I'm delighted. I shall be able to give you further particulars during our voyage out to Athens, and you will have an opportunity to get a little practice in this new-fangled pronunciation of the language, as one of my yacht stewards is a Turk.'

'Are there others with whom I am to work when I arrive in Constantinople,' Swithin inquired, 'or do you wish me to play a lone hand?'

'I should have liked you to work with Brendon. He was a very different type of fellow to yourself, but he had a lot of experience at this kind of thing and between you I think you could have found out anything there is to know. Unfortunately, however, he is out of the business now, so all I can do is to put you in touch with my old friend McAndrew. He has been established in Constantinople as a merchant for over thirty years, so he should be able to

45

give you something to go on, and he doesn't miss much of the latest gossip in the Bazaars. Apart from that, I fear I can give you little help once you arrive.'

Swithin nodded. 'Yes, I should think Bazaar whispers can prove a very useful indication in a thing like this. Haven't they given you any sort of pointer at all so far?'

'No. Frankly that is one of the things which strengthens my belief that we are up against something really big. The Bazaars are unusually, I might almost say uncannily, silent.'

'I see, but this chap Brendon that you mention. Is it quite impossible for me to get hold of him when I arrive. Even in half an hour's chat, he might be able to give me quite a lot of useful tips.'

'I'm sorry.' Sir George shook his head. 'Poor Brendon was, in a way, your predecessor, and I learned that he had been found murdered behind the station at Sirkedji only a week ago.'

6

The Jealous Lover

For the next five days, Swithin Destime lived on the top of the world. His was one of those happy mercurial temperaments which can readily forget even a serious setback provided that new prospects are opening up before them.

Twenty-four hours after he had left Sir George Duncannon, he was already telling himself that the fracas at Maidenhead had been a piece of good fortune in disguise. Up to that time he had been wrapped up in his profession, it is true, but now he looked at the other side of the question. Promotion in the Army was desperately slow, unless there was a first-class war, and there seemed little likelihood of that. With his meagre private income he would have had no chance to save, let alone marry, had he continued in the Brigade of Guards, and he would not have cared to transfer to a Line Regiment where the standard of expenditure was lower. For another fifteen or twenty years perhaps he would have carried on the old routine: route marches, rifle practice, manœuvres, courses, inspections, and leave; rising in time to be a Brigadier, if he were lucky, but more likely to be retired as a Colonel with the best part of his life behind him and insufficient capital to travel widely or buy an estate to occupy his time.

But all that was past now. He had been given a job that mattered. Something which would give him an opportunity to use his initiative and wits and all the surplus energy that was always bubbling up inside him. He was now the confidential employee of a great financial house. The sum that Sir George had suggested as his remuneration had caused him to catch his breath, it was higher than Brigadier's pay with full allowances, and Swithin felt that if he could produce an accurate summary of the information that the banker wanted, there would be other jobs for him and probably a permanent appointment to watch the firm's interests in the Near East.

That he might be risking his life on this secret mission did not cause him serious concern. He felt that the element of danger justified his acceptance of the high pay and he was fully confident of his ability to take care of himself. His luck was in again, there was not a doubt of it, and as Diana was travelling out with them to Athens in the yacht, he felt that he would soon be able to put right with her the matter of having taken the job against her wishes. They were to call at one or two places on the way, so that meant at least half a dozen days in her company.

He lunched with Peter Carew on his last day before leaving England, and to account for his high spirits announced that he had been invited to spend some weeks cruising in the Mediterranean on Sir George Duncannon's yacht.

'I know—Diana told me.' Peter nodded his fair head. 'She's got a young party, hasn't she. The Claydon-ffinchs, Boo-Boo Skelton, Harriet Helm, and Conkey Malvern—I forget who else. Oh, that writer chap, Cæsar Penton, and that other little filth, Waldo Nauenheimer. I should hardly have thought you would find much in common with that crowd.'

Swithin's spirits were a little dashed. Not having seen Diana since his visit to Belgrave Square, he had forgotten her mention of a party, and he had been blissfully picturing himself as her sole entertainer during halcyon days of glorious sunshine while the yacht steamed through the blue waters of the Mediterranean. As he could not disclose his projected activities in Constantinople, he contented himself with the bald statement that he had never met any of them.

'Haven't you?' Peter wrinkled his freckled nose in faint distaste. 'They're not a bad crowd really, I suppose, only a bit wet, if you know what I mean. Hado Claydon-ffinch is something on the Stock Exchange. He can be rather an amusing bird, but his wife's a kind of cooee-stupid blonde. They are being taken so that she can chaperone the party, I expect. Old Lady Duncannon hates the sea, so she never goes on these trips. Boo-Boo Skelton's darned attractive, but a most colossal snob. She's determined to be a Grande Dame or nothing, and Peers without money need not apply. She's been trying to hook young Malvern for the last few months. I expect that's why Diana asked them both—to give Boo-Boo her chance. You must have met Harriet Helm before. She's got a hellish tongue, but I suppose that's why people invite her everywhere. She was Lady Verdmont for the inside of a year; then when he lost his money she chucked him up and reverted to her maiden name. Waldo Nauenheimer is her boy friend at the moment. He fairly stinks of money, but I've always thought him a pretty dirty piece of work. Hitler slung him out of Germany, and if he's a fair sample of the type for whom the Germans have no use, there's a case of sorts for Hitler. Cæsar Penton's a pretty smart young man. Clever enough to write the sort of thing that's hailed as genius by the literary lion-hunters, so society has taken him up. Diana's always been keen on books and Cæsar's not bad-looking, so he has been making the running pretty well with her. She's evidently taken it into her head that she'd like to hear him do his stuff about the stars in the Adriatic, on the boat deck, for her especial benefit. So where you come in, I don't quite see—unless it is to act as runner-up to Cæsar—and make him jealous.'

'Perhaps that's it.' Swithin agreed modestly. 'But you seem pretty bitter about them all. Are they really as bad as that or is your liver out of order?'

'Neither,' confessed Peter. 'You'll probably find them quite an amusing bunch, but I've had some bad news this morning so I'm feeling pretty grim and unusually malicious, I suppose.'

'I'm sorry. Is it anything where I could be a help?'

Peter shook his head and smiled lazily. ' 'Fraid not—it's just the governor up to his usual tricks.'

'What's he done—cut down your allowance?'

'No, but you know I'd planned to go to Biarritz. Well, he's put that up the spout. He wrote me this morning that, owing to his efforts with the powers that be, His Gracious Majesty has seen fit to entrust his well-beloved servant, Peter Heriot Carew, with a Foreign Office bag—and that I'm to report at the F.O. on Monday.'

Swithin's blue eyes twinkled. 'Well, I may be an old fashioned soldier, but honestly I don't blame him.'

'You wouldn't.' Peter's lazy smile came again. 'Still, I suppose there are worse fates than tagging round Europe with dispatches for the Embassies.'

'Of course,' Swithin consoled him, 'and you'll meet any

was not a nervous man, but at that moment he felt dis-
number of interesting people on your trips.'

'Oh, to hell with interesting people!' exclaimed Peter.
'I want to sunbathe on the beach at Biarritz.'

The information received at that lunch was the first
cloud to dim the opalescent blue to Swithin's mental horizon. The second was to learn, when he met Sir George
Duncannon on the Continental departure platform at Victoria the following morning, that they were not to travel
with Diana and the rest of the party. The others had gone
on ahead in order that the women might put in a day's
shopping in Paris and would arrive at Marseilles the night
before them. Swithin's companions on the journey were Sir
George, a young man with a bulbous forehead named Ver-
non Bentley, who was the banker's secretary, a prim-
looking spinster who acted as stenographer, and several
servants. The third cloud, immense and threatening to
obscure the whole of Swithin's mental heaven, was his
reception by Diana when he eventually arrived on board
the *Golden Falcon*.

He had been travelling all night, and their embarkation
was delayed by Sir George taking him first to his firm's
office in Marseilles, where they spent some time transacting
business. In consequence, by the time Swithin had unpacked,
bathed, and changed, it was nearly twelve o'clock. When
he left his cabin he went on deck and, guided by the sound
of laughter, made his way to the stern of the vessel, where
he found a small cocktail bar open to the deck and shaded
from the midday glare by a wide, striped awning. Beside
the bar, a little group were lounging, the women in light
frocks, the men in flannels. Diana, enchanting in pale blue,
was among them.

As Swithin turned the corner, she was carrying on a laughing discussion with a tall, good-looking young man who he
afterwards learned to be Cæsar Penton. She caught sight of
Swithin at once, but ignored him for the moment in order
to finish what she was saying to the writer, then she turned,
gave him the most casual 'Good morning' and, having airily
announced, 'You know all these people, of course—don't
you,' turned back to continue her conversation.

'I'm sorry, but I don't,' Swithin said, a trifle curtly. He

tinctly awkward—which probably accounted for the fact that his voice sounded louder than he intended.

A sudden silence descended on the little group, and they stared at him with faintly hostile curiosity. Diana introduced him to her other guests and suggested that he should order himself a drink. The rest gave him a lazy nod and then resumed their chatter with fresh animation.

Swithin asked the barman for a Gin-Fizz and glanced at Diana, but she was deep in her argument with the beautifully tailored Mr. Cæsar Penton again and never gave him another look.

He stood there for a few moments trying to think of some suitable remark by which to open a conversation with Lord Malvern and Miss Boo-Boo Skelton, who were standing nearest to him. They were talking of someone called Wendy Polkington and another person, presumably male, whom they referred to as 'Rabbit'. Swithin gathered that Wendy and Rabbit were living in sin together and the question was —how long this presumably blissful state of affairs would continue.

When there seemed to be no further speculation to be made upon the point, Swithin broke the short silence that had fallen by saying, 'I am looking forward tremendously to seeing Athens. Do either of you know it at all?'

Miss Skelton regarded him with a faintly surprised look in her enormous blue eyes and shook her beautifully poised head; while Malvern replied, with a shrug of his narrow shoulders, 'Why, no—but what does it matter where we go as long as we get good bathing—or are you an archæologist?'

'Good Lord, no!' Swithin hastened to assure him. 'I'm only an old-fashioned soldier, but I should like to see the Acropolis and all the rest of it just the same.'

'Would you.' Lord Malvern pulled nervously at his little fair moustache. 'I'm afraid I don't care much for ruins and I loathe the hordes of tourists who're always swarming over them, so I shall probably give it a miss.'

There was another brief, rather awkward, silence, then they both turned simultaneously away from Swithin, and the young man asked the girl, 'Have you had any news of Jeremy lately? The last I heard was that he had tucked up with Georgina Doublethwait and they had gone to earth in a Paris studio. Isn't it queer how some people still have

51

that ostrich complex?'

Then they entered into a long and involved discussion about Jeremy and Georgina, while both ignored Swithin as though he were no longer there. Having listened to them with rising irritation for some moments, he swallowed the rest of his Gin-Fizz and, seeing that all others were equally engrossed in their respective conversations, left the sun-parlour bar as unostentatiously as he could.

That first encounter with his fellow guests was a fore-taste of their attitude towards him throughout the voyage. Their rudeness to him was in no way deliberate; in fact, they would certainly have thought that anyone who criti-cised their manners was only joking. It was simply that they had not time for anybody who was not a member of their set. Their sole topic of conversation consisted of the doings of their intimates. A faintly malicious and never ceasing commentary upon Benjy, Poodle, The Hetman, Wimple, Diddles, The Thug, Letchie, and twenty others, so that if, like Swithin, one did not know these minor members of the aristocracy by their curious nicknames, one could not contribute to the idle chatter and had, perforce, to stand there dumb.

During the first day out, while they cruised quietly past the islands of Hyeres, towards Cannes, Swithin hovered on the edge of the party hoping to get Diana to himself if only for a few minutes; but he was unsuccessful, and equally so the second day when the yacht swung lazily at anchor off Nice. He simply could not draw her from the company of those detested friends whose atmosphere she seemed to have assimilated like a protective wall, and if she was not with the crowd, the immaculate Cæsar Penton was always at her side or else she was playing chess with Waldo Nauen-heimer.

By the third day, when they had turned south towards Corsica, he was in such a state of irritation with his fellow guests that he was itching to insult the men and spank the women, if only to observe their reactions to assault, and in the days that followed he would certainly have done some-thing desperate if he had not constantly reminded himself that he was a guest himself and also Sir George's paid employee.

In the banker's society he found some consolation, for

52

Sir George allotted an hour or two each evening to giving him extremely informative talks on Turkey, its people, their outlook, religion, trades, and the policy of the present Government. For the rest of the day, however, the banker was rarely visible. He even had his meals served in the private dining cabin of his suite and, shutting himself up in his own quarters, spent hours on end discussing the sheaves of radio messages which came in constantly with the secretary, or dictating seemingly endless documents to his stenographer.

The afternoons Swithin spent with the Turkish steward, who had been relieved of certain duties in order to coach him in the new pronunciation of the Turkish language, and the rest of the time he either tried to read or spent in listening to the vapid conversation of the others if Diana were among them, yet he was miserable in her company in such circumstances, but equally unhappy out of it.

Sir George was apparently in no hurry to arrive at his destination, for the yacht lingered three days at Ajaccio while the younger people made an excursion up through the wild grandeur of Corsica's rugged mountains and beautiful chestnut forests to Corté, in the interior.

Swithin did not accompany them, although Diana threw him a casual invitation to do so at dinner the night before they started. Since she had changed so utterly from the delightful girl he had met at Maidenhead to a hard-boiled young woman who snubbed his every approach with some caustic witticism, he was not altogether sorry that his talks with Sir George and the necessity of practising his Turkish while he could detained him on the yacht. He did not care a fig about the rest of the fools who made up the party, but her treatment of him rankled badly. It seemed so mean-spirited of her, he thought, to take it out of him like this just because he had gone against her wishes in the matter of the job.

After leaving Corsica they proceeded to Palermo, and a further four days elapsed during which he saw little of the others since they spent most of their time bathing or dancing in the hotels on shore. Then the yacht weighed anchor again and, passing the Straits of Messina, entered on the dead run across the Ionian Sea.

By that time Swithin wished that he had been sent to

Turkey overland, or that the others had remained idling the days away in Palermo. The luxury yacht, the sparkling sea and sun-scorched decks by day, the myriad stars and soft, dark velvet warmness of the nights were all just as he had imagined them in London. The food was excellent, the drinks abundant, the attendance perfect, his cabin all that any lover of comfort could desire, but the constant proximity of these inane loungers who did not even display any interest in hunting or fishing, let alone the wide world and all the multitudinous activities in it, proved a source of continual irritation.

Above all, Diana showed no sign of relenting. She and Cæsar Penton had become as thick as thieves by this time. They did not get up till nearly midday, dozed side by side in deck chairs most of the afternoon, and apparently spent the best part of each night on deck together. Sir George, immersed in his business, seemed neither to notice or care how his daughter amused herself and Mrs. Claydon-ffinch did not even pretend to play the part of chaperone. She had started an affair with Waldo Nauenheimer, while her husband, who reminded Swithin of a large, sleek ginger cat, had apparently been told off to keep the hawk-nosed Harriet from making trouble.

Swithin thought the young Jew by far the most human member of the party. He was the only one who ever troubled to go out of his way to draw him into a conversation, and although they had little in common, on the few occasions when they chanced to be alone together they found plenty to talk about.

Diana appeared to like Waldo, too, since she continued to play chess with him and selected him by preference as her companion on the rare occasions when Cæsar was absent from her side, but between dinner and bedtime she devoted herself entirely to the author.

Night after night, she sat with him on a pile of rugs in a secluded corner of the vessel's stern while Swithin, after ten o'clock each evening, tossed restlessly in his cabin tortured by jealous imaginings to such an extent that he could neither read, study his Turkish, or get to sleep until the small hours of the morning.

They came to Piræus late in the evening after they had already dined. Swithin was leaning on the rail smoking a

54

cigar and watching the lights of Athens, which twinkled half a dozen miles away above the port, when Sir George sent for him. They held a final conference which lasted well over an hour, and at its conclusion, the banker said:

'Call on McAndrew as soon as you arrive. Having lived there as a trader for so many years, he is certain to be able to give you some useful tips, and send your reports to my brother Allan Duncannon's house, at Bebek, by private messenger. They will be forwarded on to me at once. Remember, too, that you are not to use Tyndall-Williams at the Embassy as a post office except in a case of great emergency.'

'I understand, sir.' Swithin smiled quickly. 'I've got it all docketed in my head.'

The banker nodded and held out his hand. 'That's right, my boy. I've told the Captain you will want the launch first thing in the morning, so I expect you will be off before the rest of us are about. Take your time over your inquiries, because if you are once suspected you would immediately be in grave danger, and I don't want you to take any risk that you can possibly avoid—Good luck to you.'

'Thanks, sir. I promise you I'll be careful.' Swithin gripped the banker's hand, smiled again, and left the cabin.

As he packed his gear, all except his night things, he hummed cheerfully to himself, a new mood now upon him. All the bothersome preparations for his mission were over and he would not have to suffer any longer the maddening frustration of having Diana always within hail yet hopelessly inaccessible. Tomorrow, he would be on the train as it wound its way in and out of the desolate sun-baked gorges up through the mountains into Macedonia. Two days more and he would have begun his task of unravelling the jealously guarded secrets of those strange half-Eastern and half-Western people—the Turks. If he succeeded he would have opened a new career for himself; Sir George had virtually implied as much on the voyage out, and Swithin had made up his mind that, even if he had to run very serious risks indeed, he would not leave Turkey without the information that the banker wanted.

Now that the yacht was at anchor, it was stifling in his cabin despite the circulators, so before turning in he went on deck for a last breath of air. The sound of dance music over the wireless came from the after part of the ship, and thinking that he had better make his formal adieus to his fellow guests, he turned in that direction. As he did so, two figures emerged from a nearby hatchway and he found himself confronting Diana and Cæsar Penton.

'I was just coming to say good-bye,' he announced.

'Why? Where on earth are you off to at this hour of night?' the author asked.

'I'm going ashore first thing in the morning,' Swithin told him, 'and as I have business in Athens which may take me several weeks, I don't suppose we shall see each other again.'

'Run along, Cæsar,' Diana said abruptly, 'I want to talk to Captain Destime. Order me another Grenadine and I'll join you again in a few minutes.'

'Oh, all right! So long, Destime—good hunting to you.' Penton turned and strolled away.

'Thanks,' Swithin murmured. Then he stood waiting for Diana to speak, his eyes searching her face in the semi-darkness.

'So you mean to go through with this?' she shot at him suddenly.

'Certainly—why not?'

'Despite the fact that I begged you not to and that you do not even need the money?'

'As it happens, I do,' he confessed. 'That rich uncle I told you of is a complete myth and I've hardly a bob that I can call my own—so I need it very badly. I'm sorry to have deceived you about that, but it should not be difficult for you to guess why I wanted you to think that I was amply provided for.'

'I see,' she said softly. 'You did hint as much, but if you had only said so at the time I could easily have persuaded father to find you another job, and I had the strongest reason for not wishing you to take this one.'

His eyes hardened as he replied swiftly, 'Thanks, I prefer to earn my pay, and I've had ample evidence on the voyage out regarding your "reasons". Perhaps it will give you a laugh to know that when I first learnt this business might prove dangerous, I was fool enough to believe that you wanted me to cut it out because you were concerned for my safety.'

'Well, that was my reason—what other could there be?'

'You've made it pretty obvious in the last ten days.'

She shrugged and answered coldly, 'I suppose you are annoyed because I have not been able to devote any of my time to you, but I warned you that would be the case before we started. If you have been miserable on the voyage out, it is entirely your own fault. You behaved like a bear from the beginning, following me about and staring me out of countenance twenty times a day until I'm tired of the sight of you. Anyhow, that does not affect the fact that I tried to stop you going into this business solely because I knew the risks you would have to run.'

'I'm sorry, but I find it difficult to believe that—now.'

'What other motive could I have had?' she demanded angrily.

'No woman likes being told the truth,' he said calmly, and Diana could cheerfully have smacked him for the even tone and supercilious smile on his face.

'I do,' she flashed, 'if you can tell it!'

He did not appear to hear the taunt; 'Very well,' he agreed. 'This is the situation as I see it—every girl likes two strings to her bow, but she can only use one at a time. If you had persuaded me not to take this job, you could have had your fun with Penton on the trip and kept me dangling on a string in London—I feel I ought to apologise for upsetting your schemes, but I assure you . . .'

'Oh, you are intolerable!' she flared.

He laughed a little bitterly. 'Well, anyway, I've got the job.'

'Yes, you've got it, you fool!' she flung at him. 'But don't you realise that you know nothing of this part of the world. You have only visited Constantinople as a tourist. The counter-espionage people will spot you the moment you begin your investigations and knife you—as they did poor Brendon—or else you'll sit there doing nothing for a couple of months and then come crawling back to father, with your tail between your legs, to confess your failure. That's the most likely thing and it may serve to reduce your incredible conceit.'

She turned angrily away, and that was the last Swithin saw of her before he left the yacht.

7

The City of the Sultans

Two days later, in the broiling sunshine of the mid-afternoon, the Orient Express covered the last stage of its journey to Constantinople.

Swithin had joined it that morning at Kuleli Burgas, the junction just south of Adrianople, and as he sat coatless in the corner of his carriage, even the discomfort caused by the heat and dust was not sufficient to prevent him admiring the magnificent approach to the city of the Sultans.

For the last twenty miles the train ran along the shore of Lake Khalkali and then followed the coast line of the Marmara Sea until the great wall, built by the early Byzantine Emperors, appeared in the distance. Its ancient brick, mellowed for centuries by the sun, had faded to a delicate brownish cream, and stretching from the sea upon the right to the far distance on the landward side, with great square towers rising from it at every few hundred yards, it stood out clear cut and beautiful against a brassy sky of brilliant blue.

Having passed through the wall, the vista on either hand was suddenly shut out by masses of irregular wooden buildings crowded against each other and so ramshackle in appearance that they looked as if it only needed half a gale of wind to bring the whole lot tumbling to the ground. Men, women, and children swarmed among them, wrangling in the narrow courts, stumbling up rickety outside stairways, and leaning indolently from countless balconies or the flat rooftops to watch the passing train. Swithin remembered this human rabbit warren from his earlier visits a number of years before; the scene remained much as it had been for centuries, yet somehow it was changed, and in a manner for which he could not, at first, account. Then the explanation flashed upon him. Many of the *jalousies* behind which the women used to sit had disappeared and given place to open windows, evidently in deference to Mustapha Kemal's ordinance, and the women themselves were no longer wearing veils.

At the Sirkedji station, the manner of receiving trains remained unaltered. Tall Kavasses, from the hotels, big business houses, and Embassies, dressed in smart uniforms, stood alert but dignified along the platform, keeping a look-out for the passengers they had been sent to meet, while a horde of tattered *hamals* flung themselves upon the baggage, fighting furiously for every piece as it was handed out from the windows of the train.

Swithin found the Kavass from the Pera Palace and pointed out his pieces. The man escorted him to a waiting car and dealt swiftly with the ruffianly porters who piled his gear on board.

The station being in the old city of Stamboul itself, the street which led from it was of that strange characterless variety only to be found in the East. It was neither a residential, shopping, or business thoroughfare, but a mixture of all three. Gaunt, old-fashioned warehouses stood cheek by jowl with modern office blocks, and dilapidated mansions between isolated retailers where oil or sweetmeats had been dispensed for generations from little, dark, cavernous shops.

Swithin was struck by the smart new taxis which were speeding through the streets until he remembered Sir George having told him that at one period Kemal had transported every available cab, however derelict, from Constantinople to his new capital, Angora. Evidently the old metropolis had benefited by the order, some big motor manufacturer having taken advantage of it to equip the city with a brand new fleet.

The sun was sparkling on the waters of the Golden Horn as he crossed it by the Galata Bridge, and that centre of the city's life was thronged as usual; but it presented a very different aspect to when Swithin had last seen it. Then, every true believer, police, dark-coated business men, and even the ragamuffins of the gutter had worn that emblem of his religion, the fez. Now, they looked queerly unattractive in bowlers or cloth caps. Previously, peaked headgear had been the certain sign of the infidel—Jew, Christian, or Greek; the sacred word of the Koran laid it down most clearly as an abomination, yet despite that dread injunction Kemal had ordered, and Turkey had obeyed. Many of the women, too, had abandoned either their brightly coloured *ferjis*, or dark flowing robes, for western tailor-mades and hats of felt or straw, while all were now unveiled.

Reaching the Pera side of the Bridge, the car swiftly mounted the hill, leaving the Street of Steps leading up to the White Tower which dominates the city on the right, and entered the modern European quarter. A few minutes later, it drew up outside the Pera Palace Hotel.

To his satisfaction, Swithin managed to secure a room on the fourth floor at the back, away from the din of clanging tram bells and motor horns in the busy street, giving him a splendid view over the intervening rooftops, which sloped down the hill to the edge of the Golden Horn. That splendid waterway, which has played a part in the history of Constantinople equal to that of the Grand Canal in Venice, showed a wonderful variety of colourful traffic and beyond, above the mass of buildings on the Stamboul shore, rose the domes and minarets of the ancient mosques, like a scene from the Arabian Nights, against the evening sky, where the sun was now sinking rapidly to rest.

By the time Swithin had unpacked, bathed, and changed, it was too late for there to be any chance of him catching McAndrew at his office, so he decided to dine quietly in the hotel and spend the evening browsing through the latest Turkish papers and periodicals, which although controlled by the Government were certain to reflect something of the interests and temper of the people.

In the lounge, he found a bookstall presided over by a young woman, so he asked her for the *Istanbul,* the *Millujet,* and the *Ulus,* then he looked at her a second time. Most men would have, for she was attractive enough to have caught the eye of the most hardened misogynist.

'*Etès vous Français, Monsieur?*' she asked with a shy smile as she handed him the papers.

'*Non, Anglais—et vous, Mademoiselle?*'

'I have no country,' she replied at once in excellent English. 'By birth I am a Russian, brought here as a little girl with the refugees at the time of the Revolution. I cannot return. I would not if I could, and although the Turks permit us to stay here, they refuse us Turkish nationality.'

'You speak English very well,' Swithin remarked. 'Have you ever been in England?'

'No, never. But I had an English governess from the age of five to ten, when we were forced to leave my home, and I have kept it up by practice with the many English here.'

He nodded sympathetically. 'The Revolution must have been a terrible experience for people like yourself.'

'Yes, for the old ones especially. They, who had been used to comfortable homes and good food and clothes and servants, still miss such things, but I do not remember much of the troubles and our escape from Russia.'

'I suppose you were lucky to come through at all,' said Swithin thoughtfully.

'Why, yes,' she smiled, 'and compared to many others, I am lucky now to have this good job in the hotel. Most of my friends have been living how they can for years in abject poverty. I break my heart for them.'

'You must find it pretty dull though if you are cooped up behind this bookstall for hours on end every day?'

'Oh, it is not so bad. I close it soon now. My time is up at eight o'clock, and sometimes there are English, French, or German gentlemen staying in the hotel who are a little lonely. If they do not care for the professional women who are to be picked up at the night places, they ask me out to supper with them.'

The girl's words were an obvious invitation, and Swithin did not doubt that, when offered, it was rarely rejected, but he skilfully avoided it by replying.

'I should like to ask you to take pity on me one night, but unfortunately I am here on business, and I am afraid that most evenings I shall have masses of figures to go through.'

'Ah, well!' she gave a little shrug. 'That is a pity, because I like to talk with the English when they are as you—a gentleman. It makes me forget for a time the difference that the Revolution has made to my life. The drudgery of my job and the beastly little flat where I live with my mother.'

'What is your name?' he asked casually.

'Vorontzoff—Tania Vorontzoff, and my mother is the Baroness. We are Ukrainians and come from Karkoff.'

He smiled and picked up his papers. 'Well, if work permits, I shall hope to see something more of you, but now

61

I must be going in to dinner. Good night.'

She smiled in return, shaking back her dark curls with a little lift of her pointed chin. 'Don't work too hard—Good night.'

Next morning at half-past ten, Swithin presented himself at the offices of McAndrew, Shorn & Co., General Merchants, in Tophane Street, with his letter of introduction from Sir George.

The senior partner of the firm saw him at once, and Swithin discovered him to be a lean, cadaverous-looking man with eyes almost as blue as his own and pale sandy hair that was just fading into grey.

Having perused the letter, the Scot glanced up from beneath beetling brows which sported hairs as long as the feelers of a good-sized prawn.

'So ye're fra' Duncannon and ye've come to this city of sin to find oot the present feeling amongst these misbelieving Turks?'

'That's it,' Swithin agreed, 'and Sir George said that you might be good enough to give me your help.'

'Not I!' exclaimed the other quickly. 'I've a use for me neck, and although they've stopped bowstringing and impaling folk these last few years, these sons of Belial are still uncanny handy with a rope.'

'Perhaps I put it a little strongly.' Swithin smiled. 'I meant that I'd be very grateful for any tips you care to give me.'

'Ei—now ye're talking. Duncannon's an old crony of mine and if I can prevent ye making a fool of yersel' by a little advice, I'm willing, though I doubt ye'll take it all the same.'

'Try me and see. Honestly, I'd be grateful if you will.'

'Ei—so you say and maybe ye mean it, but I've learnt noo to expect that these forty years sin'. Are ye staying at the *Pera* or the *Tokatlian* now?'

'The Pera.'

'Ei—I thought it would be one of those swagger hotels.'

'You think I should be less likely to be watched if I move to a smaller place?'

'Better still, take a wee place of yer own. Then ye'll be free to come and go in yer own guid time, with God's permission, and no one the wiser.'

'Right, I'll go round the house agents and see what they can offer in the way of quiet little flats.

'Ye don't need to wear oot yer shoe leather that way,' the dour McAndrew replied abruptly, 'as a sideline I keep a wee list of flats to feu mesel', so we'll combine business wi' pleasure—if ye can call it pleasure when a decent body as ye appear ta be wants to try conclusions with that treacherous rascal Kazdim.'

'You mean, the Chief of Police. Sir George told me something of him. He was a Palace Eunuch at one time, wasn't he?'

'Ei—and a Eunuch he remains, so he can breed no more of his kind, God be praised. But the Palace has gone the way of lots of things since the Sultan was smuggled oot of the toun in a British Red Cross van, wi' the family jewels and an umbrella that got stuck in the door as he tried ta climb in.'

Swithin could not help laughing at this mental picture of the unfortunate Vaheddin, last Imperial Ottoman Sultan Emperor of all the Turks and Terror of the World, fat, flabby, and useless, escaping out of his rebellious capital under the protection of the British. Then he remarked seriously: 'But what an extraordinary thing that a Eunuch should have risen to become the Chief of the Secret Police.'

The merchant had taken a shabby black book from a drawer and was flicking over the pages. He paused to look up sharply. 'And fer why should ye think that now? Spying's the natural business of a Eunuch. In the big harems there were scores of bonnie lassies wi' only one husband between the lot of them and no natural ootlet fer their passions. At times they'd go fair mad fer the lack of a man, so every harem was riddled wi' plots to smuggle in some lusty young *hamal* or soldier fer an hour. 'Twas the job of the Eunuchs to match their cunning against that of the women, and the clever ones made a mint o' money at the game. Think of the opportunities fer blackmail in sich a poseetion, mon! When one of these onnotural creatures had nosed out a love affair, he'd play the woman like a salmon trout by threatening ta tell the master if she did not find him sil'er enough to still his tongue, or if she were rich, he'd encourage her to play the whore provided he made a guid thing oot of it. But all the time he'd have to go canny as a cat, fer if the woman

63

were caught at her tricks he'd be called on ta answer fer it, and if his brother Eunuchs found him out, they'd tell on him to curry favour with their boss, so he stood a double chance of having his fat neck wrung. Can ye tell me a better school than that fer a secret-service man?'

'Of course you're right,' Swithin agreed. 'I hadn't thought of it quite like that.'

'No, I didna' suppose ye had, and if ye want my opeenion ye wouldn't have lasted a fortnight at the job yersel'!' After this crushing remark, McAndrew returned to the study of his small ledger, then he spoke again:

'Here's the vera thing for ye. Small, self-contained, three-roomed, furnished flat. Free of vermin. No. 19 Rue Tatavla —that's just north of Pera. It belongs to a Frenchman who works in the Crédit Lyonnais. The young fool started going with some Greek houri who was kept by a Bulgar, and the Bulgar caught him entertaining the lady one night—minus his trews, so he threw him out of the window. His bank gave him six months' sick leave, so here's his flat furnished and to feu. I can let it ye fer 80 Turkish pounds—that's about £13 10s. British—the month, and it's cheap at the price. Will ye take it or no?'

'Certainly. It sounds the very thing.'

'Ei—an' seein' ye come fra' Duncannon, I'll assume ye ta be a respectable body fer the moment so we can dispense wi' references.'

'Thank you.' Swithin managed to suppress his mirth with difficulty, and inquired: 'What else do you recommend me to do?'

'Keep yer room at the *Pera* if you can run to the expense and occupy it part of the time. If ye are watched, then they'll think it's yer pairmanent address and that ye are just a gay European who goes out certain nights wi' the ladies. Ye'll be free then to use the flat fer meeting people you wouldn't care ta be seen with in the cafés, and as a bolthole in case of necessity.'

'All right, I'll do that. Now can you put me on to any places where I am likely to pick up the latest political gossip. The cafés where journalists, ex-deputies, and minor officials meet, I mean?'

'Ei—there's the Foscolo Bar and the Petits Champs, but

sich places are always full o' police spies and *agents provocateurs* these days, so the other folk who use them keep a guard upon their tongues. I doubt ye'll learn anything that's not common knowledge if ye sit in them for a sen'night.'

'Surely there are places where the opposition and the discontented elements get together to discuss their grievances?'

'There *is* no opposeetion. The Wolfman at Angora hanged all that mattered of it years ago. As fer the discontented, they're all mixed up with the other folk, just as in other countries, and if some of them meet now and agen, it's in private—else the police would be on their track.'

Swithin nodded. 'On the face of it, then, it does not look as if there is anything in Sir George's idea that a drastic change is about to sweep the whole country?'

'It does not, and God forbid that it should. I'm a cautious mon when it comes ta giving an opeenion, but it's my belief that Kemal is seated firmly in the saddle now, and although he's an ill-living man in himself, he's done great things for Turkey. Tho old people take it hard that he's smashed their religion and customs, mebbe, but the young and progressive are wi' him to a mon; so if Duncannon has it in his head that there's an anti-Kemalist revolution brewing here and sent ye ta get details, it is a wild goose chase ye're on, I'm thinking.'

'That was only one idea,' Swithin demurred. 'Sir George also thought that it might be some new move which Kemal is contemplating himself. A *volte-face* to Islam again perhaps, or an attempt to regain the old Turkish territories which have been taken away piecemeal ever since the first Balkan war.'

McAndrew shook his sandy head. 'Why should he want to do that now? He's unshackled his country fra' the fetters of ignorance and superstition which have hampered it for centuries. My, it's almost unbelievable the miracle he's performed! He's changed the outlook of a whole people! Ye can no appreciate that as I can who have lived here all these years, an' he'll not go back on that even ta make hi'sel' Caliph and Sultan and Sheik El Islam rolled into one. He's more powerful as Dictator than he would be wi' fifty trashy titles if he had to submit ta the

Mullahs and the word of the Koran again.'

'Perhaps, but what about the suggestion that he is preparing for a war?'

'Not he. If he'd ha' wanted war, look what an opporrtunity he had when the Greek Revolution was in full swing. The Greeks are the hereditary enemies of his country and he's fought them fer a dozen years of his life. There's not a man East of the Adriatic who could hold a candle to him as a general; in fact, he's probably the greatest living soldier in the wurrld today an' he's got a well-equipped standing army full o' veteran fighters who'd jump at the chance of a scrap. While the Greeks were slaughtering each other, he could ha' seized Thrace overnight and smashed the Bulgars in the morning if they'd tried to intervene. But he didna'. He stuck to the Balkan Pact whereby Turkey, Roumania, Jugo-Slavia, and Greece agreed ta maintain the *status quo*. Kemal stands fer a Turkey free and independent within her own borders, and he'd even fight the British Empire if we tried to interfere wi' her—but he'll not set one foot outside the boundaries he's fixed hissel'!'

'Well, there it is.' Swithin smiled and stood up. 'I may be here on a fool's errand, but Sir George is convinced that something queer is going on and it's my job to either find it out or reassure him beyond all question that his fears are groundless. Since you can't help me further, I must just mix with every class I can and slowly sift any evidence that I manage to gather. It's going to be a long business and a dull one, I'm afraid.'

'Mebbe,' the Scotsman rose to his full lanky height, 'and I hope so fer your sake, but queer things are apt to happen ta folk who go poking their noses into other's business in this town, so me last piece of advice is ta go canny about it.'

'Thanks,' murmured Swithin, preparing to depart. 'I'm anxious enough to keep a whole skin, I assure you. When shall I be able to take over this flat?'

'I'll send the keys up ta the hotel this forenoon wi' a note fer the body who's acting caretaker; an' a letter of agreement which ye can return wi' a cheque fer the first month's rent. I'd prefer that ye don't come here agen fer I can no afford ta be mixed up in this secret business ye are on.'

'I understand, and thanks again for the hints.' Swithin held out his hand.

The dour Scotsman took it and held it for a moment, while an internal struggle seemed to be raging in his breast. Then suddenly an extraordinary kindly smile transformed his lean horus features.

'If ye get into trouble,' he said, 'real trouble—me house is in Moda, just across the Bosphorus—Yagourtchi Street, No. 110. I'm trusting ye not ta use it onless ye are scared of your life—but at a pinch I might be able ta get ye out.'

Late that afternoon, having rested through the hottest hours of the day, Swithin paid his first visit to the Tobacco Depot to take over, which was the nominal reason for his presence in Constantinople. From the Galata Bridge he was rowed by sturdy oarsmen into the open straits and up the Bosphorus. He could quite well have taken a motor launch, but as he had ample time he preferred the more leisurely pace of the ancient *caïque*, which better enabled him to enjoy the scenery.

It was not impressive as long as they remained near the Pera shore, for the wharves and warehouses, comparatively modern products of the last half-century, differed little in appearance from those of any great port in northern Europe, and Swithin knew that on a rainy day, when mist shut out the distinctive buildings of the city on the rising ground beyond, they could be as depressing as the water-side in Hamburg, Liverpool, or Rotterdam. After a little while, however, distance lent enchantment to the view, and Pera, dominated by the White Tower on its hilltop, took on the aspect of a fairy city, yellow, white, and cream, inter-sected with spaces of garden greenery, set between a sky of cobalt and a sea of deepest blue.

They passed the Dolma Baghtche Palace, rowed on for half an hour, and then just past Ortakeuy, pulled in to a small private wharf below the Tobacco Depot.

It was a long, low, two-storeyed wooden building set in what at one time must have been a beautiful garden. Swithin knew from his conversations with Sir George that in the old days it had been one of the minor properties of the Shah of Persia, and used by him on his occasional visits to the Turk-ish capital. The wide windows overlooking the gardens and the Bosphorus still contained traces of the lattice work which had shielded the ladies of the harem from the gaze of the curious, and Swithin knew that a number of them had remained in residence there until as recently as 1922.

The manager, a Greek named Lykidopulous, whom Swithin had warned of his visit, came down to greet him with low bows, much anxious rubbing of hands, and many servile phrases.

Swithin cut him short by explaining that he did not understand one word of Turkish, a subtle piece of craft since the fellow was babbling away in Greek and naturally concluded that Swithin was equally ignorant of that as well.

He broke into quaint but understandable English on the instant, and his servility gave place to a friendly, almost patronising air.

When the other members of the office staff were duly presented, Swithin found that none of them could speak a word of English, and when he tried them in French, he purposely made his own pronunciation so bad that they could not understand him. Lykidopulous grew more friendly and patronising than ever, and Swithin was astute enough to guess the reason.

Evidently the Greek had been dreading that this visit by the English Bank's representative might bring some small malpractices to light, but since Swithin was unable to question any of his staff, he now felt reasonably sure that nothing would be given away to his discredit.

Coffee was served with due ceremony in the office, and excellent cigarettes, the product of the firm, then Lykidopulous stood up.

'I show you the factory—yes-please. This side. I lead, yes-please, you not mind—I thank.'

'Please,' murmured Swithin, and he followed the Greek through several smaller chambers to what had once been the magnificent reception room of the Palace. Now it contained not a scrap of furniture, but along each wall men and women sat cross-legged on mats, busy grading the dried leaves from the tobacco plants. A great pile of the golden herb was heaped up in front of each worker, and these they were rapidly sorting into three smaller piles apiece, while overseers walked silently up and down supervising their labour. Lykidopulous explained the various processes in his queer English, and Swithin found the next hour a most interesting one.

Afterwards they returned to the office for more coffee and cigarettes. Then Swithin took his departure and was rowed back in the *caïque* down the Bosphorus. For half an hour, the men swung rhythmically at their oars until they approached Stamboul again, now peculiarly lovely in the evening light, its mosques and minarets forming a tracery like lace above the massed buildings growing each moment more indistinct as the veil of twilight hid them in the mystery of the coming night.

By the time he reached the Pera Palace darkness had fallen, but in the lounge all was brightness and animation. Travellers of both sexes, business men of a dozen different nationalities, officers of the Turkish Army and smart demi-mondaines, Greek, French, Russian, Jewish, Bulgarian, and Serb, sat laughing and drinking at the rows of tables. Their chatter in a dozen languages filled the great room with a babble of sound and almost drowned the jazz band which played in a far corner.

As Swithin made his way over to the lift, he glanced towards the bookstall. Tania Vorontzoff was there, darkly beautiful. She flashed him a smile of recognition, displaying two rows of small, even, very white teeth, and then turned back to the man with whom she had been talking.

That night Swithin dined quietly again in the hotel. Afterwards he went up to his room and spent a couple of hours studying a large-scale map of the city. He felt that an intimate knowledge of its topography might prove invaluable in an emergency.

It was not, of course, that he was definitely operating against the Turkish Government, but he was there to nose round, and he might well stumble on matters which it would most strongly resent any foreigner finding out. In that event he would find himself up against the organised police of the country and its formidable chief, the Eunuch, Kazdim Hari Bekar. They would arrest him for espionage if they could, and Sir George had made it quite plain what would happen to him then, ten years in a fortress—or worse, he would be knocked on the head one dark night and flung into the Bosphorus.

Swithin was under no illusion regarding the risks his job entailed, and he had already made up his mind that on the least suspicion that the police were taking an interest in his movements he would go to earth. It was either that or getting out at once, but he had no intention of throwing in his hand and having to confess defeat before Diana.

Having undressed, he flung wide his window to gaze out on the myriad lights that twinkled from the shipping in the Golden Horn and the houses of the darkened city.

'What secret did it hold,' he wondered. That he had not been sent there on a wild-goose chase, as McAndrew seemed to think, he felt certain. Sir George had filled him with his own forebodings that trouble was brewing in this capital of bygone empires which, despite its surface modernity, still held all the beauty, cruelty, romance, and intrigue of the timeless East.

8

The Drudgery of the Quest

All through the latter weeks of July and early August,
Swithin laboured at his task. The days were sweltering, the
nights oppressive, and his only relief from the heat and
flies and dust were his frequent trips up the Bosphorus to
the Tobacco Depot.

Always having believed that the secret of successful disguise lay in actually living the part played for the moment,
he flung himself as wholeheartedly into the affairs of the
Tobacco Company as if he had been a banker's investiga-
tor all his life. He asked endless questions and continually
pestered Lykidopulous for lengthy reports, so that the
Greek grew to loathe the sight of him. Of the technical side
he naturally remained profoundly ignorant, but he surprised himself by the quickness with which he came to
understand the general situation of the business, and was
able to comfort himself with the thought that, owing to
his activity in it, no member of the firm could possibly
suspect his stay in Constantinople to have any other
motive.

Moreover, since he was able to read such correspondence as Lykidopulous put before him, and was not dependent on the often deliberately inaccurate translations of the
Greek, he soon spotted just how the manager was making
a good thing out of it for himself, and it pleased him to
know that he would at least have this criminal leakage to
report to Sir George Duncannon when his real business
was concluded.

That real business did not prosper, however, despite
the hours he spent both day and night scraping casual
acquaintance with a hundred different types in every
quarter of the crowded cosmopolitan city. At the Pera, he
became, for a little time, a daily frequenter of the bar,
where he rubbed shoulders with Americans, English,
French, Italians, Germans, and talked of Turkey to them

by the hour. But all seemed convinced of Mustapha Kemal's pacific intentions, that his break with Islam had been final, and that, Dictator though he might be, his rule was now firmly founded upon a recognition by the majority of the people that he had saved Turkey from final partition by the victorious Allies and welded the remnant of the empire into a new and virile nation.

Obviously these people could tell him nothing, so he abandoned the bar for the cafés, which in the old days had been the centres of political discussion, but here he found that McAndrew had accurately assessed the situation. He met many interesting people and they talked freely enough upon stock-market quotations, the prospects of the tobacco, maize, and wheat crops, chess, football, which was now being played in every Turkish village, the broadcasting programmes, food, history, past wars, and a variety of other subjects, but immediately the name of Mustapha Kemal was mentioned loud protestations of admiration for his Government were promptly followed by a change of subject.

Swithin then took to wandering in the Grand Bazaar, that wonderful enclosed market with its high domed ceilings and small dust-covered windows through which the sun hardly penetrates. The uneven, badly paved streets, if placed end to end, would measure several miles in length, although all housed under one vast roof, and a thousand merchants displayed their wares there every day: jewellery, hardware, sweetmeats, boots, antiques—mostly from Hamburg or Birmingham, with an occasional genuine piece—oriental rugs, ready-made clothes, and a hundred other commodities. The more wealthy traders had lock-up shops, with glass windows, of their own; the middle sort spread out their goods each morning on open stalls; and the riff-raff hawked tawdry rubbish in the gutters.

Even on the hottest day it was cool in there, and he spent many hours bargaining for small purchases over innumerable cups of coffee and side-tracking the conversation from commercial matters when he had the opportunity, but he learnt little.

Once, when he returned to renew his bidding for a rug over which he had opened negotiations three days before, he found the dealer, an old and bearded man, admiring his reflection in a hand mirror with a worn fez set jauntily on his head. Immediately he caught sight of Swithin he whipped it off, stuffed it guiltily under a cushion, and resumed his bowler. The old chap was so rattled that he let Swithin have the rug for a hundred and fifty piastres less than he had offered on the previous occasion without a word of protest, but it would have been unreasonable to attach any undue importance to the episode except as an example of the fear in which Kemal's secret police were held owing to the rigour with which they enforced his ordinances.

On numerous occasions Swithin visited the Mosques of Ahmed, Soulyman, and Saint Sophia. The mighty spaciousness of the latter never failed to fill him with wonder and awe. Built as a Christian Basilica, it had been despoiled of its famous frescoes on the taking of the city, but it had been impossible for the victorious Turks to convert it properly to the use of their own religion. It is oriented according to the Christian formula, towards the East, and since the followers of the Prophet must face Mecca when they pray, all rugs and Mosque furniture have of necessity to be placed at an angle to the edifice, thus giving to its Mohammedan occupation a curiously makeshift and temporary appearance despite the fact that they have worshipped there for half a dozen centuries.

He manged to get into conversation with a few of the Mullahs and sought to learn how they had taken Kemal's attack on their revenues and curtailment of their privileges. They were not communicative on those points, remarking merely that the Gazi had laid no restraint on the continued exercise of their religion, and that the faithful saw to it that they wanted for nothing; he did, however, secure one piece of interesting information.

A devotee who had just come from listening to a reading of 'the word' one day, boasted how greatly the congregation had increased again of late, and Swithin verified that statement by talking to the beggars who sat outside the holy places. With them, business was on the upgrade, and after lean years they were thriving once more.

Several times he crossed the Bosphorus to Scutari, and once landed farther down at Moda, since he thought it as well to find out the exact position of the address that McAndrew had given him.

The house was a double-fronted, solid-looking property set in its own garden, and of a type which is to be found in many of the better London suburbs. Its neighbours were built on similar lines, and it seemed highly incongruous to find streets of such houses dumped down on the edge of Asia, but the British merchants of the eighties had built them thus and their successors continued to occupy them, as Swithin was aware. Having made careful note of the quickest way to reach it in an emergency, he left it sleeping there, apparently untenanted, in the strong sunshine of the afternoon.

As the days passed, his first enthusiasm began to wear a little thin. This scraping of acquaintance with strangers, accompanying them on sight-seeing expeditions, and giving or accepting odd meals here and there, all for the purpose of carrying on interminable conversations which never led to anything, seemed a completely futile waste of time. It irked him terribly that he could not get his teeth into the job, and he began to wonder if Sir George had not been barking up the wrong tree after all. Yet somehow he felt in his bones that, hidden under the teeming life of the city, something unusual was going on if only he could get a lead to it.

At last he decided that, much as he hated the idea of dressing up like some amateur detective, he must do so in order to try and make contact with the lower strata of the population.

Buying a piece here and a piece there, he gradually collected a strange assortment of second-hand clothing at his Tatavla flat, and then one evening he sallied forth to parade the streets as an apparently verminous ruffian.

For a night or two he was content to wander in the streets perfecting his make-up by watching the manner and bearing of other down-and-outs. Then he essayed the making of a few acquaintances in this new role, and for the purpose went into the poor quarter of Haskeuy, which the thousands of Russian refugees who found themselves marooned in Constantinople after the revolution have adopted for their own.

He could not, of course, pretend to be a Turk—his vivid

74

blue eyes would have given him away immediately; so he chose the character of a destitute Austrian who had been captured by the Russians in the latter part of the war, come down with the Whites as a refugee to Constantinople and, learning that he had lost both his money and his family, remained there ever since. His German was good enough to pass muster with a Russian or a Turk, and the population of Constantinople was a mixture of so many races that such a story had far more plausibility than it would have done in any other European capital.

Noticing a low, vaulted drinking shop which was fairly full of people, he went in and sat down at a rough wooden table which was only occupied by one man. A tousled-looking woman came up to take his order, and he asked for a Raki, then he sat silent for a little.

After an interval the man turned a pair of lack lustre eyes upon him, asked the time in bad Turkish and, on being told, got up to leave. Swithin sat on, hoping that other customers would come in to share his table and presently three new arrivals sat down at it. They were a cheerful trio and soon drew him into their conversation. Two of them were Russians but, in deference to the third, they talked in Greek. Swithin discovered that all three were employed in the Naval Arsenal nearby. The two refugees made no pretence to nobility; they had been simple soldiers at the time of the revolution with a belief in God and the Czar; in consequence they had remained loyal to their officers and eventually been driven out of Russia with them in 1920. Life in Constantinople was no harder for them than in any other place and as long as they retained their jobs they were content with such simple pleasures as they could afford.

For a week he went to the same drinking shop nightly, met his new friends again, and through them a number of others. It was dreary work sitting for hours in the heavy smoke-laden atmosphere, eking out a single drink, or at the utmost two, until closing time, because few of them could afford more in one evening. The talk was mostly of their chances in the lotteries, boastful references to their occasional successes with cheap women, bawdy stories, and now and then the resurrection of some oft told episode in the War which had been the outstanding period in

all their lives. They were vaguely Socialist but their grievances were more against the petty tyrannies of foremen
and low scales of wages paid by the masters than against
the exisiting Government, and they were almost entirely
ignorant of conditions in any country outside Turkey.
One man maintained that Hitler was the Kaiser's son, and
another, that Egypt was a part of India. Naturally Swithin
refrained from drawing attention to himself by any display of knowledge and risked no more than a casual word
now and then to keep the conversation upon politics
whenever they spoke of them.

One thing he noticed in these weary sessions was that
when these *émigrés* did speak of Turkish affairs they
talked far more freely than the Turks and on three occasions different men stated vaguely that they thought a
change was coming. He tried to draw them out but it was
soon obvious that they knew nothing and could not even
suggest what form the change was likely to take. Whatever happened could make little difference to their
wretched lot and they all seemed to regard the future with
hopeless apathy.

After a time, convinced that he could learn nothing of
importance from these simple Russian working men,
Swithin abandoned his evenings with them and turned his
attention to the Jewish Quarter round Galata.

Here he met with greater difficulty since he could not
possibly pass himself off as a Jew and the fact that most
Constantinople Jews are of Spanish origin provided an
additional handicap. Had they been German Jews he
might have understood fragments of their conversation
but as it was their gibbering was completely meaningless
to him except when they used Turkish or Greek.

He managed to make a friend of one however, a half
Italian and half Jewish bar-tender who had spent some
years in the United States. The man was undoubtedly a
bad hat and the place a shady haunt, but he had a sense of
humour and delighted in airing his broken English.
Swithin dressed slightly better on his visits to this place
and posed as a commercial traveller left stranded in
Constantinople because his firm had gone bankrupt.

One night the Italian-Jew got drunk and confidential.
The gist of his maudlin meanderings was that 'Somebody

was up to something as Swithin would very soon see. Every one of his Jewish friends was selling—selling—selling, and prices were coming down—down—down. They were unloading their goods now at stupid prices but still they continued to sell and, what was more, all the money was being smuggled out of the country'.

Outwardly Swithin's expression never altered but inwardly he began to get excited. It really looked as if he were on the verge of finding out something at last. Casually, in a low voice, he led the conversation round to Kemal and suggested that the Turks might be about due to revolt against his dictatorship, but the drunken Jew solemnly shook his head.

He agreed that plenty of people would like to slit the Dictator's throat, particularly those of his own race who had always used Turkey as a milch cow in the past and were now no longer able to do so except at considerable risk to their skins; but maintained that the Jews were far too shrewd to finance a rising. 'Kemal, miles away in Angora, is safe enough from assassination,' he said, 'and has troops, machine guns, airplanes, at his disposal. He would smash any attempt at revolution as easily as you could kick the top out of an old hat, so it would just be chucking money down the drain to try anything against him—no, it certainly is not that.'

At this juncture the Armenian-Jew proprietor of the place arrived on the scene, cursed the bar-tender for his condition with truly oriental fluency, and told Swithin to 'get out!' When he returned the following night, in the hope of renewing the conversation, he found a gazelle-eyed youth with greasy black curls behind the bar and learned that his drunken friend had been given the sack. The man's departure without leaving an address was unfortunate since it prematurely closed this promising line of investigation.

Within a few days of his arrival Swithin had sent in his report to Sir George, giving a *précis* of McAndrew's view of the situation, his own first impressions of the Tobacco Depot, and the information that he had secured extra accommodation which made him independent of his room at the *Pera*.

In his second report, a fortnight later, he had little of

77

interest to tell except that a quiet but steady religious revival was in progress, and that vague rumours supported Sir George's own suggestion that a big change of some kind was impending. Swithin gave full details of each episode upon which these general statements were based because he knew from his military training that small happenings which may be practically meaningless to the observer can sometimes confirm important conclusions at headquarters when collated with reports from other sources, but he was far from satisfied with his work.

He continued to sleep most nights at the *Pera*, only using his Tatavla flat when he returned to it late and felt too tired to change again in order to make a respectable reappearance at the hotel.

With Tania, at the bookstall, he became on the most friendly terms although he resisted her blandishments and hints that she would not be averse to supping with him, for his every night was occupied with his dogged but wearisome attempts to secure information.

On one occasion he tackled her on Turkish politics, since she seemed an extremely well-informed young woman, but she said at once that it was wiser not to talk of such things and, swivelling her dark eyes in the direction of a bowler hatted individual nearby, whispered that he was a detective.

At the Tobacco Depot he kept his ears open in the hope that the conversation of the workers might tell him something, since they had no idea that he could speak their language, but they talked little and, although he kept up his visits there for the sake of appearances, he learnt nothing.

After a further three weeks, his depression at his lack of success had sapped all his natural gaiety for, with his mercurial nature, it preyed upon his mind that he seemed to be taking Sir George's money to loaf about Constantinople week after week without apparently achieving anything. Had it not been for Diana's taunt he would have been tempted to throw the whole thing up and confess his failure, so it was in an unusually evil temper that he sat down to compile his already overdue third report.

Outside the apparently baseless remarks of the Russians, that something or other was in the air, there was nothing to show for three weeks grinding work except the statement of the Italian-Jew bar-tender. Swithin had confirmed the fact that commodity prices had been falling steadily for some months past, but Sir George would naturally be aware of that already, and Swithin had no means of checking the suggestion that the Constantinople Jews were busy smuggling their money out of the country.

As he sealed the letter he was as far as ever from being able even to hint at the cause or object of this rumoured 'change' which he had come out to fathom.

He sent it off, as he had the other two, in accordance with his instructions, by Kavass to Allan Duncannon, the banker's brother who lived outside the city at Bebek. Then, the following day, to his complete amazement, he received an acknowledgement of it from Diana.

9

The Impulsive Student

It read:

> I have your letter, Father is still in Athens but I have come on here to stay with my cousin Ursula. He received your earlier notes and told me to read any future ones from you in order to pass on the gist of them in my own letters to him. If we happen to run into one another it would be best if you do not appear to know me and, under no circumstances, are you to telephone me here. Be outside Hadji Bekir's, the *patisserie* in the Grand' Rue de Pera, at 4.30 tomorrow afternoon.
>
> D.
>
> P.S. You will destroy this—of course.

With mixed feelings he re-read the brief note. After surprise his first emotion was delight at knowing her to be in Constantinople, but he had not forgiven her yet for her abominable treatment of him on the yacht so, although the lapse of time had taken the edge off his indignation, his pleasure was short lived.

Thinking things over he had to concede that if she were so deep in her father's confidence she could not be quite such an empty-headed little fool as she had made herself appear on the voyage out. Then—as he realised the significance of her postscript—he smiled.

Why should she think it necessary to ask him to destroy her note? Since it concerned secret business it would have been crass negligence to keep it any case and she would certainly know that in such circumstances all correspondence is destroyed immediately as a matter of routine. The obvious inference was that, despite their angry parting, she still thought that some personal tie existed between them and that he might keep it from sentiment. Swithin laughed as he struck a match and lighting the single sheet of paper watched it flame into blakened ash.

The following afternoon he was outside Hadji Bekir's at the appointed time and so disturbed at the thought of seeing her again that he did not realise until afterwards that she had not kept him waiting for a single minute.

On the stroke of half-past four a private car drew up. The chauffeur flung open the door and Diana and another girl stepped out.

Swithin had his back to them, for he had taken up his position outside the shop and was apparently studying the notice which declared Hadji Bekir to be: *'Fournisseur de l'ex Cour Impériale et Khediviale. Créateur du Raehat-Locoum, utilisé depuis des siècles dans les Harems en Orient,'* although actually watching the reflection of the traffic in the glass.

He knew at once that she had seen him but remained as he was until she reached the door of the *patisserie* then, just as she dropped her bag and stooped to retrieve it from the pavement he turned and forestalled her. Their heads almost touched and he caught her whisper 'Try the University,' then he handed her the bag, received her smile of thanks and—she was gone.

He turned back to the window, studied the cakes for another moment, then walked away.

'God! she's good-looking.' That was the thought which dominated his mind all the way back to the hotel. Even then it was only with the greatest resolution that he put it out of his head to consider her suggestion and he had to admit that to be sound.

Students in Eastern countries take to politics with all the enthusiasm which their Western contemporaries reserve for physical development or sport, and Swithin knew that every Balkan University had its secret societies for the liberation of its fatherland from the 'foreign yoke' or 'despot' of the moment. Such youths with wild, ill-directed patriotism were the first to fill the streets on any 'national' day to aid in rowdy demonstrations, and it was from the unbalanced in their ranks that anarchist organisations recruited the fanatics who believed they could earn a martyr's crown by sacrificing their lives in some dastardly political assassination. But youth is often indiscreet and Swithin realised that there was just a chance of his securing first hand information of this trouble that was brewing if he could make a few friends at the Stamboul University.

That evening, as a first step, he inquired from the Head Porter at the *Pera* what lectures were being given in the University Quarter which were open to the public, and learned that a certain Mr. Mufid Yessari, B.Sc. (Oxon), was giving a series upon 'The Turkish Race, its Origin and Development' one of which was announced for the following night. Obviously this was one of the side lines in the Kemalist Government propaganda for strengthening Turkish nationalism. Mustapha had initiated the campaign in 1928 by acting schoolmaster himself and appearing with a blackboard to introduce the latest 'development'—his substitution of Latin characters for the old Turkish script —to the notables of Constantinople.

Swithin bought a back seat and attended, confident that a certain number of students would be among the audience. The lecturer, a short tubby man, who wore a suit of plusfours evidently imported from England, was obviously a master of his subject and a very competent speaker. The occasion was the fourth in a series of six talks and he had arrived at that period of Turkish history when the vast ramshackle Empire was tottering to its fall. Ferdinand of Bulgaria was casting covetous eyes on Macedonia, George of Greece on Crete, Peter of Serbia on Uskub, the ancient capital of his country, and Nikola of Montenegro, like any other bandit, ready to join with them for what he could get out of it. The four Christian Kings had sunk their differences, preached the Ninth Crusade, and come down like wolves on the Turkish fold. In all but Thrace they had driven Turkey out of Europe and, after bitter fighting among themselves, divided what the Austrians and Italians had left of her Western Empire between them.

On the face of it this sounded a sad tale of woe but the Government subsidised speaker treated it with extreme skilfulness. 'What had they lost?' he asked. 'Great areas of territory perhaps, but by whom was the territory peopled? Not Turks to any appreciable extent but alien races in an almost constant state of insurrection. It had cost far more money to police these countries and defend them from their Christian neighbours than they had ever got out of them in taxes; and the best men in Turkey had wasted their lives to keep them in subjection. Now they were free

82

of that burden and able to devote their wealth and energy bettering their own condition. Even the small percentage of Turkish nationals who had passed under foreign rule by these apparent disasters were not to suffer permanently. By Kemal's new scheme for the repopulation of Thrace, which had been practically denuded of human beings owing to twelve years of almost continual war, the Turks in the Balkan peninsular were all to be repatriated and settled in model farms and villages. Thrace would blossom once again and their brothers, brought out of captivity, still further strengthen and unify the new Turkish nation within its natural borders.

Swithin knew the whole story already, but he admired the able way in which the speaker put it over, for it could be no simple task to convince a patriotic people that the loss of its entire empire was for its eventual benefit. Yet the majority of the audience obviously accepted the lecturer's statements and a certain number of them even showed enthusiasm. However, here and there groups sat silent with watchful strained faces and Swithin judged that these would have vented angry criticisms had they not feared arrest for showing open hostility to the policy of the Government.

Some of these latter were obviously young students such as Swithin had expected to find at the meeting and one, apparently unaccompanied, was sitting on his immediate left. He was a tall dark young man with thick-lensed glasses and stooping shoulders. His nose was beaky and his chin slightly receding, which gave him an eager impulsive look, and his long-fingered hands fidgeted perpetually as though he was itching to stand up and make a protest.

As the lecturer spoke so glibly of settling Macedonian Turks on Thracian farms the young man suddenly sprang to his feet but before he had time to open his mouth Swithin had grabbed his arm and pulled him down again:

'Quiet you fool,' he whispered, 'this is no place to air your own opinions.'

Two stewards came hurrying up to inquire what was the matter. The young man looked worried and flustered so Swithin came to his rescue. 'My friend is ill,' he explained, 'and we would like to leave but do not wish to disturb the meeting—is that permissible?'

A passage was made for them at once and the stewards courteously escorted them to the entrance of the building. Outside the young Turk began to mop the perspiration from his face and turned to Swithin:

'I am most grateful to you. If you had not prevented me, my anger would have led me to say something stupid and then these devils would probably have arrested me. My name is Reouf. You speak Turkish well—but you are a foreigner—are you not?'

Swithin explained that he was an Englishman whose business had necessitated a long stay in Constantinople and that having seen how promptly the authorities dealt with interrupters at similar meetings he had felt it only decent to intervene.

Reouf thanked him again and suggested coffee. Swithin accepted readily enough and they were soon seated together at a nearby café. The Turk proved to be a student as Swithin had supposed and, in addition, a very charming and loquacious person. Over the tiny cups of sweet, black, scalding coffee he praised England loudly and lamented that owing to lack of proper trade agreement with Britain the bulk of Turkish business was falling into German hands. Like many Turks he hated Germany, since he considered her responsible for the ruin of his country in the War.

Swithin dared not turn the conversation to current politics for the moment, but as they talked of the past he learned one piece of history; the fatal decision which had resulted in tying the Turkish Empire to Germany's chariot wheels.

'In 1914,' said Reouf, 'Great Britain was building two big warships for Turkey. When the crisis came they were ready for delivery *and they had been paid for*—yet, at the urgent request of the Russian Foreign Office Britain detained them in her yards. On August 4th the British Navy was the stronger by two battle cruisers of the latest type but she had alienated the whole of the Turkish nation. Those ships had not been built and payed for by Budget money but by patriotic subscription to which even the widow and the orphan had contributed their mite. Turkey might have been kept neutral but for that stupidity. As it was even the children felt they had been robbed by Britain and the nation stood behind Enver Pasha's pact with Germany to a man.'

'A sad blunder on our part,' Swithin admitted, 'but even so Turkey would have done better to forget her battleships and remain out of the War.'

Reouf agreed heartily to that and admitted that there was some excuse for Britain acting as she had in such an emergency; but pointed out that, in the low state of education general in Turkey before the War, the people could not be expected to appreciate anything except that they had been deprived of those two glorious ships, paid for by self-denial and the nation's pocket money.

For nearly two hours they sipped successive cups of coffee and talked upon a variety of subjects with mutually growing interest and esteem, so that when Swithin suggested another meeting Reouf replied at once:

'I was about to ask if you would give me the pleasure of showing you something of the city during your stay. Have you yet been out to the old wall of Stamboul?'

'No,' Swithin confessed, 'but I should like to very much.'

'Then if your business permits will you meet me tomorrow at, say twelve o'clock, by the Golden Gate of the Fortress of Yedi-Koula?'

'Yes, I am free all day tomorrow as I visited my Depot today.'

'Good. Then we will make the excursion and take a picnic lunch.'

As they left the café and paused to shake hands outside it the young Turk added: 'The old fortifications are full of interest but also they have many lonely spots where we can talk freely. You are an Englishman and intelligent. My friends and I wish that Englishmen like yourself should know our views as to where the true good of Turkey lies. Changes are coming very shortly now and if you understand our motives you can explain them to others on your return and win for us the sympathy of your countrymen.'

'I should be only too happy,' Swithin replied with joy in his heart and, as he turned away, he felt that through this encounter he was at last about to gain the key to the secret which had baffled him for so many dreary weeks.

10

The Tower of Marble

As Reouf had declared the Great Wall of Stamboul was well worth a visit. One of the most imposing ruins in Europe it rose out of the dusty plain in a great double step, the inner of which was sixty feet in height and, in many places, broad enough to drive a chariot along its top; a vast buttress protecting the ancient portion of the city.

Swithin's guide met him at the Golden Gate and they entered the great tangle of masonry and courtyards, known as the Castle of the Seven Towers, which dominates the wall's south-western point. Then, climbing the broken stairway of a deserted tower they surveyed the magnificent panorama from its summit.

Below them as they faced the town were massed acre upon acre of squalid buildings, wood, brick, and stone, intersected with tortuous alleys which teemed with the slum population but beyond they gave place to tier on tier of splendid domes and a stone forest of minarets, while still further off, hazy in the quivering heat of midday, the slopes of Pera were just visible across the Golden Horn.

To the left, rising and falling over hills and hollows, curving a little here and there, broken at intervals by squat square towers, and gradually mounting with the level of the ground, the double tiered wall stretched away inland to the northward as far as the eye could see. Yet the prospect to the south was even more beautiful. On that side the old wall dipped and rose and dipped again for a quarter of a mile, then it ended in a marble tower which rose actually out of the blue waters of the Marmara.

For half an hour they scrambled from one vantage point to another, identifying the distant buildings of the city, admiring the fortifications, and gazing across the sea, intensely blue and sparkling in the sunshine, to the island of Prinkipo, which lay far out upon its faintly crested waters, and beyond, like a low bank of cloud on the horizon, the shores of Asia.

Climbing the worn stairways and across heaps of rubble in the grilling sunshine was hot work however so, as they came through a hidden passage to a great rent in the main wall which overlooked the moat and the cypress-lined road which runs parallel with it, Swithin suggested lunch.

The angle of a nearby tower made a shady spot beneath the hole; so they jumped down on to the lower wall and set about unpacking their picnic meal.

When hunger and thirst were satisfied they settled themselves with their backs to the warm brickwork below the breach, lit cigarettes and began to talk.

For a little they spoke of idle things then Swithin brought the conversation back to the point where they had dropped it the night before.

'You were going to tell me the views of yourself and your friends about the future of Turkey,' he said. 'Of course all Constantinople knows that the present state of things will not continue long but I should be interested to hear how you propose to better them?'

Reouf took off his thick glasses, peered at Swithin for a moment with his weak eyes while he wiped the lenses, and then restored them to his beaky nose. 'Yes, you are an Englishman so I can trust you not to repeat anything I tell you to the authorities—and it is very important that we should have the sympathy of as many Englishmen as possible when the time comes. You and I are only pawns in the game but if I can make you understand our situation it may be that you will persuade others of your countrymen to take a reasonable attitude and so influence your Government to the same end. You see, the Western nations have looked upon us Turks as a degenerate race for so long, I feel no chance should be lost which may help to reverse that view, and enable you to appreciate all that we feel.'

Swithin nodded sympathetically. 'Yes, it is true that many of us have always thought of Turkey as the "Sick Man of Europe" but remember how corrupt your Government had become before Abdul Hamid was deposed in 1909. Every office in the State, from Governorships to a job as a postman, and even promotion in the Army, was sold to the highest bidder. Such Ministers as would have liked to do better things had no power; each time they attempted any reform they were overruled by the Palace gang and defeated by Harem intrigue. Your country suffered in itself and in the estimation of the world, in consequence.'

'Tch! The old Red Fox—Abdul the Damned!' Reouf made an impatient gesture. 'He and his predecessors for a dozen generations were rogues—abusers of power unfitted to govern—I admit it. But that was all swept away by the Committee of Union and Progress in the Revolution. The heart of Turkey was still sound and all things would have been altered then had we been given a little time. As it was, before we had a chance to straighten out our affairs those dogs of Christians . . .' He paused with an embarrassed flush and added hastily. 'Pardon I beg—I meant no personal reference.'

'No, no—go on.' Swithin smiled reassuringly. 'You mean the Kings of Italy, Bulgaria and Greece.'

'I thank you—yes, and Peter Karageorgovitch, the Serbian who gained his throne by the murder of Alexander and his wife, and that other brigand Nikola of Montenegro. The whole pack descended on us like vultures on a dying camel. Think of what we went through in those few years before the Great War. Bosnia, Crete, Tripoli, taken from us. War in Africa. War in Macedonia. War in Arabia where the Beduin revolted and profaned the Holy City of Medina. The Great Fire in Stamboul which left forty thousand people homeless, our treasury empty, and the accursed Bulgars at the very gates of the capital. How was it possible to introduce reforms among our people when we were fighting for our very existence?'

'That's true. They must have been terrible years, and everyone knows that the Young Turk party was appallingly handicapped from the day of its birth. But there were quiet periods and during them the massacres of Bulgars and Armenians carried out on a greater scale than ever before. That had an immense effect in leading the Great Powers to suppose that the New Government was no better than the Old—and there was no excuse for it.'

'No excuse!' Reouf echoed with a wave of his slim hands. 'But, my friend, you do not understand. These Bulgar swine are very devils. They had killed by torture and mutilation hundreds of our police and troops. No

88

Turkish official was safe in their territory. Not a night passed but some unfortunate *bimbashie* was dragged from his home in an isolated village to be murdered in the streets while his women were raped to death and children hacked to pieces with saws and scythes. It is on record that one of these Christian brigands who was caught confessed that he and his friends used to partake of their sacrament before going out to raid, and that in the wine their Popes mixed the blood of Turks. No police in the world could have traced the actual perpetrators of all these slayings, so what could we do but inflict mass punishments from time to time. It is true that some who were innocent may have suffered with the guilty, but even those whose hands were not stained with our blood were guilty also, for priests, women, and children all assisted in this barbarous vendetta against us.'

'What about the Armenians?' Swithin demanded.

'Tch! there it was the same. They have made a sport of raiding lonely Turkish posts for generations. They are not human those people but wild beasts whose one delight is cruelty. They are like jackals who creep up to a wounded ox in cowardly packs to disembowel it. No kind treatment or appeal to live in amity makes any impression on them. They only understand the whip and bastinado. You would agree with me if you knew them.'

'I do—a little. I was stationed in quite a number of Armenian villages after the Armistice.'

'Well then!' Reouf's white teeth flashed in a smile of triumph. 'Judge you between us. How did they treat their animals?'

'It made me sick to see them,' Swithin confessed.

'Exactly, whereas the poorest Turkish farmer cares for his horses as himself—and the children in those villages— what of them?'

'Poor mites, they fared little better as far as I could see. On one occasion I had to use my riding crop on a great brute who was beating a child till it bled because the poor little devil had allowed another to steal the *baksheesh* it had been sent to beg in our camp.'

'There then!' Reouf spread out his elegant hands again. 'Now, tell me, have you ever seen a single Turkish child crying in the streets of Istanbul for any reason other than it had hurt itself?'

'No, now that I come to think of it I haven't and I must have walked through miles of streets since I arrived here six weeks ago.'

'Then that proves my contention that we are a gentle people. We love children, horses, dogs, and protect them from all ill. In that we are like you English, who will never tolerate unkindness to the weak and helpless; and surely that is a true test of whether a people is fitted to rule others who have not yet advanced to such a high level of conduct.'

'Yes, fundamentally I suppose it provides a genuine criterion.'

'Good, then consider our old subject races and their habits in such matters. Besides, we Turks are a Great People! Look at our history! What other nation has ever produced a line of ten successive sovereigns, father to son, each one personally outstanding as a soldier and statesman. When Western Europe was still a collection of petty states, governed by uncouth, warring robber Barons, Othman was a power in Asia Minor. Orchan, his successor, made the Sea of Marmara a Turkish lake. Murad, third of the line, took Byzantium, gave new life to its ancient civilisation and carried our banners nearly to the Adriatic Sea. In the reign of each succeeding Sultan for three hundred years our Empire spread until, under Soulyman the Magnificent in the sixteenth century, it extended from Algeria to the Persian Gulf and from Poland to Kartoum.'

'That's a mighty long time ago though,' Swithin commented softly.

For a moment the fire died out of Reouf's eyes behind the thick spectacles. 'Yes,' he admitted sadly. 'As you will know it is believed that during the reign of Soulyman the Royal Bed was desecrated and that Selim the Sot, with all those who followed after as wearers of the Sword of Othman, were not of the same blood.'

Swithin nodded. 'In any case it is a fact that the race of Sultans has degenerated ever since.'

'But not the spirit of the people,' Reouf protested, his eyes lighting up again. 'Just as you English are a nation born to rule so are we Turks. We proved it for many centuries, and should have proved it again after the Revolution, had we not been handicapped by wars which were not of our seeking and our Empire finally torn to pieces in the world struggle. But now we have recovered from our wounds and soon we will show again the stuff that we are made of.'

As these dark prophecies rolled from the young Turk Swithin almost held his breath lest he should interrupt the flow of bitter confidences, but he need not have been anxious, Reouf hurried on with a fresh spate of passion.

'Above all we are a governing people. For six hundred years there have been careers for the men of all good Turkish families in administering the provinces. Now we have provinces no longer. How would you feel in England if India and all your Crown Colonies were taken from you? Each year you send out thousands of public school men later to become Magistrates, Police Chiefs, State Engineers, Judges—and the Heads of Hospitals, Universities, Railways, Museums, Architectural Institutes, Customs, Religious Foundations, Agricultural Colleges, Postal Services, not to mention those who officer the Fighting Forces which you keep up in these countries and the thousands more who run the big business-houses under the protection of your flag. How would England feel then, I say, with no jobs left to give her young men of position and education?'

'It would be a pretty nasty problem for us I admit,' Swithin agreed hastily.

'Very well then. That is the situation in Turkey today and why England should be the first to understand our case and sympathise with us. How my blood boiled to hear the cowardly doctrine which that Government propagandist talked last night. Just think of the thousands of Turkish families who are now compelled to live under foreign rule.'

'But I understood him to say that they were being repatriated under this scheme of Kemal's for the repopulation of Thrace.'

'Tch! a few perhaps but not five per cent of their total number!'

'What would you do then?' Swithin put the question with a lazy smile but inwardly he waited, taut with expectancy for Reouf's answer.

'Do!' exclaimed the young Turk without hesitation. 'I would wrest the Government from this traitor Kemal who has been led into making criminal pacts by his admiration for Western Nations.'

'So,' thought Swithin, 'the cat is out of the bag at last,' but no muscle of his face relaxed as Reouf went on hotly:

'Kemal did much for Turkey in the War and after, but he has sacrificed the soul of our nation for the material trappings of the West. We are not a European people and we never shall be. No wearing of bowler hats, jazz music and co-education will ever make us so. We are Asiatics and and the ways of our fathers which endured for centuries are those best suited to our needs.'

'Yet you admit that sweeping reforms were long over-due.'

'Truly—and they have now been carried out—but that could have been done without laws which force us to sin fifty times a day in the sight of Allah, or treaties which tie us down to the permanent acceptance of territorial limitations making us into a Third-Class State.'

Swithin knew that it was vital to find out if Reouf's view represented those of only a small group or if they were widely accepted throughout the country, so to lead the young man on he shook his head and said:

'You are an idealist and I understand your personal feeling, but surely the great bulk of the population has accepted Kemal's reforms quite willingly.'

Reouf grinned suddenly. 'You think that eh? All right, meet me tonight at the lower end of the Street of Steps in Pera. Be there at eight o'clock and I will take you to a meeting. There you will see for yourself many others who think as I do, and realise that this movement, for which I speak, is a living thing springing from the heart of the whole nation.'

'I would like to come very much,' Swithin said softly.

'Good. I am glad, for after tonight you will under-stand how determined we are to go through with our pro-gramme. I will introduce you to my brother Arif who will be there but you will saying nothing of our talk please. Many of my comrades think that all things should be done in complete secrecy. I also think so but that we should make exceptions to our rule with people like yourself. Later, when we have accomplished our revolution we shall have to face the hostility of all our old enemies in the Balkans, but if a dozen men like yourself know the truth and would speak it fearlessly England might use her influence in our favour and perhaps persuade the other powers to do likewise. You and I are but pawns as I have said before but we are both earnest men and if we work together we may at least do something towards fostering good feeling and understanding between our countries.'

Swithin sat silent for a moment, to all outward appearances just enjoying an academic discussion as he leaned, smoking a cigarette, with his back propped up against the wall, but his brain was ticking over like the engine of a racing car.

There was actually a Revolution brewing then. That was at the root of all these vague signs of unrest which he had noted. Probably no more than a few hundred students and fanatics were concerned but it behoved him to find out every possible detail that he could and, particularly, the strength behind the movement. His inward excitement was intense, now that he felt himself to be really getting to the core of the mystery, but his voice was quite steady as he remarked casually:

'You speak of a Revolution, but how can you possibly hope to overcome Kemal. He controls all the armed forces of the country and has a swift way of dealing with such outbreaks.'

The young Turk sunk his voice a little. 'Listen, this is very secret but it is necessary that I tell you in order that you may appreciate the importance of our talk. This movement is a highly organised one. We speak of it ourselves as the Kaka, which is an abbreviation of The Brothers in Allah of the Sword and Crescent. In every regiment in the Army and squadron of the Air Force there are members of it. Many officials, big business men, journalists and teachers belong. In fact, wherever there are intelligent patriotic and determined men the Kaka has its representatives sworn to carry out its ideals.

'And Kemal, how will you deal with him,' asked Swithin softly.

Reouf laughed mirthlessly again. 'When the time is ripe —and it is not far distant—we shall dispose of Kemal as he has disposed of so many others.'

'You speak of the Gazi,' cut in a thin piping voice above them suddenly.

Reouf sprang to his feet as though he had been stung and Swithin whipped round his head with equal quickness. There, above them, his enormous bulk almost filling the great breach in the wall stood one of the strangest looking individuals they had ever seen. He was a tall man with immensely powerful shoulders but the effect of his height was minimised by his gigantic girth. He had the stomach of an elephant and would easily have turned the scale at twenty stone. His face was even more unusual than his body for apparently no neck supported it and it rose straight out of his shoulders like a vast inverted U. The eyes were tiny beads in that great expanse of flesh and almost buried in folds of fat, the cheeks puffed out, yet withered like the skin of a last year's apple, and the mouth was an absurd pink rosebud set above a seemingly endless cascade of chins.

'Well?' he questioned. 'Am I not right.'

Reouf had gone deathly white under his tan. His slender hands trembled as he strove to draw a cigarette out of his case. Swithin too was wondering anxiously how much of their conversation the stranger had overheard :

'Yes,' he admitted. 'Is it forbidden?'

The big man stood there framed in the ragged oval of brownish creamy brick, his vast protruding paunch on a level with their heads. Suddenly his absurdly small mouth twitched into a smile: 'Not for foreigners and I guess you English—am I right? You come here to see the wall, eh? I speak English. I will show you all there is to see.'

'Yes, I am English,' Swithin admitted, 'and although we went over the Towers before lunch we were just thinking of having another look round. Are you a professional guide?'

'Hardly that, sir,' the high piping voice came again, 'but I could find my way blindfold through most of these passages and I know much of the history of this old wall.'

'How interesting,' remarked Swithin guardedly. Something about the big stranger filled him with intense distrust but the obvious policy was to be civil in case the man had overheard much of their talk.

The stranger nodded so that his multitudinous chins creased more sharply. 'Interesting, yes,' he repeated and it seemed like a ventriloquist's trick that the tiny fluting voice could really come from this mountain of a man. 'And I delight to be guide for an English visitor. Come I will show you everything.'

'Thanks, that's nice of you,' said Swithin with a cordiality he was far from feeling. Then, followed by the young Turk, who had now more or less pulled himself together, he scrambled up into the hole in the great wall.

'This wall,' began the other, 'is made in the reign of Emporor Theodosius the Second by Anathemius, Prætorian Prefect of the East in A.D. 413.' He suddenly paused and switched round on Reouf. 'You do not mind that I do not repeat in Turkish. You understand English, yes—and very well—I hear you speak.'

Swithin felt a little shiver go down his spine and again he wondered anxiously how much of Reouf's disclosures this sinister person had overheard, but the young Turk replied now with commendable calmness. 'Oh, yes, people are kind enough to say that I speak English very well. I took an honours pass for it at Robert College.'

The big man grinned and his little eyes almost disappeared between their encircling rolls of fat. 'So you are from Robert College, eh? The education there does honour to our city. Oh! so many clever young men come from Robert College and if they are not too clever they get big position later. If they become *too* clever though sometimes they make the big mistake.' His great body suddenly shook with silent horrid laughter.

'What was it that you were going to say about the Emperor Theodosius?' Swithin intervened quickly. He was reasonably certain of being able to keep his own end up in this unpleasant situation but scared that Reouf might perpetrate some stupidity owing to fright, which had turned his face to a sickly, palish green again.

'This way—you follow please.' Their guide turned and led them back through the dark passage in the wall out into a sunny courtyard. Then, with frequent chuckles at his own jokes he gave them an outline of the history of the fortifications.

Reouf stood by, suspicious and uneasy, but Swithin's eyes

never left the big man's face. He laughed at the right moments and asked numerous questions until, after a while, both became easier in their minds and satisfied that their new companion was only a talkative busybody.

'Now,' he exclaimed at the end of his dissertation. 'Follow me please, and all points of interest I will show.' Then, with surprising agility for one of his enormous bulk, he led the way up a flight of steps to a tower top from which Swithin had already admired the view earlier in the day. Next they descended again, passed through some dark arches and, with the aid of the big man's torch, groped their way down a narrow passage to the rows of cells where prisoners had been held captive, far from light or sound, in the very heart of the great wall.

'Just think of being cooped up in these dreadful places for months on end, perhaps,' Swithin remarked. 'It's nice to know that civilisation has at least made such horrors impossible in these days.'

The other chuckled: 'Yes, all things are speeded up now. Either a man is tried and released if he is innocent or if that is not convenient he is not tried but dies at once. Come, there is another point of interest that I will show.'

He led them out into the sunlight from the Castle of the Seven Towers by a low gateway, down a tree-lined road to the railway embankment which cut the fortifications at right angles to enter the city, under it by a narrow tunnel, and so on to the wall again, where it runs for its last four hundred yards towards the sea. They entered another black hole in a bastion, stumbling down a long flight of crumbling stairs and eventually arrived in a circular chamber which echoed to a peculiar hissing sound.

The vault was lit by long slits in the walls through which, in ancient days, archers had loosed their shafts upon beseiging foes. Glancing through one of them Swithin realised that they were now in the Tower of Marble which, projecting from the main fortifications, was built out into the sea. Three sides of its base were washed by the waters of the Marmara and only the fourth linked it with the shore by the structure concealing the passage through which they had come.

The repulsive-looking fat man stood there pointing to a great hole in the middle of the floor. Swithin stepped forward and peered over the edge. This then was the explanation of the hissing sound; forty feet below the chamber where they stood the seething waters rushed and tumbled through a channel right beneath the centre of the tower. It was an *oubliette* and Swithin realised its deadly purpose. Reouf did also, and after one glance backed away towards the wall.

Again their self-appointed guide chuckled as he looked from one to the other of them. 'When it was not convenient to try people they were brought here. These walls could tell lovely tales for us of screaming men, and women too, their hands tied behind their backs, flung down into the water. Better than a dungeon that eh? All over in one minute and none ever returned to tell of their experience.'

For a moment all three of them regarded the sinister black hole in silence while the sound of the rushing waters from which there could be no escape came up to them. Then the big man suddenly laid his plump hand on Reouf's arm.

'I have known such things happen even in my lifetime,' he said softly, 'and such things might happen to those who are so clever that they make the big mistake.'

II

Old Lamps for New

From the first appearance of the big stranger, Swithin's apparent interest in the fortifications had only been dictated by caution. At last, after all these weeks of unsuccessful prowling he had secured, in one short hour of conversation with Reouf, real confirmation of Sir George's fears for the stability of Turkey. It yet remained to be seen how wide the ramifications of the conspiracy were but he felt that his news should be passed on with the least possible delay so, as they left that sinister chamber in the Tower with its horrid shaft down which men had been hurled to death in the sea below, he glanced at his watch, appeared surprised to find that it was after three, and begged the others to excuse him.

Reouf seemed disappointed that he could not remain to drink coffee with him at a local café before returning to Pera, but their self-appointed guide offered himself jovially as a substitute and, since the young Turk could not refuse his company without being openly rude, Swithin was able to leave the two of them together, having confirmed his appointment with Reouf for that evening.

He hastened back to the *Pera* and scribbled a line to Diana saying that he had urgent news which he preferred not to commit to paper. He added that he would remain in the lounge of the hotel until a quarter to eight so that she could appear to run into him casually there if she wished or, if she thought that too public, would she send him a message stating some other place where they could have ten minutes talk together.

Having dispatched his note by messenger he passed the time of day with Tania, purchased a sheaf of the latest periodicals from her, and settled himself with them at a table in the lounge which commanded a good view of its entrance.

How long he would have to wait he had no idea. Diana

might be out when his note arrived, or kept by some engagement, yet he felt certain she would manage to come or send him a message somehow before a quarter to eight. She had gone up immensely in his estimation since their brief meeting two days before outside Hadji Bekir's. She might be a hard-hearted-Hannah, he felt, but she was no fool; her suggestion about the University had already borne magnificent fruit and she was obviously taking a keen interest in her father's affairs.

He watched the clock tick round from four o'clock to five with reasonable complacency feeling that in any case he could hardly expect her under the hour then, at half-past five, he ordered himself a second tea in the hope that she might arrive in time to join him, but by six he had finished toying with it and she had not yet appeared.

By seven his optimistic mood had passed. Twice he had been to the porter's desk to make certain that there was no message for him so he began to wonder if she had been out all afternoon and not yet received his note.

He thought of telephoning but did not like to go against her instructions. Then he began to wonder why she had laid it down so definitely in her note that he should not do so, and a new idea filled him with sudden apprehension. Perhaps with this great network of police spies in Constantinople she suspected that there was one among the servants in Allan Duncannon's house. If so, the fellow might have means of supervising all correspondence and for some purpose have deliberately delayed the delivery of his note. It seemed a rather far-fetched idea but the prohibition against his telephoning supported it and Swithin felt that in the sort of business in which he was now engaged even improbabilities should be taken into consideration. He was doubly glad that he had refrained from giving written particulars of his news and began to wonder, reckoning the theory of a spy among Allan Duncannon's servants as a possiblity, what course he had better adopt if Diana failed to turn up by a quarter to eight.

It meant that he would have to go to his appointment without passing on his information. The few hours delay were of no great importance, but there was just a chance that the unexpected might happen at the meeting. If Kemal's Secret Police were better informed than young

Reouf and the dreaded Kazdim Hari Bekar chose that evening to round up the conspirators, Swithin saw himself being caught among them and thrown into prison with the rest. It would prove an extremely difficult business then to get his warning through to Sir George yet the conspiracy would go on and perhaps catch the banker unawares.

He admitted to himself that there were no real grounds for such morbid fears, either of a spy in Allan Duncannon's house or that the meeting of the Kaka would be beaten up that evening, but he did not want to take any chances and as he pondered the matter he suddenly had an inspiration. He would use Tania as a post office.

It was twenty to eight now and still no sign of Diana so he went over to the desk and wrote out a telegram to her. 'News of the World which you ordered urgently just arrived please collect. Vorontzoff Pera Palace Bookstall.'

That, he thought, should evade the attention of any possible spy at Allan Duncannon's and ensure Diana calling at the bookstall next morning if he chanced to be arrested with the conspirators that night.

Then, on another sheet of plain paper he gave a brief account of all that he had learned from Reouf concerning the Kaka, left it unsigned and sealed it up in a blank envelope, feeling that he could trust Tania to pass it on to Diana.

When he had finished he dispatched his telegram to Diana and with the letter in his pocket strolled over to the bookstall.

'Tania,' he asked. 'Will you do me a favour?'

'Certainly, my nice Englishman.' She smiled serenely upon him as an old friend now.

Lifting a paper from the stall he dexterously slipped the note underneath it so that only she could see what he did, then he said softly:

'That letter is for a friend of mine. She is rather tall, very fair, and has lovely dark eyes. I may not be back to-night and if I'm not she will call here tomorrow morning and ask for a copy of the *News of the World*. I want you to give her this note for me and promise that under no circumstances will you give it to anyone else. You see—' He proceeded with the romantic fiction he had concocted to secure her interest. 'Her father does not like me a little bit and if he saw the telegram in which I've told her that I have left this letter with you he might send somebody to fetch it and that would get both her and myself into a whole packet of trouble.'

'I understand.' Tania raised her sleek dark eyebrows. 'So that is why you would not take me out to supper?'

'Yes,' he confessed with a smile. 'But I'll stand you and your best boy friend the finest supper that's to be found in Istanbul if you'll help me out in this.'

'Of course I will,' she laughed. 'Is she very lovely?'

'Very lovely, Tania,'

'Lovelier than I am?' her dark eyes narrowed.

'Some men adore fair women and some dark,' he replied diplomatically. 'So the two of you could divide the whole race of men between you.'

Tania's red lips curved into another smile. 'You are enchanting!' she exclaimed, 'and your lovely lady shall have her letter in the morning.'

'Thanks Tania, you are a dear.' With a gay wave of his hand he left her and hurried away to meet Reouf.

The Turk was there, waiting for him at the lower end of that truly oriental 'Street of Steps' which curves its way up the hillside towards the White Tower, the citadel and sole remnant of the fortifications built by the Genoese merchants when Galata was a separate city, given to them by the Byzantine Emperor for their aid in driving out the Roman garrison.

'This way,' said Reouf promptly and turned in the direction of the Galata bridge.

'How did you get on with that queer bird who interrupted our conversation, after I had left you?' Swithin inquired.

'Very well.' The young Turk sank his voice to a whisper. 'He turned out to be one of us—a high member of the Kaka. We have a sign by which we can recognise such men and he showed it to me immediately you had gone. We had a most interesting conversation and finding me so enthusiastic he told me that there may be some special work which we would like me to undertake.'

'That's fine,' Swithin commented. 'I was a little afraid he might have overheard the last part of our conversation, but even if he did there's no harm done as he is in this thing himself.'

At the Galata bridge they shouldered their way through the press of people down to the quay and boarded a steamer ferry which would transport them across the Bosphorus to Scutari.

The passage of the straits is about four miles and by the time they had reached the Asiatic shore darkness was falling. The lights of Stamboul and Pera began to twinkle in the clear atmosphere across the water and above, in a black velvet sky almost free of cloud, a thousand stars appeared to jewel the heavenly canopy.

After the long day of moist heat, excitement in the sudden progress of his mission, and then the anxious hours waiting for Diana, the change to cool, restful, semi-darkness with the waters hissing softly against the sides of the small steamer, was a welcome respite to Swithin, and a new energy pervaded his limbs as they walked down the gangway on to the low quayside where the ferry berthed.

'This way,' Reouf murmured again and led him through the narrow tortuous streets of Scutari's Turkish quarter, heavy with the mingled smells of spices, cooking garlic, and unwashed humanity which pervades the Orient until, a quarter of a mile from the landing place, they paused before a small restaurant.

It was a two-storeyed, flat-roofed building without chimneys. On each side of the door a large dirty window displayed a sad collection of the edibles offered for sale within. In one smothered beneath a million flies, were ranged bowls of *Yaourt*, saucers of semolina topped with rose leaf jam, chunks of the most uninviting greyish goatsmilk cheese, and slabs of *Halva*, the oil of which was oozing through the silver-paper covering on to a wooden board. The other window was half-open and in it *Chis-Kabap* was being cooked—strips of meat, fat and onions placed in layers upon a long spike and built up from the bottom in the shape of a cone. A charcoal brazier provided the necessary firing and before it the *Chis-Kabap* was being turned constantly by a slatternly looking boy cook. Yet despite the unwholesome appearance of the place, the smell of the cooking meat which permeated the whole street was highly appetising, and at least slightly modified

Swithin's reluctance to follow his host inside.

The whole of the ground floor consisted of one big room with the charcoal cooking-braziers in a corner by the window, a rough wooden staircase at the far end leading to the floor above, and the rest of the space devoted to tables covered with American cloth, at which sat a motley collection of diners.

Most of the men were black-coated and the few women present wore dark costumes and European hats. Swithin judged them to be of the small merchant and junior official class. On one wall hung a large portrait of the Gazi, Mustapha Kemal, not in the buttoned-up military overcoat and rakish *papenka* as of old but bare-headed, his sleek hair brushed flatly back, and clad in a perfectly tailored morning coat, a dark waistcoat with a neat white slip inside its V, a long tie and a stiff white-winged collar. No minister at Westminster could have presented a more faultlessly correct appearance but the lean face was unchanged and the curious light magnetic eyes stared out of the photograph with all the old relentless determination.

A lean, older and more handsome edition of Reouf with a kindly face and heavy black eyebrows rose from a side table below the portrait and extended his hand to Swithin.

'My brother Arif—my English friend, Mr. Destime.' Reouf made the introduction.

'I am happy to see you,' Arif said pleasantly. 'Reouf telephoned that he hoped to bring you. May I introduce my Uncle Issa?' With a wave of the hand he indicated an elderly grey-bearded Turk, the only other occupant of the table.

The greybeard remained seated, his arms crossed upon his stomach and his hands hidden in the long sleeves of his coat after the old fashion of the Orient. '*Merhaba beyn. A fietesiniz Is Alah has keldiniy,*' he said with a stiff bow in answer to Swithin's greeting then he relapsed into dignified silence, but the two brothers soon made up for his taciturnity.

They seated their English guest between them, clapped hands for the waiter and, while apologising for the indifferent fare of the eating-house, pressed him to order of its best.

Swithin chose *Arbuse*, the large green water-melon with

red flesh and black pips, to eat as a first course in the English fashion, then *Tauk* which he knew to be chicken, though it turned out to be a very scarecrow of a cock and so overcooked that the meat was falling from the bones, and *Kadaieff*, an inoffensive sort of cake. The others joined him in the melon, then had *Kebap*, with rice cooked in fat, and afterwards a *compote* made of dried fruits—except for Uncle Issa who ate nothing. Arif explained to Swithin in a whisper that the old man was very devout and at present fasting.

During the meal Reouf spoke of the meeting that was to follow. It was not political he said but a small social society which had been established for a number of years. They met twice monthly and, certain of their members being amateur musicians of some skill, enjoyed a little music, also recitations, and sometimes a debate. It was the trend of the latter which would, he felt certain, bear out all that he had said to Swithin that afternoon.

As they ate their desert the tables began to empty and most of the patrons, instead of leaving by the door to the street, went up the wooden staircase. Arif settled the bill and, with Uncle Issa still gloomily silent leading the way, they followed.

Swithin caught a glimpse of some small fusty rabbit-warren rooms on the first floor and then, after climbing a steep ladder, came out upon the flat roof above.

The summer night air was cool and refreshing after the stuffy food-laden atmosphere of the restaurant, and the stars gleamed like powdered diamonds in the dark purple bowl of the sky above. About twenty people were assembled on the roof-top which, apart from the star-light, was only lit by a few small oil lamps where a coffee maker sat busy at his task in one corner.

They walked over to him and were served with little cups of the dark aromatic brew, then mingled with the rest. Arif and Reouf exchanged greetings with a number of other members of the society, introducing Swithin as their guest, while Uncle Issa joined a group of elderly serious-looking men and sat down with them cross-legged against the low coping of the wall.

There was no air of conspiracy about the men whom Swithin met, they were polite and friendly people, gathered apparently for a pleasant social evening. They spoke freely of their affairs, asked Swithin his impressions of Istanbul, and listened with interest when he told them of the Tobacco Depot which he had come out to supervise. In their grave discourse he could trace no sign of discontent, they made no mention of Kemal's government or foreign politics, much less of the secret organisation that he had hoped to find out about.

After half an hour the number of people on the roof had increased to about fifty, the trap-door to which the ladder gave access from below was closed and a little group of people began a rhythmic clapping of their hands.

A space had been cleared in the centre of the roof, cushions laid out in it, and in the semi-darkness half a dozen men, each carrying a stringed instrument, took their places there.

After a few hesitant notes silence fell and the sextet broke into a jumble of weird discordant sounds which to Swithin's unaccustomed ears had no trace of melody in it.

Quiet applause followed as their music ceased. They rose and bowed solemnly, then sat down to play again. Suddenly the tinny jangle of a jazz tune from a radio set in one of the houses across the street cut through the wailing of the stringed instruments. There was an irritated murmur from the listening crowd. The players struggled on for a little and then, giving up the unequal contest, brought their music to an abrupt conclusion. The roof-top positively buzzed with angry whispers.

'Why don't you send someone across to ask those people to stop their wireless?' Swithin inquired to Arif.

'It would be dangerous to do so,' the Turk replied. 'The Government wish to change our music as they have changed so many other things. If we complain we should be sure to get the worst of it but look—we are about to see some dancing.'

The cushions were being collected from the centre of the roof, only one player remained and, as Arif spoke, he begun to draw thin notes from a long reed pipe. A slim female figure emerged from the shadows almost as though she were floating on air. She span, hesitated, and then drifted on making the circle of the onlookers and almost touching them as she skimmed past on her toes.

Swithin caught a breath of her heady perfume and in the faint light saw that she was naked but for the filmy veils that shrouded her delicious limbs, yet a *yashmak* curved from ear to ear below her kohl-laden eyes and he realised with a little shock that this was the first veiled woman he had seen since his arrival in Turkey.

She returned to the centre of the circle and remained there, a picture of grace, gently swaying from the hips in time to the cadence of the music. That dance was a perfect example of the Eastern art and would have been a thing of sheer delight, captivating the senses, luring the imagination to subtle mysteries and binding the watchers like a spell, but for one hideous discord which cut across its fascination and destroyed its thrall; the mechanical monster opposite made the night hideous with the revolting crooning of some western barbarian brought on the unresisting ether from Midland Regional or Madrid.

The veiled odalisque fluttered to a final obeisance, rose, and floated away into the shadows once more. The applause broke out afresh but many heads among the audience were turned in furious remonstrance towards the blaring horror across the way and savage imprecations almost drowned the clapping.

A short stout man then took the centre of the open space and began to declaim in what, to Swithin, were queerly unequal periods, and an accent which was somehow strange, but after a moment he realised that the orator was reciting poetry and in the old Turkish which had been the everyday speech in the capital when he had visited it before. As he listened he found that he could understand most of it and the theme was very similar to that of the French troubadours who told in the middle ages, of old heroisms and past wars. The fat little Turk was delivering a classic epic about the greatness of their nation when they had stamped the Bulgars in the dust and the star and crescent had waved from Christian castles in many distant lands.

As he ceased the applause broke out in greater volume and Swithin felt the first tingle of excitement run through his veins. The meeting was now pervaded with an almost electric atmosphere. Another speaker took the fat man's place and announced that Zainee Hanoume would now address them on the new marriage laws.

With eager expectancy the crowd shuffled for fresh places. The wireless had at last been switched off and, as an elderly woman came to the front, a pin could have been heard to drop in the shadowy silence that now enveloped the gathering on the roof.

Madame Zainee spoke quietly but she was obviously a practised orator. For a little while she talked of Turkey as it had been in the past and the monotonous existence led by women of good family. They had been treated unfairly, she declared, and prohibited from undertaking many useful services to their families and the State but, though all had agreed that these conditions should be altered, such changes should not have necessitated their becoming irreligious or lending themselves to the immorality of Western ways.

Then for the first time Swithin heard the arguments of an educated woman for the maintenance of polygamy. She cited her own history. Married at the age of sixteen to the son of a wealthy Pasha she had been a first wife—petted and adored. For seven years, at which, as a doctor and observer of humanity, she placed the limit of sexual attraction of two average persons for each other, she and her husband had lived in the utmost felicity. During that period she had borne him four children and at its end she knew, as every woman in the east must know sooner or later, that the time had come when her husband should have another bed-fellow. There was no question of divorce, such a barbarous custom had never been heard of except by mutual consent after a husband and wife had found it impossible to live happily together. Instead, in accordance with the age-old precedent she had been responsible for negotiating the marriage of her husband to a second wife. With care and diligence she had sought for many weeks until she had found a young girl who possessed beauty, a fine dowry, and came of a good family. With loving care she had prepared the girl for the marriage-bed and in the early days of matrimony instructed her in all things which might aid her lasting happiness. The child had responded with sincere affection and the respect which was due to the first wife of her lord. All three had lived in amity for a further term of years. The husband happy in the possession of a beautiful young wife and a well-ordered home. The girl happy in her love time, with no household cares to burden her youthful shoulders and destroy tranquility. Herself happy in her growing children and as the undisputed mistress of the house who ordered all things for their mutual comfort. When the second wife had borne three children a third wife had been added and, after that pleasurable excitement the household had settled down once more. As first wife she had remained mistress still with all the respect and devotion of the other two yet relieved of her most onerous duties, now that she was advancing in age, by number two; who in turn was able to devote more time to her young children; while number three provided that relaxation for their husband which even a middle-aged or elderly man must need at times.

And now! This admirable ordered scheme of things had been entirely wrecked. Under the new law a man was allowed only one wife. Either he must remain tied to the first and when the flesh moved him, go whoring after shameless women to the loss of his self-respect, or he was forced to a succession of these hateful divorces; leaving his older wives, the mothers of his sons, even though he loved them tenderly, to go out shamed and lonely into a strange world bereft of his sympathy and protection.

That women should be free to follow careers if they wished Madame Zainee most heartily supported. They had brains as well as men and should be given every opportunity to use them but, she maintained, that was no reason for this senseless destruction of the home. Monogamy might suit the West perhaps although even that was doubtful, and she produced statistics to hammer home her point. France, England, Germany, the United States, all possessed legions of sterile, unmarried thwarted women and legions more who through divorce now lacked any natural protector and settled home for their declining years. In Turkey, until recent times, as a natural course of events every girl had at least shared a marriage-bed, and had her chance of motherhood with such security from want as was afforded by her husband's means. Above all, she insisted, Turkish women were naturally unsuited by temperament for either the sterile or insecure existence which appeared to satisfy so many of their sisters in the West. Yet that in future was to be the lot forced upon many millions of them unless these shameful marriage laws could be annulled.

It was a long speech and so admirably built up that Swithin had to admit the logic of the speaker's views—at least as far as the people she represented were concerned. If these Eastern women were content to share a man, as they had done for centuries, why should they not be allowed to continue to do so and, now that many of them were taking up careers there seemed a better reason than ever for two or more to divide the labours entailed by children and a home between them. Of course few Western women, he realised, would be content to accept so short a sex life, that was the big snag, but apart from it and the question of Christian morality, the system if adhered to, appeared wholesome when compared with the scandalous fraud and collusion which arise from the English divorce laws or the casual liaisons which are openly indulged in throughout every country in the West.

About the opinion of the gathering, there could be no question. They crowded round Madame Zainee, pressing her hands to their foreheads and murmuring enthusiastic approval of her address. The coffee-maker in the corner got to work again, trays of *Rahat Locoum,* stuffed dates and an assortment of fruits crystallised in sugar were handed round, and then the meeting began to break up.

Reouf took Swithin by the arm. 'Arif has to see my Uncle Issa to his house, he said. 'He lives here in Scutari, as we do also not far from him, but Arif will join us again later. You and I will go on ahead and secure a table at a little place in Pera we frequent for supper, if you are willing.'

'Splendid,' Swithin agreed. 'Your brother is a charming fellow and I should like to see more of him.' Upon which they made their adieux to the rest of the company and left the rooftop.

On their return journey to Galata, the ferry steamer was less crowded and they found a deserted spot near the stern where they could talk at ease.

'Well, what did you think of it?' Reouf inquired eagerly.

Swithin was leaning over the rail gazing at the foam in the steamer's wake, which sparkled with phosphorescent fire as the screws churned it up, leaving a lane of dancing silver in the dark waters of the Bosphorus. 'I found it most interesting,' he answered thoughtfully. 'Are all those people members of the Kaka?'

The Turk smiled in the darkness. 'I do not know for certain, but I think you can rest assured that at least eighty per cent of them are and the others soon will be. There are gatherings like that going on all over Turkey now and you saw for yourself the trend of popular opinion.'

'Yes, you convinced me of that all right, but would those people who were there tonight really carry much weight politically?'

'Why, yes. They were representatives of the class that is the backbone of the nation. Not necessarily wealthy, but solid, respectable people, landowners, merchants heads of departments in various services, the type that in the past has sent its sons to administer in the provinces. My brother is a good example. He is chief of the goods yard at Haidar Pacha station, the great terminus of the Baghdad railway, where it comes to an end on the Asiatic side of the Bosphorus.'

Swithin nodded. 'He'd be a pretty useful man, then, to have with you in the event of a revolution. I liked him awfully, he is such a pleasant chap to talk to.'

'But he is not happy,' Reouf cut in quickly. 'He is in love and would like to marry, but it is not possible.'

'Why, is he married already?'

'Oh, no, but she is the mistress of a man of great importance, one of Kemal's friends and a general in the army.'

'Can't she leave him?'

'That would be dangerous. She would like to, but he might kill her or at the least have her deported, for she is a French woman whom he brought from Paris. She acted as his secretary there, then he made her his mistress and brought her to Turkey. She is very beautiful, you will see her tonight as she is free for supper. It is for that reason we cross to Pera, where she lives.

For a little Swithin pondered the miserable position of the unfortunate Arif, deeply in love with a woman who was compelled to give herself to another man, their only hope of happiness that in time this general might tire of his beautiful Parisian plaything. In the meantime, what agony for them both, and how Arif must loathe this Kemalist general.

His thought turned for a moment to Diana and he wondered if she had yet received his note, then the dark bulk of the shore became less vague, a skyline formed—etched against the starry heavens, the minarets and domes of Stamboul rose up in front of them, and the steamer berthed just below the Galata bridge.

At the tiny restaurant they found a table for four and ordered lager while waiting for the others. Reouf, who was a practising Moslem, denied himself wines and spirits in deference to his religion, but told Swithin that he did not consider himself to be jeopardising his salvation by the enjoyment of an occasional glass of beer.

The café was thronged with people, so they talked no more of the meeting, and twenty minutes later Arif joined them, bringing with him a rather startling platinum blonde whom he introduced to Swithin as Mademoiselle Jeanette Foureur.

She proved a pleasant, natural girl, with few pretensions and an irrepressible fund of vitality and humour. With her elbows propped on the table and her plump little pouter-pigeon bust pressing against its edge, she smoked incessantly, chaffed Reouf, ogled Swithin in a purely friendly way, and pressed her knees against Arif's under the table.

Arif was obviously intensely proud of her, and Swithin thought that she would probably make him an excellent wife. Being a French woman, she would doubtless settle down quite cheerfully to middle-class domesticity and, with the shrewdness of her type, handle his finances with an astute economy. She was by no means 'very beautiful' as Reouf had said, at least according to Swithin's standards, but she was cleverly made up, and her black and white check tailor-made was distinctly chic. It was probably her vivacity, which had made the Turkish general consider her worth importing and later played such havoc with Arif's affections.

The pilaff of veal they had for supper was excellent, although Jeanette boasted that she would cook Arif a better one when they had their own kitchen, and over the meal she kept them in continuous fits of laughter. Swithin had not enjoyed an evening so much during all the weeks that he had been in Constantinople. Yet, noticing suddenly that it was nearly eleven o'clock, it occurred to him that there might be a letter from Diana waiting for him at the Pera Palace by now. It was even possible that she had given him an appointment for a few moments at one of the dance places that night, since he had said that the matter was urgent. So he drank up his coffee and moved his chair back preparatory to excusing himself from his new friends and wishing them good night.

He said how sorry he was to have to leave them, and Arif at once produced a card giving the address at which he and Reouf lived in Scutari, with the hope that they would meet soon again. Then, just as Swithin pocketed it, well satisfied with his evening's work, a shadow fell across the table, and turning, he recognised the gigantic man who had acted as guide to Reouf and himself on the old wall that afternoon.

'Good evening,' piped the mountainous newcomer in his thin falsetto; addressing Reouf. 'Please forgive me if I disturb your party, but that of which we spoke together has happened. Is it possible for you to give me your assistance now—tonight?'

'Ho! ho!' thought Swithin, 'the affairs of these conspirators move swiftly, but never mind, if there is anything important in the wind I'll have it out of Reouf tomorrow, sure enough.'

The young Turk rose to his feet, adjusted his thick glasses on the bridge of his protuberant nose, and murmured, 'Certainly.' Then with a smile at Swithin and a word of farewell to his brother and Jeannette, he followed the big man from the café.

Swithin had risen, too, and then his eye fell on the girl who was sitting on the opposite side of the table. Her face had gone deathly white, the patches of rouge stood out upon her cheekbones in sharp contrast to her pallor; her plump little hands gripped the edge of the marble-topped table, the painted crimson nails cursing the ivory of her taut knuckles.

'What is it—are you feeling ill?' he asked quickly.

'No—no,' she stammered, 'but that man—what does 'e want with Reouf?'

'*Ma chérie*, whatever is the matter!' exclaimed Arif,

placing a protective arm about her shoulders.

'*Mon Dieu!* why 'as 'e taken Reouf,' she stammered desperately, her lips trembling with sheer terror. 'I am afraid —I am afraid.'

'Why—d'you know him?' demanded Swithin. His blue eyes had suddenly gone hard and cold. 'Who is he?'

'Oh, do you not know?' she almost wailed. 'That is the Chief of the Secret Police, Kazdim Hari Bekar, the Eunuch of Stamboul!'

12

The Gifted Amateur Bungles Badly

'What if he is?' said Swithin quickly. 'Reouf is not a criminal wanted by the Police.'

'But Kazdim!' breathed the girl. 'That man is a monster of sadistic cruelty; 'e 'as never missed an execution an' delights in carrying them out 'imself!'

Arif had one pale. He looked up at Swithin doubtfully. 'Reouf's no criminal, but—well, there are other things.'

Swithin wished that he could have reassured them. It seemed pretty certain that Arif was a member of the Kaka, and it would have set his mind at rest if he knew that Kazdim was in the conspiracy also, but to say so would have necessitated Swithin admitting his own knowledge of it, which was directly contrary to Reouf's strict injunctions, so instead he said, 'I don't think you need worry. Your brother told me that he had a long talk with this fellow Kazdim this afternoon and that they agreed to meet again about some business they thought of undertaking together.'

'I see.' The taut muscles of Arif's face relaxed slightly, and although Jeanette's eyes were still filled with anxious forebearing, there was nothing else which Swithin could do, so repeating his farewells, he left them.

Little time had been lost by those swift exchanges and, although Reouf's doings were not strictly Swithin's affair, he wondered if the young Turk were aware of the identity of his sinister companion. Hoping that he might be able to catch him and get him aside for one moment to give him a word of warning, he hurried out into the street.

It was crowded, with a slowly drifting throng enjoying the cool darkness after the long day of damp semi-tropical heat. Taxis, private cars, and old-fashioned horse vehicles swarmed in the narrow roadway. He glanced swiftly up and down, but there was no sign of Reouf or the enormous Secret Service Chief. They had been swallowed up in the crowd, or perhaps driven off immediately in a waiting car.

Swithin realised at once that there was no chance of tracing them through the labyrinths of the vast cosmopolitan city, and consoled himself with the thought that the young Turk probably knew who the Eunuch was and his evil reputation already. In any case, they were both mixed up in the same business, so there was no reason to fear that any ill would befall the young man. With a little shrug—the outward sign of Swithin's Latin temperament which accepts finality philosophically—he hailed a taxi and ordered the man to drive to the Pera Palace.

As the car bumped over the cobbles of the uneven streets and swerved to avoid the clanging trams, he reviewed the situation afresh. That there was a conspiracy to overthrow the Kemalist Government, he now had no doubt. Apart from Reouf's word, the whole atmosphere of the meeting he had attended that night had confirmed it.

These people he had met had been business men, responsible officials, people with a stake in the country. Their attitude to the wireless, their enthusiastic reception of the fat man's patriotic saga, their complete agreement with the woman who had preached the restoration of polygamy, all proclaimed their rooted antagonism to the reforms of the present government.

Yet, as Swithin considered the matter, he felt that Reouf had probably been grossly exaggerating when he had said that there were similar groups all over Turkey and members of the Kaka in every regiment of the Army and squadron of the Air Force. The wish was doubtless father to the thought, and actually the conspirators consisted of no more than a dozen or so circles operating in the principal cities with a few discontented officers among them. If so, it was hardly likely that they could succeed in overthrowing Kemal, who had all the resources of the State behind him even if they managed to engineer a revolution. However, there might be a nasty flare-up and Swithin decided that he could congratulate himself on having at least run to earth the cause of Sir George's forebodings. It remained for him to make a thorough job of the business and worm full details about it out of Reouf.

As he entered the hotel, his step was jaunty and his smile of greeting to the head porter far gayer than usual. He was happier than he had been for weeks now that he felt himself to be nearing the source from which sprang all these rumours of coming troubles.

With cheerful confidence he asked at the desk for the message he expected, but to his dismay learnt that there was nothing for him. 'What the hell has gone wrong?' he wondered angrily, and with a little shock of fear—'could anything have happened to Diana?'

Hiding his perturbation under a smile, he turned away and began to debate the next move as he went up to his room. He could go to his flat, of course, change into rags, and endeavour to reach her by playing burglar at her uncle's house. But if he were caught by the servants, he would look a pretty fool and he could imagine the cynical amusement she would derive from helping him out. He might be spotted by the Turkish police, too, as he scaled the wall and that would be almost worse—nothing accomplished and a month in a bug-ridden prison for his pains—what an ignominious end to his adventures. On the other hand, he could write a fresh report and take it to Tyndall-Williams at the British Embassy for dispatch to Sir George in the Athens bag, but the banker had been most insistent that he should not use the Embassy except as the last possible resort. Was this an emergency which would justify his taking such a step? He hardly thought it could be considered that at the moment, besides a message might arrive from Diana yet. Obviously, then, despite his anxiety to pass on his news, he must remain where he was until morning in case she still tried to get hold of him there.

As he switched the light on in his room, he saw that it was only a quarter-past eleven, early to go to bed, particularly as there was a chance that he might be routed out again in the next hour. He picked up a book and, with the idea of going downstairs again to read for a bit, turned back to the door.

'Got you!' said a voice behind him suddenly.

In the same second he dropped the book and spun round. It was Diana standing in the doorway of his bathroom, tall and slim and golden. She regarded him with an enigmatic little smile.

'Lucky for you I'm not one of Kazdim's people, isn't it?' she said sweetly. 'If you have really found out anything worth knowing and they've rumbled you, one of them might have caught you beautifully just now.'

'Lucky for you that you're not,' he replied a little grimly, 'or you might have got a lump of lead where you keep your dinner.'

'Dear me, what a rude and ruthless person you have become.'

'No, it's just that if a nervy fellow like myself is taken by surprise, these things are so darned likely to go off.' Withdrawing his hand from the side pocket of his coat, he displayed a small but quite deadly automatic.

'I suppose it was stupid of me to play that joke on you,' she remarked, as he pushed back the safety catch of the pistol and laid it on a table beside the bed. 'But somehow I can't help thinking of you as the hero in a secret-service romance.'

Despite his face-saving exhibition with the gun, Swithin knew that she had really caught him napping. That had ruffled his vanity and annoyed him into a rudeness that he did not intend, so he seized the proffered olive branch immediately.

'It's very flattering that you should think of me like that.'

'Do you find it so?' A little frown creased her brow. I'm afraid I only meant that the gifted amateurs of fiction know nothing of the game. Of course, despite every sort of gaff, they always get out on their luck—but that doesn't often happen in real life.'

He walked over to the cupboard, from which he produced whisky, Evian, and some glasses. 'Why the hell need she have said that?' he wondered, and then a delicious idea came to him for getting a dig back at her.

'I forgot,' he remarked quietly, 'That you must have read all Cæsar Pentons novels, where the man is always an honest fool and his brilliant girl friend saves his honour or his life. It's only natural that you should enjoy dramatising yourself as one of Cæsar's heroines—have a drink?'

'Thanks.' She took the glass he offered. A moment before, she had been regretting that some imp of cynicism had prompted her to compare him with the sort of fool who gaily shot his way through penny dreadfuls or a thriller play. Now, she said icily, 'Cæsar's very competent at his own business.'

'And you think I'm not at mine?' he flashed. 'Well, as your father's agent, I'm doing my stuff. Apart from that, you're probably right. If I knew my business as far as you are concerned, I'd turn up your skirts and spank you right away.'

'That would be a most chivalrous proceeding in view of the circumstances in which I happen to be in your room—wouldn't it? If I began to yell, bang would go the last shreds of my reputation, so I'd have to take your beating with a towel between my teeth.'

'Oh, damn it!' he exclaimed, angry that even in jest she should infer him to be capable of taking advantage of her. 'You know I didn't mean that—but if we can't be friends, at least let's be business-like. How did you get up here anyway?'

'In the lift, after which I slipped the floor-waiter a crinkly note to let me wait in your room.'

'Then you've lost your reputation already as far as he is concerned. I'm sorry about that.'

'You needn't be. He doesn't know me and I thought it was less risky than for us to be seen talking together in the lounge. You said that it was urgent.'

'It is. Sit down and I'll tell you about it.' He pushed forward the armchair and she sank into it, adjusting the little satin cape, which matched her frock, carefully round her bare shoulders. Then he perched himself on the side of the bed and gave her a detailed account of his activities since his first meeting with Reouf at the lecture.

She listened without once interrupting him until the end, then she said quietly, 'I do think you've done awfully well. After having practically nothing to show in six whole weeks, it is marvellous to have made all this progress in the last two days.'

So much had happened in the interval, it was difficult for him to realise that he had met her outside the teashop only two days before, but as that flashed into his mind, he immediately jumped to the conclusion that she was comparing his previous lack of success with that which he had achieved as the direct result of her suggestion. He shrugged a little bitterly:

'Oh, I take no credit for it. I'm quite aware that we should be just as much in the dark as ever if it had not been for your tip to try the University.'

'That wasn't kind,' she replied quickly. 'You know I didn't mean that. Why will you deliberately misinterpret everything I say?'

'I don't deliberately, but I must confess that I find you pretty difficult to understand at times. It's probably my third class brain. Soldiers are always supposed to be stupid —aren't they? At least, I gather that lots of people think so.'

She shook her head impatiently. 'Don't pretend to belittle yourself like that—it's childish. You are not a fool and you don't regard yourself as one. Why must you behave like a sulky bear?'

'I just say frankly what I think—that's all.'

Her profile hardened, then she turned her eyes on him. They seemed enormous in the pale, delicately bred face, but they had a hard, flinty look. 'And since you've taken a dislike to me, you have made up your mind not to let me forget it—haven't you?' she asked sharply.

'I have never taken a dislike to you.'

'Well, you haven't forgiven me yet for what you considered to be my neglect of you on the yacht.'

'There is nothing to forgive. You had planned a pleasure trip and I just did not happen to fit in to your party— that's all,' he replied evenly.

Diana's upper lip curled a trifle. 'So you think it was entirely pleasure?'

'Well, what else?'

'Surely you realise by now that I help father quite a lot? I should not be able to do half so much for him unless I camouflaged myself by mixing with that crowd of half-wits.'

Swithin did not speak for a moment. His pulses had quickened to a new tempo. If she were speaking the truth, he had behaved like a halfwit himself. Of course, there were probably all sorts of bits of information she could pick up for Sir George if everyone believed her to be an empty-headed little butterfly. But who had there been worth angling for in the party? Not a soul, he decided. She was just bluffing, probably because she found herself a little bored in Constantinople and thought that even if they had to confine themselves to secret meetings, it would be rather fun to have him on the string again; but he had been bitten too badly the first time to care about giving her a second chance to hurt him as she had before. His pulses slowed down to normal, he raised his eyes to that slim, tantalising piece of devilry lying back in his armchair, and said lightly:

'So you really considered them all halfwits. I must say it's interesting to have your true opinion of Cæsar Penton.'

Next moment he could have bitten out his tongue. What an utter imbecile he had been to bring Penton's name into it again. Trust her to attribute it to the jealousy he had felt, and she was on him like a flash.

'So that's what made you look so sick! Well, if you want to know, I had quite an amusing time with him, but you're a poor sort of secret-service man if you couldn't spot anyone better worth studying than Cæsar on the voyage out.'

The truthful reply would have been that the whole of his time which had not been taken up by Sir George and the study of Turkish had been devoted to bitter thoughts about herself, so that he had hardly noticed the others, except in the mass, but he did not care to make it and began instead, 'Then who . . .'

'Oh, please forget it,' She stood up suddenly with an angry flush. 'I don't care to be cross-questioned about my actions, and I can't stay here all night. Let's get back to the business in hand.'

He darkened under his tan, his quick eyes searching her face. Her 'actions'—the phrase stuck in his mind. What were they and what had they been? Apart from her flushed cheeks and angry eyes, she looked cold as marble. Her bare arms and shoulders would, he knew, be cool and infinitely refreshing to the touch, but that wide mouth of hers seemed capable of any devilry. Had she really been occupied in negotiating some delicate affair on the yacht or as infatuated with Cæsar Penton as she had appeared? He wished desperately that he could make up his mind, but before he had a chance she spoke again.

'What do you intend to do now?'

'Find out all I can about the organisation of the Kaka,' he replied, wrenching his mind back to business. 'How many people are in it, at what rate their numbers are increasing, and if possible the names of the men who were responsible for starting it.'

'Armaments?' she suggested.

'Yes. They will need arms if their rising is to be successful. Even if a portion of the Army is involved, they will have to make some sort of show before any troops go over to them, so it's a hundred to one that they are smuggling in arms from somewhere.'

'And their zero hour.'

'Yes. That is important, too. From the way Reouf talked I should imagine they are nearly ready, but I can't think that they stand any real chance of success.'

'No, Kemal is a hard nut to crack,' she agreed slowly, 'Yet the Eunuch is in it. He is a big man and a very shrewd one.'

'I hardly think we should attach too much significance to that. Kazdim is naturally a reactionary at heart. As one of the old school of thugs and grafters, the reforms Kemal has brought in have probably robbed him of a fortune, so he would be among the first to sympathise with the aims of the Kaka.'

She shrugged. 'I think you are underrating the intelligence of your enemy, and remember he is that now. If he once suspects that you have got on to this thing, he will not scuple to employ his secret police against you to ensure his own safety. They would probably try and frame you on a charge of espionage, and if they did we couldn't help you—so for goodness' sake be careful.'

'I will,' he promised, 'but I don't think you need fear that the Kaka is strong enough to plunge Turkey into Civil War. It will probably only lead to a couple of days' upset.'

'I only hope you are right,' Diana murmured, but she shook her fair head pessimistically, and added, 'I have a feeling now that it is something really big we are up against.'

He smiled reassuringly. 'Well, now that I'm on the trail I'll dig into it again tomorrow and find out as many further particulars as I can.'

'Good.' As she moved towards the door, she returned his smile and added, 'I meant what I said about your having done awfully well. Father will be terribly pleased, I know, but do keep out of danger all you can.'

'I will,' he repeated cheerfully. The tension had gone out of the atmosphere, and he felt now that he was talking with a level-headed comrade as he might have with another man.

She drew the little cape round her shoulders and then paused. 'By the by, did you know that Peter Carew is in Constantinople?'

'No—really!' His face brightened at the name of their mutual friend.

'Yes, but only for a day or two, I think. He was given a Foreign Office bag just about the time we left England and his job happens to have brought him here.'

'I know. He told me the day before I sailed. I'd love to see him again, but I suppose he is staying at the Embassy and at the moment that is out of bounds for me.'

'No, I met him in the Grand' Rue this afternoon, and he told me that as the Embassy is full up he had had to take a room here, but I don't think you ought to see him, all the same. He has no idea that you are in this part of the world and he might ask awkward questions.'

'That's true. Then I had better keep a good look-out that I don't run into him in the morning. Perhaps for the next few days it would be best if I camped out in my flat.'

Diana nodded, her hand upon the door. 'I think that would be best, and it might be advisable to slip away from here early tomorrow morning before he is likely to be about. I must go now—good luck.'

'Thanks.' He smiled again. 'I'll be careful, but I can't leave before nine o'clock—when the bookstall opens—I've got to collect the letter I told you about in my telegram.'

'What telegram?' She turned and faced him again quickly.

He stared at her in surprise. 'Didn't you get it then?'

'No, only your note. I was out all the afternoon, so I did not get it until I returned to change for dinner, then I had to dine at the American Embassy this evening. That's why I could not get here before.'

'But of course,' he exclaimed. 'How stupid of me. The telegram would not be delivered until tomorrow morning and anyway I only sent it in case my note had gone astray, to tell you that if I did not turn up here again, I had left a letter for you at the bookstall. It contained a summary of what I have been telling you about the Kaka.'

'Who—who did you leave it with?' Diana's face had suddenly gone sharp and strained.

'With the girl who runs it—Tania Vorontzoff—to be given to you personally, just in case this meeting that I went to was beaten up tonight. She's quite a decent kid.'

'Decent!' Diana's voice stung him into new attention. 'You madman! Don't you know that she is one of Kazdim's agents—planted here to report upon the guests—she will have passed that paper on to Kazdim—— Oh, Swithin! He'll know that you've found out about the Kaka by now, and he'll arrest you on some trumped-up charge to save his own neck.'

Suddenly all the hardness had faded out of her face. Her soft hands were gripping his in passionate entreaty, and her slim body was pressed against him as she cried:

'Swithin—my dear—the second Kazdim sees that letter, he will be after you. You've got to get out of here. At once! At once! At once!'

13

The Old, Old Story

During Peter Carew's two months as a King's Messenger, he had been employed on the runs to Brussels and Berlin, with an occasional trip to Warsaw, so he was highly delighted when a change of duties brought him journeying to Istanbul, which he had never before visited.

The news with which he had been greeted on his arrival at the Embassy, that they were unable to put him up owing to an unusually large invasion of important guests, had not distressed him in the least. He was only too glad to escape the usual business of having to dance attendance on the ambassador's wife and discourse upon the distinguished careers of his innumerable uncles with middle-aged diplomats. At an hotel, he would be free to amuse himself and see all that he could of the glamous old city until he was called upon to return home with fresh dispatches.

No sooner had he settled himself at the *Pera* that morning than, having bathed and changed, he hastened down from his room in search of a guide-book. The purchase of one could have been effected in about ninety seconds, seeing there was a bookstall in the lounge, but as it happened that Tania was behind it, the transaction occupied some twenty minutes.

Peter's knowledge of Balkan history was limited, of the Sublime Porte infinitesimal, and of Byzantine Art exactly nil. It was far more the fact of having arrived in a strange country and the romance of this city of domes and minarets fringed by blue waters which impelled him to rush out and 'see things'. He had an eye for colour, and the sight of beauty, animate or inanimate, warmed him like a glass of wine; but ten seconds in front of the bookstall were quite sufficient to sponge the fabled glories of the Yildiz Kiosk and the Seraglio Gardens from his mind. What were they after all but a skilfully erected pile of rubble and an open space dotted with cypresses. Tania had beauty—and romance, too—as he learned before the full ninety seconds had elapsed, for she made not the least difficulty about telling him her name and that she was a Russian aristocrat forced by ill-fortune to wrestle with fate for a precarious living in a strange land.

In the eighteen and a half minutes which followed, she said to him very much what she had said to Swithin six weeks before. Swithin had not been unsympathetic, but he was an older man, and had seen something of those nightmare conditions which prevailed in the Near East during the years immediately following the war, so he privately considered that she was lucky to have escaped the miserable end which overtook most of her class and more fortunate still to have secured a job which kept her decently fed and clothed. His visits to the Russian quarter since had strengthened his view, for he now knew eighty per cent of her country-women to be keeping body and soul together only as the result of working in the sweatshops and prostitution, irrespective of their pre-war rank or culture.

Peter's view of the beautiful Russian girl's situation was naturally very different. His path had always lain in pleasant places and it had rarely taken him outside peaceful England, except for occasional visits to the Continent: St. Moritz, Biarritz, Le Touquet, Juan les Pins, those playgrounds which the British have made so much their own that, apart from the mild exhilaration of being able to gamble in the Casinos, forget their own absurd drink-hour restrictions and the refreshing foreign-ness of the automatons who sell things in the shops, they hardly consider a visit to them as venturing outside their own island fastness. Even his visits to Brussels, Berlin, and Warsaw had been a matter of journeyings with a *laissez-passer*, to spend a night or two in a British Embassy, where all things were ordered with the same decency, decorum, and spacious comfort which characterised his father's fine house in Gloucestershire.

The discovery of Tania was as unexpected to him as the holding up of a Hellenic Cruise liner in the Mediterranean by Barbary pirates would have been to a spinster from a cathedral town making her first voyage in a party with the local clergyman as *cicerone*.

Tania was lovely, and not with the pale, anæmic beauty of an English miss who knits a jumper while she discusses the merits of the latest Book Society choice, or the hard, cold, chiselled features of the girls who rode to hounds at home. The red life-blood pulsed beneath the smooth skin of her cheeks and her dark eyes held a slumberous fire. Above all, she was beauty in distress. The daughter of a Russian baron, yet compelled to stand for long hours every day peddling guide-books and periodicals to keep the life in that delicately nurtured body.

Peter would have remained there longer, listening to her sad story and pouring out a lavish sympathy, had their conversation not been so constantly interrupted by a stream of other customers, but when, with gallant resignation to her fate, she admitted that very occasionally she permitted herself the relaxation of supping with some guest staying at the hotel, he immediately implored her to do him that honour that very night.

She demurred at first, but on his pointing out that he might have to return to England next day or on the following one of the latest, she smilingly consented and named the Grandpère in the Grand' Rue as a good place to sup and dance.

When she added that she could not meet him there before a quarter to twelve, he pleaded with her to make it earlier, but she explained that her invalid mother never went to bed until eleven and that before going out it was necessary to settle her down for the night. Yet with that Peter was content enough, and as he left her to sally forth into the sunlit street, he could hardly believe his amazing good fortune in having secured such a glamorous companion to sup with him within a few hours of arriving in a completely strange city.

He lunched at the *Tokatlian*, which had been recommended to him by Tyndall-Williams, the first secretary of the Embassy, but his head was so full of this absorbing adventure that he hardly noticed what he ate, and afterwards, as he came out into the Grand' Rue, he would certainly not have recognised Diana had he not run slap into her.

She asked him to dine at her uncle's if he were still in

Istanbul the following night, but he hurriedly excused himself on the plea of a previous engagement, not wishing to tie himself up in case he was still there and able to persuade Tania to have supper with him again.

When Diana hurried away to an appointment, he took a taxi down to Galata, across the bridge, and so to the mile-long wooded height which crowns Seraglio Point. There in the lovely gardens which surround the mighty palace of the Sultans he wandered the whole afternoon by lotus pools, down avenues of cypress, and through the seemingly endless buildings ranged about their three mighty quadrangles: the Court of the Janissaries, the Court of the State Receptions, and the Court of Felicity, which led to the now empty private apartments and harem; forgetful that he had meant to inspect the mosaics of Aya Sophia and Museum of Antiquities as well that day and thinking only of the night to come.

He returned to change and dine at the *Pera,* and as he sipped a glass of Kummel afterwards he caught himself cursing the slowness with which the hours dragged by—then laughed at himself for his stupidity in having allowed a pretty face to create such havoc with his emotions. He told himself that it was absurd to fall so easily for a perfect stranger of whom he knew nothing—or practically nothing, such a thing had never happened to him before—at least, not quite so suddenly, and he had had affairs with scores of girls—that is, certainly a good half-dozen, but perhaps it was the atmosphere of romance and intrigue with which this wonderful old city had been saturated for centuries that had got into his blood. He thought again of those cool, fountained courts and arcaded galleries he had visited that afternoon, of the beautiful veiled odalisques who had danced and loved and died in the great, haunted echoing chambers, of the curved sharp-bladed scimitars which decorated the walls of the Palace Armoury and the quarters of those almost legendary creatures, the eunuchs.

He would have been more than a little startled if he had been aware that one of those very eunuchs, Kazdim Hari Bekar, who had lived in that palace less than ten years before and actually slain beautiful disobedient odalisques with one of those glittering scimitars, was covertly watching him at that moment. But he did not know that Kazdim was registering his face for future recognition as a British King's Messenger whom Tania was to pump for any information he might have later that evening, and as the eunuch was partly concealed behind a pillar of the lounge, Peter was not even called on to wonder momentarily who that vast grotesque figure might be, dressed so incongruously in a modern lounge suit.

Stubbing out his cigarette, Peter stood up, suddenly feeling that it was childish to sit there for three hours mooning like an idiot over the delicate beauty of a girl's face seen for the first time only that morning. His imagination was probably playing him tricks he feared, and she would turn out to be no more than averagely good-looking when he saw her again. With a long, lazy stride, he strolled out to the head porter's desk and made inquiries about the theatres.

The head *Kavass* recommended the show at the Théâtre Français in the Istikal Djaddessi close by, so Peter told him to telephone for a seat and went round when the hour arrived.

It was not a bad performance, about of the standard that one might expect in Lyons or Marseilles, but with a faint dash of the Oriental in it, enough at least to enable any Western member of the audience to remember that he was sitting within half a dozen miles of the borders of Asia. Peter left well before its conclusion, for the Istanbul theatres play at later hours than those of London or Paris, and before the real enjoyment of his evening began he wanted to make certain that no message from the Embassy had been left for him at the hotel.

Having visited the desk at the *Pera* again, he heaved a sigh of relief on hearing that nothing had come for him and, just at the moment when Diana, in a room upstairs, was imploring Swithin to leave the hotel without a second's delay, he passed out of its imposing portals on pleasure bent.

Five minutes later his taxi set him down at the Grand-père. A brawny *Kavass* ushered him through a thickly carpeted foyer where men and women were drinking together at small tables or waiting solitarily for others to join them. Tania was not there, so he passed through into the restaurant and took a quick look round. It was newly and lavishly decorated, but old-fashioned in construction and of a type quite new to him, although familiar enough to anyone who has travelled east of Vienna. For a moment he thought it was a theatre from its loftiness and the fact that two tiers of boxes ran right round its walls, but it lacked a stage, and what would have been the well of the auditorium consisted of a wide dance floor surrounded with tables. A cabaret was in progress at the moment and a couple of dozen semi-nude girls pirouetted in the green rays of a searchlight.

As the turn ended the girls dispersed, and instead of retiring to their dressing rooms joined various male companions at the tables on the floor. The lights were turned on, a jazz band struck up, and about fifty couples moved out into the centre to dance. Peter looked round the tiers of boxes. A few held parties, but most a couple or only a single woman. Suddenly his eye fell upon one of the latter. It was Tania, occupying a box in the lower tier.

He was just about to wave a greeting when a big blond man, a Swede perhaps, dressed in the uniform of an officer in some mercantile marine, got up from a table on the floor, walked over to just below her box, and called up to her. She shook her head and turned away, then catching sight of Peter, smiled and beckoned to him. He lifted a hand to show that he had seen her, then walked round behind to join her in the box, but his smile had given place to a worried frown.

The Grandpère was obviously quite a gay spot, although few of the patrons were in evening dress, and Peter felt that it might have been good fun to visit it for a rag with half a dozen other men, or as something a bit out of the ordinary with a mixed party, but it was certainly not the sort of night club in which a decent girl like Tania should be allowed to sit by herself for even five minutes. He was a little surprised that she should have chosen it, but thought that perhaps she had never visited it before.

Immediately he arrived in the box, he apologised that she should have had to wait there alone, but excused himself on the plea that it was still nearly ten minutes before the time of their appointment.

She smiled up at him. 'No matter, I have been quite happy here watching the dancing.'

'But that sailor chap,' he protested, 'wasn't he troubling you—or perhaps you know him?'

'No,' she laughed. 'It is nothing—he only asked me to dance with him—please do not distress yourself—let us order supper.'

A waiter had entered unobserved behind them and he now produced the menu. Tania ordered a long and elaborate meal, the waiter tactfully persuading her to add dish upon dish, while Peter smiled and offered further suggestions. He was a little amused that so sylph-like a person should require so large a supper, but anxious she should have enough for ten if that would please her—for, he reflected, the poor child probably did not get a decent spread once in a month. At last the selection was completed and the waiter drew a table from the back of the box, already laid for two, with a bottle of champagne in an ice-bucket at its centre.

Peter pulled out the bottle and eyed its label askance, then told the waiter to bring a bottle of whisky.

'But it is a good wine—the best,' Tania protested quickly.

'Is it——' he replied a little dubiously. 'I'm afraid I don't awfully fancy drinking Turkish champagne—hadn't we better stick to whisky?'

'If you wish,' she shrugged, 'But I prefer to drink wine —and that is French, specially imported.'

'My dear, of course, by all means, if you like,' he agreed hurriedly, although he was doubtful if the sort of champagne the French shipped to Constantinople would be much better than the local variety—only about five times as expensive.

'Oh, you are nice!' she explained gratefully, and placed a small hand on his knee. 'I knew that I was going to enjoy myself this evening.'

He covered the hand with his own and pressed it gently. His heart was pounding with the realisation that he had not been day-dreaming in the Seraglio Gardens that afternoon. She was every whit as beautiful as he had imagined her to be and a faint delicious perfume played havoc with his senses as he leaned towards her.

'Shall we dance?' she asked abruptly, but she withdrew

her hand from his very gently, almost as though she did so with reluctance.

'Let's!' He stood up promptly and followed her from the box. It was then he noticed for the first time that her afternoon frock and smart little hat were hardly in keeping with the income which a young woman might be expected to derive from working behind a bookstall. They had a *cachet* which definitely spoke of large sums expended in the right places. Her shoes, he noted, were handmade, for he was rather a connoisseur of such things, and her silk stockings the sort his own sisters could not afford to wear except on State occasions; but a moment later they came out on to the dance floor, she turned, held up her arms, and as her body closed against his in one supple caress, he let the problem of her expensive clothing fade from his mind.

They danced, and danced again, and yet again. Never, he thought, had he met anyone possessing such a sense of rhythm, her limbs moulded themselves against his own and she swayed to his every movement with the most perfect timing.

He would have gone on once more as the band broke into a fresh tune, but she seized his hand with a delightfully impulsive gesture and, pulling him from the floor, cried with a shake of her dark head: 'No, no—I am starving—let us have supper.'

Yet, back in the box, after she had accounted for two large helpings of caviare, she did little more than toy with the elaborate dishes which succeeded one another and the champagne in her glass remained untasted.

However, the sudden disappearance of her appetite did not seem to have any ill-effects upon her spirits, for she talked and laughed with an animation that Peter found enchanting. Actually, with a skill acquired from considerable practice in handling men, she was leading him on to talk about himself without appearing to do so. She already knew from her chief, Kazdim Hari Bekar, that Peter was a British King's Messenger, and within a few minutes of sitting down to supper he had quite openly given that as his reason for being in Constantinople himself; so it was easy for her to ask him about his other journeys and those northern cities which she had never seen.

Tania had no wild idea of coaxing world-shattering

131

State secrets from the breast of her tall, fair-haired young host. She knew quite well that such things are not entrusted to junior Foreign Office officials, and that actually he was little more than a glorified postman. Her job was purely a routine one of collecting scraps of information, and she would have practised it equally assiduously with a commercial traveller or the purser of a liner, providing that they had just arrived in Turkey from a foreign State. The Press being so rigorously censored in many countries under various forms of dictatorship, the constant tapping of visitors to Istanbul provided the principal means by which the Turkish Government could keep itself correctly informed as to the true thought and feelings of foreign populations. Tania was just one of many agents employed for that purpose, and Peter having, as she soon learned, visited Brussels, Berlin, and Warsaw in the last few months was, from that point of view, an object of interest to her.

'What did he really think of Hitler?' she wanted to know. 'And how did those private citizens whom he must have met on his trips to Berlin regard the Führer? Say anything happened to him, would the Socialist propaganda merchant Goebbels come out on top, or General Goering seize power for himself?'

'Marshal Pilsudski's death had been tragic—hadn't it? Who would succeed him as Dictator of Poland? What had the Poles whom Peter had met in Warsaw said about that?'

'Poor little Belgium had had a nasty shock financially in the spring—hadn't she? How did the business people in Brussels view their country being forced off gold?'

They were all simple questions such as any person with wide interests might have asked, and Peter replied to them frankly. Even if he had suspected that he was being pumped, he would have said much the same, for he was only airing his personal views and in any case had nothing of importance to give away.

He did eventually remark what a serious person she was and how strange he thought it to find anyone so young and lovely with such a wide knowledge of international politics; but she laughed that off quite easily by explaining that sometimes there were long periods when she had no customers at the bookstall in the hotel, so she relieved her boredom by reading all the foreign papers, and knew as much about Hore-Belisha and his beacons as any English girl.

By the time they went down to dance again, she felt that she had done her duty and could compile a report of general interest which would satisfy even that exacting master Kazdim, so was free to enjoy herself until it was time to go home. She liked Peter, his long clean limbs, fair boyish good looks and charming manners, all appealed to her, so when they returned once more to their box she began to question him about himself.

He told her of his lovely old home in Gloucestershire; of the shooting in the autumn and hunting in the winter; of his vast family—nearly all soldiers or civil servants with a sprinkling of clergymen, rather strait-laced but decent people; of his mother, who was quite young but had snow-white hair and was very beautiful; of his father the General, who was a holy terror but a darned good sort; and of his sisters—all three married to promising soldiers now. Tania listened to it all with envious interest and a growing sadness so that, suddenly catching sight of the moisture in her eyes, he stopped, quite overcome by the contrast of his mother and sisters living in comfort and security, with the pathetic fate of this young girl of equally good family who had nothing but a job behind a bookstall between her and starvation—and an invalid parent to support.

In the silence that followed he looked awkwardly away from her down into the well of the restaurant. The dance floor was beginning to empty. Some of the patrons of the place were now a little drunk. The big Swedish sailor who had spoken to Tania earlier in the evening was spanking a young woman across his knee to the hilarious diversion of their party. One of the ladies of the cabaret stood with arms akimbo violently abusing a pasty-faced man in a corner—suddenly she struck him savagely in the mouth. Peter felt more convinced than ever that Tania could not have known the sort of place it was when she had suggested supping there, and blamed himself for not having carried her off directly he arrived to somewhere at least outwardly respectable.

The door at the back of the box opened suddenly. A fat, dark man with a hooky nose and fleshy lips stood there, swaying slightly.

'*A la bonheur*, Tania,' he muttered with a crooked grin.
'*Que desirez vous, m'sieur?*' Tania exclaimed sharply.
'Come and dance,' said the fat man thickly in bad French.
She stood up and went over to him, but began to protest nervously that it was impossible because she was already engaged.

Peter's French was by no means excellent, but good enough for him to catch a few of the intruder's phrases in response to Tania's low-voiced entreaties that he should leave the box. From friendly importunity, the man suddenly passed to indignant abuse:

'Why do you allow one visitor to occupy your whole evening? What if he has paid for your supper. Have I not paid myself many times for the food you waste—but I have not grudged it that you should dance for a little with another. You are a woman of the house—here every night—I am a regular patron and so to me you shall be polite—if not I will make trouble. The management shall take your box from you and for the future you shall sit with the cheap women on the dance floor to be picked up by anyone who chooses.'

'Get out!' exclaimed Peter furiously, and pulling Tania aside, he gave the fat man a violent push in the chest which sent him reeling back into the corridor. Then he slammed the door in his face.

He would have acted sooner had he not been temporarily stunned by that appalling revelation. During the course of the day he had built up a castle of illusion which had grown to magnificent proportions—now it had been shattered to its foundations in one awful moment. For a dozen hours he had allowed his romantic imagination to endow this girl with all the qualities of a fairy-tale princess, robbed of her birthright and enslaved to labour by some wicked witch's spell—only to learn that she was a professional harpie in this shoddy night resort. He saw now how she procured the money for her expensive clothes, those necessary trappings to her trade, and realised why she had ordered that long elaborate supper with the costly but undrinkable champagne; she got a percentage on the bill, of course, and the more she could induce her clients to spend, the better for her pocket. He did not grudge the money, but his vanity was wounded to the quick. Like any callow, trusting fool, he had believed her lies about her gallant struggle against fate, and that as an occasional relaxation from her monotonous life she allowed herself to go out to supper with someone whom she specially liked—yet all the time she was the property of any drunken brute who cared to buy drinks from the management of this dive. She had played up to him with the most sordid motives from the very start, just as she would have to any rough-neck sailor from the port, and her caresses were to be had by right of purchase by any vicious tough. He wondered, with a misery which almost made him physically sick, what other duties of the establishment she undertook, and concluded that few of its patrons would be willing to pay her for no more than eating supper with them.

Then with the brutality of which only youth is capable when its generosity has been abused, he pulled out his wallet and flung a banknote upon the table.

'There you are,' he sneered angrily. 'Fair payment for your evening—or something for your invalid mother if you prefer to keep up that farce. Now you had better go and make your peace with that loathsome-looking friend of yours in the corridor. I'll settle the bill on my way out.'

Not trusting himself to look at his fallen idol lest she should laugh openly at his mortification, and burning with shame at the memory of the idiotic things he had said which must have given her much food for secret merriment, he turned brusquely towards the door.

'Oh, please,' she gasped. 'One moment!'

He halted, his chin stuck out, his eyes grown hard, staring at her: 'Well?'

'I know what you think,' she stammered, twisting her fingers together nervously, 'and it's true. Not all of it—but nearly all. I do come here every night. This is my box and I rent it. I make men spend all the money that I can here and, of course, I get a rake-off. I know I lied to you—but most of the men who come to the bookstall and take me out expect this sort of thing. I didn't realise until this evening that you were different. Then you were so sweet to me that I just hadn't got the courage to shame myself by admitting the sort of life I lead. It's a rotten game—and I hate it—and the men are nearly always beastly—but I liked you so I didn't want you to know. I'm sorry about the supper and that poisonous champagne, but if we hadn't ordered it the manager would have come along and made a fuss—besides it is true about my mother. She's an invalid with heart trouble—her medicines are horribly expensive, and as she was brought up in luxury she has never got used to being poor, she is always asking me for costly things. What the hotel people give me for running the bookstall isn't half-enough. It hardly keeps the roof over our heads, so I just have to do this as well.'

After that spate of words she suddenly went silent, and Peter saw that two great tears were running down her cheeks. There was such a ring of sincerity in her voice that he could not help but believe her, and his heart melted afresh at her pathetic fate.

They were standing close together in the semi-darkness at the back of the box. Suddenly he put his arms round her and, as her dark head fell forward on his shoulder, she burst into a fit of heart-rending sobs.

'You poor little girl,' he murmured softly. 'You must have had a *rotten* life.'

14

'For Them There are Gardens Beneath which Rivers Flow'— (*The Qur'ân*)

It was past three o'clock when Tania arrived home at her apartment. She had insisted on Peter dropping her at some distance from it, since she did not wish him to see the poor, tumbledown row of houses in which it was situated.

He had watched her disappear into a dimly lit thorough-fare with considerable misgivings, fearing that her smart clothes might make her the object of unwelcome attentions at that hour of night, and he would have been even more uneasy if he could have seen her a few moments later as she turned into an evil-looking cul-de-sac; but he need not have worried, for Tania knew every broken window, garbage tin, and frowsty, shuttered shopfront in that unsavoury area, as well as most of its now slumbering inhabitants. Her income had increased considerably in the last few years, but her mother's insatiable craving for petty luxuries having increased with it, there had never been sufficient cash in hand for them to risk a move to better quarters from this sordid slum in which they had lived for years.

A baker's shop occupied the ground floor and basement of the small two-storeyed house in which Tania dwelt. The men were busy at their nightly baking and the stench of refuse in the gutters was temporarily overcome by the appetising odour of new bread. One of them called a cheery greeting to her as she inserted her key in the lock of the side door which led to the rooms above; they all knew and liked her for, having been desperately poor herself, she often helped unfortunates with a little money and was free with her piastres to the ragged children who thronged the narrow court in daytime.

There was no hallway to the house, only a steep flight of rickety, uncarpeted stairs. The place was black as pitch, but as Tania's head came level with the landing, she saw a streak of light below the door which opened directly into the sitting-room.

For a moment she feared that her mother had had an attack—although she had seen the old lady in bed and asleep before departing for the Grandpère—but on flinging open the door she found, with mixed feelings of fear and relief, that despite the lateness of the hour they had a visitor. The vast form of Kazdim Hari Bekar was wedged into their largest armchair.

He was smoking placidly and a little mountain of cigarette stubs beside him in a brass ashtray betrayed the fact that he had been there for some time.

The Baroness Vorontzoff, fat, blowsy, and dull-eyed, was seated near him on a couch, which also served for Tania's bed, since she preferred that to sharing the only other room of the apartment with her mother. The old woman was clad in a shabby dressing-gown and untidy wisps of grey hair straggled about her unnaturally red cheeks. Vanity was not her vice, the sole interest which she had retained in life after the shattering experiences of her flight from Russia was her stomach. As Tania appeared, she roused herself from her lethargy:

'Ah, there you are at last, daughter. I thought you would never come, and the Effendi Kazdim has done us the honour to visit us in this miserable hovel.'

The Eunuch slowly turned his beady eyes upon her. 'Effendi is a word no longer used in Turkey,' he said unctuously. 'All titles were abolished several years ago, as I have told you many times before.'

'Pardon,' she fluttered. 'Pardon an old woman's forgetfulness. I will refer to you as our Proctor then.' She was shrewd enough to know that this man who had spent his youth as a palace slave liked being addressed as 'Lord' and that he bitterly resented the law which robbed him of the official distinction he had gained in the troublesome times after the war.

His little rosebud mouth curved into a smile between the huge hanging cheeks, wrinkled like withered apple skin. 'Protector, yes,' he piped. 'I am your protector as long as you obey my every word—if not . . .' He made a sudden cutting gesture with his plump beringed hand, then stubbed out the cigarette it held with a slow, almost caressing finality.

'You cannot know how grateful we are . . .' began the

138

Baroness in a cringing whine, but Tania, unable to bear the sight of her mother's servility any longer, cut in.

'Do you wish to talk to me?'

He nodded ponderously, creasing his many chins, and switched his eyes meaningly in the direction of her mother.

The Baroness, catching his glance, hurriedly struggled to her feet with the aid of an ebony stick and drew her faded dressing-gown around her. 'I will leave you then,' she smirked. 'Tania is a good girl and will do everything you wish. Good night, Effendi, we are so grateful to you, and honoured by your visit.

Kazdim sat impassively smoking yet another cigarette. He made the faintest gesture with it, waving her away, but not the least sign of impatience as Tania helped her mother slowly across the room. He seemed almost a fixture there. Huge, sinister, implacable, relentless, as though the passage of time had no meaning for him.

'That fiend,' muttered the old woman, as soon as she was in the other room, 'what does he want with you at this hour? He has never come so late before.'

'I don't know, mother,' Tania replied wearily.

'You—you haven't been fool enough to displease him?' The Baroness's eyes showed sudden fear.

'No, no mother. I do my job, so he has no cause to grumble. Go to bed now, please. I mustn't keep him waiting.'

'That's right—do as he says, then your poor mother may at least die in a bed and not in the gutter. It is a pity though that you cannot make him give you more money.'

'Would you like to try *making* him give you anything?' Tania asked a little bitterly.

'No, no, don't misunderstand me. You are such a touchy girl, but in summer good fruit is a necessity. These peaches you bought yesterday were very poor, three of them were woolly ones.'

'They came from the *Tokatlian*,' said Tania sullenly, 'and the season is almost over.'

'Ah, well, it cannot be helped, I suppose. If only I were not an invalid, I would go out and choose such things myself—then we should fare better. Where is the new bottle of French cognac, a little drop would help me to get off to sleep, I think.'

Tania's shoulders sagged and her eyes closed with weariness. She had meant to bring a fresh bottle back with her from the Grandpère, where they let her have it at trade rates, but the totally unexpected scene with the young Englishman had put all thought of it out of her head.

'You—you haven't forgotten it?' The old woman's rheumy eyes filled with facile tears.

'I'm sorry, mother.' Tania suddenly felt an awful beast. She always did when her mother wept, no matter how absurd the trifling disappointment to her appetites which caused her to give way.

'I *am* sorry,' she repeated desperately. 'I'll get up early tomorrow morning and fetch it for you then. Now, please don't cry any more. There's some Slivowitz left—look, here in the cupboard. Have that instead.'

'Very well,' the old woman quavered, 'but you are not to get up early for the cognac—tomorrow night will do. As it is, you sleep too little, my dear—and what would happen to us if you were to become ill?'

Tania knew that no thought but affection for herself lay behind the words, yet she was certain that her mother would be peevish and querulous all next day unless she had her cognac. She poured out the Slivowitz, set it on the table beside the bed, kissed the old lady, and murmured, 'Don't worry about me, dearest. I'm strong as a horse, but I must go now. I dare not keep Kazdim waiting any longer.'

Having returned to the sitting-room, she lit a cigarette, leaned negligently against the big porcelain stove, and waited for the Eunuch to address her. Inwardly, she was as terrified of him as her mother, and she was searching her mind frantically as to what fault she could have committed in her work to bring him there at that unusual hour, but she would not show her fear.

'Well,' he piped, glancing up at her, 'what have you to tell me of that young man with whom you supped this evening?'

'Nothing of much value,' she replied laconically. 'He was easy enough, but he is new to his job and has only visited Brussels, Berlin, and Warsaw. I got his views on certain subjects for what they are worth, and you shall have them in my report tomorrow. Surely you did not come here to ask me that?'

'No, I am here on account of the letter which you sent me from the Pera Palace this evening.'

'It was important, then?' she hazarded.

'Very.' His great, egg-shaped face creased into a frown. 'I wish that I had received it earlier.'

'I sent it to you immediately the bookstall closed,' Tania said hastily. 'I did not dare to before in case Swithin Destime returned and asked for it back.'

'Yes, yes, my child, but I had special business to attend to this evening, so I did not receive it until after midnight. By then our bird had flown.'

'This man is dangerous then, after all?'

'He is inquisitive and has already learned too much. His letter was a report which shows him clearly to be acting as a secret agent, but for whom I have yet to find out. Do you not consider it strange that he should have lived in Istanbul for six weeks without anyone—particularly yourself—suspecting his activities?'

Tania quailed before those small, beady eyes embedded in their rolls of fat. 'No,' she managed to get out with an effort. 'You know that I could not induce him to entertain me, and he never talked of any matter of importance. Once, when he mentioned the Gazi, I did the old trick of warning him to be careful because the hotel detective was standing near. I hoped that would give him confidence in me. I think it did or he would not have risked leaving this letter with me tonight.'

'Perhaps. Did you know that he only spent certain nights in the hotel?'

She shook her head. 'How should I? My work there ends at eight o'clock. Surely it is for others to check up the movements of visitors who go out at night.'

'They do, but the fools believed this man to be harmless, and so many visitors spend their nights gambling or with women, that they never troubled to find out where he went.'

For a little time the Eunuch smoked in silence, then his high-pitched, child-like voice came again. 'This woman to whom you were to give the letter tomorrow morning. Have you ever seen him with her?'

'I have never seen him with any woman—or man—except casual acquaintances whom he picked up from time to time among the other visitors to the hotel—people staying for a few days only—but all of them are now gone.'

'You have passed on to me every word of the description that he gave you of her?'

'Every word.'

'Does it fit any woman who frequents the hotel?'

'There are half a dozen, at least, who are tall, slim, fair-haired—and that he said she was beautiful tells me nothing —he would think that whatever her looks if he happens to be in love with her. But if he does not return, she will come to my stall for the letter in the morning.'

Almost imperceptibly, Kazdim shook his enormous head. 'I think not. My men shall keep watch on the off-chance, but I have a feeling that something scared him away. He returned to the hotel a little after eleven and left again before twelve. His heavy luggage is still there, yet his dressing-case is gone even though the Kavass swears that he did not take it with him. If I am right, he will have warned the woman so she will not come—but it is *he* whom we must find.'

Again he sat silent, smoking his interminable cigarettes, while Tania waited. Then at last, he spoke again:

'How many times has this man talked with you?'

'Almost every day since his arrival.'

'Then he must have let something drop into your little ears which can be of use to me.'

'No, nothing, I promise you. He only spoke of the weather and the news in the papers that he . . .'

'Silence!' he piped with sudden vehemence. 'A chattering woman is a scourge to thought. Take heed now, did he say nothing of the purpose which had brought him to Istanbul?'

'Not a thing that I can remember,' Tania answered wearily.

'No? Let me aid your memory, then.'

'I mean that I *should* remember if he ever *had* said anything,' she corrected herself hurriedly.

'I wonder. You will try a little harder, perhaps, if I remind you that your mother and yourself are aliens, allowed to remain in Turkey only on a permit at my pleasure. This matter is important. If you cannot remember something which will assist me to find this man, I may not remember to renew that permit. Then that foolish old woman and yourself will be expatriated to Russia. The rest of your career I leave to your imagination and the Bolsheviks.'

'You wouldn't do that—you can't,' Tania pleaded. 'I've served you well—brought you lots of little pieces of useful information.'

He raised his eyebrows until they formed two semi-circles in his high, bald forehead. 'Can I not? And why? Do you think, then, that you have the only body that men will lust after in Istanbul? There are a thousand like you with whom I could fill your place tomorrow. Allah! Why is it that thou hast cursed women by making them such imbeciles? Think, girl. Think, I say! This matter is important.'

'I can't,' Tania moaned. 'Honestly, I can't think of anything he said that mattered.'

'Listen,' Kazdim spoke quite calmly again now and almost as if he was addressing a small child. 'Go over in your mind all the reasons for which he *might* have come. We know the truth now, but he must have had some ostensible reason to cover his secret activities. Was he a doctor or engineer? Did he speak of visiting the museums, which might make you think him an antiquary? Was he always eager to see the latest market reports in the papers, and so a financier, perhaps? Did he discuss the shipping in the port? Had he ever had one of those leather cases which hold samples with him? Did he express interest in aeroplanes, or clothing, or the new buildings which are going up in the city? Was he concerned with any of our industries? Carpet manufacture, scent . . .'

'Stop— I have it,' Tania exclaimed. 'Tobacco. He is something to do with one of the tobacco depots. He only mentioned it once—just after he arrived—and that is such a long time ago now that it had slipped out of my mind.'

'Well, that is something. Not much, it is true, since there are scores of tobacco depots within ten miles of the city, but at least it gives me one line of investigation.'

The Eunuch stared at Tania for a moment as he considered whether he should try to screw something more out of her, but he had decided long ago that she was not withholding anything wilfully, and now he thought it unlikely that she could help him further, however hard he pressed her.

With a sudden lurch he came to his feet, then with an astonishingly swift movement he seized the lobe of her ear between his finger and thumb, twisted it violently, causing her momentary but acute agony, chuckled gleefully as he released it, and turned towards the door.

'Take care of the young one you were with tonight while he is here,' he shot at her in his curious treble. 'He may prove a useful source of information to us later if he returns regularly to Istanbul.' Then without another glance, he left her.

Tania listened to his unexpectedly light tread as he pattered down the stairs. As the street door banged behind him, she gave a sigh of relief, and pulling off the smart little hat laid it brim upwards upon a chair. Five minutes later, she had removed the cover from the divan and taken off her clothes, crossed herself before the Ikon that hung on the wall, blown out the lamp and tumbled into bed. Almost as soon as her head touched the pillow, she was asleep.

Another who slept that night in Istanbul from sheer exhaustion was Swithin Destime. When he had woken that morning, he had known nothing of this conspiracy, heavy with fateful possibililities for Turkey, which was creeping like an invisible miasma amongst the inhabitants of the city. Picnicking on the Wall with Reouf, he had learnt of it and sensed its possible importance. Afterwards he had spent anxious hours trying, without success, to get in touch with Diana. Then there had been the meeting on the rooftop at Scutari, confirming Reouff's view that the Kaka had popular backing. Supper with Arif, Reouf, and Jeanette. His conference with Diana, which had ended in such an alarming manner. His flight from the *Pera* to his secret refuge in the Tatavla flat. Diana's arrival ten minutes later, flushed with the success of her bold *coup* in getting away unchallenged with his dressing-case through the back entrance of the hotel. Another long conference and, after her departure, his decision that he must warn Reouf and Arif from asking for him at the Pera Palace in case they got into trouble through their association with him. The labour of changing into a suitable disguise, then out again to undertake the wearisome journey across the Bosphorus. A wrangle with a boatman who suspected, from his shabby clothes, that he could not pay the fare, until the money had actually changed hands. The anxious search through dark, unknown streets to find the address upon the ornate gilt-edged card which Arif had given him, then the dropping of the note for the brothers saying that he had left the Pera Palace for private reasons that night for good, and would communicate with them the following day. Back again to Tatavla, and so—at last—to bed.

As was to be expected, he slept late the following morning, but when he woke every episode of the previous day was clear in his mind. His first thought was of Diana. He turned over in bed, lit a cigarette, and visualised her as he had seen her the night before. She had behaved magnificently, urging him to quit the *Pera* at once and leave her to do his packing. On his refusal, she had insisted on cramming his dressing-case with many useful things that he would have been loathe to leave behind, and smuggling it out herself when they left by separate entrances.

His whole view of her had changed again completely. He now had a boundless admiration for her courage tempered by a grudging regard for her efficiency. It was not that he was the least mean-natured, but for a man of his temperament and rather old-fashioned outlook, it was a bitter pill to swallow that any good-looking young woman should show herself to have a quicker and apparently more analytical brain than his own. He did himself the injustice of forgetting that, having acted as go-between for her father on previous occasions, she had far more experience of the sort of work he was employed upon than he had, and it rankled with him that from start to finish her mind had been ahead of his the night before. Not being used to playing second fiddle to a woman, he soothed his ruffled plumage by attributing her abilities to a certain hardness in her nature. That fitted in with her ill-treatment of him on the yacht, for he considered her partial explanation of it far from satisfactory. Her story of playing a part in order to keep some member of the party under observation did not hold water, for who, he argued, in that crowd had there been to watch.

She was a darned good pal to have by one in a nasty hole, he told himself, but a heartless little minx where other matters were concerned. She had played with him in England and with Cæsar Penton on the yacht; now it seemed she was more or less willing to play with him again; but he wasn't having any. . . . 'Once bitten, twice shy, and we'll stick strictly to our business,' was his final verdict.

He got up, breakfasted off a tin of sardines from an emergency store that he had laid in, and began to select some suitable clothes from his second-hand wardrobe, but it occurred to him that if he were going over to Arif's house these tattered garments would need considerable explanation. The Turk knew him only as an English business man visiting Istanbul, and had no idea of the true reason which had brought him there. Obviously, he must go dressed in his ordinary clothes, if he went at all, and that might be risky if the police were looking for him. However, it was imperative for him to see Reouf if he wished to learn more of the Kaka, so he decided to chance it.

For once the sky was overcast, so he was able to compromise by covering his lounge suit with a filthy old mackintosh, which was among his gear, without risk of drawing undue attention to himself, and which he could remove on his arrival. He completed his costume by a rather dusty bowler worn right on the back of his head, and as he surveyed himself in the mirror, he wondered gleefully just what his friends at home would think if he walked into the Club in Brook Street dressed like that.

Actually the disguise was very adequate, for far more depends upon such trifling alterations in the manner of wearing headgear and a different type of walk than theatrical false beards and moustaches, so despite the fact that his description had already been circulated, the Eunuch's men never gave him a second glance as he boarded the steamer ferry at Galata bridge, and he reached Arif's house by twelve o'clock.

A stout, swarthy-faced female answered the door through which he had dropped his note in the small hours of the morning, but to his inquiry for Reouf she shook her head:

'He is not here today,' she said slowly, 'and he did not sleep at home last night, but perhaps you may find him at the University. Allah puts it into the heads of these young students to do crazy things at times, although Reouf is a serious one and not apt to be afflicted by the Most Merciful in this way.'

Swithin then asked for Arif and elicited the information that, as usual, he could be found in his office at the Haidar Pacha terminus goods station. Arif would obviously be busy with his work and it was Reouf whom Swithin really wanted to get hold of, so he recrossed the water, walked to the old Arsenal in which he knew the University now to be situated, and after considerable difficulty managed to find a student who knew his friend. This pot-bellied young gentleman had not seen Reouf that day and could tell him nothing, so he returned to his flat annoyed and disappointed.

Knowing no other place in which he might profitably search for the young Turk, he spent the remainder of the afternoon thinking out subtle questions to ask him in the evening, for he had little doubt that Reouf, obviously having been kept out the previous night on the Eunuch's secret business, would return home by dusk and have a most interesting story to tell if only it could be got out of him.

When night had fallen, Swithin crossed to Scutari for the fourth time since he had gone there with Reouf to the meeting, made his way by side streets to Arif's house, and sent in his name by the old woman whom he had seen earlier in the day.

Arif received him in a long, low room, the furniture of which was a curious mixture of Edwardian French and Oriental. Plush, gilt-studded chairs, apparently little used, were ranged stiffly round the walls, but at one end there was a sumptuous divan; an ornate chandelier hung from the ceiling, and the electric globes with which it was fitted shed so harsh a light that the delicate colours of the fine rugs upon the floor became almost blurred when dazzled eyes looked down upon them.

The Turk promptly observed the rules of hospitality by calling for coffee, but apart from outward civility he did not appear particularly glad to see his visitor. He resumed his place cross-legged on the divan, inquired abruptly if Swithin would care to smoke and, on the acquiescence of his guest, handed him an amber mouthpiece which was attached by a long tube to the already bubbling *narghile* on the floor. Then he picked up his own pipe and began a constant nervous puffing.

When the coffee arrived, they exchanged a few sentences and Swithin inquired for Reouf, upon which Arif replied that he had not seen him since the night before. That obviously was the cause of his anxiety, yet Swithin felt once again that he dared not reassure him by saying that both Reouf and Kazdim were members of the Kaka.

Despite his European clothes, Arif seemed to have reverted entirely to the Oriental as he sat there cross-legged upon the divan. He spoke only occasionally and with grave courtesy about nothing in particular. Swithin replied with equally measured and well-considered words. Between each exchange long silences occurred and after a little the Englishman began to think that this formal procedure had its uses. He knew quite well what was in the other man's mind, but surely this stoical repose under the strain of anxiety was more dignified than striding up and down endlessly repeating futile speculations or insincere assurances that he was not really worried about his brother at all.

An hour, two hours, drifted by. Swithin sat on, determined not to leave, unless he had to, before he had seen Reouf and at least arranged another meeting. Arif, if not a glowing host, seemed at all events not unwilling that he should remain, for once when he half-heartedly suggested that it was growing late, the Turk pressed him to stay on with a sudden eagerness which showed that he preferred not to be left alone.

The footsteps shuffled in the hall. Swithin was unable to refrain from standing up; Reouf at last, he thought, it will be devilish interesting to know what Kazdim kept him busy on all this time, but instead of Reouf an old man entered. He stood there looking at Arif for a few seconds in silence, then he said:

'I grieve for you, brother. The fishermen found him. His body was washed up by the current upon the far side —about three miles blow the spot where the Wall reaches the sea. It is the will of Allah—praise be upon His name and that of the Prophet.'

Then half a dozen other men followed him into the room. They carried a bier which they set down on the floor.

148

Arif had risen. He snatched at the cloth which covered it. Reouf's face, unnaturally swollen, stared up at them. Two of the men silently turned the body over, the clothing squelched and a trickle of water ran out upon the floor. Its arms were bound behind the back with strong cords.

Swithin had a fleeting vision of the Tower of Marble, jutting out into the Marmara Sea, as he had seen it the day before, and of the sinister chamber within it, then of the gloating face of the Eunuch as he had pointed to the dark shaft below which lay the rushing waters, and described the terrible fate which had overtaken so many people in that place of ghosts—because they knew too much.

'Allah is great,' chanted the old men. 'He is the Merciful—the Compassionate—and blessed are the believers upon Mahomet his Prophet—for them there are Gardens beneath which Rivers flow, and they shall dwell therein for aye.'

15

'For These are the Fellows of the Fire and They Shall Burn Therein for Aye'
(*The Qur'ân*)

Swithin was momentarily overwhelmed by the thought that he had brought this tragedy upon the brothers, but his sense of proportion soon reasserted itself. He had been the innocent instrument through which fate had worked perhaps, but no more. Reouf's own hot-headed fanaticism and enthusiasm for his cause, which he had confessed to displaying so indiscreetly to Kazdim after Swithin left them together on the Wall, were obviously the prime cause of his death. Yet the fact that he could absolve himself from blame hardly lightened Swithin's distress, for although he had known the youth barely forty-eight hours, he had taken a genuine liking to him.

After the first shock, Swithin was brought back with a jerk to the effect this hideous business might have upon his own affairs. The body of the young Turk lying there, damp, swollen and repulsive, brought home to him as nothing had before the real gravity of his own situation. If Diana had not urged him to leave the Pera Palace on the previous night, he too might have been sent, with his arms trussed behind his back, to feed the fishes in the Bosphorus. Subconsciously, he had been a little inclined to take insufficient heed of the obvious fear with which the name of Kazdim Hari Bekar filled other people, but now he had an all too horrible example of the man's swift ruthlessness and realised that his life henceforward hung upon his own caution. One false step and he would be like that silent, still dripping thing upon the floor.

Arif gave a muttered order. The men replaced the cloth over Reouf's face and moved the bier into the centre of the room. Swithin saw that as a stranger it was impossible for him to remain there any longer; the women of the family would be coming to mourn their dead. In a low voice, he expressed his sorrow and sympathy to be bereaved Turk, bowed to the others, and then left the house.

Once in the street he walked a hundred yards, sat down on the edge of a horse-trough, lit a cigarette, and began to think things out.

For nearly twenty-four hours Kazdim's people must have been searching for him and his mission was not yet half-accomplished. So far he had only ascertained that there *was* a plot hatching against Kemal, but he knew nothing of its extent, its leaders, the methods they meant to employ in order to gain their ends, or when it was likely to come to maturity.

With fresh anxiety, he realised that he had been counting on Reouf to furnish him with all these details, or at least give him the necessary leads, after skilful pumping, which would enable him to find them out from other sources—and now poor Reouf was dead. That avenue was closed for ever, so he must start from the beginning again by winning someone else's confidence; a difficult enough business at any time, but infinitely more so now that he no longer dared move in the open for fear of being recognised by the police.

The night was still and cloudless, few people were about at this late hour, and the quiet side street would have been hushed in silence but for a distant wailing from Arif's house, where the women had already gathered in Oriental fashion to hold the wake which would not cease until the funeral took place the following morning.

Swithin had seen such ceremonies before and knew what would happen then. Even for a man of some position, there would be no coffin or hearse. His male relations, taking turns as bearers, would carry the bier through the streets, followed by a straggling procession, to the burial ground outside the town. There a rough hole would be dug, the body placed in it, sitting upright and facing towards Mecca, the earth shovelled in upon it, and every man present would cast a stone on the new grave, forming a small cairn. The Turks, being curiously callous towards their dead, no tributes of flowers would be offered, either at the funeral or afterwards in token of memory, and even if the family troubled to erect one of those queer coffin-shaped tombstones, it would be allowed to topple over in course of a few months, since they would never visit the grave again.

As Swithin pondered the problem, he saw this one hope lay in Arif. Reouf had as good as said that his brother was in the conspiracy, so somehow the Station Master had got to be made to talk—but how? He was a much tougher proposition than the younger man had been and far less likely to open his heart to a stranger unless he could be persuaded by some very potent reason. However, the attempt had got to be made, so the first question was how to get hold of him.

Swithin rubbed his hawk-like little nose thoughtfully. He could hardly return to the house in the middle of the wake, so the first chance to call would be after the funeral, but that meant waiting until the following day and time was now an all-important factor. Every hour that he spent in Constantinople henceforth would be one of danger; he must get his job done and leave Turkey at the earliest possible moment if he were to escape with a whole skin. Besides, it would have been reported to Kazdim that Reouf's body had been recovered and taken to his brother's house, so it was almost certain that the Eunuch would have the funeral spied on to ascertain who attended it. If Swithin went for the purpose of getting in touch with Arif, he considered it a safe bet that he would be recognised by the people Kazdim sent, and then his goose would be completely cooked.

After his fourth cigarette, he stood up, having decided that his best chance lay in trying to get hold of Arif before the night was out. He sauntered back to the house, cogitating ways and means. Outside it, he paused; the keening of the women was making the night hideous, obviously he could not just go in at the door and ask to be announced in the middle of this scene of grief, so he turned down a narrow, high-walled alley which ran along the side of the premises.

As he had supposed, there was no garden, for the house, built in the old style, was erected round a central courtyard and there were no windows in the wall that faced on the alleyway, only a low, nail-studded side door. He knew that Arif would not be with the mourning women, but that he must be somewhere about the place. There was just a chance that he might be up on the flat rooftop. It was the sort of spot a man might well select, rather than a stuffy room, on a hot night when unable to sleep from shock and sorrow.

Swithin picked up a stone from the gutter and weighed it in his hand. He had been a keen cricketer all his life and that now stood him in good stead. He pitched it with commendable accuracy so that it neither went too far and fell into the courtyard which was concealed from his view, nor struck the blank wall and rebounded into the lane. It landed on the roof of the two-storey building with a faint clatter which he could just hear from his position down below. He waited a moment—nothing happened—then he pitched up another.

The dark blob of a head suddenly appeared above the stone coping, and Swithin began to whistle softly: 'God Save the King'. He did not wish to give his identity away before he was certain that the person above was Arif, but hoped that if it were, the station master might possibly recognise that British tune.

'Is that Mr. Destime?' came a sharp inquiry.

'Yes—and I've got to talk to you,' Swithin called up with a cautiously subdued voice. 'It's vital that I should— about your brother. Come down and let me in.'

The head was withdrawn and a couple of minutes later a crack of light appeared down the edge of the nail-studded door. It widened, and Arif stood there peering out into the darkness.

'Thanks.' Swithin joined him in two quick strides. 'Take me somewhere where we can talk without being disturbed —will you?' He spoke firmly, showing no trace of doubt as to if the Turk would let him in.

Arif's hesitation was hardly perceptible, then he turned and led the way down a passage to a small room which contained a desk, an old-fashioned filing cabinet, a swivel chair, and a cheap Tottenham Court Road settee—obviously an office.

'Now,' he said, turning a face lined by grief to his midnight visitor. 'What is it? Why do you disturb me thus?'

'Because I know who killed your brother,' Swithin replied promptly.

The Turk nodded. 'Well, so do I. It was that hell-spawn Kazdim. The Eunuch whom Kemal has seen fit to make Chief of the Police. You were with me last night when he carried the poor boy off on some pretext—no one has seen Reouf alive since.'

'True, but do you know why Kazdim killed him?'

'Yes, that also I can guess. My brother—Allah rest his soul—was young and an idealist. Poor innocent, he meant no harm, but he had allowed himself to get mixed up with certain fools who think that they can overthrow Kemal. Perhaps he was betrayed or perhaps he gave himself away. At all events, Kazdim discovered that he was associated with these traitors, and for that reason—took his life.'

'You're wrong,' said Swithin quietly.

'Why should you think that?'

'I know it—just as I know that you yourself are one of those very traitors whom you speak of—the Kaka, who are plotting against Kemal.'

For a second the two men stared at each other: Swithin, dark, small, wiry, calm, but his blue eyes unwavering and hard as steel; the Turk, taller almost by a head, lean, muscular, but stooping a little, and not up to the same degree of fitness owing to years spent at a sedentary occupation. Swithin was quite confident that he could knock hell out of the bigger man if it came to a dust-up. Arif thought so too, perhaps, for his black eyes narrowed and he made a sudden dive towards the top drawer of his desk, but Swithin with equal quickness thrust his hand into his pocket, and the other checked his movement immediately.

'You don't need the gun you've got in that drawer,' remarked Swithin affably. 'I've got one on me, but I don't intend to use it—yet.'

Then with a quick smile he withdrew his hand from his pocket and extended the gold case that it held. 'Let's talk this matter over quietly—have a cigarette.'

Arif shook his head and backed away with a suspicious look. 'Who are you?' he shot out tersely.

'An Englishman representing others who are good friends to Turkey. I want you to believe that. If you do, no harm will come to you through me; if not—well, the last thing I want to do is to threaten, but I'm afraid you're going to have a pretty sticky time.'

'You mean to inform on me to Kazdim?'

'Not if you do as I request.'

'What do you want of me?'

154

'I want you to answer a few questions. To some of them I know the answers already, so I shall put them only as tests to see if you are telling the truth. The others concern certain points that I am still in doubt about and wish to check up.'

'And if I refuse?'

Swithin shrugged. He felt an utter beast in using such methods, but for the moment he had to put every consideration out of his mind except his job. 'If you don't,' he said firmly. 'You know what happened to Reouf— I'm afraid it will be your turn tomorrow night.'

A strained silence fell in the little room, then Arif jerked out at last: 'You cannot hope to wreck our organisation —even if I do tell you all that I know.'

'I'm quite aware of that,' Swithin bluffed on swiftly, 'But we'll start at the beginning. Give me the objects of the Kaka, please.'

'So be it.' Arif's eyes fell to the floor and the terror that the name of Kazdim inspired strong upon him, he recited almost mechanically: 'We are bound by oath to work for— the restoration of the Faith, the law as it is set forth in the Holy Koran, and our ancient Empire—for the destruction of the atheist, blasphemer and traitor, Kemal; and to obey without question all orders emananting from the chief of our cell or one who shows the signet. Praise be to Allah, the Most High, and blessed be the name of Mahomet his Prophet.'

'Ha! ha!' thought Swithin, 'so they are working this on the cell system—are they,' while he asked at once:

'What is the number of your cell?'

'Number 310.'

'Is that your parent cell or one that you have formed yourself?'

'My own.'

'What is the number of your parent cell?'

'Number 72.'

'And how many members are there to each cell?'

'Five,' Arif replied, with a suspicious look, 'but why ask me such a question when you know the answer?'

'In order to test your veracity,' Swithin countered promptly, as he thought rapidly to himself: 'No wonder this chap thinks it would be mighty difficult to wreck their organisation. If he were tortured for a week, he could not give away more than eight of his fellow plotters, the four in the cell into which he was originally initiated and the four pals that he has roped in to form a new cell under his own leadership.'

'How many cells have been formed to date?' he inquired.

'I do not know exactly, but the number is over 1,700 now.'

Swithin calculated quickly. 'Four new members to each —that meant nearly 7,000 people were involved already, and half that number were at work all over Turkey, recruiting their friends to form new cells of their own. The movement must be spreading like wildfire. It was a far graver business than he had imagined.' His eye fell upon a small old-fashioned iron safe in the corner of the room.

'I should like to see your correspondence,' he said suddenly.

'Arif frowned. 'What do you mean—you know that we have none—all orders are passed from cell leader to cell leader by word of mouth.'

Seeing he had blundered badly in his bluff that he already knew the answer to many of the questions he was asking, Swithin hurried on: 'No matter—produce your signet, please.'

With an angry shrug, Arif half-turned away. 'This is absurd,' he protested. 'You trick me into answering by pretending that you know much of our organisation and I find that you know nothing—I refuse to reply further.'

'It does not concern you in the least what I know or what I do not know,' Swithin said quietly. 'The question is—do you talk or do I turn you over to Kazdim?'

Fear gleamed suddenly in the Turk's eyes again, and he muttered: 'So be it then. Only twenty-one persons, the members of cells 1 to 5, possess the signet, so it is impossible for me, a member of cell 72, to show it to you.'

'Thank you. Now on what date is the rising against Kemal to take place?'

'I do not know.'

'Be careful.'

'As Allah hears me, I do not know!'

Swithin's eyes bored steadily into those of the Turk.

'Don't run away with the idea that because I am ill-informed on some points that I know nothing of this business,' he warned him. 'You are Chief Station Master of the Goods Depot at Haidar Pacha—aren't you?'

'Yes—but all Istanbul knows that.'

'Do they also know of the contraband machine-guns and other material which you have concealed under the heading of "Government Stores" in some of your warehouses at the Depot?'

It was a shot in the dark—initiated by the memory of Diana's question about smuggled armaments the night before, and a sudden realisation that this man, in so high a cell as number 72, and with such perfect facilities for storing contraband and ensuring its rapid distribution to all parts of Turkey, might have been made use of for that purpose—but it found its mark.

Arif flinched and paled a little under his dark skin, although he murmured sullenly: 'I do not admit that.'

Swithin saw that he had scored a hit and rammed it home. 'It is not necessary. I can easily tell Kazdim to send his men to inspect your sheds.'

'So be it, then—I am in your hands—but the date of the Jehad I cannot tell—for I do not know it. Perhaps it has not even been fixed yet.'

For one awful moment Swithin held his breath. The word 'Jehad' flamed through his brain with all its terrible possibilities. Of the patriotic ravings of young Reouf he had taken little stock, but this was a very different business. It even far exceeded the scope of the determined internal revolution of which he had learned in the last ten minutes, for a Jehad meant the preaching of a Holy War. These people were not out only to destroy Kemal and reinstate the old law of the Koran, but with all the bitter zeal of blind fanaticism, they meant to carry their full programme into actual practice. It meant the certainty of another flare-up in the Balkans, their co-religionists would probably rise in sympathy and begin massacres of Europeans in India, Syria, Palestine, Egypt, Algeria, and, taking into consideration the unstable state of things in Europe, perhaps even be the kindling spark leading to the supreme horror of a war to the death between fresh combinations of the Great Powers.

'How long do you consider it will take your army to

reach Salonica?' he asked, putting the leading question as casually as he could, and with equal casualness Arif confirmed his worst fears.

'A week perhaps, not more, since our air force could wipe out that of the Greeks in forty-eight hours. Kemal has at least forged us a fine weapon to strike with when the time comes. No one outside Turkey has any idea of the number or efficiency of our planes.'

'I see.' Swithin paused again, completely staggered by the momentous importance of this secret which he had discovered. It was clear now beyond all doubt from Arif's attitude that if these madmen gained control, they really meant to play the 'Mad dog of Europe' and start a first-class war overnight. His task had suddenly assumed immense significance. It was now more than ever up to him to get every possible detail that he could and either persuade Arif into acting with him or force him into disclosing other leads for further investigation. With the latter in mind, he said, 'I should be glad if you would give me now the names of the other members of your two cells.'

'No, that I cannot do.' Arif shook his head firmly.

'You can, since you must know them.'

'True, but I refuse. I will not betray my comrades.'

'Kazdim has not forgotten how to bastinado obstinate people, I imagine!—surely it would be wiser to speak now than wait until the soles of your feet have been beaten to a pulp.'

'I will not, I say.' The Turk drew himself up with dignity. 'I have given you the information which you ask about the Kaka because, if I can, I would save my life, but I have only done so with the knowledge that you cannot prevent its success. Even if you were to kill a hundred individuals like my brother and myself, you could not do that. It is like an octopus and for every arm you cut off a dozen more will grow; but when it comes to betraying others personally —that I will not do.'

'I'll give you two minutes to think it over,' Swithin declared, sticking out his chin. 'If you have not told me those names by that time, you know what to expect.'

'If you gave me a hundred years, my answer would be the same.'

Swithin glanced at his watch and then stood there silently.

It was pure bluff, but he had got to get every scrap of information that he could and the names of eight other men concerned in this secret movement would be extremely valuable, each could be forced for further details and other names in turn.

As he stood there, the magnitude of this menace appalled him afresh. The fact that he had spent six weeks in the city probing for something of the kind, yet finding nothing, was ample proof that when fresh cells were formed, they chose the members with the utmost care, only admitting men whose anti-Kemalist views were proved beyond question. Reouf could only have been a rare exception. And there were 7,000 of them—more undoubtedly by now, all bigoted fanatics who would stop at nothing to restore the full observance of their ancient faith, and glory in marching to war upon their old enemies, the Balkan Christian States.

The thought of grim, fasting Uncle Issa came into his mind. Men of a higher position, but very similar, would take control. Kemal's superimposed westernisation of the nation would melt away like frost before a summer dawn. A million bowler hats would be flung into the Bosphorus, long hidden fezes would come out of every drawer. The Mullahs, with their antiquated religious law, would be the final court of arbitration for the civil population once again. Women, however much they might have progressed in the last fifteen years, would be thrust back behind the *jalousies* and the old reign of corruption and bribery would be restored. Within a month Turkey would be clamouring for war and plunder, those twin excitements upon which these descendants of the Asiatic Huns had lived for centuries. Whatever their other shortcomings, no one has ever denied that they are first-class soldiers, and with the army which Kemal had trained to such a high degree of efficiency, they could overrun the Balkans in a week. France would stand by that child of her creation, the Little Entente, Italy had ambitions in the Adriatic, and before the private citizens of the world could protest, they would find that the pacts and leagues by which their statesmen had so brilliantly enmeshed them had precipitated another general slaughter.

Swithin saw it all with the same clarity as if he had been listening to the cold logic of a Staff College lecture upon

International Complications. He was no diplomat, but as a soldier he had passed out of the common rut and done his two years at Camberley, where he had listened to instructors who could give points to the average banker or big business man, when they got down to brass tacks, on the mainsprings which actuated the delicate balance of power that kept the peace of Europe. He glanced at his watch again and then produced his pistol. 'Time's up,' he said. 'Are you going to talk or must I march you off to Kazdim?'

Arif remained quite placid. The fear had gone out of his eyes now that he had formed his resolution. 'Do what you will,' he shrugged. 'Allah is my witness that I will not say one other word.'

The bluff was called and Swithin knew it. With a rueful smile he repocketed his gun, and when he spoke again his voice had a ring of genuine admiration. 'May I congratulate you on your courage—you're a brave chap, Arif, and a loyal one. And now I'll tell you something. Apart from what I've learned from you, I don't know the first thing about the Kaka. In fact, I did not even know that it existed until Reouf told me of it yesterday.'

Suddenly Arif's lips went greyish white with furious anger. 'It was you, then, who betrayed him,' he almost screamed.

'Quiet for God's sake!' Swithin held up a warning hand. 'I never had any intention of handing you over to Kazdim, and please believe me, on the word of an Englishman, I had no hand in the death of your brother.'

The Turk let out his breath with a sharp hiss of relief, but he persisted doggedly: 'Who betrayed Reouf, then—if it was not you?'

'I can tell you. That's why I came back here tonight. I admit that I've tricked you into telling me certain things. I had to, because it's my job to find them out, but before you think of turning me out of your house I want you to remember this. When I came here I only suspected that you were a member of this secret league against Kemal, now I know it—and the numbers of your cells, so if I wished I could now lay an information against you far more effectively than I could have a quarter of an hour ago. But I'm not threatening you now and I give you my word that your secret is perfectly safe with me. I only state that because whatever you decide to do, you must give me a hearing.'

'Well?'

'Reouf was not executed by Kemal's Secret Police.'

'By whom, then?'

'By your Brothers in Allah of the Sword and Crescent. They killed him because, poor boy, he talked too freely—they thought him dangerous and so they decided to eliminate him.'

'I do not believe it.'

'I can prove it to you. He wished to gain my sympathy as a foreigner who might influence outside opinion in favour of your movement—so he talked to me—with the best intentions, perhaps—but of things that he should not have done. That did not matter, but he did the same to someone else. That person was a member of one of your high cells. Thinking the boy a danger, he praised his enthusiasm, showed him the signet, and told him that he should be given special work to do. Reouf told me this himself. Then under that pretext, he was decoyed away last night and murdered—to still his tongue.'

'Who was it?' demanded Arif fiercely.

'Kazdim, of course! He's in this thing himself, he must be, how otherwise would he have possession of the signet—and the final proof is the manner of Reouf's death. It was no execution in a prison yard, but murder done in secret at the Marble Tower by your fellow conspirators because they feared that he could betray them by his indiscretion.'

The Turk covered his face with his hands and sank down in a chair. 'Allah!' he moaned. 'Allah—Father of All—how can thy servants be guilty of a deed so foul.'

'Listen.' Swithin placed his hand on the distraught man's shoulder. 'Your eyes are open now. You, and probably thousands of others, have been most terribly misled. As idealists, you have believed yourselves to be working for your religion and the restoration of the ancient glories of your country. That is not true, you are being used as puppets to break Kemal, who has saved for you all that is left of Turkey and whose efforts to clear up all the abuses from which the country has suffered for a hundred years are the admiration of every power that counts in the world today.

'If you succeeded, what would happen? Only just re-covering from a dozen years of war, you would be plunged into war again. You couldn't win, even under Kemal's leadership, because war is far more a matter of possessing adequate stocks of the right raw material than bravery today, and without him you would be beaten before you started. The Greeks and the Bulgars and all your old enemies would be only too glad of the excuse to have an-other cut at you, and they'd have the backing of the Great Powers behind them. There could only be one end to it—the final dismemberment of Turkey—and you would all become a subject race under some Mandate from the League of Nations.'

Arif uncovered his face and began to bite nervously at the nails of his left hand.

'Damn it, you've got to listen to reason,' Swithin went on, throwing every ounce of persuasion of which he was capable into his voice. 'You and your friends have been fascinated by this chimera of restoring the ancient glories of your country—but it's an old saying in England that outsiders see most of the game. I'm a foreigner, and I know what other people in France and Germany and the United States think about Turkey as well as my own friends at home. If this revolution is successful, you will have the whole world against you and by getting rid of Kemal you would simply be making a rod for your own backs.'

'You really think that,' Arif murmured, looking up with tear-dimmed eyes from under his heavy brows.

'I'm certain of it, man—besides, think what Turkey would be like to live in if any portion of it were left to you after the dust-up. You've lived in security for fifteen years under Kemal, so you've forgotten what life was like here before he took control. All the old abuses and corruptions would start up again, and the terrorisation of the man in the street by the high officials. You know how ruthless they used to be when they had a grudge against a man—and there was no justice to be got. It would be the same again, and they'd bowstring or impale the people they didn't like. Think of your brother and what they have done to him—even before they are in power. Doesn't that open your eyes? And that devil Kazdim is high up in this thing, so he will be one of your new rulers. Surely you are not mad enough to wish to make a Minister of your brother's murderer.'

'You are right,' Arif gasped, suddenly standing up. 'I have been mad—blind—besotted—but Allah has opened my eyes in time. If they would do this to an innocent boy they are unfit to govern. Better a thousand times that we should continue under the atheist Kemal.'

Swithin's heart was pounding with excitement. He knew that at last he had won the Turk over. 'You'll help me, then?' he exclaimed. 'Help me to fight these murdering devils!'

Arif straightened himself. For a moment he glanced in the direction of the door, and in the ensuing silence the wailing of the women could be faintly heard as they mourned by the body of Reouf in a distant room.

'For them there are gardens beneath which rivers flow,' he quoted solemnly. 'But these are the fellows of the fire and they shall burn therein for aye.'

16

The Stopped Earth

In the late afternoon of the following day, Swithin boarded a motor launch which lay waiting for him at a broken-down pier on the little frequented waterfront just to the north of Scutari.

He was dressed in greasy overalls and a rakish check cap which had seen considerable service: a portion of his second-hand wardrobe which Arif had brought over from his Tatavla flat earlier in the afternoon.

The Turk stood on the slimy steps of the landing stage. It was he who had arranged the hire of the launch and that it should be left ready at this quiet spot. As Swithin started up the engine, Arif tossed a bundle down to him in the boat and, with a quick glance round, started off up the jetty.

Swithin slung the bundle into the small cabin that occupied the rear of the launch, cast off from the landing stage and turned her nose up the Bosphorus. On reaching the landward end of the pier, Arif glanced over his shoulder. Swithin, too, was looking back; both raised a hand simultaneously in a farewell wave, and then the Turk disappeared among the boat sheds and low buildings.

The launch settle down to a steady chug, making a good pace against the current, and Swithin decided that Arif had done his business well. The Turk had put up a good performance in more than one way since their mental tussle which had taken place in the small hours of the previous morning. Once Swithin had convinced him that his brother had been murdered by the very men he was endeavouring to place in power, the station master's whole attitude had changed. His actual knowledge of the conspiracy was little more than Swithin had already forced out of him, but he had promised his unreserved assistance in securing further details and helping to checkmate it.

He had been devoted to Reouf, and the thought that the

boy had been done to death for a simple indiscretion, where a sharp warning would have proved sufficient deterrent to his making further rash confidences, filled him with bitter anger and an implacable hatred for those unknown chiefs of his organisation who must have ordered the murder.

Swithin had spent half the night alternately trying to console him for his loss and goading him to a white-hot resentment against Kazdim and his associates, so that when both were nearly dropping with fatigue, Arif had willingly put him up for the rest of the night and, in the morning, agreed to undertake various matters for him.

As he was wanted by the police, Swithin felt that it would be a needlessly risky proceeding to cross the Bosphorus in the daytime, yet it was essential that he should arrange a meeting with Diana. In consequence, he had decided to lie low at Arif's house until late in the afternoon, while the Turk went to his flat and collected some of his disreputable clothes, arranged for a motor-boat, and dispatched a note to Diana, asking her to be at the Tobacco Depot without fail by six o'clock.

Arif had had to attend his brother's funeral in the morning, but directly he returned from it, he had set about making Swithin's arrangements with an efficiency which delighted the Englishman, who in addition to his personal satisfaction was only too glad to see that by busying himself with active measures against the enemy, his new friend's mind was temporarily distracted from his bereavement.

By a quarter to six Swithin's launch lay just below Ortakeuy, under the shelter of a bank fringed with aloes and cactus. He moored it there and disappeared into the cabin, where he undid the bundle, which contained his ordinary clothes, and pulling off his overalls changed into his lounge suit. Then he accomplished the last half-mile up to the Depot.

At the wharf, he found that Diana must have passed him while he was changing in his cabin, for she was just landing as he rounded the last bend, and he saw the Greek manager, Lykidopulous, coming down through the garden to receive her.

In response to his hail, they turned and strolled back to the water steps, arriving just as he came alongside. The Greek displayed a mixture of bombastic importance and servility as usual, rating Swithin with forced playfulness for not having visited the place for a week in one breath and exclaiming how honoured he was to receive Lord Sir Duncannon's daughter there in the next. Diana looked cool and lovely in an outrageously fashionable hat with an enormous brim and a gauze-like summer frock, the outer layers of which ruffled as she moved, caught up like green foam by the gentle breeze which comes with evening down the Bosphorus.

Lykidopulous was pointing out the beauties of the old palace and speaking of the Shah of Persia's association with it in his hardly understandable English, while Swithin puzzled his wits how to get rid of him for a few moments in order that he might talk privately with Diana, but she saved him further worry by inquiring of the Greek: 'What are those lovely flowers over there?'

'Honourable Lady—you like—yes-please?'

'They smell heavenly,' she said, casting him a bewitching smile. 'Might I have some to take back with me. You give me some—yes-please?'

Swithin had his work cut out to suppress his laughter as she simplified her request into the Greek's limited vocabulary without the flicker of an eyelid, but the great thing was that the man understood, and declared enthusiastically: 'Yes, yes. I pull flowers very nice for Ladie Duncanno.'

Diana felt that it was useless to explain that she was not Lady Duncannon, and time was precious, so directly he moved away to pick her a bunch, she turned questioning eyes on Swithin.

'I'm on to it now,' he said swiftly, 'and it's a real big thing. I thought it safer to meet you here than risk going into Pera in the daytime. This Greek fool is going to be a nuisance, but fortunately he doesn't understand much English, so if we use the longest words we can think of, I'll be able to tell you my news while he shows you round without his catching on to what we're talking about.'

'What do you mean by "big",' she asked, 'is the movement likely to become really dangerous?'

'Very. There are over seven thousand of them in it and as far as I can gather, they're all picked men. The programme is to do Dictator Kemal in and run Turkey on Republican lines. That is the theory, so there is no question of bringing back the ex-Sultan, but they mean to restore their religion to its former place in national life, so they will appoint some member of the old Royal House to the Caliphate. Actually, of course, the Republican part of the business is all fiddlesticks and the country will be run by a *junta* as corrupt and unscrupulous as any Palace gang in the bad old days of the Sultans. But that's not the worst of it. These birds are religious fanatics and once they have seized power they intend to preach a *Jehad*—you know what *that* means.'

She threw him a sudden startled glance.

'Yes,' he went on grimly, 'I was pretty rattled myself when I found that out. Salonica is their first port of call and with Kemal's trained forces to do the job, they'll pitch the Greeks into the Mediterranean unless I'm a Dutchman.'

'They will have Bulgaria on their hands if they try that and the rest of the Balkan countries as well.'

'Don't I know it! But there's no reasoning with these birds, I tell you, and they're mad keen to start out on one of their good old Christian slayings.'

Diana frowned. 'If certain Powers seek their own advantage by backing the Turks, there is going to be first-class trouble.'

'Of course, and you may bet your life they will. It is just the excuse they have been waiting for.'

'It's awful to think of,' she exclaimed. 'I'll send a code radio to father tonight—the minute I get back—he will pass it on to our Foreign Office and they will tip off Kemal.'

'Yes—that's the best hope of stopping it, but we've got no proof to offer, since we can't give away the source of our information.'

'Who told you this—Reouf?'

'No.' Swithin paused for a moment as Lykidopulous rejoined them with a big bunch of sweet-smelling Tuberoses, then he concluded his sentence. 'Houdini was a marvellous fellow, he could get out of any hempen tangle, but my friend wasn't quite so good and when they pressed him to give an aquatic exhibition he was a dismal failure—so he has retired from business.'

'Thank you—thank you most awfully,' Diana gushed to the Greek; then she glanced at Swithin. 'Poor fellow—how terrible. Who stage-managed the show?'

'I forget the fellow's name, but you know him. He is remarkable for his avoirdupois, a circumference about two ells, and weight nearly up to that of a Brontosaurus.'

'You see factory—I show—yes-please,' beamed Lykidopulous.

'Yes-please,' Diana nodded, as they turned towards the building; then she asked casually: 'Why did the Brontosaurus provide this work for a mortician?'

'Because he fear t'other fella spilla da beans.'

'Pot-belly is in this racket, then?'

'You've said a mouthful.'

'Whence the lowdown if our ewe lamb failed to survive the arctic douche?'

'A scion of the same house—likewise a bomb-chucker—but converted now and out to relieve Bronte of his red corpuscles.'

The coffee-maker had already prepared for their reception in the office, and after having partaken of his brew Lykidopulous led them through the ante-chambers to the big room where the hands were still at their work, seated in long lines against the walls with the golden tobacco leaves heaped up before them. '*Salon de Polais*,' he explained. 'Now workroom. I lead—you follow—yes-please.'

'How interesting,' Diana murmured—and then, 'Hast heard aught of divers contraptions by the use of which Homo Sapiens render each other suitable to be placed beneath the subsoil?'

'Yea, verily. Such lie in well-timbered erections, camouflaged as agricultural implements awaiting distribution to the liege lord's serfs, in the place where chariots propelled by aqua pura brought to 240 degrees Fahrenheit—depart for the Garden of Eden.'

As Swithin delivered his involved reply, he overheard the Greek say to one of the foremen in his own language: 'Go get Mr. Stikolides. Tell him to come to me at once.'

Then for a few moments they had to listen to him as he showed them how the tobacco leaves, having been sorted and graded, are made up into small packets between two strips of wood, and these, being placed together, make up the bale which is then pressed, wrapped in hessian, and pressed again.

'Aren't the leaves a marvellous colour—just like piles of bronzy-gold,' Diana remarked. 'What time does the balloon go up?'

'Yes, but their colour is not a patch on your hair,' Swithin replied, momentarily carried out of himself by a fresh wave of admiration for her loveliness; then he added quickly, 'I'm not on to Greenwich yet.'

'Think so,' she murmured. 'Well, I'd do a year in prison if I could have your eyes. It's a sin that eyes as blue as yours should be wasted on any man; but getting back to the chessboard, what move does the Red Knight, now clad in grey, mean to make next?'

'Whatever he moves he will be in danger from the White Queen,' Swithin replied promptly. Then, at that moment, she dropped her parasol, and as he picked it up their eyes met. Hers were full of mocking laughter, and as he turned away he kicked himself mentally for his folly in carrying on this game with her, yet he could not resist the temptation of adding: 'How shall the hunted avoid the snare of the hunter?'

'If you refer to the goddess of my name, her arrows are weak weapons against the armour of a knight,' she replied, 'but if to the "Beast" every precaution is requisite. Has not the Red Fox his earth. Let him seek it and go not abroad for a season.'

'It is essential that he fraternise with late bomb-chucker number two in order to receive further *communiqués*.'

'Hope you, then, for further tidings from that source?'

'Yea, the bereaved one hath a "moll" who is a stenog to one of the Mighty, who imported her as a bedworthy piece of goods himself. This Nabob is a big shot in the tunnelling company, or at least so bereaved one thinks and, as the trollop is an outlander, her boss confideth to her certain papers for taping out on the old machine. Their nature is, so far, like next week's weather to us, but our jealous and love-sick swain hopes to matriculate thereon. If his superstition is correct, we may be able to fill in quite a piece of our little crossword.'

'Would this Nabob place such fateful matters in the handy-pandies of a chit?'

'Why not. She had no connection with Christmas pudding. Her sister danceth in the Folies Bergère, and she probably knoweth nought of the true import of her labours.'

They had passed now from the big room to smaller ones beyond, where the bales of tobacco were stored, and Stikolides, one of the clerks from the office, joined them. Lykidopulous duly presented him and then, as they moved on, spoke rapidly to him in his own tongue.

Between the rhythmic thudding of the presses Swithin just caught the words: 'Where have you been all this . . . We have him now . . . at once, they can get here from . . . in ten minutes. I will keep them talking while . . . Hurry now, Stikolides!'

For a second Swithin stood quite silent. The presses thudded on, the drowsy hum of bees came from the garden, and a marvellous scent of flowers drifted in through the open windows. Then, without looking at Diana, he said in a swift whisper:

'Lucky he thinks I don't understand Greek. I just heard him tell that other chap to telephone for the police. Evidently my description has been circulated. I've got to get out of here—and mighty quick.'

He turned as Lykidopulous rejoined them and said casually, 'Have you heard yet from Constantinos regarding our offer?'

'Constaninos—yes,' beamed the Greek. 'He write . . .'

'Fetch me his letter.'

'But I tell . . .'

'No, no,' Swithin protested blandly, 'the letter—you bring—translate for us here—show Lady Duncannon the good business we make—yes-please.'

Lykidopulous paused for a moment, but Swithin's air was so smilingly innocent that the Greek felt he could not possibly have any suspicion of his recent orders. He nodded quickly. 'I bring—I show—fine business—you wait.'

No sooner was his back turned than Swithin whispered to Diana, 'When he returns, tell him I'm suffering from the heat and that I've gone into the garden for a breath of air. Then ask him to give you more coffee in the office and say I said I'll join you there. It's thin, but keep him with you as long as you can—even a few minutes may help.'

'Yes, yes,' she replied impatiently, 'for God's sake don't waste time—go!'

He opened a little side door and peered out. The coast was clear, but he did not leave at once. Instead, he turned to her with a cheerful grin. 'I'm awfully sorry to have let you in for this, but I don't think the police will worry you. As Sir George's daughter, you have a perfect right here, and they are not to know you are aware that I am anything but one of the firm's employees.'

'Oh, for God's sake go!' she repeated anxiously, 'and *do* take care of yourself.'

'I will,' he promised, and slipped out into the garden, closing the door softly behind him.

No one was about, and under cover of a row of young ilex trees, he reached the landing stage unobserved, unmoored his boat, and jumped in; a moment later he was heading for the centre of the Bosphorus.

Once in mid-channel, he turned the launch down stream and, aided by the current, it skimmed through the water under the feed of a fully open throttle. Then, seizing a piece of twine, he lashed the small wheel into its set position and dived into the cabin. When he emerged, he was in the dirty dungarees and check cap again.

Within fifteen minutes of leaving the Tobacco Depot, he was opposite the Dolma Baghtche Palace, and turning in to the steps just south of it.

As the launch grazed the stonework, he flung a looped rope over a bollard, jumped ashore, and scurried into a nearby alley. Then he made his way up the steep hill, past the gasworks, across the open space, through the old cemetery by the Armenian Hospital and so to Tatavla.

As he pushed open the street door leading up to his flat, he gave a sigh of relief. The escape had been a narrow one. If he had not overheard the Greek, he knew that he would have been occupying a cell in Ortakeuy police station by this time.

He climbed the stairs slowly, since he was rather tired, having had little sleep the night before owing to his long discussion with Arif. On the landing he paused, smiling at the thought that no one could find him in this hideout, then he let himself into his hall sitting-room.

'Welcome,' piped a high, thin voice. 'When they telephoned me that you had left the Tobacco Depot, I thought that you would come here.' It was the Eunuch, smoking placidly in the best armchair, and beside him stood two of his men, who drew their automatics and levelled them at Swithin's stomach.

17

Trapped

For a moment Swithin was completely nonplussed. If he had come face to face with Kazdim in the open street he could at least have made a bolt for it, but to find the Police Chief here, in his secret hideout, placidly waiting for him to put in an appearance, left him temporarily gaping and witless.

'Hallo!' he exclaimed awkwardly; then realising that he must make some attempt to appear innocent, however useless it might prove, he added, 'I don't remember giving you my address when we met the day before yesterday on the old wall.'

The Eunuch's rosebud mouth twitched into a smile. 'That was an omission which I found it comparatively easy to repair.'

'But what are you doing here with these desperadoes?' Swithin waved a hand towards the other two Turks, who stood stolidly by, their dark eyes watching his face intently and their pistols still pointed at his midriff, 'and how did you manage to get into my flat?'

'We are the police.'

'I see. For the moment I was afraid that this was some kind of a hold-up, but if you're the police I suppose you have the right of entry. Anyhow, you might restrain your friends with the heavy armaments. A little carelessness and one of those things might go off.'

'Both of them would at a sign from me, but my people are so used to handling firearms that you need have no fear of any genuine *accident*. Sit down. I wish to talk to you.'

Swithin sat. There did not seem to be much option, but as he did so, he remarked with absurdly forced cordiality, 'Well, fire away. If I have been unconsciously hobnobbing with some criminal you're after, any information I can give you will be a pleasure.'

'It is information about yourself which I require,' piped the Eunuch.

'Indeed, I was not aware that I had broken any of the laws of your good city.'

'That we will discuss later. You will tell me, please, the true purpose of your visit to Istanbul?'

'Certainly,' Swithin agreed, with a heartiness he was far from feeling. 'As you apparently know already, I have just come from the Tobacco Depot which was once the Palace of the Shah of Persia. Sir George Duncannon's firm hold a controlling interest in that concern, and I was sent out by him to supervise its finances.'

'Do not trifle with me, please.' The Eunuch's little beady eyes gleamed momenarily between their rolls of fat. I asked the *true* purpose of your visit?'

Swithin was mentally berating himself for ever having walked into this trap. He recalled Diana's taunt about amateurs who knew nothing of the game and it stung him afresh. No doubt an experienced agent would have taken measures to ensure his knowing if his hiding place had been broken into each time he returned to it. An inconspicuous piece of cotton sealing the door, perhaps, but in this case that would have been useless, as Arif had visited the place earlier in the day to secure the soiled dungarees which he was still dressed in. Now that he had been caught, he did not disguise the fact from himself that the chances of his getting out of the Eunuch's clutches were extremely slender, but it seemed that a bold front was the only attitude to maintain, so he shrugged and repeated, 'Sir George Duncannon sent me out to supervise the finances of the Tobacco Depot. *That* is the purpose of my visit.'

'So—and you have no other?'

'None.'

'Now!' Kazdim hoisted his enormous bulk forward in the chair. 'You have a room at the Pera Palace Hotel. Is that not so?'

'I *had* until two nights ago.'

'Yet you rented this flat under another name immediately on your arrival here—early in July.'

'Yes, why not? I am a romantic soul and felt that I would like to see something of the city under conditions which are not possible to any tourist.'

'Why did you give up your room at the Pera Palace so suddenly two nights ago?'

'I thought that I would like to live here instead.'

'Explain, please, why you did not notify them of your intention and left all your heavy baggage behind?'

'Because I haven't actually given up my room there. I shall return to it later.'

'A contradiction, Malik—note that,' Kazdim glanced up at the wiry little man who stood on his right. 'First he said that he had a room there *until* two nights ago—now that he had not yet given it up—as to his returning to it—we shall see.' His great moon-like face broke into a smile of evil enjoyment as he slowly crushed out his cigarette with that air of terrible finality.

Beneath the smile which was beginning to feel stiff and frozen on his face, Swithin felt a cold chill of real apprehension. He knew that he was properly up against it, and that all these *pourparlers* were only due to the fact that the huge man before him took a subtle delight in playing with his victims.

In his mind, he sought desperately for a way of escape, but he could think of nothing. Again Diana's taunt came back to him, and he wondered miserably just what those gifted amateurs of fiction did when they had walked blithely into the arms of their enemies. Bulldog Drummond, he supposed, would have tackled the present situation with fantastic ease. Having the courage of a lion and the strength of a rhinoceros, he would have risked the bullets, grabbed the two 'tecs', one in each hand, brought their heads together with a skull-shattering crack, and seizing the twenty-stone Eunuch, carried him off across his shoulders as a memento of the occasion. Bulldog might not be exactly subtle, but at times he certainly possessed the advantage of being devastatingly heavy-handed. Then there was that other fellow, an infinitely more dangerous gentleman adventurer, 'The Saint'. Swithin had followed his amazing prowess in many countries, through fifteen novels, and admired him greatly. The remarkable flow of cheerful badinage which he managed to sustain even in the most desperate situations was a joy to read, and his methods a perfect example of how matters should be handled in the present instance. How the 'Saint' would revel in an encounter with Kazdim; his old enemy Chief-Inspector Claud Eustace Teal would lack flavour on his epicurean palate ever after. Swithin could almost hear the tall, slim, modern buccaneer burble one of his carefree witticisms as he placed an index finger gently in the middle of the Eunuch's stomach. Then, doubtless, a seraphic smile lighting his dancing blue eyes, he would lay his free hand upon the nearest pistol with lightning rapidity and reverse it, remarking brightly, 'Brother, permit me. You are not holding that correctly—it should point the *other* way.'

Those were the sort of things he should be doing, Swithin knew quite well, but as it was he sat there staring dumbly at the Eunuch, while the great brute placidly lit another cigarette and puffed at it thoughtfully, watching him with that unwinking stare by which a snake fascinates a bird.

He tried to nerve himself into attempting something, but he had neither 'Bulldog's' strength nor the 'Saint's' quick wits, let alone the courage of either, and although he had an automatic in his pocket, he felt certain that he would bungle the job if he tried to draw it. Filled with the bitter, hopeless misery of defeat, he knew that sudden violence would be simple suicide, for the two plain-clothes men would shoot him like a rat before he could hope to get through the door.

Suddenly Kazdim spoke again. 'You wear now the costume of a working man—why?'

'To keep the oil off my clothes. I came down from the Tobacco Depot in a motor-boat.'

'Indeed, and how do you explain all the other rags we have found in the cupboards of this flat?'

'Oh, I've always had a passion for dressing up,' Swithin replied with an attempt at brightness.

'You think such conduct in keeping with your responsible position as Sir George Duncannon's financial representative?'

'Now look here,' Swithin stood up slowly, 'I don't know what you think I've done, but there's no crime in having rented a flat as well as a room in an hotel, or in possessing a collection of second-hand garments.'

'Did I say there was?'

176

'No, but you are questioning me as though I were a criminal, and I advise you to be careful. If you have anything to charge me with, you can do it at the nearest police station. If not, you had better clear out or I shall be compelled to seek the protection of the British Ambassador.' Swithin realised the futility of his bluff even as he made it. Sir George had fully impressed the fact upon him that he would be playing a lone hand, and that in the event of his coming to grief he must expect no help from official sources. Now that he had been caught nosing into the highly dangerous personal secrets of the Eunuch, he had little doubt that his double life would be used against him as a frame-up on a charge of espionage, and the chances of him escaping a long spell in a Turkish fortress, looked extremely slender.

'I do not propose to charge you with any crime,' the big man bleated in his high, thin voice. 'You have committed none as far as I know. But it is a pity you did not take the warning which I gave you when we visited the Marble Tower together the other day. Do you remember? I spoke of the unpleasant fate which, in this old city, has so often overtaken those who know too much.'

'What the deuce do you mean?' Swithin protested; but he knew only too well what the words portended. They did not mean to take him off to prison. Instead, when night fell, he would be bundled into a car and driven across the city to the old wall, his arms corded behind him, and then, despite his frantic struggles, he would be pitched head foremost down that rocky chasm in the sinister tower. His hands went damp at the thought of that awful death which awaited him, gasping in vain for air, a dozen feet below the foaming surface of those rushing waters.

The Eunuch had taken a paper from his inside pocket. He smoothed it out carefully on his enormous lap and held it up for Swithin to see.

'Do you recognise this?' he asked quietly. 'It is the letter which you left two nights ago at the Pera Palace bookstall. It was to be called for by a lady, I believe.'

Swithin shrugged and answered promptly, 'I've never seen it in my life before.'

'A lie, Servet—note that,' Kazdim glanced up at the tall man who stood upon his other side, then he turned back to his prisoner. 'Have you not? How strange, then, that it should be in your writing. You see, I have had the opportunity to compare it with some of your notes on the Tobacco Depot which we found here in your desk.'

'Well, have it your own way. What are you going to do about it?' Swithin said desperately.

'I am going to send you on a long journey to a place where you will have no further opportunity to meddle in Turkish politics.'

For a second, Swithin's eyes lit with hope. There was just a chance that, as he was a foreigner, the Eunuch meant to deport him rather than risk the necessity of making awkward explanations if his body were discovered and possible trouble with the British Government. No country allows its subjects to suffer the extreme penalty without a protest, even if they are guilty of espionage, unless they have first received fair trial; much less their secret murder.

'Do you mean that you are going to send me out of the country?' he asked evenly, 'or, as they say in the United States, "take me for a ride"?'

'A "swim" would perhaps be a more correct description in this case,' the Eunuch chuckled.

Again Swithin heard in his imagination the hissing of those dark waters below the *oubliette*. He held his breath and wondered how long the horrible business would take. The fall must be about forty feet. Would it seem seconds or years before he struck the surface of the torrent? Would he hit the water with his head or turn a somersault in mid-air? The wall-like cleft was narrow—if he did turn over in his fall, it was probable that he would be bashed against the rocky walls. If he hit his head, he would probably be unconscious when he went under, a thing to pray for perhaps, because whatever people might say about drowning being an easy death, he wasn't quite so sure. It might be if one's faculties were numbed from the exhaustion of long efforts to keep afloat, but that sudden icy plunge with one's arms lashed behind one's back seemed too horrible to contemplate.

'You do not like the idea apparently,' Kazdim was still smiling. 'Then tell me the name and whereabouts of the tall, fair-haired lady who was to have collected this note?'

'If the writing *is* like mine—it's a forgery. I don't know anything about it—or any fair-haired lady.'

'Allah sees fit to fill your mouth with foolish talk. Tell me that which I ask and I may reconsider my decision about yourself.'

'I don't know anything about it,' Swithin repeated doggedly, 'and if I did, I wouldn't tell you with any hope that you would keep your word.'

The Eunuch shrugged. 'No matter. I do not press you, since my men will easily find her if she is still in Istanbul, and we will send you for a swim. There is good bathing in the Marmara Sea. A few miles down the coast there is a little place called Floria, where all Istanbul bathes every summer. The season opens always upon the sixth of August. The beaches are black with people on that day.'

'But why the sixth of August?' Swithin asked, catching at any straw which would deflect his thoughts, even for a moment, from those ghastly pictures which had been forming in his brain. 'It's marvellous weather here from the middle of May on—why wait until the summer's half over?'

Kazdim very slowly shook his great head. 'I do not know, but that is the date. Only mad dogs and Englishmen enter the water before then.'

'I see,' said Swithin, and again he fell to frantic speculation upon possible methods of escape. If only there were a chance of someone arriving at the flat to create a diversion, but only two people even knew of its existence, Arif and Diana. Arif now, *he* had been there earlier that day, say he had managed to secure further particulars of the conspiracy through Jeanette. He might take it into his head to call. But if he did, how would that help. He would ring the bell, which would give Kazdim's people plenty of warning, then when they let him in he would be taken as completely by surprise as Swithin had been himself. Even if he were armed and put up a fight, he could not possibly hope to overcome Kazdim and his two men. Of course, if that did happen, Swithin knew that he would chance a bullet himself and leap into the fray, then the odds would be two against three and reasonably sporting. The third, too, would be the Eunuch, who could almost be counted out. He was probably very strong if he got a grip upon anybody, but so unwieldy that it would not be difficult to place him *hors de combat*. With mental relish, Swithin decided to be thoroughly un-English and, at the first sign of a diversion, to kick him. He selected the spot with care and enjoyment; he could almost feel his boot go home in that great mass of blubbery flesh. Then his new enthusiasm evaporated instantly, as he realised with appalling suddenness that the hope of Arif arriving was almost fantastically unlikely, and that even if he did he would certainly be taken by surprise and find himself at the absolute mercy of Kazdim's gunmen.

Then there was Diana, but it was even more of an outside chance that she would put in an appearance. She had never visited him there, and the fact that she had seen him only a couple of hours before made it even more improbable that she would do so now. As Swithin realised that, he felt it to be at least one blessing, for courageous as she was, she could have done no earthly good, and Kazdim would be sure to recognise her from the description of the woman who was to have collected the letter he left with Tania. They would seize her as his accomplice, and . . . but the thought was utterly unbearable. He thanked God again that she was safely out of it.

She had behaved splendidly again that afternoon. He knew from the fact that no sign of unusual activity had appeared at the Depot when he last glimpsed at it, that she must have played her part with Lykidopulous and held the fort for at least ten minutes. He was glad now —devilish glad that he had said that nonsense about the White Queen. He only wished that he had said more and told her that he didn't give a damn whatever she had done on the yacht, because he never really thought of her as any different from what she'd seemed that night when he had first met her at Maidenhead.

Suddenly he realised that the Eunuch had not spoken for a long time, and glanced up at him. That monstrous caricature of humanity was still seated there, imperturbably smoking his endless cigarettes. A little pile of butts lay at his elbow, fifteen—more—twenty, at the least, and the two plain-clothes men still stood on either side of him, holding their pistols at the ready.

'What could they be waiting for, Swithin wondered, then

it dawned on him that the shadows in the room had lengthened. It must be nearly nine o'clock. That human devil in the chair was only marking time until darkness had fallen; then under cover of night he would add one more murder to his long record of sadistic crime.

Swithin began to study the faces of Malik and Servet, the two plain-clothes men, consciously for the first time. It occurred to him that if only he could get one of them alone, he might be able to bribe him. But how could he set about it? The peril in which he found himself seemed to have robbed him of his wits, for he could no longer think clearly. With fresh bitterness he realised anew how right Diana had been and how hopelessly unsuited he was to the job he had taken on.

The men hardly seemed conscious of his presence. Their faces were quite expressionless and set like masks of wax. If he asked to be allowed to go into the bathroom, Swithin thought, it was unlikely that they would both be sent with him, and he had big money in his belt, enough to tempt a dozen ordinary Turkish policemen into condoning some small irregularity. The fellow might contrive some blunder which would give him a chance to escape—if he could knock out the Eunuch—and take the other by surprise. But that was hardly a small irregularity, and these were not ordinary policemen. In fact, they were not acting as policemen at all. It was quite obvious from the manner in which Kazdim had displayed the letter and spoken of his intentions, that his two lieutenants were also members of the Kaka, so it was equally in their personal interest to put an interfering foreigner, who knew too much about it, out of the way for good. Their own lives and safety depended upon taking ruthless measures against such people as himself; and as that fact sank into his mind, he saw how futile it would be to waste his breath in trying to bribe either of them into giving him a break.

The clock upon his desk was ticking loudly, unnaturally so it seemed to him, and as the twilight deepened he knew that it was ticking out the moments of his life. The heart in his breast seemed to be hammering in time with it, and the fantastic thought came to him that the clock would still be ticking there all through the night for many hours after his heart was still.

One thing he was resolved upon. When the time came, he meant to fight. That they would shoot him down was as good a certainty as that the Derby would be run again next year in England, but it was better to go out like that than submit tamely to the death they intended for him. If only he could draw his gun, but it seemed hopelessly inaccessible in the hip pocket where he carried it.

During the next twenty minutes he thought of many things. His boyhood in summer holidays; Sandhurst and nights in London. His first day with the regiment, manœuvres on the Plain; good days out hunting; a girl that he had met in Leicestershire; another down at Pau; Prince Ali eyeing Diana that night in the ballroom at Maidenhead; another dance, another girl; then Diana again, as he had seen her that afternoon.

Kazdin stirred his great bulk and stood up. Twilight had vanished and the night had come. The room was now lit only from an arc lamp in the street below. It had never been in anything approaching genuine darkness.

Without a word Swithin sprang. The Eunuch went down under the impact. Frantically, Swithin grabbed at his hip pocket, endeavouring to wrench out his gun. It came free and was half-lifted when a blow like a hammer descended on his wrist. He felt the weapon slip from his nerveless fingers, and almost in the same second another smashing drive caught him behind the left ear. His head swam, but he turned and lashed out with his only sound fist; the other hung limp and useless, aching horribly. His jab went home, and Malik, who had caught him in the neck, staggered backwards with a gunt, but Servet, who had maimed his wrist, was now behind him and with a second savage blow brought down the butt of his pistol, this time on Swithin's head. His knees gave way under him, his whole body crumpled, and he slipped to the floor.

He could not have been out for long, but when he came to he found that his arms had been tied behind him and a gag thrust into his mouth. Malik was slapping his face, by no means gently, to bring him round, and as soon as he opened his eyes he was jerked to his feet.

Kazdim had already left the room and was tripping lightly downstairs; the other two thrust Swithin after him. Next moment they were in the street and pushing him into a waiting car.

He was bundled into the back seat beside the Eunuch; the other men clambered in, and the car set off. Fortunately, perhaps, Swithin was only semi-conscious during the first part of that journey. The side blinds of the car were drawn, but he could see ahead over the driver's shoulder, and vaguely realised the route they were taking. In a haze of pain, he recognised a street sign in the Hamal Bachi and, supreme irony, the gates of the British Embassy, then he was dazzled by the bright lights of the Grand' Rue de Pera.

He closed his eyes. His head, neck and wrists were throbbing madly, the cords cut into his flesh, and he was forced to sit awkwardly forward owing to the doubled-up position of his arms behind his back. He knew that they were speeding down the hill, and when he opened his eyes again, they were crossing the Galata bridge.

His full senses returned to him then, and he jerked himself upright. This was fantastic, impossible, it could not be true that they really meant to kill him, yet the car raced on. They were passing the Fire Tower of the old University and, on the other side, the Grand Bazaar.

He tried to struggle to his feet, but the Eunuch thrust him back by jabbing a great elbow in his chest. He realised then that he must pull himself together—and think clearly —that was his one chance of saving his life, yet coherent thought simply would not come.

They had passed out of the Laley Djami now and turned left along the Avenue Moustapha Kemal Pasha towards the sea. He thought wildly of endeavouring to attract the attention of the people in the streets and collected his breath for a stentorian shout, but when he gave it, the gag prevented any sound except an uncouth rumble coming from his mouth.

In a quarter of an hour—ten minutes—it would be too late. He knew that with a horrible certainty as he gritted his teeth and strained at the cords that bound him. They had turned right again and were running along Maslak Vlnga Street—the direct road to the Castle of the Seven Towers. It was horrible, unthinkable, he felt, that his life should end like this; never to see the sun again or hear the whinny of a good horse impatient for a gallop—he must think of something—do something—before it was too late.

His breath was coming in painful gasps and the cold sweat of stark, ungovernable fear was running down into his eyes in little rivulets.

The speed of the car had increased now that they were free of congested traffic. It was roaring along the straight through Samatia Street, its klaxons howling to drive the slum population from its path. Five minutes now and they would be there.

Swithin groaned behind his gag. All sense of pain in his head and arms had been driven from him by the one appalling thought which now came fully home to him. There *was* no escape. They really meant to do him in. He was going to die. Soon—terrifyingly soon—within a few minutes now. The car had entered Imrahor Street—the last lap—they would reach the Wall in under a hundred seconds. He tried to persuade himself that he was suffering from a nightmare, that he would awake cheerful and well to another glorious day of health and life in the bedroom at his flat or in the *Pera*; but he knew that this was no ghastly dream, he was awake and sane. This terrible thing was happening to himself and they meant to kill him—to blot him out—so that never again would he see the faces of dear friends or know joy in this existence. It was true!—true!—true!

In the whirling panic of his brain he wished desperately that they had killed him in the scrap. A bullet would have been different. No one cared to die that way either when there were so many wonderful things still to do; but as a soldier he had grown up all his life with the knowledge that he stood a fair chance of going out like that, and it was a decent sort of ending—whereas to be pitched head first down that ghastly well . . .

The car took a side turning and ran on a little, parallel with the Wall, towards the Marmara. He could see it now, huge and foreboding, towering above them. Again he sought frantically for a way to save himself, but no thought would come except that of icy rushing water.

He knew that they had arrived at their destination, yet it gave him a fresh shock of horror when the car actually halted; but he was given little time for further thought. The door was flung open and the two gunmen dragged him out. The Eunuch followed, calm and imperturbable as ever, still smoking his endless cigarettes. He produced a torch and led the way over the rough, uneven ground, and as Swithin, hustled along by Malik and Servet in his rear, caught a whiff of the fragrant tobacco, he almost cried out at the thought that he was never to savour the serene delight of smoking any more.

Dark shadows were all about them as they approached the frowning wall. They climbed some steps and entered a narrow passage. It was black as pitch inside, with only the beam of the Eunuch's torch in front to light their stumbling feet. To Swithin, it seemed that they walked a mile in that close, musty darkness, then as he staggered down a flight of broken stairs, he saw lights ahead, another moment and he heard again that ceaseless hissing sound, and then he was in the vaulted chamber of the tower, staring at the black hole in its floor.

The lights came from flaring torches placed in sconces on the walls. For a second their glare blinded him after the darkness of the hidden tunnels in the fortifications, then he saw that two other men besides the Eunuch and his guards were present. Both were huge negroes, naked to the waist, their black skins shiny and glistening, their white eyeballs staring at him with dumb animal curiosity.

Kazdim spoke to them in his high falsetto. The mouth of one opened in a half-imbecile grin, and Swithin realised dimly, through a wave of sickening horror, that the man had no tongue—and that they were mutes, old henchmen of the Eunuch's from his Palace days perhaps, the instruments of many hideous crimes under his orders, if they could only tell of them.

Malik and Servet stepped back. The negroes took their place at Swithin's sides. One of them wrenched the gag out of his mouth. He tried to speak, but his tongue was so swollen that the words would not come. The other pushed him forward to the edge of the hole.

The Eunuch stepped up to him and, pulling the flat check cap from his head, folded it round a piece of broken brick, then dropped it down the shaft. For what seemed an eternity, they all stood there listening. The hissing continued unabated, then at last there was the faintest 'plop'.

In a sort of blur, Swithin glimpsed the Eunuch's face, pasty white and grinning in the torch light, a mask of unutterably cruel enjoyment.

So this was the end, thought Swithin, and whatever way a man left this world, he should endeavour to make a decent showing. He was quite a little man, so the top of his head barely came level with the shoulders of the huge negroes, but he stiffened himself and stood upright, then all the terrible fear that he had suffered in the last hours seemed to fall from him. As the mutes seized him again by his bound arms, he even managed a nod of farewell that had half a smile in it to the two watching policemen.

Suddenly the negroes jerked him off his feet and, lifting him high into the air, pitched him with one heave head foremost into the gaping hole.

He felt himself falling—falling—falling, then with a stunning blow his head hit the torrent, he was twisted violently in its grip, and the waters of death closed over him.

18

The Desolate City

A violent shudder ran through Swithin's limbs as he plunged down—down—down into the icy depths. He had struck the water with such force that it seemed as if he would never stop in that smooth gliding descent. The top of his head felt as though it had been split open with a hatchet. It seemed to have become bigger than his whole body and to be opening and shutting in agonising spasms. Blinding lights and whirling circles flashed before his eyes. Apart from that, he was conscious of nothing but the searing pain in his cranium and the appalling cold.

Suddenly he knew that he had stopped moving downwards. The current had caught him and turned him on his side. Normally he could swim fairly well under water, so automatically he opened his eyes. Not a ray of light penetrated the darkness and the utter silence was the most terrifying thing he had ever experienced. It was as if he had been struck blind and deaf in the same instant.

For a second he thought 'so this is death,' but the sense of feeling still remained to him and the smooth pressure of the water upon every portion of his body told him instantly that he still had to suffer final dissolution.

Next moment the constriction in his chest confirmed that horrible knowledge. He had yet to face the agony of gulping down great draughts of water when he could no longer hold his breath and began the hopeless fight for air.

The underground current bore him swiftly onwards, turning him like a sack, first one way, then another and rolling him over half a dozen times in as many seconds so that he could no longer tell if he was face downwards or on his back. Then, without warning, something seemed to leap at him out of that terrible silent darkness. The subterranean torrent had whirled him violently against a snag of rock.

The pain of the blow was so great that he opened his mouth to cry out, the water filled it and he forced it shut again, but he was compelled to swallow the gulp he had taken. It tasted salt and bitter.

He could hear nothing, see nothing, yet he knew that his clothes had been ripped from his side and the cold water was now flowing against the bare flesh of his thigh as he was rushed headlong forward again in the grip of the racing tide. The awful pressure in his chest was growing. A stabbing pain had started behind his eyes, and then his last desperate fight began.

It was automatic rather than conscious, for so strong is the fear of oblivion in men of every race and temper, that when the mind has ceased to function, instinct takes control and battles wildly for the physical survival of the body it holds dear.

Steel bands seemed to be tightening round his chest, an awful drumming thudded in his ears, but his legs began a frantic kicking and he felt himself shoot out of the current. He had no idea if he had yet been swept from under the tower into the open sea; he did not even think of that or realise the hopelessness of his efforts.

The only impulse that animated his semi-conscious brain was to battle his way to the surface, regardless of the fact that he could not swim a stroke, since his arms were lashed behind him, and that even if he succeeded he must slip back into the depths after one last glimpse of that now remote world above.

With the strength of madness, he lashed out with his feet, stabbing the surrounding water with mechanical jerky strokes. His ear-drums seemed bursting, his eyes starting from their sockets, sledge-hammer blows pounded inside his head and his brain seemed to have come loose in it, sogging from side to side as he fought his way upwards. He could contain his breath no longer, it burst from his strained lips in a great bubble of air and the water gushed down his throat. He felt himself choking, his body was one aching mass of pain, then he hit the surface.

His head was above it for no more than a second, just long enough for him to gasp in a great draught of heavenly air which served temporarily to restore his full consciousness, then, as he sank again, he knew that his stupendous effort had only served to prolong his agony.

The constriction of his chest began again almost immediately, and the pressure behind his eyes and on his eardrums. His reason told him that he should hold himself still, so that he might sink for good and escape his torment quickly, but the instinct to fight on had him in its grip again. Once more a violent jerking of his limbs brought his head above the water.

For a moment, while he trod water desperately, he glimpsed the stars, but he knew that with his arms pinioned he had no possible hope of keeping afloat. He strove madly to burst the cords but they only cut deeper into his flesh. The exhausted muscles of his legs gave up the uneven struggle, a wavelet splashed in his face, and he went under.

Suddenly he felt a fresh stab of pain, this time in his shoulder. He was wrenched sideways and drawn up, the whole weight of his body hanging on the boat-hook which had caught in his clothing.

In a hazy way he knew that hands were grabbing at him, felt himself being hauled in over the low gunwale of a boat, and collapsed upon its floor-boards. Then blank night descended upon him.

When he came round his arms were free and a man bent above him in the darkness, pouring some fiery liquid down his throat. He coughed and endeavoured to sit up, but flopped back again against the thwart.

'Allah be praised—for he has restored you to us,' said a voice. 'Be patient now, and in a little time you will be yourself again.'

Then he knew that the man who was bending over him to be Arif, but it was some moments before he recovered sufficient strength to whisper: 'Thank God—you spotted me —but how did you get here?'

The Turk sat down beside him and said softly: 'I blame myself for all that you have been through, but by Allah's mercy at least I have been able to save your life.'

Swithin shuddered. 'It was—horrible—but what do you mean—you blame yourself?'

'When I went to your flat to get your clothes today I found a letter lying on the mat, so I put it in my pocket intending to give it to you, then like a fool I forgot. Later, when I found it again, I opened it. Knowing that you were living there in secret I thought it might be important. It was a blank slip of paper with only three words typed upon it, they were in a foreign language and their meaning I do not yet understand. I felt that you should have it without delay, so I crossed at once to Pera and visited your flat.'

'What time was this?' asked Swithin.

'About eight o'clock.'

'By Jove, you arrived then when Kazdim and his men had me cornered there.'

'Yes. I heard voices when I was just about to ring at your door, and fortunately I paused to listen.'

'I see; you guessed what had happened, and what they meant to do to me, so you chased off to get a boat and hang round the Marble Tower with it in the hope of being able to pull me out.'

The Turk nodded. 'There was nothing else I could do. I should have been shot like a dog if I had tried to rescue you by force, and the lights in the Tower told me when they were making ready to do this ghastly business.' He paused for a moment and almost choked on a sob, then added: 'We know from experience that the bodies of victims who are dealt with thus are swept from under the Tower by the flowing tide, to be washed up on the beaches of the Marmara. It was a fair chance therefore, that you would come up to the surface for a moment some twenty yards below the Wall.'

'It was mighty lucky for me you took that letter,' Swithin said feelingly. 'If you hadn't, Kazdim would have found it, and and I should be dead by now. Can you remember the words that it contained?'

'Yes, they were spelt like this—G-E-T—O-O-T—M-O-N——'

Swithin chuckled suddenly as he saw what must have happened: Kazdim's men had evidently searched the registers of all the house agents in the city for recent 'lets'; particularly those made in the last two months to foreigners. The good McAndrew had been unable to prevent them scrutinising his books and, noting their interest in the occupant of No. 19 Tatavla Street, had sent a warning, transcribing his own broad Scots on to paper in order to befog anyone who examined it if it fell into wrong hands.

He felt horribly sore and battered. The places where the

cords had cut into his arms burnt like bands of fire, his head ached intolerably, an angry throbbing in his thigh came from the place where he had been hurled against the rock, and he twitched every time he moved the shoulder which had received a flesh wound from the boat-hook but, despite his wretched physical state, he was cheerful and optimistic. After all, he was still alive and with good friends like Arif and old McAndrew to stand by him, he thought he might get even with Kazdim yet. Squelching as he moved in his sodden clothes, he sat up and looked about him.

The Tower of Marble now lay behind them—the lights of its narrow windows had disappeared. It stood out black and sinister against the starlit sky that hung above the Marmara. The four oarsmen in the boat were pulling with strong even strokes, back along the Stamboul shore towards the heart of the city.

'Well, what's the next move?' he asked softly.

'To hide you, surely,' the Turk replied in a low voice. 'I would offer my own house, but I fear to do so since they may guess my bitterness over—over Reouf's death, and have it watched to see who I receive there.'

'No, no,' Swithin protested quickly, 'that's nice of you, but I couldn't let you take the risk—you have done more than enough for me already.'

Arif shrugged impatiently. 'There is no question of enough or too much, brother. If last night's happenings had not opened my eyes, our talk afterwards would have done so. Between us we will serve this spawn of Iblis, Kazdim, as he has served others. In the sight of Allah I have dedicated my life to it.'

Swithin was now desperately cold. He had considerable difficulty in preventing his teeth from chattering, but he felt a spiritual warmth as he heard that bitter declaration. Then he glanced forward, and laying a hand on Arif's arm, muttered, 'Hush—the boatmen—they will hear you.'

'Have no fear. They are Frenchmen from the port and know no Turkish or anything of our business. I picked them up just as they came to spend an hour or two ashore from their steamer. They are well paid for their work and that is all they care about.'

'That was clever of you,' Swithin nodded, 'but have

191

you any suggestion as to where I can hide for the night? I shall be all right again tomorrow—but just at present—I'm feeling pretty grim.'

'I do not wonder. You should be put to bed between warm blankets, but I fear that is impossible, for you would not be safe in any *han* and it is your safety which matters above all things. However, I thought of a place on my way down from Tatavla—you know the Kutchuk Hamam quarter?'

'That is part of the great area in the centre of Stamboul, which was burnt out in the big fire of 1911, isn't it?'

'Yes. But for the wars it would have been rebuilt, and certainly later, had not Kemal made Angora the new capital which has diverted much finance and initiative from Istanbul. As it is, many acres of it remain to this day covered only with wreckage. Beggars, thieves, and outcasts have built themselves hutments among the ruins, but even so there must be a thousand places there in which you could remain hidden for weeks.'

'Sounds pretty safe,' Swithin agreed, but his saturated garments were now drying like boards on his body, and he was feeling desperately ill, so he added slowly, 'I've got to find a change of clothes, though, and get some warmth inside me somehow.'

Arif kicked a bundle in the bottom of the boat. 'I thought of that also, knowing it would be necessary if we had the good fortune to save you.'

Swithin controlled his chattering teeth and grinned faintly, 'By Jove, you must have hustled after you left Tatavla.'

'Allah gave me time. I knew that if they took you to the Tower it would not be until after dark, and the shops by the port were still open.'

The boat grated against some stone steps lapped by the tide, and the French sailors made it fast.

'Here we are now,' Arif added, 'can you manage the bundle while I pay off these men?'

Picking it up, Swithin staggered ashore. He was feeling ghastly and collapsed again on the top step. A moment later the Turk joined him, relieved him of his burden, and pulled him to his feet.

'Where are we?' he murmured with a groan.

'The Psamatia wharf. Courage now, ten minutes' walk through Soulou Monastir and we shall be there.'

'All right,' Swithin muttered, 'I'll make it somehow,' and with Arif's hand supporting him under the arm, he began the dreadful march to his new quarters.

It may, as the Turk had said, only have been ten minutes, but to Swithin it seemed a dozen years as he staggered up the gently sloping hill, through the twisting streets of Soulou, to the quarter which had been ravaged and left desolate by the great fire nearly a quarter of a century before. Then, when they reached the heart of it, he had to endure a seemingly interminable wait while his guide nosed about among the ruins.

With his back hunched against a wall he crouched in a corner, shivering as though a fit of ague were upon him, unheeding of the dark shapes that flitted past, or the sound of quarrelling voices which once disturbed the silence.

At last, Arif rejoined him and led the way down what had once been a narrow court, but was strewn with fallen beams and debris now overgrown by rank verdure. A small brick building stood at the far end. It lacked a roof and upper story, but still had its four walls standing.

'You should be secure here,' Arif announced, 'for this place has no sign of occupation, and Kazdim's men might hunt for a month through this wilderness of rubble without coming upon you. Strip now, while I undo the bundle.'

Swithin did as he was bid, but not without difficulty for his thigh and shoulder both hurt him badly. Yet once he had cast his sodden garments on a weed-covered mound, he felt a little better. Their clinging dampness had restricted his circulation and in this sheltered spot the night air still held something of the lingering heat from the past day.

'Dry yourself with this,' said Arif, handing him a coarse blanket from the bundle and, despite his hurts, he rubbed himself vigorously until some real warmth was restored to his cramped limbs.

The garments which the Turk had procured for him were rough sailor's wear from a slop shop down by the docks, but they were clean and thick so that once he had donned them, he felt more himself again—except for his splitting head.

Arif had purchased three blankets and having spread

these on the coarse grass between two hummocks in one corner of the ruin, he said, 'Lie down now, and I will roll you up.'

Nothing loath, Swithin stetched himself out. It was a hard couch, but infinitely welcome, and it was a glorious sensation to be able, at last, to relax. His companion tucked him up like an infant, and then produced a tin of biscuits and a flask of Raki. 'Eat and drink,' he ordered, 'while I talk to you, then you shall sleep.'

Swithin set to work on the biscuits and found that he was ravenously hungry. He had not eaten since midday at Arif's house, and as he sipped the Raki it coursed through his veins bringing heat and comfort to his exhausted body though it made his swollen lips smart. Meanwhile the Turk crouched beside him on the ground, and told his news.

'I have seen Jeanette,' he announced, 'for half an hour nearly, before I visited your flat. She works for her Pasha still—may the fire eat out his bowels—but she says that the papers which she types mostly concern a charity. Lists of donations received—with numbers against them—and the names of hospitals to which they are distributed in bulk. That does not need great intelligence to interpret, the donations are *subscriptions* towards the Kaka contributed by each cell and the *hospitals* the places where the armaments which the money purchases are stored.

'Of that I am certain because, when I pressed her to search her memory, she said that last month 360 Turkish pounds were given to the Hospital at Haidar Pacha. She remembers noticing the amount particularly, having thoughts of myself in her mind since she knows that my work lies there. Now last month, I received 360 cases of munitions for storage from the Kaka and they lie in my Depot at this moment labelled as parts of motor ploughs.

'Tonight she will go through his files with this new outlook in her mind, for—may Allah pour perfume on her eyelids—she feels about the manner of my brother's death even as I do myself. Tomorrow we meet again. Then I shall learn from her everything which she has discovered and—if Allah wills—we may then have much that is useful to go upon.'

'That's good work,' murmured Swithin, 'but I wish we could get some proof in black and white; that is what we need to break up the Kaka. I suppose it's not possible for her to secure a list of members since this chap is such a big noise in it?'

Arif shook his head. 'She would attempt anything—willingly, for in addition to her love for me and distress at Reouf's death, she sees in this an opportunity to be revenged on this dog of a Pasha who has debauched her—but how could she procure a list. No man has that, not even those who belong to Cell No. 1. That is the way in which the Kaka protects itself. None of us knows the names of more than eight other members. The four in our parent cell and another four in that which we have formed ourselves.'

'Of course, I had forgotten that for the moment,' Swithin said drowsily, 'anyhow it is great to have Mam'selle Jeanette working for us. We must wait now until we learn if she was able to get hold of anything tonight.'

'That is so, and you are weary my poor friend.' The Turk stood up. 'Do not move far from here when you wake in the morning otherwise you might miss your way among this tangle of ruins, and then I should not be able to find you when I come again. I will bring food—and news if there is any—about midday. Sleep now, and the Peace of Allah be upon you and about you.'

'Thanks—thanks a thousand times for all you've done for me,' Swithin replied, but the Turk had already disappeared into the shadows and next moment he was asleep.

When he woke the sun was already topping the broken wall of his roofless hiding-place. He rolled out of his blankets, stood up stiffly and looked about him. The place in which he had spent the night had apparently once been a small forecourt. A broken fountain, so overgrown with weeds that it was hardly recognisable, rose from a basin in its centre. Arched openings in the far wall led to inner apartments but each displayed the same silent desolation.

He walked a few paces and found that the bruise on his thigh still pained him, also that his shoulder was swollen and tender. His skin felt hot and dry yet he shivered spasmodically, and eyed the biscuits and Raki which Arif had left, with distaste. All he craved for was a hot bath and a cup of tea, but, with an effort he pulled himself together and limped out of his retreat to have a good look round.

From the roadway he could see quite a big portion of

this dead city as it sloped towards the Golden Horn, and thought it one of the strangest sights that he had ever seen. For a mile or more it stretched away before him in range after range of broken walls and great hummocks. Few traces of the fire were visible now, weather and vegetable life had dissolved the charcoal and camouflaged the blackened beams. The whole area was a uniform greenish yellow, so that the ruins melted into one another, and, for a moment, his military mind played with the idea of how fine a place it would be to conceal khaki-clad troops.

Here and there a few people were moving among the green-topped walls and in the far distance he could see a stream of traffic crossing the side road on which he stood by some main thoroughfare cutting through the desolated area. None of the people in his neighbourhood displayed any interest in him, doubtless considering him, from his ill-fitting sailor clothes, to be a down-and-out, like themselves. Numerous birds which were not visible cheered him with their morning song.

He returned to his corner and, since he had nothing to read or do, slept again, partly as a method of killing time and partly because he could stop his shivering under the rough blankets.

When he awoke again the sun was high in the heavens, the old brick near him scorching to the touch, and the stonework sizzling. He moved over into a patch of shade and surveyed the scene afresh: the birds that he had heard singing in the morning were silent now, enjoying their noonday rest, but the ground was alive with insects. Grasshoppers twittered incessantly and little *fliegers* of a hundred different varieties buzzed and hummed. For a few minutes he watched a party of ants, carrying their enormous burdens, as they proceeded in single file along their well-worn pathway to a cranny in the wall; then the greeny-golden lizards with their flickering tongues, darting from side to side or sunning themselves on the warm brickwork caught his attention.

His watch had stopped owing to its immersion the night before, but from the position of the sun he judged the time to be a little after midday. He had sweated while he slept in the sun and felt distinctly hungry now—less chilled and feverish. He began to hope that Arif would soon put in an appearance.

An hour or more drifted by and then in desperation he tackled the biscuits and the Raki as a stop gap. By the time he had finished he guessed it to be about two o'clock and as Arif had said that he would return at noon his failure to turn up being to cause Swithin considerable uneasiness.

He wandered out into the road again; not a soul was in sight, even the beggars and vagabonds who had their lairs in this strange wilderness were still taking their siesta. A brooding hush hung over the whole district, so that it seemed impossible to believe that he was standing in the centre of a city with a population of over a million inhabitants and the greatest for a radius of nearly a thousand miles.

As the afternoon wore on his anxiety increased, and having nothing with which to distract his attention, he could not free his mind from the fear that some calamity had befallen the Turk. When his neighbours began to move about again, he retreated to his hiding-place, but at every footfall on the roadway he peered hopefully out, and at about half-past four, with immeasurable relief, he saw Arif approach, turn off the road into the long grasses that grew knee deep in the outer court and, with a cautious look round, slip through the rounded arch of the doorway.

The Turk's eyes were gleaming with excitement and, without pausing to explain his lateness or inquire how Swithin felt, he burst out immediately:

'We have to act, my friend—act very quickly—or it will be too late. I received a visitor at my office this morning— the leader of my parent cell who is also a member of one much above it. He gave me orders for the distiribution of the arms which I have concealed for the Kaka. They are to be dispatched on lorries and delivered to various addresses throughout Scutari, Haidar Pacha, Kadikeuy and Moda, tomorrow night.'

Swithin's face suddenly went grave. 'That means they intend to make their *coup* soon now—within a week or so I suppose?'

Arif nodded. 'Only the members of the first hundred cells know it yet, and they because to them fall all the necessary arrangements, but it is fixed for midnight on the twentieth.'

'Good God! Swithin exclaimed, 'and today is the eighteenth! We haven't got a shred of evidence against the Kaka yet, and only forty-eight hours left before the Revolution sweeps the whole country.'

19

The Lion's Mouth

Arif began to unpack a parcel he had brought. It contained bread, cold meat, fruit, a bottle of water and some sherbet.

'I am sorry that you should have had to remain hungry for so long,' he apologised, as he spread out the things on a fallen block of masonry, 'but I was kept at my office far later than I had expected owing to this visit, and then I had arranged to see Jeanette at half-past three, so it was impossible to get here before.'

'The great thing is that you've turned up after all,' Swithin remarked thankfully, as he sat down and helped himself to the food, 'I was becoming really scared that something awful had happened to you. Now what the devil are we going to do? If the Revolution is timed to start at midnight on the twentieth, we're up against it good and hard and proper. The authorities will never disorganise the running of the whole country and order all sorts of precautionary troop movements on our bare word alone. It would be different if we had some real proof of the existence of the Kaka that we could show.'

'Allah has been gracious,' the Turk replied, drawing a paper from his pocket. 'Here is the proof that you need. Jeanette secured it last night. Look, it is a complete list of the *hospitals* among which the *donations* have been distributed.'

Swithin took the paper eagerly. glanced quickly down it, and then shook his head. 'This would be extremely valuable if we had something else to go with it. Mam'selle Jeanette has done marvellously to get it for us, but I'm afraid it's not a proof of anything. You or I might have typed this list and it bears no signature. We must have some paper which has been signed by one of the heads of the conspiracy. It does not matter what, as long as it is a document dealing with the organisation of the Kaka.'

Arif's heavy brows drew down into a frown. 'I have already told you that it is impossible to procure such a thing. No documents exist. There *is* no correspondence. All orders are conveyed from cell-leader to cell-leader by word of mouth, so nobody ever signs anything—except . . .' he paused suddenly.

'Except what?'

'The oath to the Kaka.'

'There is a list then?'

'No, but when any member forms a new cell, he is given a small pentagonal paper. The oath is written in its centre and the five members of the cell each sign their names, one in each of the five angles. The cell leader does not pass it on, so those above him never see it, but he keeps it himself as a guarantee of the good faith of the others.'

'You have one yourself, then?'

'Yes, I will show it to you.' Arif took out his pocket-book, and produced a thin pentagonal wafer no larger than a five shilling piece. It had minute writing in its centre and an involved scrawl in each of its corners. The signatures were in the old script, a jumble of involved arabesques, so Swithin could not have read them without considerable labour even had he wished, and he noted that the almost transparent little document was made of rice paper, so that it could be swallowed in an emergency.

'By Jove,' he murmured, 'If only we could get hold of the Pasha's. Mam'selle Jeanette is er . . . well very intimate with him—isn't she?'

Suddenly and viciously Arif spat. 'Let us be frank. She is perforce the mistress of this dog. If she repulsed him, she would be thrown out of Turkey and never again should we brighten each other's eyes—or worse might befall her.'

'Then surely—it's a hundred to one that he keeps his on him—as you do. Couldn't she find an opportunity . . .?'

'I will speak with her of it when I see her again tonight. She has courage—may Allah protect her— and it may be that she can find a way to search him.'

Swithin's blue eyes glinted. 'This Pasha must be a member of one of the highest cells if he is responsible for collecting all the contributions from the others and distributing the munitions that they pay for. On his wafer there must be the names of four other big men in this business. The oath signed by five of them would be proof enough to convince anyone, and if only Mamselle Jeanette could get it for us we'd smash the Kaka yet.'

'I see little chance of that, unless Allah grants us time by a postponement of their plans,' Arif murmured despondently.

'Do you think there is any prospect of that?'

'None. The organisation is so excellent that all things run like clockwork.'

'Still, you'll do your damnedest to persuade Mam'selle Jeanette to try everything she knows tonight in the hope of discovering where the Pasha keeps his wafer—and securing it, if possible.'

'She will need no persuasion knowing that her success would mean a rope round that sadist's neck and her freedom to live with me in happiness.'

'Good. Now this thing.' Swithin held up the wafer which he had not yet given back. 'Are there occasions when you have to produce it?'

'No, never.'

'May I keep it then?'

Arif suddenly drew back. 'But you would not have me betray my comrades!'

'No, that we can get over by a little skilful alteration of the signatures, I think. Enough to disguise the names without materially altering the appearance of the thing. Since it concerns cell 310, which is a long way down the list, the disclosure of the names on it would not materially harm the Kaka in any case, but the oath is written in its centre and it might prove extremely useful as a specimen.'

'So be it then—if you wish.' Arif took out his fountain-pen. 'Give it to me and I will see how the lettering can best be altered.'

While Swithin finished his picnic meal, the Turk worked silently upon the wafer, converting the flowing arabesques which decorated the five corners, by adding curls and little dots, into other letters. When he had finished he handed it back and stood up. 'I must go now. You will remain hidden here until I come again?'

'No, I must get in touch with the British interests—those friends of Turkey—whom I told you that I represent. You can help me there, if you will, by despatching a message for me.'

'By all means. Have you paper?'

Swithin nodded and drew out his notebook. Most of its pages were still sodden in the centre, but he had dried the top few sheets in the sun that afternoon and he began to scribble a note to Diana.

He wanted to see her urgently in order to pass on his news, but Bebek was nearly nine miles away—right out beyond Pera—so he doubted if his message would reach her much before dinner-time. Then there was the difficulty of suggesting a suitable place to meet her. If she had been a man he could have made it any street corner after dark, but being in Constantinople, he could think of nowhere which would be all right for her, except the lounge of some hotel or dance place—yet into those he dared not go himself. Besides, even if he were prepared to chance it, he knew that they would not let him in unshaven as he was and dressed in his present shoddy rig-out.

Thinking it over, he realised that Diana could have no idea what had happened to him since they last met, so she would not be expecting an urgent summons and might quite well be dining out, in which case she would fail to turn up even if he risked lounging at the entrance of the *Tokatlian* or the *Pera*. Moreover, since he still lacked any vital proof which he could pass on to her, she could do nothing except report the movement of arms for the following night and that the balloon was timed to go up forty-eight hours later. No action would be taken without proof, he felt certain, unless he or Arif were prepared to give evidence at first hand, so although the delay was irritating he decided, all things considered. that it would be better to ask her to meet him next morning. He could be sure of her getting his message in time to keep the appointment then, and there were plenty of places where it would not matter about her walking through the streets alone in daylight.

Seeing his hesitation, Arif remarked: 'You look worried, my friend—can I, perhaps, help you in some way?'

'I am a bit,' Swithin admitted. 'I should have liked to fix a meeting for tonight, but that seems impossible, so I must leave it till the morning. Where would you suggest as a good place to run into someone as though by accident—

somewhere where there is a good-sized crowd with which it would be easy to mingle for a few moments?'

The Turk thought for a little, then he said: 'Why not at the Mosque of the Sweet Waters? Tomorrow is Friday—our holy day—so the Dervishes will dance there at eleven o'clock. The government still permits it as one of the sights of the city, and many foreigners go there, which enables the Blessed of Allah to collect funds for their support.'

'Excellent!—the very place.'

Swithin finished his note and dated it the 20th, putting a heavy circle round the figure in the hope that she might guess its meaning when she received it that night, addressed the folded sheet, and handed it over.

'If you will have that sent to Miss Duncannon by a trustworthy messenger she will arrange for the person I wish to see to meet me in the morning,' he said, not wishing to involve Diana herself further than was absolutely necessary, even to Arif. 'Then I will pass on the list of *hospitals* which Mam'selle Jeanette secured for us.'

'It shall be done and without delay.' Arif pocketed the note and added: 'Now I must leave you, but there is one thought which comes to me, since you go to Pera in any case tomorrow; would it not be better for us to meet there also? Now that I am so pressed for time—both Jeanette and yourself to keep in touch with—also my work which I cannot neglect entirely, this place presents great inconvenience and the loss of precious hours, since I have to cross each time either from my office in Haidar Pacha or from Jeanette in Pera.'

'By all means,' Swithin agreed. 'How about place and time?'

'The Bridge at Galata—the Pera end. That is always a busy spot, there is a restaurant there which is a meeting-place for Greek business men—the Café Athéné it is called—whichever of us arrives first can sit at one of the small tables behind the box plants outside, and for time, let me see . . . I do not know at what hour Jeanette will be free to see me tomorrow until I have spoken with her tonight. It will not be before the afternoon and perhaps in the latter part of that. If we said six o'clock that should allow me a safe margin.'

'Right then. Six o'clock at the Café Athéné near the Pera end of Galata Bridge.'

'I shall be there, and in the meantime, may Allah protect you.' Arif turned away.

'And you,' Swithin replied. Then he watched his friend stalk through the long grass and down the roadway until his tall figure had passed out of sight.

Swithin packed up the remainder of the food and stowed it in a corner. As he did so, one thought was beating in his brain. The 20th. Saturday night, and this was Thursday evening. In little over forty-eight hours now the Revolution was due to break out. Once it started, who could say where it would finish? The Kaka was very powerful and admirably organised. He knew that now, beyond a doubt, and its leaders were men like Kazdim, Chief of the Secret Police, that, of course, was why no rumour of it had leaked through to Kemal. The Eunuch would take good care to delete any hint of it from his men's reports. Then there was this Pasha who kept Jeanette against her will, for his amusement. When he had first been mentioned. Swithin remembered poor indiscreet Reouf talking of him as an important official. With such men behind the movement its chances of success were very considerable, and if their *coup* did come off anything might happen. The Jehad would be preached and the legions of the Faithful come flocking to the green banner of the Prophet. There would be war in the Balkans within a week and that might spread into a universal conflagration.

If he had had definite proof to offer, Swithin would have taken it straight to the British Embassy. They would, he knew, have forwarded it immediately by 'plane to Kemal. The Grey Wolf of Angora would then spring before his enemies could rise, and the continuance of peace would be secured.

But even if Jeanette succeeded now in stealing the precious wafer from her Pasha, Swithin saw that it could not be in her hands before the following night and that would be too late to get it to Kemal—miles away in Asia Minor—before the smuggled arms of the Revolutionaries had been distributed.

The more he thought of it the more certain he became that he ought to take action now—immediately. He could go to the authorities with the list of secret munition stores and if he could only make them believe his story, those could be raided and the contents confiscated. That seemed to him the only possible chance of stopping the Revolution, and stopped it must be, he felt, it it lay within his power to do it, whatever risks he had to take himself. It meant that he would have to confess to being a spy, and if they refused to believe his statement about the secret menace of the Kaka, he would be properly sunk. It was no light matter to accuse a man like Kazdim, the actual Chief of the Police, of being up to the neck in a conspiracy against the Government, without a shred of proof. Swithin knew that he would probably be regarded as a lunatic and thrown into prison for his pains, but he still felt that the responsibility of endeavouring to stop this outbreak which might lead to so many horrors, lay on his shoulders.

For half an hour he wrestled with the problem. Then he made up his mind. He would set off at once, and bribe or force his way into the presence of the Military Governor of Constantinople. If the gods were kind the man might prove intelligent and credulous. In any case, he, Swithin, would say what he had to say and implore him to take adequate precautions against a coming rising.

Leaving the ruin, Swithin set off at a brisk walk down the sloping road towards the Golden Horn. He judged the time to be about half-past five, and he hoped to reach the Harbieh Military School, beyond the end of the Grand' Rue de Pera, where the Governor had his office before it closed at six.

His thigh still hurt, so he moved at a quick limp, but his shoulder no longer pained him and he pushed on gamely, thinking of nothing but the importance of getting hold of the General Commanding the Forces in the City at the earliest possible moment.

He reached the Rue Top Capou, which crosses the burnt-out quarter, and turned right along it until he reached the still standing shops and houses. In Murad Pasha Street he managed to pick up a taxi and ordered the man to drive at top speed to the Harbieh Military School.

A quarter of an hour later he was questioning the sentry on the gate. The man was a simple, friendly fellow and passed him without difficulty, but at the enquiry office he met with the red tape that he had expected. His rough clothes and sprouting beard were hardly calculated to inspire confidence or respect, and his request to see the Governor's secretary on urgent private business was curtly refused by a bulbous-nosed sergeant.

Swithin wasted no time arguing, but immediately produced a substantial bribe, upon which he was allowed to proceed upstairs where he interviewed a clerk. Again he met with insolent opposition, but another bribe did the trick and extracted the information that the General's secretary had gone for the night—so, he also ascertained, had the General. Another crinkly note secured the address of the General's private residence, in Nichantache, just north of the Military School. He hurried downstairs and out into the street, five minutes later he stood before the door of the General's house.

The man on the door was not a soldier but a Kavass in ornate livery. He admitted that the General was at home, but protested that his master never received callers without an appointment. Swithin produced yet another bribe and was allowed to wait in the hall while the Kavass went off to fetch the major-domo. This individual appeared after a short wait, a portly person who on one glance at Swithin broke into pompous expostulations. One note silenced those all right, and another, after some consideration, produced the statement that since the matter was vitally urgent, something might be managed if certain persons could be persuaded, with Allah's blessing, to give their kind assistance.

Swithin parted with a third and still larger note that these unknown forces could be brought into play on his behalf, although he shrewdly suspected that it would remain in the company of the other two. Then he was led through to a small library and told to wait in patience.

He did, for ten minutes or more, then the door opened again and he heard the voice of the major-domo, cringing and persuasive.

'This person is a filth who soils our carpets, *Hanoume*, as your peerless eyes will discover for themselves, but he speaks of tidings which mean life or death. If you would but see him yourself for one moment and judge whether it is fitting that he should be admitted to the presence of our Master.'

'Just as you wish, Rustam,' came the quiet reply, obviously from a woman, and the next moment she entered the room.

Swithin gave her one look and then his mouth dropped open. It was Jeanette, and the full meaning of that appalling discovery flashed upon him. This was the house of the General Commanding the Forces in Constantinople—but it must also be the house of the Pasha of whom Arif had spoken—they were one and the same person—and the General, Kemal's trusted lieutenant, was himself a member of the Kaka!

Jeanette stood staring at him white-faced and wide-eyed. She knew him again instantly, despite his shoddy clothing, by his bright blue eyes.

'What is it?' she whispered. 'Arif *as tol*' me of the work you do, but—*nom de Dieu*—why 'ave you come 'ere?'

Before he could reply, a door on the other side of the library was flung open. The General, clad in a grey uniform, stood on its threshold.

'Cocktails, my dear,' he cried in French. 'It is not fitting that you should keep me waiting.' Then, seeing Swithin, he advanced into the room and added sharply: 'Who is this fellow?'

Swithin was bareheaded, so his disguise consisted of a one-day beard and his sailor clothes. He could do nothing but offer up a frantic prayer that he would remain unrecognisable—for the General was his old enemy—Prince Ali.

After one astonished glance, a murderous hatred leapt into the Prince's eyes and his fists clenched convulsively as he shot out: 'Allah be praised for delivering you into my hands—Captain Destime!'

20

Cocktails for Two

There was only one thing for it. Swithin saw that instantly. No bluff could serve him here. He had come determined to expose the Kaka but, even if the Prince had not been a member of it, there was their personal quarrel. Ali was not the type to forgive a man who had once struck him and, to have that man at his mercy in his own country, meant flaying for the man. In this case discretion was by far the better part of valour, and after one glance at the Prince's dark, malevolent face, Swithin bounded from the room.

Jeanette gave an hysterical scream as he leapt past her —then, with extraordinary presence of mind, flung her arms round the Prince's neck.

With a savage movement, Ali broke her grip, whipped a silver whistle from his pocket, and blew upon it with all his force. The piercing blast shrilled through the house.

Out in the hall the fat major-domo cowered back, his eyes bulging from his head in terror as he saw the ruffianly-looking visitor he had admitted dash from the library, but the tall Kavass straightened as the whistle blew and sprang up the half-dozen steps from the vestibule.

Swithin hit out, but it was a running swipe and he was partly off his balance when he made it, so his fist only scraped the Kavass's cheek instead of landing beneath his jaw. The fellow flung himself forward—grabbing at him, staggered under the impact, then tripped on the topmost stair and fell—dragging Swithin with him. Next instant they were rolling over and over down the short flight of steps, locked in each other's arms.

They came to rest against the front door, with Swithin on top. He drew back his right fist and, with every ounce of strength he had, struck the Kavass a smashing blow under the heart. The man grunted. Swithin slammed in another terrific jab and scrambled to his feet.

Pandemonium had broken loose in the hall above. Prince

Ali was still blowing piercing blasts on his silver whistle. He had only paused in the library long enough to grab an automatic from his desk, and now stood on the topmost step brandishing it fiercely, his face suffused by anger to a dusky purple as he endeavoured to thrust Jeanette aside so that he could use his pistol freely. Jeanette was screaming as though she was going to have a fit, yet in fact, with all her wits about her, endeavouring to hamper the Prince's movements. The major-domo was shouting 'Murder!' in a deep bass voice, a great wolfhound bounding from a nearby door broke into furious barking, while the sound of answering shouts and running footsteps coming from the back of the house added to the general din.

As Swithin seized the latch of the front door, Ali fired. Almost simultaneously with the report of his pistol a bullet thudded into the woodwork only an inch from Swithin's ear. The Kavass staggered to his feet. Ali fired again, but Jeanette, apparently hysterical, fell against him knocking aside his elbow as he pressed the trigger. The bullet went through the Kavass's shoulder and he sprang into the air with a howl of pain.

'At him, Salim!' roared the Prince, and just as the door latch gave way under Swithin's fumbling fingers the wolf-hound launched itself upon him. He turned, but too late; the dog's teeth snapped into the forearm that he raised to protect his face, its heavy body swung against his middle and the latch clicked to again behind him.

Half a dozen other menservants had now appeared upon the scene. At their master's cursing order they surged down the steps in a body. One seized Swithin by the collar while he was still trying desperately to fight off the dog, another hit him in the face, the heavy boot of a third caught him on the shin then, still struggling wildly, he was pulled down and the whole lot threw themselves in a heap on top of him.

He struck out blindly and felt his fist land with a softish crunch upon the nose of one of his assailants. It began to bleed and the drops of blood fell warm and sticky on his neck. Someone trod on the dog and it yelped dismally. Then for the next few moments Swithin was powerless under a rain of blows. They kicked, cuffed and shook him until they had beaten every ounce of breath out of his body and finally hauled him to his feet, battered and gasping.

'Bring him here,' ordered the Prince, and Swithin was pushed up the steps with his arms held fast behind him. Ali raised his open hand and brought it down with a ringing slap on his helpless prisoner's face. 'Captain Destime,' he sneered, 'you must learn humility.'

Swithin winced under the blow. Normally he could have taken it perhaps, but he was still choking for breath and half-dizzy with the battering he had received. Ali grinned maliciously and struck again, then having apparently eased his feelings for the moment he flung out curtly to the servants: 'Take him into the library and tie him to a chair.'

They hustled Swithin inside, thrust him into a stiff-backed seat and lashed him to it, then Ali ordered them out of the room and sent Jeanette, who had ceased her screaming, to fetch the cocktails.

For a few moments he regarded his prisoner in silence with ironical curiosity, then he said suddenly:

'So you came all this way to try and assassinate me because I had you dismissed from your army, eh?'

'You did not have me dismissed—I handed in my papers,' said Swithin. The short respite, while Ali had been staring at him, had enabled him to get back his breath and with it some semblance of calmness.

'There is little difference—and you came here to be revenged.'

'No.'

'Well, what are you doing in Istanbul then?'

'I'm doing my best to get you hung,' Swithin replied smoothly. There was something about Prince Ali which goaded him into defiance. The day before, when he had been trapped by the Eunuch, his feelings had been entirely different. Kazdim was so completely Oriental—subtle, sadistic, but so certain of himself and showing so little of his emotions that it had seemed a waste of breath to bandy words with him, whereas the Prince was so much more a Western type that Swithin felt almost as if he were up against an exceptionally depraved and brutal specimen of his own kind.

'To get me hung,' Ali repeated slowly; 'and how did you propose to do that?'

'You'll see before you're three days older.'

A new expression, half fear and half amazement, came into the Prince's eyes. 'What the hell d'you mean?' he thundered.

'Just what I say.'

Ali raised his fist. 'Speak, you rat,' he snarled, 'or I'll . . .'

'*Les cocktails!*' Jeanette's voice came, suddenly urgent behind them. He turned and stared at her. 'All right—put them down and leave us.'

He marched across the room, his spurs jingling and his footfalls heavy on the parquet. With an unsteady hand he poured himself a drink.

'Thank you,' said Swithin, 'I'd prefer a whisky, but I could manage one of those.'

The Prince paused with the glass half-way to his lips, he raised his eyebrows disdainfully and was about to speak when Swithin cut him short.

'Just as you wish, of course, but when I was an officer, my Regiment entertained you at Maidenhead. As a member of the Club I naturally paid my share of the champagne you appeared to appreciate so much, and I've always understood that no Turk cared to fail in returning hospitality.'

A flicker of astonishment passed over Ali's smooth features, and his whole expression changed. 'I'm sorry,' he said, then he bowed stiffly from the waist, filled another glass, and carrying it over, carefully poured it into Swithin's mouth.

'Thanks,' Swithin murmured. 'It's queer to think we'll both be dead within a week—isn't it?'

Again that look suspiciously like fear showed for an instant in the Prince's eyes, yet he squared his rather sloping shoulders and replied: 'As far as you are concerned you can put it at much less than that, but in my case you have no need to worry.'

'I'm not,' Swithin declared promptly, 'yet you are going to die just the same—so you had better make up your mind to it.'

Ali frowned. 'What is your object in making these absurd statements?'

'I thought you might like a chance to prepare yourself for the fate which is going to overtake you—*and* certain friends of yours.'

'Who?'

'Why, the Brothers in Allah of the Sword and Crescent.'

The Prince was helping himself to another cocktail. He banged down the shaker, spilling a portion of his drink, and exclaimed: 'So you *do* know about that?'

'Yes, I know all about the Kaka.'

'How the hell did you find out?'

'Does it matter? Anyhow, I've had the pleasure of furnishing full details of your precious conspiracy to Kemal.'

'Allah strike you—that's not true!' Ali stepped back across the room and stood glaring down at him.

Swithin only grinned. His baseless predictions of the Prince's death and the flat lie had had just told about having given full information concerning the Kaka to Kemal, were solely inspired by the fact that Ali obviously meant to kill him anyhow. He could not possibly hope for another miraculous escape from death such as he had had the night before so, whatever he said, he felt he could not make the situation worse, and, in the meantime, it afforded him considerable pleasure to have got Ali so badly rattled. It looked as if he had at least destroyed any possibility of sound sleep for his enemy until the Revolution had actually done its work.

The Prince turned suddenly and seized the telephone, bawled a number down it, and jammed it back.

'Getting on to your old friend Kazdim?' inquired Swithin maliciously. 'He's going to swing by the neck too. My one regret is that I shan't be there to see you dangling side by side above Galata Bridge.'

'Silence,' snapped the Prince. The 'phone tinkled and he snatched it up again. 'Give me Kazdim Hari Bekar,' he shouted into the instrument.

There was a pause, then the Prince spoke again. He gave a quick description of Swithin and demanded if anything was known of him—another pause—then he gave an impatient curse and cried: 'That is impossible. He is here, I say—you must be mistaken and speak of someone else.'

'Bring him along,' suggested Swithin. 'He'll think he's seeing a ghost and probably have apoplexy—I'd like to see that brute die in a fit.'

'What!' Ali turned to stare at him. 'It is not true—you

cannot be the man he says was executed at the Marble Tower last night?'

'Not executed,' Swithin corrected mildly. 'They sent me for a swim, but I've got nine lives like a cat, so whatever you try I'll live to see your namesake Bald Ali, Kemal's hanging judge, do your business yet.'

'You are lying—no one has ever come alive from that exit to the Marble Tower—it was some other spy.'

'Liar yourself,' retorted Swithin rudely; he was now keyed up to a state of nervous recklessness which transcended fear.

The Prince turned back to the telephone. 'You will come here at once—and bring your guards to remove this man,' he added, then slammed down the receiver.

'Now, now, don't get in a temper,' Swithin admonished him. 'You might break a blood-vessel and cheat the executioner—which would be a pity. Still, that may be your end yet. As you are a sort of royalty Kemal will probably make a special example of you and hang you by the heels instead of the neck.'

'Silence, you filth!' Ali roared and then he jabbed a finger on a bell.

A footman answered it, one of the mob who had mauled Swithin by the front door. The Prince thrust his pistol into the astonished man's hand and said curtly:

'Take this. If that dog in the chair speaks one word to you your answer will be to shoot him through the head—understand? Kazdim Hari Bekar will be arriving shortly. Tell him that I have gone up to change and that I will be down in due course.' Without another glance at either of them he stalked out of the room.

Swithin studied the face of the man who had been left to guard him, but it was mean and narrow with close-set eyes. The fellow was watching him suspiciously and had a nervous finger on the trigger of the automatic. It looked as though he meant to use it on the slightest provocation, so there did not seem much hope in that direction.

Five minutes passed in uneventful silence. However slender his chances of remaining alive for another twenty-four hours, Swithin did not care to ask deliberately for a bullet through the head. Then, behind the man's shoulder he saw the door through which Prince Ali had first entered begin to open very slowly.

He watched it fascinated, a new tension in his limbs. The cautious, silent, stealthy opening of that door could only mean one thing. Jeanette was behind it, coming to his assistance. The footman could not see it from where he stood and Swithin felt certain that if only Jeanette had the pluck and did not bungle, she would be able to crack the man over the head from behind before he even knew what hit him.

The door opened another foot. The man remained unsuspicious. Swithin began to pray. If Jeanette succeeded in knocking out his guard, he knew that she could free him from the cords that bound him in two minutes. Once free, with Ali upstairs and well out of the way, he could grab the gun, scare hell out of the other servants, plug any of them who tried to stop him, and be out of the house before the Prince had the least idea what had happened.

He saw, of course, that he would have to take Jeanette with him, which might prove a handicap later when they were in the streets, but he could not possibly leave her to face the music. That would destroy their one chance of getting the Kaka wafer from Ali, as she could not have had much opportunity to find out where it was and steal it yet—which was a pity—but it could not be helped. They might run slap into Kazdim and his boy friends, who were due to arrive at any moment, on the doorstep too, but if that happened Swithin thought grimly that, with a loaded pistol in his hand, he could at least see to it that the Eunuch did not survive to participate in any forthcoming celebration in the event of his Revolution being successful. The door opened a few more inches. Swithin held his breath and waited.

Suddenly Jeanette's platinum head came round the corner. Swithin blinked at her to show that he was ready, but he dared not say a word. She stared at him for a second and nodded, then moved her head in the direction of the guard, placed her finger on her lips to enjoin silence, and disappeared.

Swithin sat tense and expectant. She had evidently re-connoitred the position to her satisfaction and now gone to secure some weapon with which to bash the footman over the skull. The door remained open—which was proof that she meant to return. If only Kazdim did not arrive in the meantime. The next two minutes seemed to spin themselves into hours. Then at last Jeanette's head and shoulders appeared again.

21

The Cat with Nine Lives

Jeanette's right hand was still hidden behind the door so
Swithin could not see the poker or stove rake that he felt
certain she had secured in her absence, but in her left she
carried a white sheet of foolscap paper with some words
printed on it in large capitals. She held it up for him to see
and he read the sentence in one glance:

'JE SAIS OU IL LE CACHE.'

He had expected some instruction as to how to aid her
when she made her attack, but was thrilled to learn that
she had already found out where Ali concealed the Kaka
wafer. Perhaps, he thought, she had even managed to get
hold of it. To escape and carry that off as well would be a
veritable triumph, but he was burning with impatience for
her to attempt his release. He blinked violently again and
swivelled his eyes in the direction of the guard.

Jeanette glanced at the man's back, then she made a
little helpless shrugging motion with her shoulders and
withdrew as quietly as she had come—closing the door
silently behind her.

With bitter distress Swithin suddenly understood that
all his wild hopes had been completely groundless. She
had never intended to attempt his rescue, but only to pass
on that piece of information in case he could manage to
escape on his own. His disappointment was intense, absolutely physical. He felt his heart slip downwards in his
chest and his whole body relaxed despondently under this
shattering blow.

Another ten minutes slipped by in silence, then there
were voices in the hall. He recognised the high, fluting
falsetto of the Eunuch, the door opened and Kazdim came
into the room followed by his bodyguards, Malik and
Servet.

For a second all three stared at Swithin with unbelieving eyes, then Kazdim's little pouting mouth broke into a smile.

'It is true then,' he piped. 'The ways of Allah are surely past the understanding of mankind. I never thought these eyes would behold your face again.'

'No,' Swithin agreed grimly, 'I don't suppose you did.'

The footman delivered his master's message and left the room. The two guards took up their positions one on either side of the Eunuch as he seated himself gingerly on the nearest chair. He continued to stare at Swithin with intense interest and a certain admiration in his little black eyes. Then the chair creaked under his great weight as he leaned forward and inquired amiably:

'How comes it that you survived the waters of the Marmara?'

Swithin kept a perfectly straight face, and replied seriously:

'Because, as I have just been telling Prince Ali, I have nine lives like a cat.'

'Indeed,' beamed the Eunuch with equal seriousness. 'Then we shall have to give you a drink of strychnine, stick a knife into your liver—shoot you through both lungs—impale you on a stake—hang you by the neck—cut your throat—and, finally burn your body. Thus will we dispose of the eight lives which you have left, and if I exercise some care, you will, I trust, remain conscious up to the seventh operation—although each would prove fatal in itself after a lapse of time.'

'You can't think of any alternatives, I suppose?'

'Why, yes. I have not spoken yet of bowstringing—cutting off the head—flaying—suffocation by pillows—starvation—sewing up in a sack with wild cats—snakebite—or feeding you to the rats in one of the old cisterns—another eight, you see—all of which modes of death, with many others, I have witnessed in my time. But some of these latter are lengthy processes, whereas my original suggestions could all be carried out within half an hour—if so Allah will—and in these days I have much business to attend to.'

'In that case I'm quite agreeable to dispensing with the wild cats and the rats.'

'I am obliged,' said the Eunuch politely.

'Not at all,' replied Swithin, with equal courtesy, 'you are to be congratulated on your profound knowledge of the subject.'

'Thank you. I had the good fortune to study under the illustrious "Twisted Beard" Pasha when I was a youth—which accounts for much. His fame as a director of executions may even have reached your ears, perhaps. He was Comptroller of the Household to His Majesty the Sultan Abdul Hamid who now sleeps in the bosom of Allah.'

Swithin nodded, and his blue eyes twinkled. This fantastic conversation on death did not seem to be a really personal matter, and he thought he had a good one up his sleeve as he remarked: 'If you knew "Twisted Beard" Pasha you would also have known His Highness the Grand Eunuch Djevher Agha.'

'Surely, he also taught me much.'

'Do you remember the manner of *his* death?'

'He was hung with "Twisted Beard" and a number of others above Galata Bridge when the Young Turks deposed the Sultan. By the mercy of Allah I had been sent to Tiflis to make purchases of Circassian concubines at that time.'

'You are wrong, my friend, he was not hung. A man I know was in Istanbul then and witnessed the execution. The Grand Eunuch Djevher Agha was a man much like yourself, of royal proportions and many chins. When it came to his turn, the gipsy executioners could not get the rope properly round his throat; in consequence, when they pushed him off, he died neither from strangulation nor a broken neck.'

'How then?'

'By the gradual pull of his own enormous weight until the tendons of his throat stretched to breaking-point and choked him with his own blood. It took quite a time—so my friend told me, and when Djevher Agha was still at last his head was nearly a yard from his shoulders and his great carcass suspended by a rope of neck not thicker than my wrist. I hope you will remember that when Kemal sentences you to be hung.'

Swithin saw from a flicker of Kazdim's puffy eyelids

that he had got home, but the Eunuch suppressed it almost instantly, and smiled again as he said:

'But tell me please of your escape last night. I am much interested and a little proud of you. The execution of most prisoners is quite dull, whereas yours, the method having failed for the first time, has made history.'

'I'll tell you the trick if you will let me throw you down the hole,' Swithin offered.

'No, please,' Kazdim shook his vast bald head. 'All my life I have preferred to experiment on others, and I am too old to change my habits now. It was the woman, I suppose?'

'I don't know what you're talking about.'

'He! He! He!—note that, Malik, it is a joke.' The Eunuch's enormous sides wobbled and shook as though they were made of jelly. 'Surely,' he tittered, 'you have not forgotten the tall fair miss with the dark eyes. She who was to have collected that letter from the Pera bookstall?'

Before Swithin had time to make a denial, Prince Ali came clanking into the room. He was dressed in full uniform, with sword, top-boots, stars and medals, evidently about to attend some official function, and Swithin had to admit to himself that the Prince made a fine figure of a man.

The Eunuch slipped from his chair and, with unexpected agility, salaamed almost to the floor, so also did his henchmen. This excessive deference surprised Swithin for, although Ali was of Royal blood such considerations had long since ceased to count under Kemal's regime, and it seemed strange that the Chief of the Police should actually grovel even to a very highly-placed General but when Kazdim addressed the Prince as 'Most Exalted one' Swithin suddenly understood the true position. Ali came of the line of Sultans—only such were eligible under the religious laws to occupy the Caliphate, he was also a high member of the Kaka—the Kaka meant to restore the Caliphate, and it had evidently been arranged that immediately the Revolution was accomplished Prince Ali was to be proclaimed Caliph of all the Faithful.

'Is this the man you spoke of?' Ali barked at Kazdim after the barest acknowledgment of the salutations.

'It is indeed, Most Exalted One—and a miracle that he

should have escaped—but the matter shall soon be rectified.'

'It had better be—he knows too much—he even speaks of having communicated certain things to the Unbeliever. Can there be any truth in that?'

'None, Most Exalted One, pray accept reassurances from your servant. He was but on the fringe of matters which it were better not to speak of now.'

'You are sure of that?'

'Certain, under Allah's will, O Blessed and Holy Descendant of the Prophet. A young student whose unfortunate demise occurred four nights ago was guilty of certain indiscretions to this foreigner. Yet what can he have learnt that could cause a flutter of your exalted eyelids?'

'I have your word for it that he has had no opportunity to communicate with the Unbeliever—that is the vital thing?'

'My oath, O Dispenser of Felicity. The posts in that direction are watched with the utmost care and any private message would surely have been intercepted by those who delight to serve you in the Unbeliever's entourage.'

The Prince heaved a sigh of relief, then he said quickly: 'I have a personal interest in this man, so wish to witness his execution myself. Also, I desire that he should be bastinadoed in my presence before he is put to death. Tonight I attend a banquet and after, I have a private appointment, so the matter had best be concluded tomorrow morning.'

'To hear is to obey,' bleated the Eunuch with a low obeisance.

The Prince moved as though to leave the room, then he turned and spoke again. 'How was it possible for him to survive a visit to the Tower of Marble—even if some fool was careless with the cords that bound his arms?'

'By a chance in a thousand, Most Exalted One. His confederate must have known of our intent and waited below the Tower in a boat—again a hardly conceivable coincidence, but he must have risen to the surface within a few yards of the boat's position—and so was hauled to safety while still alive.'

'This confederate you speak of—what of him?

'It is a woman, O Blessed of Heaven! We intercepted a letter from him to her three days ago.'

'Has she been dealt with?'

'Not yet, Descendant of Divinity.'

'Who is she? Have you discovered her identity?'

'She is Miss Duncannon, Most Exalted One, who stays with another of that name at Bebek.'

Swithin's heart almost stopped beating. It was an appalling shock to him that the Eunuch should have discovered Diana to be the woman to whom the letter left at the bookstall had been addressed, and next moment his fears for her were increased a hundredfold by the sudden interest that leapt into Prince Ali's eyes.

'So,' murmured the Prince, 'this is extremely interesting,' then he smiled maliciously at Swithin.

'Would you like to see her flogged—you may, perhaps, after I have done with her—if it does not mean delaying your own execution too long. I have not forgotten that she, as well as you, displayed insolence towards me when I was in England.'

Swithin bit his lip and remained silent, half-stunned by the ghastly mental picture which had risen before his eyes.

Ali turned back to Kazdim. 'Why—if you knew this woman—has she not been arrested?'

'I did not think it necessary or diplomatic at the moment, Most Exalted One. She acts only as a post-office for this man, so without him she is harmless. Also, she has many friends in high places, and there would be immediate protests to the Unbeliever if I sent my men to the Duncannon house. However, if it is your Felicity's desire, it will be simple to arrange that she disappears when next she goes abroad.'

'Arrange it,' snapped the Prince, 'and see that it is done tonight. I hold you responsible for her safe keeping, and immediately she is taken see that she is sent at once under guard to me.'

'To hear is to obey, O Flower of Holiness,' cringed the Eunuch, bowing again almost to the ground. 'And the execution of the prisoner here is to take place at my police barracks at nine o'clock?'

'The time is to stand, but take him to your own house. He will be equally safe in the private cell there if he is well guarded, and that will be more convenient for me tomorrow morning. Allah be with you!'

Among a murmur of answering salutations, Prince Ali left the room, and the Eunuch's men immediately began to unlash Swithin from the chair.

Ten minutes later, with his arms still tied behind him, he was hustled into the Eunuch's car and they drove off towards the Bosphorus. Kazdim was in a conversational mood and tried to joke with him again, but all the nervous resilience which had sustained him in the last hour had now drained away. He could think of nothing but Prince Ali's hideous threat concerning Diana.

The journey was a short one, little more than half a mile down the hill to a big villa behind the Dolma Baghtche Palace. When they arrived, Swithin was bundled out, marched through a side door in a high wall, across a good-sized garden, down a few steps to a semi-basement entrance which had a balcony running the whole length of the house above it, along a few yards of passage, and so to a bare, stone-walled room. Malik and Servet pushed him through the door, then slammed and locked it behind them.

He looked round desperately. The place boasted two chairs, a table, and a plank bed. It was about twelve feet square, but little more than seven feet in height, so that the sill of its one window was on a level with his shoulders. He ran to it and peered out. It was heavily barred and faced on to a blank wall opposite, but by thrusting his head as far as possible between the bars, he could just see that below the window there ran a cobbled alleyway. Owing to the house being built on the slope of the hill, the alley was at a lower level than the floor of his room, so no passer-by could look in, and from the window-sill to the cobbles was a ten-foot drop. The bars were thick and solidly set in the ancient stone.

Evening sunlight still flooded through the window at an oblique angle and he guessed it to be about eight o'clock. Diana might be going out to dine or dance at any moment and the Eunuch's men would already be lying in wait for her. The thought was agonising.

For a quarter of an hour he paced frantically up and down, no longer conscious of his hurts, but suffering a far greater mental agony as he bludgeoned his tired wits for some way to break prison in order that he might get a warning to her.

In a fresh wave of distress, he suddenly realised that he was personally responsible for having given her away. Kazdim had traced her easily, of course, through Lykido-pulous. By his own stupidity in asking her to meet him at the Tobacco Depot, he had laid the perfect trail for the police to investigate and follow up. The Greek had known who she was from the beginning, so what could have been easier than for Kazdim to check his description of her with that of the woman who had been going to call for the letter at the *Pera* bookstall—and draw the obvious conclusion? Swithin came near to raving when he fully understood just what his folly in appointing the Tobacco Depot as a place to meet Diana had involved her in. He could easily have selected a dozen other places where no one who saw them would have known her identity and address.

The door opened and Malik came in, bringing a platter of food and water, which he set down on the table. Then he unbound Swithin's arms and bade him eat.

For a second, Swithin thought of grappling with him, but he knew that he had no chance. His arms were still so stiff that it pained him abominably even to move them, so how could he hope to overcome the wiry little Turk, even discounting the fact that the policeman's automatic re-posed, handy in its holster, by his side. Then into the chaotic welter of Swithin's thoughts came the forlorn hope of trying bribery. There was no time to weigh the chances of success, as Malik was already moving to the door.

'Hi! One moment,' Swithin called, and unbuttoning his coat groped with stiff fingers in a pocket of his money belt for a biggish note. It rustled as he pulled it out.

Malik turned and his face showed a quick cupidity as he saw the money. Then, before his prisoner had a chance to parley with him, he drew his gun and snatched at the note.

'Hands up,' he rapped, 'or there is going to be an accident.'

Livid but helpless, Swithin painfully raised his arms shoulder high while the Turk, still covering him, unbuckled his money belt and seizing one end, wrenched it from his waist with a violent jerk.

Swithin made one grab at it and broke into furious protest, but Malik only laughed, jabbed him savagely in the ribs with the barrel of his gun and, having momentarily winded his prisoner, turned contemptuously away. When Swithin got his breath back, the Turk had left the room, locking the door again behind him.

With blinding fury in his heart, Swithin collapsed upon a chair. He felt that he had behaved like an utter, senseless, weak and stupid fool. It had been sheer madness to expose his money to a man whom he was far too weak to tackle—absolutely asking to be robbed—and he had got his full deserts.

His body ached dully from the beating he had received in Prince Ali's house, his head was a whirling nightmare of impotent rebellion. 'Diana and Ali—Diana and Ali—Diana and Ali,' was the one thought which beat like a hammer in his brain. He knew that he had got to do something—do something quickly, not sit there like a senseless imbecile—or he would go stark staring mad. He must hang on to himself and think! think! think!

Only one sane memory emerged from that stupendous effort to concentrate. It came to him that Kazdim's men had not bothered to search him, so he still had the paper giving the list of the Kaka's ammunition depots on him—and the Kaka wafer signed by the members of Arif's cell, yet altered now so that the signatures were unrecognisable. Could he make use of that?—it was just a chance.

Cell organisations work two ways, as he was swift to see, once he thought of it. There were seven thousand people or more who were now members of the Kaka, and the majority probably lived in Constantinople, the ex-capital which had been robbed of its dignity and importance by Kemal. None of them knew with any certainty more than eight of their fellow conspirators, and few of them would even suspect that Kazdim Hari Bekar, the Chief of the dreaded Secret Police, was himself one of their number.

Swithin got out the wafer and gazed at it fascinated. The odds were long, but it held an outside chance. He snatched a crusty piece of bread from the table and, hurrying over to the window, began to scan the alleyway as far in each direction as he could see with straining eyes.

Few people had passed it when he had been peering out before, only two women, a man with a laden ass, and a small boy, in the ten minutes or more that he must have stood there. Now it was silent and empty.

Holding the big hunk of bread ready, he waited anxiously, knowing that the coming of darkness would rob him of this last chance. He must have been in the cell for over an hour already and the light was failing. A woman came into sight just within the orbit of his vision. No good—he let her pass. Five minutes drifted by, a man appeared, a surly looking *hamel*. Swithin was desperately tempted—but refrained, hoping that someone more likely to be a member of the Kaka would come along. As the seconds passed, he cursed himself for having been so slow-witted as not to think of his scheme before, and bitterly regretted that wasted hour of useless raving. Once darkness had fallen, he could say good-bye to any faint hope of his plan succeeding.

A youth on a donkey-barrow laden with vegetables passed beneath the window and, almost immediately after, a young girl went by; then for an interval the alley remained deserted. Swithin stamped with impatience. The sun had set, only its afterglow lingered upon the blank stone opposite, deep shadows were converting the alley into a black-walled pit, then came the sound of shuffling footsteps. A neatly clad old gentleman appeared, hobbling along bent over a stick. Swithin was almost in despair; it was hardly likely that the frail old man could help him, but he knew that this was his last chance, another two minutes and the cobbles would be blurred from his sight by the blackness of the oncoming night. He threw down the piece of bread.

It fell just in front of the old gentleman's feet, he looked up startled and paused in his walk. Swithin stretched out his arm to its full extent between the bars. In his finger and thumb he held Arif's fragile Kaka cell wafer. He released it and it fluttered to the ground.

The ancient stooped painfully and picked it up, examined it by bringing the thing to within a few inches of his short-sighted eyes, and then looked up again.

As he peered down from between his bars, Swithin's heart pounded in his chest. 'Help!' he whispered hoarsely.

'Help! I have been taken prisoner by Kazdim's Secret Police. In the name of Allah, listen. Carry a message for me, I beg—Allah will reward you!'

In that quiet spot the old man must have heard unless he was stone deaf, but he did not reply. He lowered his gaze and shuffled on again until he had disappeared from sight, without once glancing back.

Swithin's grip on the bars relaxed, he staggered away from the window, and collapsed into the chair once more. He had shot his bolt and failed. Despite his Latin temperament, he was not a man given to demonstrative emotion, even when alone, but now he buried his face between his arms upon the table and rocked himself from side to side as the darkness closed about him.

He had failed—failed utterly from the very beginning. By not foreseeing that Tania's was such a likely post for the police to plant a spy, he had given himself away to Kazdim through entrusting her with that letter. By failing to catch and warn Reouf of Kazdim's identity that night when they left the café together, he felt that he had been largely responsible for the poor boy's death. By not troubling to take the most elementary precautions at his flat, he had walked blindly into the arms of the enemy, then, when almost miraculously his life had been spared, he had been crazy enough to place himself in Ali's clutches, where the veriest tyro would at least have taken care to find out the name of the Military Governor of Constantinople before risking a visit to him—and now, by his supreme folly in asking Diana to meet him at the Tobacco Depot, he had given her away to Kazdim, too.

He had failed not only in carrying out his mission, which he realised now was a thing of comparatively small account, since it only concerned investing certain sums of money, but through his incompetence new wars were to be sprung upon an unsuspecting world, and above all—a thing far nearer home—that woman whom he had considered hard and selfish, but who was brave and proud, and whom he now knew that he loved so that he would go down to hell itself to help her, was to be humiliated, befouled, broken and tortured, in body and spirit. His cup of bitterness brimmed and spilled over when he recalled his refusal to take her warning—that he had not the brain or nerve for the job he had taken on so arrogantly—and knew it to be true.

His body exhausted, his brain bemused, tortured by the most horrible imaginings as to what might be happening to Diana, no longer able to string his thoughts together consecutively, he dropped into a nightmare doze, then his head rolled sideways on the table and he was sound asleep.

He awoke with a start, not knowing how long he had slept, but with a feeling that it must be hours later. His mouth tasted horrible, but his brain was clear. The cell was pitch black as he looked round wondering what had roused him, then it came again, a low call from the window.

Lurching to his feet, he groped his way towards it, a man's head and shoulders showed vaguely on the far side of the bars. When he saw Swithin, he spoke in a quick whisper:

'Hist!—my father sent me.'

'Help, brother—help!' muttered Swithin, all his wits flooding back to him. 'These dogs of police seized me and have detained me here. I must escape or send a message, for I am entrusted with Allah's business.'

'I know it—watch the door,' whispered the other. 'I have a file. Cough if you hear anyone coming.'

Swithin said no more, but hastened to the other side of the room and bent, straining his ear for any approaching footfall, while he blessed the inspiration which had led him to drop the Kaka wafer at the feet of the old gentleman. Behind him at the window, the steady music of a grating file as it bit into the iron bar sang a hymn of possible deliverance.

How long he remained crouched by the door he could not tell. It seemed to be for nights on end and it was actually a little over two hours. At last the low call came again and, although he had not realised it with the gradual lightening of his cell, he saw that dawn was not far distant. The window was a square of light and the dark outline of his deliverer's head was now framed in it.

He ran softly across the room and, with the fierce strength of frantic urgency, helped his unknown friend wrench aside the two bars which had been sawn through. Then, feet first, he performed the by no means easy feat of wriggling between them. The stranger lent his aid and pulled him down

227

on to a short ladder which was propped against the wall. Another moment and he was standing in the alley, free— free at last.

His rescuer proved to be a burly youth hardly out of his teens. Swithin asked him his name, but the young man only shook his head and said, 'There are things which Allah's children do for each other in the sight of Allah—and Allah knows all.

Then he returned the Kaka wafer, swung the ladder up on to his shoulder, and marched away as the full light of dawn broke over the surrounding houses.

The faint cry of a Muezzin from a distant minaret, calling the Faithful to prayer, drifted to Swithin on the fresh morning breeze, but he was too accustomed to the musical chanting to take any notice of it. He had already rendered brief but heartfelt thanks for his amazing escape, and now his every thought was centred again on Diana.

If she had not gone out the night before, he might yet warn her in time, and his need to know if she were still safe or not was so pressing that he began to run up the silent alleyway where the full splendour of the new day was now gilding the ancient walls and rounded arches.

He ran and ran through the quiet streets, only slackening his pace, when he had to for lack of breath, to a quick walk, hoping every moment that he would come across an open shop or restaurant, but he covered nearly two miles and reached Galata before, down by the port, he saw an all-night café.

Unheeding the slovenly looking waiter, who was swabbing up the floor of the now empty dive, he barged his way through the stacked-up chairs to a public telephone which hung on the wall at the rear of the premises.

Whatever Diana's orders about never ringing her up, he meant to disregard them on this occasion. He prayed that she might still be sleeping, for even if he roused her what did that matter as long as she was safe? He found the number, gave it, and waited impatiently.

He heard the bell ringing in the house at Bebek, and clung to the wall to support himself, still panting heavily after his long race. It went on ringing—insistent but unanswered.

At last the line clicked and an angry voice came in Turkish: 'Hallo—who is that?—why do you disturb us at this hour?'

Swithin controlled his panting as well as he could and spoke with curt authority: 'I wish to speak to Miss Diana Duncannon. The matter is very urgent.'

'I regret, sir,' came the reply of the startled servant, 'but Miss Duncannon left here last night and she has not since returned.'

22

Love at the Sweet Waters

Swithin plumped himself down at one of the tables in the empty café, beckoned over the waiter, and ordered coffee, European fashion with milk, and rolls. His instinct urged him to dash off again to Prince Ali's house, break in before many people were about, and chance his luck in being able to find Diana; but he knew that, unarmed and single-handed as he was, there could be little hope for such a crude attempt at rescue. Acting on impulse had proved so disastrous before that he now felt it vital to consider every aspect of the situation prior to deciding on his next step.

One thing stood out clearly. Diana had not been arrested—but abducted, and as she was not guilty of any offence against the established government, her detention was illegal. The obvious thing on the face of it, therefore, was to seek the assistance of the police; but Kazdim controlled the police and was using them on behalf of the Kaka, so any appeal in that quarter was worse than useless. Kazdim's direct superior, the Minister of the Interior, would be with Kemal three hundred miles away in Angora, and even if Swithin could have got in touch with him, he saw that the report about Diana's disappearance would only be referred back to Kazdim—who would promise every assistance in tracing her and then promptly sidetrack the inquiry—*unless* the Police Chief were actually charged with her abduction and complicity in the revolutionary conspiracy. That was the course which Swithin felt had the best hope, but the devil of it was that he still lacked any proof to support an accusation against the Eunuch. After looking at the problem from every point of view, he decided that his first move must be to inform Tyndall-Williams at the British Embassy, and thus secure official assistance.

Finishing his coffee, he paid the waiter out of the small change which Malik had left to him, and finding that he had just enough money remaining for a taxi, he hurried out to get one. It was still early yet, however, only a quarter to seven, so no cabs were to be seen, but people were now fairly numerous in the streets and the trams were running. He hopped on one which took him up the hill, covered the last few hundred yards on foot, and turned in through the gates of the British Embassy.

The magnificently clad Kavasses who guard its portals by day were not yet on duty, and the night porter, judging Swithin by his villainous appearance, gave him anything but a cordial reception. Being in no mood to suffer delay, calmly he adopted his most authoritative manner, and insisted on his name being taken up to the first secretary despite the fact that worthy was reported to be still in bed and asleep.

Grumbling a little, the porter showed Swithin into one of the small rooms off the Chancery, and sent a servant who was polishing the floor upstairs to rouse Tyndall-Williams.

On being woken half an hour before his time, the diplomat swore gently to himself, but recognising Swithin's name pulled on a dressing-gown, ran a comb through his sparse brown hair, and came downstairs to interview his visitor.

'So you are Swithin Destime,' he said quietly, once they were alone together. 'Sir George Duncannon told me in a letter two months ago that you might turn up here if you found yourself in some especial difficulty, and Diana has mentioned you to me several times in the last few days in connection with this Kaka business you have unearthed for us.'

'It's about Diana that I'm here,' Swithin shot out at once. 'She's been kidnapped by these devils.'

'Dear me!' Tyndall-Williams' mild blue eyes showed a pained distress. 'That's bad news—however, I think you had better tell me all about it from the beginning.'

'But it's urgent!' Swithin insisted. 'Desperately so! We've got to do something and devilish quick!'

'Of course,' the diplomat soothed him, 'but all the same, since you have been working with her, I should like to hear what you've been up to from the beginning, then I shall be able to place the facts clearly before His Excellency.'

Swithin nodded. 'All right, then. Tell me how far you are acquainted with the work I have been doing and I'll go on from there.'

'Diana told me of her talk with you at the Tobacco Depot two days ago and, from all she said of the Kaka then, it sounds a pretty serious business. We are very anxious to hear more.'

'It is,' Swithin agreed quickly, and launched into a full account of his adventures. At first he had been impatient at Tyndall-Williams' quiet, unhurried air, yet as he proceeded with his story, the diplomat displayed a youthful keenness which he usually concealed under an appearance of bored but distinguished middle-age, and Swithin found considerable comfort in being able to pour out his tale at last to such sympathetic ears.

When he had finished, Tyndall-Williams sat back in his chair and said feelingly, 'By Jove! You *have* had a time!'

'I've made a pretty fine mess of things,' Swithin muttered bitterly.

'Mess! Not at all. I think you have done remarkably well.'

'What? I've been thundering lucky in getting away with my life, of course, but look at this ghastly situation Diana is in—entirely through my stupidity.'

'Don't feel too badly about that,' Tyndall-Williams said earnestly. 'Anybody might have made the same bloomer, and the fact does remain that you have performed a pretty remarkable piece of work in getting all these particulars of the Kaka for us.'

'But damn it, man! What are we going to do about Diana?—that's what's driving me insane.'

The diplomat's mild blue eyes hid the fact that he had soon assessed Swithin's personal interest in the missing lady, but his voice was very kind as he said, 'I know—I can guess what you must be feeling, and if you are right about Prince Ali I agree that the affair doesn't bear thinking about. Still, he must be very heavily occupied with this revolution so close at hand, and the probabality is that he won't have any time to devote to his fair prisoner for the moment. I'll get on the telephone to Allan Duncannon's house and find out all the particulars about her disappearance that I can. As a matter of fact, I am rather surprised that they have not reported it to us already.'

He got the number, asked a few questions, listened intently for a little, then hung up the receiver and turned back to Swithin.

'That's queer! Allan Duncannon did not return home either last night, nor did his daughter Ursula. They both went out with Diana after dinner—about nine o'clock.'

Swithin brightened. 'Well, it's some consolation to think that her uncle is with her, anyway.'

'I take an even better view of it than that. Tyndall Williams remarked hopefully. 'Quite possibly all three of them stayed the night with friends.'

'Surely they would have telephoned to the house if they decided to do that.'

'Not necessarily. There is no one else in the family who might be alarmed for them, and if it were late, after a dance perhaps, Duncannon may not have thought it worth while digging the servants out of bed to say that they did not mean to return until this morning.'

'How about clothes?'

'They would send for those this morning—it's early yet —only a little after half-past seven, you know.'

Swithin shook his head gloomily. 'It's possible, of course, but rather unlikely, unless there was some special reason which kept them out very late quite unexpectedly.'

'Maybe. Anyhow, this is a good sign. You know the revolution hasn't taken place yet, so Ali and Kazdim are not actually in power. They might risk staging the disappearance of a single girl like Diana, and offer half a dozen different reasons to account for it. A secret romance for one, with the suggestion that she had eloped with somebody, or that some Turk had developed a passion for her and taken extreme measures—such things have happened in Istanbul before now, you know—or even that she had been white-slaved—but I hardly think they would risk kidnapping a prominent man like Allan Duncannon and his daughter into the bargain. That would be infinitely more difficult to explain away.'

'Perhaps you're right,' Swithin agreed despondently, 'but we can't remain in this awful state of uncertainty. What the hell are we going to do?'

Tyndall-Williams stood up and laid his hand gently on

Swithin's shoulder. 'You are going to leave things to me for a bit while you come upstairs, have a good hot bath, and then a few hours' rest on my bed.'

'I can't.' Swithin protested. 'I've got to find her somehow, and if your inquiries don't bring any result I'm going out myself to have a cut at Prince Ali's house—can you lend me a gun?'

'No, only a safety-razor. You're just about all in, my dear fellow, so if you want to be any real help you must take a few hours off to get your wind back while I rout round and have a talk with H.E.'

Swithin was horribly reluctant to give in, but his common sense told him that Tyndall-Williams was undoubtedly right. He had been through so much during the last forty-eight hours that he was virtually at the end of his tether. Only by taking a short spell off could he possibly hope to recruit his energy sufficiently to enter the field effectively again.

Upstairs, he dragged the thick sailor clothes from his stiff limbs, shaved his two days' beard, and tumbled into a warm bath, where he luxuriated for a quarter of an hour. Then he returned to Tyndall-Williams' room and found that the bed had been remade with clean sheets and pyjamas laid out for him.

The diplomat came in just as Swithin was climbing into bed. 'I've spoken to the chief,' he said, 'and he is going to get on to Kemal personally. That is the devil of the Gazi having shifted the capital to Angora. It means our running two Embassies. Of course, we live at Angora in the winter, but it is a god-forsaken spot and impossible in the summer, so we come back here, and then we are always up against the difficulty of having to use the long-distance telephone instead of being able to see people on matters of urgency. We are sending a report through and the list that you secured for us of secret ammunition stores—which are to be distributed tonight—by special plane. He should receive them by midday.'

'If only he'll take your word for it,' Swithin muttered. 'It's a tall order to expect him to believe that his own trusted friends—people like Prince Ali—are out to do him in, when we can't offer a shred of proof.'

234

'Well, we may have some news by the time you wake up.'

Swithin turned over in the comfortable bed. 'Look here, I want you to promise me one thing. I meant to ask you downstairs.'

'What is it?'

'To wake me in two hours from now. That will be enough sleep to put me on my feet again, and I can't bear the thought of being idle longer while we don't know what's happened to Diana.'

'All right, I will.'

'Thanks.'

As Tyndall-Williams made the promise Swithin shut his eyes. The very next moment, it seemed to him, the diplomat was shaking him by the shoulder and saying. 'Your two hours are up.'

He stirred and rolled over as the other added, 'I've got some good news for you. Sir George Duncannon is downstairs.'

'By Jove! Where did he spring from?' Swithin exclaimed, wide awake at once.

'He came in on his yacht last night, and he sent for his brother Allan and the two girls immediately he arrived, so that he could hear the latest news. They did not get on board till half-past ten and sat talking until well past two; then, as it would have taken them an hour or more to get back to Bebek, they decided to spend the night on the yacht.'

'Diana's safe, then?'

'Yes.' A kind smile lit the diplomat's mild blue eyes for a second. 'I'm afraid you've had your scare for nothing. But Sir George is anxious to see you, so if you feel fit enough, you had better get up now.'

'Rather. I'm still a bit sore and stiff, but that two hours' nap has made all the difference.'

'Good.' Tyndall-Williams pointed to some clothes neatly folded on a nearby chair. 'I thought Kazdim's people might recognise you in your seaman's get-up next time you go out, so I got these instead. They are hardly likely to be looking for a chauffeur in plain livery. You'll find some money in the inside pocket, too, as they cleaned you out.'

'Thanks most awfully!' Swithin scrambled out of bed

and began to don his new disguise. The uniform was a little large for him, but that was a minor matter, and a few minutes later he followed Tyndall-Williams downstairs.

Sir George was with the Ambassador, Sir Francis Cavendish, a short, rotund, red-faced little man, to whom he introduced Swithin at once, while Tyndall-Williams disappeared to make a telephone call. Then the banker said heartily:

'My dear Destime, I'm proud of having discovered you, but I knew the very moment I saw you that I had picked the right man for this job. You have rendered an inestimable service, not only to British banking interests but also to your country.'

'That's nice of you, sir.' Swithin hesitated. 'I was afraid that I had bungled things pretty badly—especially last night.'

'On the contrary, Captain Destime,' Sir Francis Cavendish remarked. 'I think you have put up a remarkably fine show. If only Kemal will act on this information which we have been able to supply through your efforts, it may be the means of averting an extremely grave situation.'

'Your Excellency is most kind, but that seems to me the real trouble. *Will* Kemal act without any proof that my whole story is not a complete fabrication.'

The Ambassador nodded. 'I appreciate your point, and unfortunately the people in Angora tell me that Kemal left there last night for an unknown destination; but I spoke to Ismet Pasha, whose loyalty is beyond question, on the telephone this morning, and he will receive your list of the secret armament depots by midday. I understand, too, that you have hopes of securing this—er—Kaka wafer before tonight, and *that,* signed by five leaders of the conspiracy, will be absolute proof of their treasonable intentions.'

'Yes, sir. It bears the actual oath of the Revolutionaries inscribed upon it, and this French woman in Prince Ali's household has found out where he keeps it. The only thing is that, even if she succeeds in her part of the job, I cannot get hold of her until this evening. Won't that be a little late for it to be of any use to us?'

'No, no. Night-flying over the mountains in Asia Minor is unfortunately impossible, but I shall arrange for a private plane to be ready to leave at dawn tomorrow. Kemal, or

Ismet in his absence, will receive it by about nine o'clock in the morning, and as the Revolution is not due to break out until midnight, there would still be time for them to take measures against it.'

'In that case, sir, of course I'll do my very best to bring this vital piece of evidence in.'

'Fine—my boy—fine!' beamed Sir George, 'and I cannot congratulate you too heartily on the splendid work you have done. Diana was giving me details of it last night—a most glowing account.'

'Diana,' cried Swithin suddenly. 'Where is she?'

The Banker looked puzzled for a moment, then he said, 'Why, she left us when we came ashore and went off on her own—but, of course—she was going to pick up a further report from *you* at the Mosque of the Sweet Waters.'

'Good God! but don't you realise . . .'

'Of course!' Sir Francis cut in. 'If she is wandering about on her own, Kazdim's people may arrest her.'

'Surely not!' exclaimed Sir George. 'She has not committed any crime. The police can have nothing against her.'

Swithin shook his head quickly. 'They had nothing against me *officially*, but they arrested me just the same—and tried to kill me. They meant to arrest Diana last night, and can only have refrained because when she went down to the yacht her uncle was with her.'

The Ambassador nodded. 'Yes. They evidently didn't like the idea of arresting Allan as well, and knew that if they took the girl without him, he would have come straight here. Then they would have had to answer an immediate protest from the Embassy.'

'But in broad daylight . . .' Sir George began.

Swithin snatched up his peaked cap. 'She will be in danger every moment she remains in Istanbul, now they know that she has been working with me against the Kaka. I must try and get hold of her at once.'

'If you find her, bring her back here. She will be safe in the Embassy, but nowhere else,' Sir Francis called after him as he hurried from the room.

In the hall he caught sight of a clock. It was a quarter past ten, and he knew that he would have all his work cut out to reach the 'Sweet Waters of Europe' by eleven o'clock, the time of his appointment with Diana. He fled down the steps of the Embassy, along the drive, and dashed out of the gates.

An empty taxi was just passing at cruising speed, so he leapt on to the running board, told the taxi man where he wished to go—and to drive like hell—then he swung himself into the cab.

As he turned to bang the door behind him, he suddenly caught sight of Malik, staring at him from the pavement just outside the Embassy gates. Kazdim's lieutenant jumped into the roadway, shouted to a policeman on a nearby street corner, and they both began to run after the cab, yelling and gesticulating.

By the mercy of heaven, Swithin's driver, already visualising a large tip from his passenger's request for speed, had not seen them, and almost immediately switched his cab down towards the *Petits Champs*. The taxi was new and fast, it turned another corner, and Swithin sat back with a sharp breath of relief.

Malik, he guessed, had been sent to watch the Embassy, to see if he tried to take refuge there and if so arrest him before he could get in; knowing that once he was inside he would be able to claim immunity from arrest as being on English soil. Only the fact that he had come *out* instead, which Malik was obviously not expecting, and the speed of his sudden exit had saved him; but it had been a narrow squeak, and he realised with new apprehension that his last bolthole had been closed to him. If he attempted to go in again, they would get him for certain.

He leaned out of the window and gave his driver a new direction, telling him that he had changed his mind about going to the Sweet Waters and would go out there another day. Then halfway down to the Old Bridge, he stopped the cab and, blessing Tyndall-Williams for his thoughtful provisions of new funds, paid the man off. The driver might think him a mad Englishman, but that did not matter; if Malik had taken the number of the cab and telephoned police headquarters to have it stopped, they would not find him in it when they caught it.

He dived round another corner on foot, picked up a second taxi, ordered the man to drive to Kassim Pasha Street, abandoned the second cab there, picked up a third immediately the second was out of sight, and told the new man to drive as though Iblis were after him to the Mosque of the Sweet Waters.

By these manœuvres Swithin felt fairly certain that he must have thrown Malik off his trail, and his thoughts immediately reverted to Diana.

His principal fear was that she had been recognised when she came ashore that morning and followed by Kazdim's men immediately she separated from her father. If so, she had been in their net for the past hour. On the other hand, the Sweet Waters being right up at the extreme landward end of the Golden Horn, it took the best part of an hour and a half to reach them by *caïque* from Galata Bridge. She could not have landed much before half past nine, so the chances were that she had set off up the Golden Horn at once, and if she had escaped recognition by the port police, it would have to be a very evil chance indeed for her to be spotted in a small boat on the water.

The taxi rattled on past the Naval Arsenal at Haskeuy and through the suburb of Abouselam, but he could only guess the time, and that filled him with additional anxiety. If Diana had escaped the police at the port, but failed to find him when she arrived at the meeting place, she might assume that he was not coming and return to the centre of the city. The Eunuch would be sure to have men on the look-out for her at the *Pera*, the *Tokatlian*, Allan Duncannon's house, and all the places which she was likely to visit, so she would then fall into their hands owing to his lateness in keeping the appointment.

At last the taxi pulled up in front of the wooden Mosque by the confluence of the two rivers where they flow into the Golden Horn at the place of the Sweet Waters. As Swithin jumped out, a man came up to him and asked if he wished to see the Dervishes dance. He replied that he did and was led inside.

It was a large building and its interior was similar to that of an ordinary Mosque except for a wide, very highly polished floor in its centre, which was enclosed by a low rail. Beyond, wooden platforms covered with piles of Persian rugs formed accommodation for the congregation, and seated on them were a considerable number of guests—principally Turks.

Swithin ran his eyes quickly over them, but could not see Diana. He found to his relief that he was in good time after all, so he prayed that she was on her way, but had not yet arrived. Along the wall behind the rostrum was a row of windows latticed in wood from which he knew, in the old days when they were secluded from any eye except that of their husband, Turkish women used to watch the ceremony. Thinking it a good place to keep a look-out for Diana without being observed himself, he made his way to one of the windows through a series of little side rooms.

The ceremony was just about to commence. Twenty male dancers of all ages and types, dressed in long flowing robes, barefooted and befezzed, entered the main room in single file. On the far side of the floor was seated the Mullah, and the leader of the dancers having bowed before him moved off, slowly gyrating in a circle at a speed rather like that of a top at the end of its spin. One by one, the others followed, and within a few moments all twenty of them were whirling round and round in their own orbit, each keeping an equal distance from his neighbour, and all travelling in a uniform oval formation round a wide elipse.

Swithin kept an anxious watch on the main door, only glancing now and again at the dancers. As they span, all consciousness seemed to fade from their faces and they became like lifeless bodies obeying some strange unknown law which kept them spinning round and round without any reason known to the human mind. Beads of perspiration trickled off their feet until the entire track of the elipse was slippery with human dampness. Sometimes they increased their pace until their gowns swirled about their waists. Some of them span with their arms stretched upright above their heads and at times they leant outward until their bodies seemed almost parallel with the floor.

Suddenly Swithin saw Diana come in. Overjoyed to know that she had escaped so far, he left his post and, hastening round, managed to intercept her before she reached the crowded rostrum.

'So the Red Knight has kept his tryst,' she said in a low voice, smiling as he came up to her.

'Yes, by the luck of the gods,' he grinned. 'He has been taken twice since we talked chess at the Tobacco Depot, but he managed to pop out of the box and back on to the board again—but we've got to get back to Pera. The White Queen is in danger.'

She shot him a quick glance. 'From the Red Knight?'

'I wish he could think so and that she had nothing worse to fear—but the Brontosaurus is after her—come on!'

'Is the danger here?'

'It's everywhere now in Istanbul except at the British Embassy, and I've got to get you there as quickly as possible.'

She smiled again and followed his lead—dropping their verbal imagery. 'If it is not actually coming round the corner then, do let's stay here for a few moments. I'd like to watch the dancing.'

He hesitated. 'I'd rather we headed for the Embassy right away.'

'No, please. I'll come quite quietly now you have turned policeman—but it is two days since I have seen you. Surely you don't dislike me so much that you want to get rid of me immediately?'

'Good Lord, no!' he exclaimed fervently. 'It's only that I have been absolutely worried out of my wits about you.'

'I've been worried about you, too,' she confessed, 'and I can see you've been fighting from all the horrid cuts and bruises on your poor face. Do tell me what you've been up to.'

'All right, then, but let's get behind the scenes and watch the show from one of those latticed windows. Then if anyone we don't want to see does walk in, at least we shall have a chance of spotting them before they see us.'

Swithin led her through the side rooms, and when they were comfortably ensconced in his old position, he gave her a brief account of all that had happened to him. The Dervishes were still gyrating. Some of them were now frothing at the mouth. After a time, one suddenly collapsed and fell face downwards on the floor. He lay there inert, but the dance continued. Another fell and then another, until there were no more than a dozen left whirling round the slippery boards. All at once the remaining dancers stopped dead in their tracks, formed into single file, passed before the seated Mullah, bowing low, and walked right out of the building. The others, rigid insensible forms, remained outstretched upon the floor. The ceremony was over.

'You poor dear—you have had a ghastly time,' Diana exclaimed as Swithin finished his recital, 'but you have performed marvels.'

'You really think I've—well put up a fairly decent show?' he asked, flushing with pleasure.

'I've never met an old hand at the game, or a new, who could have done better.'

'Do you—do you really mean that, Diana?' he insisted, half afraid that she was only mocking him again, yet impressed despite himself by the ring in her voice.

'I do,' she assured him. 'Of course, it's easy now to take back all the rotten things I said to you, and you won't think any better of me for it, but I was very mean and stupid and unkind, when I ought to have tried to encourage and help you more in a most difficult undertaking.'

'Nonsense!' he protested. 'Once we really got started, you did everything for me that you possibly could. You've been marvellous.'

She shook her head. 'I wish I could think so—but anyhow, thank goodness it's all finished now. We'll go and sit in the British Embassy until the trouble is over. Neither of us has done anything against the Turkish Government, so we have nothing to fear and in a few days we will be on our way home again.'

'I'm afraid it's not quite finished yet,' Swithin demurred. 'I've got to meet Arif tonight and get Ali's Kaka wafer from him—if Jeanette managed to get it. If I can pull that off, I really shall have succeeded—but not before.'

'No! no!' she turned to him impulsively. 'You have done enough—more than enough. It's someone else's turn now. One of the regular people from the Embassy can meet Arif.'

'That wouldn't be much good. None of them know him and even if they recognised him from my description he would never trust them. I've got to go myself. Besides, that piece of paper is Prince Ali's death warrant, so I've a personal interest in collecting it.'

'No . . . please,' she begged, 'you mustn't. It is a desperate risk now that they are hunting for you all over Constantinople. Please don't, Swithin—you simply mustn't take any more chances. Not knowing what has been happening to you these last two nights has been hell—please don't—I love you so.'

For a second he could hardly believe that she had said those words. Then he looked at her and saw that her eyes were brimming with unshed tears.

'Diana! Do you really mean that?' he asked breathlessly.

'You pig! Of course I do!' The tears brimmed over and came running down her cheeks.

'Oh, my dear! I didn't know—how could I?'

'You—you—you never believe anything unless it's thrust in front of you—do you—and you hate me, anyway,' her voice ended in a sob and she half turned away.

'Hate you! Good God, I adore the very ground you walk on!' He gripped her arms and pulled her clumsily towards him.

Then, sheltered from view by the lattice which had screened the ladies of the harem in years gone by, they clung together, greedy for each other's caresses; unheeding of time, place, or danger, in the ecstasy that the opening of the floodgates of their long suppressed emotions had let loose.

At last they drew apart. Diana dried her tears on a minute handkerchief and stammered, 'You—you stupid little man—why didn't you say you—you cared for me before?'

He laughed happily. 'You great big gawk of a girl. Why didn't you give me half a chance? You never have since that afternoon when we had tea together at Belgrave Square—and I did my stuff that day.'

'But I hardly knew you then and I had to be certain.'

They stared at each other, blind to their surroundings and everything except their own happiness; kissed again with sudden mutual passion and remained locked together with closed eyes. Then, breathless from their embrace, they separated again, and Diana said faintly, 'We needn't go back yet, need we? There is a ruined palace here and lovely gardens—aren't there? Let's stroll round them arm-in-arm so that I can really feel I've got you with me for a little while. I'll have to be alone and desperately anxious for you again so soon.'

'Whatever you wish, my sweet.' He drew her arm through his, opened the fingers of her hand, and passing his own between them pressed his palm to her. Then they sauntered back through the dim side chambers of the old Mosque to its front entrance. 'Darling, I want to hear you say "I love you so" just as you did before,' he said suddenly.

'I love you so,' she murmured. 'I have from the very beginning, I think.'

'Even on the yacht?' The second he had said the words he could have bitten out his tongue for asking the now pointless question, but she had already unclasped his hand and withdrawn her arm.

'So you still don't trust me?' Her voice was high-pitched, resentful, bitter, but he had no chance to answer.

As they came out into the sunshine they both saw Sir George Duncannon and Tyndall-Williams walking towards them from a big closed Daimler which was parked some fifty yards away. Then another car came racing round the corner and pulled up with a jerk. Swithin recognised the driver immediately. It was the first taxi that he had taken when he ran out of the Embassy. Almost before it was at a standstill, Malik and two other policemen jumped out of it.

'Quick,' he cried, grabbing Diana's arm and pulling her back into the entrance of the Mosque. 'The police—they've traced my taxi and followed in it.'

She wrenched him forward again. 'This way! Daddy's come in the Ambassador's car—it's the same as Embassy soil—we'll be immune from arrest if we reach it—for God's sake, run!'

Tyndall-Williams, Sir George, Swithin, Diana, Malik, and the other policemen all started forward together from different directions. They collided about ten yards from the Daimler, Diana dodged one of the policemen neatly and jumped on to the running board. Tyndall-Williams got in Malik's way and they both tumbled in a heap. Sir George added to the general confusion. Swithin shook off the man who grabbed him—thrust Diana into the car and sprawled in beside her. A moment later, Sir George joined them.

Tyndall-Williams picked himself up, lightly dusted down his grey lounge suit, and then turned his attention to Malik, who was angrily protesting against this obstruction of arrest.

'If you care,' said the diplomat quietly, 'to report the matter through the proper channels, doubtless your protest will receive the attention of the Embassy in due course.' Then he turned his back and calmly got into the car.

The Daimler's engine purred and, with a superior glance at Malik, the cockney chauffeur let in the clutch. The Turk stood watching with impotent fury blazing in his eyes. He would cheerfully have given five years of his life to be able to draw his gun and haul Swithin out of the car at the point of it—but he dared not. A small silk Union Jack fluttered gaily from a slim silver staff on the Daimler's bonnet. No policeman—be he black, white, yellow, or brown, lays hands with impunity upon the property of His Britannic Majesty's accredited representatives the wide world over—and Malik knew it. Stirred by profound emotion, he spat, while Swithin, no less stirred by the portentous meaning of that little flag, looked away quickly and lit a cigarette.

As the Daimler gathered speed, Tyndall-Williams glanced back out of the rear window and remarked, 'It was darned lucky for you H.E. had the idea of sending me after you in his car, but they are following us. What do you intend to do now?'

'Drive straight back to the Embassy,' said Sir George promptly.

'That's all very well—but if we once take Destime in, they will arrest him immediately he comes out again—and he has got to be down at Galata this evening on a very important matter.'

'I know,' Swithin agreed. 'You must drop me somewhere on the way. Then I'll lie low till I have to turn up for my appointment with Arif.'

'No, no!' Diana exclaimed. 'Those policemen behind will see you get out. I won't let you.'

Tyndall-Williams was still peering out of the small window at the back. 'They've only got a taxi,' he said, 'and we're gaining on them already. Tell our man to drive as fast as he can, Destime—then we'll increase our lead. If we can put a few streets between us when we come to the houses, you ought to be able to drop off without being seen.'

'Right!' Swithin gave swift instructions to the driver, and the big car leapt forward. Then he turned back to Tyndall-Williams. 'Look here—there is one thing you can do for me.'

'What?'

'Swop clothes. They will be looking for me in this chauffeur's uniform, so if there is another agent on the gate, he will think I have gone to earth in the Embassy again when he sees you drive in, besides I should be far less likely to be spotted in your lounge suit.'

For a moment the diplomat stared blankly, then he glanced at Diana.

'Go on!' she said sharply. 'I've seen thousands of men in nothing but their bathing shorts—what *does* it matter if I see you in your pants.'

'All right,' he murmured. 'But I'm glad that secretaries to the Embassy don't have to do this every day.'

As the Daimler sped through Abouselam the two men exchanged clothes. Another few moments and they were entering Haskeuy. The taxi had dropped out of sight behind them.

'I'm getting out here,' said Swithin, putting his hand on the door latch of the car.

'Oh, darling!' whispered Diana, and her eyes were full of tears again.

Her father looked at her in mild astonishment and she caught his glance. 'Darling,' she repeated. 'That's what I said. The man's a jealous, untrusting brute—but I call him darling just the same.' In nervous misery, she clasped her hands together and clenched them tightly.

They were in a quiet street. The car slowed down. Swithin smiled at Diana, then while it was still moving at a running pace he dropped off on to the pavement. Its speed increased again and it sped away. Diana only caught his parting murmur of 'Bless you, sweet,' and the next moment he had disappeared from view up a narrow alley.

By devious ways, learned weeks before when he had been a nightly visitor to the Haskeuy quarter, Swithin made his way to the small wine shop which he had frequented for a time with the Russian workmen.

Having reached it safely, he dived down the few steps from the steet and took refuge in the gloomiest corner of the low, vaulted room. It was dark and cool in there after the glare of the midday sun, but he feared for a moment that the clothes he was now wearing, ill as they fitted him, would attract unwelcome attention from the sullen waitress who came over to take his order. The sartorial elegance of Savile Row must be a rare phenomenon among her shabby customers. However, she served him without any manifestation of interest, and, as he settled himself with as much outward calmness as he could muster, he blessed her dull, apathetic brain.

Fortunately, the vault was practically deserted and remained so. A few men in blouses entered it now and again, bought a drink, talked together for a little, and then went out again. None of them came near Swithin's table and, after half an hour, he was able to take fresh courage from the thought that he had eluded Malik successfully. It was now a matter of patience. Just sitting there doing nothing until the time came when he would have to venture forth to meet Arif.

He repeated his drink order, and asked for a double portion of the greasy pilaff which was the main dish on the day's bill of fare, thus guarding against any inclination on the part of the owner of the place to turn him out after he had been there a certain time, then, when he had eaten, he lay back in his corner against the wall and pretended to go to sleep.

Although he never allowed himself actually to drop off, he remained for a long time in a semi-doze, but all his thoughts were conscious and centred about Diana. If only he could get safely through this business, what times they would have together! His dash of Latin temperament almost made him cry himself as he thought again of the tears she had shed in the Mosque. In his imagination, he could feel them damp on his cheek as they had been when he had first taken her in his arms and pressed her face against his own.

At three o'clock, he roused again and ordered another drink. He reckoned that it would take him no more than an hour to reach Galata, even on foot as he meant to go, so there was no point in leaving the wine shop before five. It was far safer to remain there in comparative security than to risk wandering about the open street.

For a long time he considered what his next move had better be if Jeanette had succeeded and Arif was actually able to hand over the Kaka wafer. The approaches to the British Embassy would almost certainly be guarded again by Kazdim's men. Swithin wished now that he had thought of that before jumping out of the Daimler, and asked Tyndall-Williams to have the car sent to meet him somewhere so that it could run him safely in, but the time they had been together had been so short and almost entirely occupied by changing clothes. Eventually he decided that it would be madness to risk trying to get into the Embassy again and that a far better plan would be to slip quietly off to the *Golden Falcon* and lie low there until Sir George or Tyndall-Williams could join him.

The last hour of his wait seemed never ending, but it dragged itself away in time, and towards the end of it he began to get restless and excited. His nerves were keyed up to the highest pitch by the knowledge that Diana loved him. He felt himself omnipotent—capable of quick thought and swift, sure action.

Just before five he ordered a final drink, eager now for the final effort that lay before him, and pulling Tyndall-Williams' smart Homberg well down over his eyes, left his refuge.

The journey to Galata was uneventful. He kept to side streets practically the whole way, and there were plenty of them in that teeming quarter of the city. At the bridge, he found the Café Athéné without difficulty, but was a little worried at the thought that Arif had not suggested a more discreet meeting place. Beneath its striped awning five rows of tables occupied the broad pavement; most of them were taken, and inside the building quite a number of people were already seated at an early evening meal, but his momentary anxiety at the publicity of the spot was forgotten in his delight at finding that Arif had kept the appointment and that Jeanette was with him.

They were at a table in the back row, right at the end and partly sheltered from observation by a row of small bay trees in brass-bound tubs, which divided the Café Athéné's length of pavement from that of its next-door neighbour.

As Swithin joined them and took a chair with its back to the street, he thought that Jeanette looked pale and tired, and Arif grey-faced and miserable, but they both cheered up on his arrival. The Turk ordered him a coffee from a passing waiter, and then, leaning forward, said in a hasty whisper:

'So you are safe. We were out of our wits because Jeanette told me that you had been . . . well, after that which befell you last night, we feared not to see you again. We came here not knowing what else to do. Allah has indeed been merciful.'

'He has,' Swithin agreed in a low voice. 'Last night I thought it was all up with me, but I've been counting all day on Mam'selle Jeanette having heard that I got clear this morning, and letting you know. I'm darned glad you came here this evening on the chance of my luck holding. Have you . . .'

Arif nodded. 'Jeanette has got it.'

'Well done!' exclaimed Swithin.

She tapped his knee under the table and then pressed a small flat parcel into his hand. He took it quickly and slipped it into his inside pocket, as he inquired eagerly, 'Where did our friend keep it?'

'Roun' 'is neck,' she murmured, 'in a locket—on a ribbon. 'E was a little drunk when 'e come 'ome lars night an' I made 'im more so. Later, when 'e was asleep, I cut the ribbon an' take it off 'im.'

'She stole out of the house and came over to me at Scutari in the middle of the night,' Arif added. 'She dare not go back. The police will have been hunting for her all day and I tremble to think what those devils will do to her if they catch her.'

'That's bad,' Swithin made a wry grimace. 'What do you mean to do?'

'I have drawn all my money out of the bank and we must leave Turkey at once—but how?'

Swithin considered for a moment, then he said softly, 'There is a yacht in the harbour. It is called the *Golden Falcon* and belongs to Sir George Duncannon. I am going off to it as soon as I can. You would be safe there—anyhow for the time being. I think it would be best if we separate at once, though. As they are looking for Mam'selle and myself now, there will be less chance of us being caught if we do not remain together.'

She nodded quickly, and Swithin went on, 'The *Golden Falcon,* remember, owned by Sir George Duncannon. When you arrive, ask for the captain. Harold Wortley is his name, say I sent you and tell him I said that you were to remain there until I turn up or you have seen Sir George. He knows all about this business, so he will look after you both if I fail to make it. You had better go now. I'll pay for the coffee and remain here until you have had a good start.'

They both stood up. 'I thank you, my brother,' said Arif. 'I have entrusted my future wife and myself to you, and you have not failed us. We are very deeply grateful.'

'Nonsense,' Swithin replied, a trifle self-consciously. I'll see you again under the hour, I hope—good luck.'

When they had gone he sat on for a little, toying with his coffee. As he pressed his upper arm against his chest, he could feel the little locket which held the wafer, a small, hard bulge in his breast pocket. The joy of success warmed him like a glass of wine. If he could only reach the yacht safely, he was through with his share in this desperate business now.

Casually he looked through the half-lowered glass screen at the early diners seated at the long rows of tables in the interior of the café. One man was stuffing macaroni into his mouth with amazing speed. Arif's body had concealed him from Swithin's view before. The man's profile seemed vaguely familiar.

Suddenly he turned his head and looked straight at Swithin. Recognition was instantaneous and mutural. It was Lykidopulous.

The Greek bounced up from his table, dropping his fork with a clatter. Swithin sprang to his feet a split second later and barged his way out through the crowd on to the edge of the pavement. As he turned to the right, he caught a glimpse of Lykidopulous in the doorway of the café, shouting:

'Stop! Police!—that man is wanted by the police! Stop him!'

Dodging through the crowd, Swithin covered thirty yards in as many seconds, then he glanced back. The crowd in front of the café were staring after him. Half of them were already on their feet. A table crashed over in the middle of them. A policeman had appeared and was blowing his whistle. Lykidopulous was on the pavement pounding after him, a small mob of people at his heels, all yelling at the top of their voices.

Swithin thrust a man out of his path, dug his elbows into his sides, and began to run—literally for his life.

23

The Man Hunt

Swithin had turned to the right as he dashed from the café.
Now he turned right again into a narrow street leading
away from the waterfront. A moment later, he realised that
he had blundered. It ran steeply uphill, bad going for a
hunted man with fresh pursuers likely to join the mob at
every street corner. However, he was free of the crowd, so
able to increase his lead a little before the others reached
the turning.

As he padded up the hill, he threw a swift glance over
his shoulder. A policeman was leading, with a lanky
youth beside him. Another policeman was not far behind,
and then came a bunch of people headed by Lykidopulous.

With fury in his heart, Swithin wished damnation on the
Greek. He saw that it was natural enough for the man to
take delight in raising this hue-and-cry after the way he had
pried so persistently into affairs at the Tobacco Depot, but
what evil luck to have come to the Café Athéné as a
rendezvous, and that Lykidopulous should have been feeding there that evening. Then he cursed himself for not
having thought of such an eventuality when Arif had first
mentioned it as a meeting place for Greek business men.
It was only just round the corner from Tophane Street,
the heart of the business quarter, and he should have remembered that Lykidopulous came in to negotiate deals
there at least twice a week. But self-reproach was useless
now.

Halfway up the hill he caught sight of an arcade on his
left and, swerving, dived into it. The easier going gave
him a chance to increase his lead still more. He flew down
its fifty yards of deserted length and dashed out of the far
end just as the shouting mob entered it after him. Again he
turned right, up towards Pera, but this time he had little
option; a small crowd blocked the way lower down outside
a cheapjack shop where a street auction was in progress.

As his pursuers surged out of the arcade the street auction broke up at this new excitement, and the idlers who had been watching it joined in the chase.

Swithin glanced back again. The knot of a dozen people who had started after him from the waterfront was now a bunch of thirty. The policeman and the lanky youth were still leading—from the ease with which he ran, the latter looked as if he were a trained athlete. Lykidopulous had dropped behind and was hidden in the pack. Again Swithin cursed his ill-luck in having been spotted by the Greek and realised that his change of clothes with Tyndall-Williams had been responsible for landing him in this wretched situation.

If he had only remained in the chauffeur's uniform, or been dressed in one of his old rigs as seaman or mechanic, it was highly improbable that he would have been recognised, but Tyndall-Williams' light grey Savile Row production was very similar in colour to his own lounge suit in which he had visited the Tobacco Depot so often. Naturally Lykidopulous had known him again immediately.

He shot into an alley to the left, and again made easier going on the level stretch. Fortunately his long years of army training had kept him strong and supple. He had been battered about pretty badly in these last two hectic days, but he knew that he must have slept several hours the night before in the cell at the Eunuch's house and, in addition to his long rest in the wine-shop all that afternoon, he had had a spell of real refreshing sleep at the Embassy in the morning, so he was feeling far better than at any time since Kazdim had had him thrown down the shaft in the Marble Tower.

Suddenly he came out of the alley into the Street of Steps and found himself about two-thirds of the way up it. In gradient it differed little from the others he had just traversed in the same direction. Each step was shallow and separated from the next by a yard of cobbles. Before he noticed a policeman who was slowly walking up towards him, he had bounded down two of them. Then, knowing that the man would be certain to try and intercept his wild flight, he pulled himself up with a jerk, spun round, and bolted up the hill again.

As he passed the alley he had just come down he saw that

he had lost a good twenty yards of his lead. The athletic youth had now outdistanced the others, who followed some way behind, jammed together in the close-walled passage.

Swithin put on a fresh spurt, managed another eighty yards of the hill, and switched down a narrow turning to the left. To his horror he saw that it contained a small fruit and vegetable market, where a number of people were making purchases from stalls erected in front of a row of grimy shops. He hesitated a second, thinking of continuing up the Street of Steps, but that last dash up the slope had taken it out of him badly. The mob was straggling up the hill and the rear of it was still pouring out of the alley, but the tall youth was thirty yards ahead of the rest and no more than twenty from the entrance of the market. Swithin's momentary pause decreased the distance by a half, and seeing it was too late to turn he dashed forward among the shoppers.

From the first stall in the street he grabbed an apple, then he turned suddenly and flung it. Once more his cricket ing days stood him in good stead. With the velocity of a rocket it struck the pursuing youth full in the right eye. He let out a yell, slipped sideways, and went sprawling in the gutter.

'That's settled him,' thought Swithin savagely, and then, 'poor kid, he's not to blame—I'm devilish sorry'; but the shop assistant at the stall had seen the episode and with a loud cry roused the whole street.

People paused in their bargaining to look round, and saw a panting, sweating, hatless figure in grey come charging in amongst them. One man tried to trip him and got a blow on the ear for his pains which sent him crashing sideways, another grabbed at his shoulder, but Swithin had played rugger as well as cricket, and side-stepping with practised skill raced on.

He was nearly through the market when the original mob entered the street at the far end. Some of the shoppers had joined in the chase and there was now the best part of a hundred angry, shouting people at his heels. His wind was going and he knew that unless he did something desperate he could not remain free for more than a couple of minutes.

Someone threw a potato which struck him on the back of the neck. Other missiles began to fly. A man leapt at him from the last stall in the street, but as the man jumped a carrot, thrown by someone in the rear, struck him in the mouth. He lost his balance, grabbed wildly at his stall, and fell upon it.

The stall was old, rickety, and heavy laden. It gave with a sharp splintering sound and went down under the man's weight. In a second a cascade of purple, pink and golden fruit was pouring into the narrow street. Baskets, boxes, punnets, all disgorged their loads and bounded over the cobbles. As Swithin, wild-eyed, breathless, panting, darted round the corner, he knew that providence had given him one more slender chance of escape.

The leaders of the pursuit slipped up on the sea of figs, lemons, peaches, plums, apricots, and nuts that had been scattered by the hundred. They tumbled right and left among the fruit, crates, and baskets, bringing down more people in their rear and holding up the rest of the mob in a scene of indescribable confusion. Only two got through without tripping, a big, black-bearded fellow in a blouse and the policeman whom Swithin had nearly run into on the Street of Steps.

With the perspiration streaming down his face, he panted on, darting and thrusting his way through a new throng of people. He saw that he had reached the brow of the hill and came out into the open space about the great White Tower of Galata. Round, massive, and smooth-walled, it loomed above him; its four-storeyed top, like the stages of a birthday cake, each smaller than the one below and ringed with arches.

The pavements were crowded and the roadways full of traffic. Even if his straining lungs could have enabled him to keep up his former pace, he knew that it was not possible to maintain it in this moving multitude. He wondered desperately if he would stand more chance of getting away by taking the next turning in the hope that it would be less crowded, or by relaxing to a walk and endeavouring to shake off the pursuit by mingling with the passers-by.

Another swift glance back showed him the black-bearded man and the policeman still hard on his heels. At the sight of him they both raised their hands and shouted. He sped on and, fearing to be knocked down by his onrush, the people in his path gave way to right and left—opening a passage for him.

Only one man tried to stop him in the next twenty yards and with a violent thrust Swithin sent him reeling into the roadway; but at that, as though by a signal, the crowd about him started forward, and he knew that in another moment they would be on him like a pack of wolves.

With sudden decision he floundered off the pavement in front of an oncoming car. Its wheels missed him by inches. A cursing drayman strained at his reins and pulled up his horses. Swithin ducked beneath their tossing heads, but dashed into a bicycle—sending its rider spinning. He fell as well, was nearly run over by a car coming from the opposite direction, but saved himself by rolling over into the gutter, staggered to his feet and stumbled on again through the crowd on the far pavement.

For a moment he had thrown off his pursuers, but only for a moment. The furious cyclist had picked himself up and was yelling after him; fresh heads were turning to stare in his direction. Breathless and exahusted he reached the southern end of the Grand' Rue de Pera with a fair lead but with a new mob after him.

Sometimes in the gutter, sometimes on the pavement, he dodged and darted through the shifting crowd. Seeing a temporary gap in the traffic he crossed the road again. The vehicles closed up behind him giving him fresh hope for another moment. There was a big store one block further on, and he felt that if he could only reach it before the pack got across the street he might be able to throw them off altogether, but as he pushed his way through the swing doors a moment later he saw, over his shoulder, a policeman holding up the traffic and the mob streaming across the roadway in full cry.

Once in the store he stopped running and fought to control his laboured breathing. It was coming in quick, gasping sobs, and he feared that it would attract the attention of the people as he pushed his way in amongst them. As quickly as he could he slipped through three departments, turned left and so by another entrance out into a side street. He was almost certain that he had done the trick but, next second, he was disillusioned. The black-bearded man and one of the policemen, guessing his ruse, had let the mob surge into the front entrance of the store while they dashed round to prevent his exit from its side.

They were no more than fifteen feet from the door as Swithin came out into the street, and both rushed at him together. It was too late to dash back into the store so he stood stock still and waited, his feet planted firmly, determined to put up a fight for it.

As the policeman charged in Swithin hit him with all his force. The straight left landed on the fellow's chin and he went down like a ninepin. The workman grabbed at Swithin's arm but he brought his right round with a smashing body blow, tore his arm free, and took to his heels again. Thirty seconds later he was back in the Grand' Rue.

The burly workman grunted painfully, gave one contemptuous glance at the huddled body of the policeman and set off after Swithin, hullaballooing in a deep bass voice. Another policeman who was on guard at the front entrance of the store heard him as he reached the corner and before Swithin had got fifty yards the hunt was up again.

He was feeling the strain badly now. His heart was pounding in his ribs, his breath came in rasping gasps, and his lungs seemed to be bursting. His head was swimming, and he could hardly see out of his eyes. He stumbled and fell, losing a precious moment, but picked himself up and forced himself on again at a loping run.

Suddenly he realised that he was running parallel with a tram and just ahead of it. The front platform where the driver stood was open to accommodate extra passengers with standing room during rush hour traffic. Only two women stood on it at the moment. He halted, grabbed the stanchion as the tram went past, and swung himself on.

With a gasp of relief he fell against the partition which separated the seated passengers from the platform and stood there panting, white and shaken. For a moment he could think of nothing but endeavouring to get back his breath, then he tried to force his thoughts on to where he had better head for.

The yacht was now out of the question. Kazdim would have been telephoned to by this time and told of his recent appearance in the vicinity of the port. On that, the Eunuch was quite shrewd enough to suspect his intention of trying to escape by water and ordering a special lookout to be kept down at Galata. The Embassy was temptingly near, Swithin saw that he would be almost passing its front gates in a moment, but it was completely barred since Malik would undoubtedly have resumed his watch there, and be praying for another chance to intercept him. The thought of McAndrews' house occurred to him but he instantly dismissed it. To reach Moda he would have to cross the Bosphorus and he had already ruled out the neighbourhood of the port as highly dangerous. He decided that his best chance was to slip into a small cinema and lie low there until night had fallen, then steal a boat from one of the unfrequented piers above the Customs House and attempt to reach the *Golden Falcon* under cover of darkness.

In the two minutes since he had boarded the tram it had been swaying along at a fine pace so he felt sure that he had given his pursuers the slip at last, but he was still sucking in his breath with painful gasps and the two women on the platform were eyeing him curiously.

Suddenly he heard a loud commotion in the passenger compartment behind him. Whipping round he stared through the glass partition. The devilishly persistent black-bearded man and another policeman must have chased the tram and leapt on to its rear platform. They were forcing their way through the excited passengers and their faces, just beyond the glass, were only six feet from Swithin's own.

The tram had almost reached the junction of the Grand' Rue and Hamal Bachi Street. The driver, unconscious of what was happening in his rear, applied the brakes. Swithin sprang off before it had ceased moving, jumped from in front of a car on to the pavement, and began to run again. Blackbeard and the policeman followed a moment later, yelling at the pedestrians to stop their quarry.

As he charged headlong into the crowd, Swithin knew that he could not last much longer. The respite on the tram had been so brief that it had done little but stave off complete exhaustion for a few more moments. Every muscle of his body ached as though it had been bruised and beaten, a blood vessel hammered in his head as if it were about to burst, and his legs were failing under him. He thrust a man aside who had heard the policeman's shout, bumped into a small boy who stood gaping at him and careered on in a wild zigzag.

There was only one thing to do now. Immediately round the corner, only twenty yards away, lay the British Embassy. Malik would be waiting outside the gates, that was almost a certainty, but Swithin knew that he was absolutely at the end of his tether, and could not cover another hundred yards before they caught him.

Another man hunt had started up. People on all sides were shouting 'Stop him! Hold him!' but he took to the roadway, preferring the risk of being run down to that of being grabbed by the people on the pavement.

One last exhausted spurt and he was round the corner. He caught a glimpse of two gorgeously robed Kavasses standing in the gateway of the Embassy. Then Malik's face loomed up before him, barring the way to safety.

Only ten yards separated them. Malik drew his gun. 'Would he use it?' was the only thought which seared through Swithin's dazed mind. To shoot a British subject in cold blood outside the gates of his own Embassy would take some explaining whatever charges they might trump against him afterwards in an attempt to justify the act.

With sudden inspiration Swithin thrust his hand into his breast pocket and drew out the packet containing the all-important Kaka wafer, flung back his arm, and hurled it over Malik's head into the Embassy garden.

'Halt!' yelled Malik. 'Halt or I fire!'

But Swithin was past weighing chances. The supreme knowledge of victory now blazed in his brain. Whatever happened to him he knew that he had outwitted Kazdim and succeeded in the thing that he had set out to do. With his last ounce of strength he launched himself at Malik's knees.

It was a rugby tackle in the best tradition; swift, fearless, and direct. Malik, taken completely off his guard by this unorthodox attack, went crashing to the ground. Swithin, twisted as he fell, kicked out, and rolled into the very gateway of the Embassy.

Next moment there was a general mêlée. The pursuing policeman sprang forward on to him. Blackbeard arrived panting on the scene. A dozen others came rushing up and people on all sides began to run towards the gateway.

In it, an extraordinary struggle was proceeding. Swithin, utterly finished, no longer had the strength to raise a finger, but one of the great swarthy Kavasses had grabbed him by the collar as he rolled into the gate, and the other by the wrist. Both were endeavouring to haul him inside while the policeman, astride his body, and Blackbeard, who had a firm grasp on his ankles, tried to pull him back on to the pavement.

The crowd edged in, shouting and waving their arms excitedly as they abused or urged on the combatants. Malik had staggered to his feet. He thrust his way through them, his small dark face livid with anger, rushed in beside the policeman and grabbed at Swithin's shoulder. One of the Kavasses pushed him back. The other gave a violent jerk at Swithin's collar and hauled him another yard. Malik made as if to follow. Then as from a great distance Swithin heard a quiet voice say:

'You can't come in here, you know!'

Blackbeard released his legs, the other policeman was now standing beside Malik, the two Kavasses lifted Swithin to his feet, and he saw that it was Tyndall-Williams who had spoken. The diplomat was just behind him. He was calmly smoking a cigarette and his face showed no trace of excitement or emotion.

'I want that man!' Malik declared furiously, pointing at Swithin. 'I have a warrant for his arrest.'

Tyndall-Williams shook his head. 'I'm sorry, but I happen to know that this gentleman is a British subject, and as you are aware, it is quite impossible for me to allow you to execute your warrant here. If you submit it through the proper channels the Embassy will surrender him to you, of course—providing you can show bona fida grounds for his arrest.'

'Twice!' shouted Malik. 'Twice you have abused your privilege to obstruct me in the execution of my duty. You will hear more of this!'

The crowd outside had swelled to nearly a hundred. Tyndall-Williams ignored Malik and glanced towards the head Kavass. 'With all these people in the street I think you had better close the gates for half an hour.' Then he took Swithin's arm and supported him as he stumbled up the drive.

As the gates clanged to behind them Swithin's dazed brain began to function again. 'Did you get the packet?' he gasped.

'Rather, a second after you threw it. Fine work that, but lucky for you it occurred to me that you might have trouble getting in here again and thought of keeping a look out for you at the gate.'

'You—you were expecting me then?'

'Yes, you told me if you remember that your appointment was at six o'clock—I hardly thought that you would get here so soon though!'

Swithin grinned feebly. 'I meant to try for Duncannon's yacht—but they spotted me at the port—and I ran all the way.'

'Well done—take it easy now—you'll be all right in a minute.'

In the entrance hall Swithin halted, his chest still heaving painfully. 'It was—devilish sporting of you,' he said jerkily, 'to have the Kavasses there and—get me in like that. But won't there be hellish trouble—about this abuse of privilege, I mean?'

Tyndall-Williams smiled slowly. 'I don't think so. It is most irregular of course. We should never dream of trying to prevent an arrest like that in the ordinary way, but the circumstances are quite unusual. H.E. feels that most strongly. Some people think he's slow, just a nice old boy who gets on well with Johnny Turk—but he's a bit more than that when it comes to a time of crisis. We have been in communication with the F.O. and they take that view as well, so the old man has got his hackles up and is prepared to stretch diplomatic privilege as far as it will go.'

'Good for him. Wouldn't it be as well if we had a look at this Kaka thing though—just to see that it is—what we want?'

'Yes—here it is.' Tyndall-Williams drew the small packet from his pocket, tore off the paper, and displayed a gold rimmed locket. Under the glass lay a pentagonal wafer.

Swithin gave it one glance and nodded. 'That's it all right. With that inscription in the middle—Kemal will have enough proof to hang the people who signed it—in the five corners—a dozen times over.'

'It is a pity it is too late to send it tonight but he or Ismet will have it by breakfast time tomorrow. I've made all the necessary arrangements.' As Tyndall-Williams thrust the locket back in his pocket he added: 'Feeling fit enough to walk upstairs now?'

'Yes—I'll manage.' Swithin took a firm grip of the bannisters.

'Good! Then I'll attend to this at once. You know where my room is. Lie down there for a bit. H.E. dines at half-past eight. He told me that if you turned up I was to give you his compliments and express the hope that you would join him.'

Swithin grinned. 'Really! That was nice of him, but it sounds terribly like getting out the village band—to welcome home the conquering hero. Fortunately I have an easy let out—no evening clothes.'

'I think I can manage to fix you up.'

'Thanks awfully—but I've ruined one suit of yours already. Look—it's in a filthy state.'

'Nonsense,' smiled the diplomat. 'It only needs cleaning and pressing.'

'But honestly,' Swithin hesitated. 'I'd rather not dine with His Excellency. Would you mind very much making my excuses and saying that I'm all in.'

'Oh, if you wish. I shall be very happy to take Diana in to dinner myself.'

'Eh!' Swithin exclaimed. 'That's another matter. Where is she? I'd like to see her now for a moment—before I go up.'

'Well, you can't unless you are prepared to appear in Lady Cavendish's drawing-room in your present state. She has some friends here this afternoon between six and eight for a little music, and naturally Diana is with her. Far better save your thunder until after you've had a bath and change.'

'In that case you're dead right. You might let Diana know that I'm here though.'

'I will. Now be a good chap and go and get some of that muck off yourself. You've got an hour before you need think of changing. Take it easy while I deal with this Kaka thing, and I'll come up to you later.'

'Thanks—thanks awfully,' Swithin muttered and turning away he slowly climbed the stairs.

For a long time he lay easing the strain of his aching limbs in the comfort of a hot bath and deriving infinite pleasure in the knowledge that he had succeeded in his mission. Succeeded beyond his wildest dreams, for he had actually secured incontestable evidence of treason against the five leaders of the Kaka.

It now remained to be seen what use Kemal would make of it—and if he would be able to act in time to prevent the Revolution. Swithin doubted if he would. The arms were to be distributed that night, so even if the Kaka leaders were arrested some time next day, final orders for the rising would probably have gone out by then and it would take place as planned at midnight.

It looked as if they were in for exciting times during the next few days, but Swithin knew that he had played his part and Diana, bless her, was safe in the Embassy. They could only be onlookers now, while the fate of Turkey hung in the balance.

Tyndall-Williams arrived with the Naval Attaché, a man whose shorter stature more closely resembled Swithin's, and between them they fitted him out with evening clothes. Though still a little bruised when he went down the broad heavily carpeted staircase at twenty past eight he was feeling absolutely on the top of the world.

At that moment precisely Tania Vorontzoff was descending the steep wooden boxlike stairs of her back street apartment. A bell pealed when she was half-way down and, opening the door at the bottom, she found her visitor to be the Eunuch.

'I wish to speak with you—go up,' he said curtly.

She turned and reascended the stairs, with him labouring up behind her. In the small sitting-room the old Baroness rose stiffly to her feet at the sight of Kazdim.

'Greetings, Effendi,' she smirked. 'We are honoured by your visit.'

'Would you leave us, Mother,' Tania said quickly. 'We wish to talk business and I am already late for my appointment.'

'No—it is not necessary.' The Eunuch looked old, tired

and evil tempered as he sank heavily into the only arm-chair. 'It is as well on this occasion that your mother should hear my words. I thought that you always spent the evening with her. Why tonight, are you going out so early?'

'It is an exception.' She faltered, already apprehensive at this unexpected visit. 'This is my last opportunity to see Mr. Carew. He leaves tomorrow afternoon for England, and we had arranged to meet at the usual time, but he came into the *Pera* just before I left and said that he had received fresh instructions. First he will make the trip to Angora and back by aeroplane—departing from Istanbul at five o'clock in the morning. He must have a few hours' sleep before he sets out so he begged me to meet him at half-past eight instead of half-past eleven.'

'And so I am to be left alone,' muttered the Baroness peevishly.

'Oh, mother—just for once . . .' Tania began, but the Eunuch cut her short:

'Silence! Quibbling women are as the grating of a pencil on a slate. Tell me now, you have a fondness for this young man—have you not?'

Tania turned her glance from the little black eyes in his great puffy face. 'Why should you think that?' she answered guardedly, filled with instinctive dread now that he displayed this interest in her relations with Peter.

'Have you or have you not?' he piped. 'I am in no mood this evening for jesting or delays. Speak, and speak quickly.'

'I prefer his company to that of most men whom you order me to keep in touch with.'

Kazdim nodded his bald head and his many chins rippled down towards his chest. 'I thought as much. This man Carew has now been four days in Istanbul. You supped with him on Tuesday and on Wednesday night, and in neither case were you home before three in the morning. Yesterday, Thursday, was your half-day off. You left your stall just after midday and spent seventeen hours alone in his company—returning here only with the dawn. You could not have acted so from professional interest alone.'

He paused, puffed at his cigarette for a moment, and continued slowly, 'It matters to me not at all if it amuses you to sleep with him or another. . . .'

'We drove out to the forest of Belgrade,' she interrrupted quickly, 'dined there, walked in the woods for hours afterwards, and returned to watch the sun rise over the Bosphorus.'

'That you are a prude and he is a fool who chooses to miss his opportunities interests me even less.' Kazdim shrugged. 'My point is that should you allow sentiment to interfere with the execution of the orders I am about to give—you will have cause to regret it all the days of your life.'

'What are your orders?' Tania asked nervously.

'Listen.' He hunched his great bulk and sat forward. 'The man Destime, may Eblis gnaw out his bowels, has been the cause of far greater trouble than I anticipated. With the aid of one whom you do not know he has stolen a golden locket from a very high personage. That locket contains a paper of extreme importance. Destime succeeded in delivering it to the British Embassy less than two hours ago. They intend to transmit it to Angora at the earliest possible moment but any 'plane that set out so late this evening would have been overtaken by darkness in the mountains so—by the mercy of Allah—it is not to be sent off till dawn tomorrow.'

He paused again, crushed out his cigarette and lit another, then went on with cold deliberation: 'This packet is only a small thing but, should it reach Angora, incalculable harm will follow. It must be got back therefore and restored to its owner—the high personage of whom I speak. I have sworn by the blood of the Prophet that this shall be done. The young man Carew is to take it. I care not if you love him or no. You will get it from him for me tonight.'

The blood drained from Tania's face. This was infinitely worse than anything she had imagined. 'But—but perhaps he will not have it on him,' she stammered.

'He will,' the Eunuch snapped. 'My people are everywhere—even among the servants in the Embassy. If he were sleeping there it would not have been given to him before morning, or at least until his return tonight, but he sleeps at the *Pera* and will have to be up by four o'clock so the first secretary—whose wits Allah must have been graciously pleased to fuddle—handed it to him in a sealed envelope within half an hour of Destime's arrival with it.'

'Suppose—I am unable to get hold of it,' Tania faltered.

'It is for that reason I wished your mother to be present at our conversation. If you fail she will know who is to blame when I refuse to renew your permit to remain in Turkey, and you are both sent back to Russia as renegade aristocrats for the Bolsheviks to deal with.'

'Oh, Effendi—Effendi, you would not do that,' the Baroness quavered.

'Peace, woman,' he squeaked angrily. 'I will do that and more. You shall go to Russia alone so your daughter's fine eyes will not be there to make a special pleading for you with the Komissars, and I will send her to Bitlis as a plaything for a Kudish chieftain of my acquaintance. A man whose only pleasure is to inflict pain upon soft bodies. She will have aged thirty years by the time she has been his mistress for six months.'

Madame Vorontzoff began to wring her hands together and the easy tears trickled down her reddish face. 'Tania!' she moaned. 'Oh, Tania!'

'That is one side to this question,' the Eunuch went on more calmly. 'The other is that if you succeed Allah will prompt me to be generous. Your permit shall be made permanent. I will require no further services from you, and even allow you a small pension in lieu of the money which you would have earned. Now choose—for the sands of time run low.'

Tania stood there white to the lips, appalled at the horrible choice which was being thrust upon her. 'But if you are mistaken,' she pleaded fighting off the issue.

'I am not mistaken,' he answered testily. 'The man Carew has this small packet on him now, and he would never allow such a thing to go out of his possession. If you fail—you know the penalty, and by so doing you will not protect *him*, for I shall take other measures.'

'What—what do you mean by that?' she whispered.

'I will have him killed if necessary. But that packet must be in my possession before the morning.'

'Oh, Tania!' wailed the Baroness, 'how can you be so heartless as even to hesitate.'

Tania felt as if she were choking, but that threat to kill

266

Peter put an end to her resistance. 'All right,' she stammered dully, 'I will do my best.'

'That is well,' Kazdim nodded. 'And you must return here with it by eleven o'clock.'

'But that is not possible—it is our last night together. Even though he has to leave at five o'clock he will not wish to part from me before midnight at the earliest.'

The Eunuch heaved himself to his feet. 'You must make some excuse to get away from him. I can allow you no longer. If you do not return it by eleven other arrangements will have to be made.'

'I can't,' cried Tania desperately. 'He trusts me and—Oh, I love him—I can't—I can't.'

The Baroness beat her hands feebly on her knees. 'You must Tania—you must. Think what this means to us. I implore you to do as the Effendi bids you.'

'Effendi!' he echoed in his thin falsetto, then he smiled. 'I have told you not to address me thus, but there is a rumour that titles are to be revised in Turkey soon. In a few days it may be again permissible for you to call me Effendi or perhaps—even Pasha.'

'Please— I beg you to give me any other work—anything—anything,' pleaded Tania.

Kazdim shook his great head. 'No. The stage is set for you alone. I leave you now to the persuasion of your mother. If you succeed—a permit to remain for good, no more such work will be required of you, and a pension; but if you fail me—your mother sets out in a cattle boat alone for Russia tomorrow morning. You shall be sent to the Kurd, and I will kill your lover.' Once more, with that air of terrible finality that Tania knew so well, he slowly crushed out the butt of his cigarette—and left them.

24

When the Heart is Young

Peter Carew waited impatiently for Tania in the lounge of the *Pera*. He was utterly miserable at the thought that he must leave Constantinople to return to England next day and furious that, at the last moment, the Embassy should have foisted on him the job of doing a five hundred mile 'plane journey to Angora and back, before he collected his bags and caught the express for home.

The Aerodrome at San Stefano was on the far side of Stamboul, a good twelve miles away, and he had been told that the pilot who was to take him to Angora had orders to start at crack of dawn. That meant he would have to leave the *Pera* by four o'clock at the latest, and so had put paid to his plan of making a last night of it with Tania.

If there had been some prospect of sleeping in the 'plane he would have cut out any idea of going to bed at all, but he knew that sleep would be impossible while flying over the mountainous country in Asia Minor which is full of air pockets; and as he had made do with less than half his usual allowance of sleep ever since he arrived in Constantinople he felt that he definitely must get a few hours before he started out on his journey.

He glanced at the clock. It was a quarter to nine already and, when Tania had left her bookstall at eight, she had promised to go straight home, arrange things with her mother and return by half-past. He wondered angrily what could have kept her. Every moment of this last night was precious, it was appalling to see it ticking away, slowly but inexorably, like this.

She had been sweet about it when he told her of his ill luck, and agreed to desert her invalid mother for the evening in order to meet him there hours earlier—and thus enable him to get to bed by one—although he doubted whether, when it came to the pinch, he would not keep her with him until the very last moment before leaving for the airport, however ghastly he might feel next day.

How he hated the thought of leaving Constantinople. This fairy city of golden sunsets, blue waters, white mosques, great curving arches, and dark mysterious alleyways. When, if ever, would he return to these scented gardens lined with their tall cypresses, see again the *caïques* on the sparkling waters of the Golden Horn, or smell the strong spicy Eastern perfume that emanated from the narrow, old fashioned shops.

The thought that he had only been living there for four days seemed fantastic, utterly absurd. He felt that he had known it all his days, or lived before in some somnolent chrysalis state, waiting to burst his cocoon and wake to glorious life in this city of romance.

'Tania—Tania—Tania,' he murmured the name over and over again to himself. 'God, how sweet she was. How utterly desirable. The embodied essence of this place of dreams.' And now he had to say good-bye to her.

After their first evening together, at the Grandpère, he had met her for lunch the next day, and had it out with her, demanding to know the limit of her duties in that questionable resort. It was an impertinence upon so short an acquaintaince, as he realised afterwards, but he was determined to know the truth or see no more of her and he was so earnest when he spoke of it that she did not resent his questioning. She could not tell him that owing to her Secret Service work the Eunuch's protection enabled her to cold shoulder patrons of the place, without offending the management, when they became too pressing, but satisfied him by pointing out that if she were prepared to be any man's mistress there were plenty of people in Istanbul who would be only too pleased to give her a comfortable flat, excellent clothes, and a reasonable income upon which to support her mother; in which case it would be quite unnecessary for her to continue her long hours at the bookstall or nightly excursions to the Grandpère.

The statement was so logical that it immediately convinced him, and after that he had given a free rein to his first impulse, thinking of her more than ever as some fairy Princess who had been enchained to servitude by some wicked witch's spell.

Except for the very few hours which he had spent

in sleep Tania had never been out of his thoughts, and actually in his company every free moment of her time, since the first day of his arrival. They had supped together again on his second night, at the Tokatlian, danced, laughed, swopped reminiscences, and grown far more intimate. Then his third day had been Tania's half holiday.

He had hired a car and they had driven out to Floria, the lovely little *plage* on the Marmara coast below Stamboul. Lunched there in the broiling heat of midday on a shady vine-covered terrace that overlooked the azure sea. Bathed from a secluded beach a mile farther down the coast in the afternoon. Lazed in the sunshine on a deserted silver strand cupped in a little cove, through the hours that followed. Dressed again, driven back through the city and out of it once more to a wayside inn on a cross roads in the Forest of Belgrade. Dined off red caviare from Odessa, salty-sweet fresh caught Marmara lobsters, and luscious Anatolian pears. Then hand in hand they had strolled through the moonlit woods behind the Inn, found a mossy bank and lain down upon it; kissed and fallen silent, then kissed and kissed and kissed again, while the short warm summer night folded them in its scented cloak and the hours crept slowly by. Until the coming of the faint grey light they had lain embraced, the world forgotten and only glorying in their nearness to each other, so that it seemed a sacrilege ever to leave that place of joy, yet abandoning it at last to return to Pera in time to see the gorgeous colouring gild the sky as a new day came up over sleeping Istanbul out of the far hills of Asia.

'What a day—what a day—what a day.' Peter glowed at the very thought of it. In his imagination he could see her slender golden body as she splashed and tumbled in the creamy breakers, and feel again her gentle breath as her soft lips clung to his, her face upturned and patterned by the moonlight that filtered through the foliage of the trees in that silent enchanted forest. Then the glow faded as he recalled the aftermath.

When he had crept into bed that morning he had made up his mind to take Tania back to England and marry her. He had toyed with the idea first when they had been lazing on the sands after their bathe the previous afternoon. It had come to him from seeing then a new side to her nature—a fun-loving simplicity which had not been apparent in the artificial atmosphere of the restaurants—but he had dismissed it as impossible.

The thought of his enormous overbearing family had proved too much for him. The strait-laced Aunts, the rigid soldier Uncles, his old dragon of a Grandmother, would never receive Tania with anything but hostility. The connections which she claimed might or might not be valid they would say—the fact remained that she was a penniless Russian and that he had picked her up at some place in the Near East. If she had been some plain, dowdy little thing he knew that it was just possible he might have got away with it—but she was not. She was beautiful—*too* beautiful for them ever to believe her also good. That was the tragedy.

Although he had put the thought out of his head it had come again at dinner, then played with devilish persistency in his mind all through the hours that they remained together, and their night in the woods had set the seal upon it.

He would defy his family and take her home, away from this ghastly life of wage slave and semi-cocotte which was her portion. His mother would understand. He knew that, gentle, sweet-tempered, beautiful herself, he could count upon her to the limit. If his father did not like it he could lump it and the rest of the family could go to blazes. Tania was so gay, so tender, so marvellously lovely that to have her with him always would be worth any trouble that he might have to face, and at the close of their wonderful day together, when he parted from her in the dawn-lit street near her apartment he was convinced that never in his life again would he meet any girl so utterly desirable.

He had said nothing to her, only having finally made up his mind after he had left her. Back at the *Pera* he had undressed and tumbled into bed, slept for about three hours, and then suffered the most vivid, real, and terrible nightmare.

It seemed to him that a long line of ghostly figures stood swaying at the foot of his bed. They were staring down upon his recumbent form with unutterably cold contempt and disapproval on their faces. He knew them instantly for the astral bodies of his nearest relatives.

One of the tightly corseted aunts spoke first in grim disgust. Her voice was thin and unsubstantial but he heard it plainly.

'To think that he should have allowed himself to be taken in like this.'

Another answered, 'A Russian too they tell me. It is most distressing.'

The shade of a portly uncle, one of His Majesty's Honourable Corps of Gentlemen at Arms said heavily, although his voice came faint and attenuated to Peter's ears 'Can't you get hold of this trollop and buy her off, George? Cost you five hundred or a thousand, perhaps, but worth every penny of it.'

Peter's father, the General, tall, frowning, grim, replied: 'Buy *her* off! Cut *him* off you mean. And I'll see he doesn't get a shilling from his mother—the weak-minded young fool.'

The Bishop, another uncle, swayed forward. 'No marriage which is based on lust can possibly bring happiness,' he declared severely.

'Plucked eyebrows!' murmured an aunt.

'Good-looking though, in a sort of foreign way,' remarked her husband. 'I remember when I was in Vienna in '04 a man I knew there took me to a night club and introduced me . . .'

'Herbert!' rapped out the lady acidly. 'If you have such dubious reminiscences kindly reserve them for your visits to your Club.'

'Talking of night clubs,' cut in Peter's Uncle Max, the black sheep of the family; 'Last year when I was on that cruise we called at Constantinople. I visited a place there named the Grandpère. There was a young woman in a box. I forget her name but she was one of the *filles de maison* —do anything for a five pound note you know—and this girl is most awfully like her.'

'TANIA VORONTZOFF,' cried the whole line in a horrid shout.

'Good Lord!' Uncle Max's wraith almost swayed out of line with excitement. 'That's it—Tania—and by Jove she was hot stuff. But damn it, this must be the same girl. Look here we can't let the boy marry a tart.'

'Cost you five hundred!'

'An insult to us all!'

'He'll not have a penny from me!'

'Blood red finger nails—Anyone could see . . .'

'Lust!'

'Cut him off!'

'Tart!'

'LUST!'

'TART!' came the appalling chorus of voices, curiously thin as though coming from a great distance, yet ringing with vicious menace and profound condemnation, while the ghostly line of figures swayed slowly back and forth like reeds in a gentle breeze.

Then the ghost of Peter's grandmother administered the final *coup de grâce*. In her thin high treble she said coldly: 'I regret, but under no circumstances could I attend the wedding.'

At that he had woken, sweating, shivering, his fair hair wet and matted about his temples. The ghostly parade which had tortured him by their abuse of Tania and vile innuendoes had vanished—the light of full day was streaming through the curtains of his window. Further sleep had been out of the question but those thin bitter voices still sounded in his ears, and with black despair in his heart he knew that he dare not take Tania back to England with him.

As he sat now twelve hours later in the lounge of the *Pera,* he felt grim and despondent, knowing that within a few hours he must leave behind him this girl who had brought a mad exaltation and vibrant colour into his life beyond all others that he had ever met.

He glanced at the clock again. It was five to nine. The precious moments were flying. What could have happened to her he wondered anxiously, and then he saw her coming towards him, slender, pale-faced, her chin high, her shoulders thrown back, with the carriage of a Princess.

'Tania!' he exclaimed hurrying forward to meet her. 'I thought you were never coming. You're looking awfully white. Is anything the matter? Why are you so late?'

'Mother,' she said with a sob in her voice. 'She has had an attack— I could not get away before.' It was a lie, but she had to explain her distraught appearance somehow.

'Darling, I *am* sorry.' He took both her hands and pressed them. 'You—you'll want to go back at once then,

273

you only came to tell me. It's tragic that this should put paid to our last chance to be together. But of course I understand—if she's really ill.'

Tania shook her head and smiled faintly. 'No, she is better now and friends are looking after her—but I must be back by eleven. They cannot stay later.' Even as she was thinking how sweet it was of him to offer to forgo their evening so unselfishly her lie developed automatically. The perfect excuse to ensure him allowing her to leave him and be back on time.

'Thank God!—we've got two hours then anyway.' He spoke with incredible relief. 'Listen, I'd booked a table at Therapia before I knew about this filthy business of having to go to Angora—and an electric launch to take us up there. We still have time to dine in the garden and spend half an hour on the water afterwards if we leave at once. Would you like that?'

'I should love it,' she said softly as, with complete disregard for the people watching them, he drew her arm through his and led her from the lounge, 'I am terribly upset though that our last evening together should be cut short like this.'

He patted her hand and then pressed it in his own. 'We're lucky to have even these two hours really with your mother ill and that tailor's dummy Tyndall-Williams at the Embassy. He wanted me to sleep there on a shakedown in his office tonight, and was huffy as blazes with me when I flatly refused.'

'Why did he wish that?' she asked although she already knew the answer to her question.

'Because he says this thing I'm taking to Angora is of the first importance, and I suppose he was afraid that if I went out tonight some lovely wicked spy would steal it from me. As though such things happened in these days. I've never heard such fantastic rot.'

Tania felt sick and ill as she climbed into the taxi which was to take them down to the pier where the motor launch was waiting. He was so sure of himself, so contemptuous of that possibility which she knew only too well to be a very real and present danger. She laughed shakily as he went on angrily:

'When I refused to dine and sleep, he wanted to keep the

wretched thing in the safe at the Chancery, and make me get up half an hour earlier to call for it before I left. Look! He produced it from his inside pocket. 'It can't even be an important despatch.'

'Oh, guard it carefully,' she urged spontaneously, leaning against him in the cab. The casual way in which he showed it to her filled her with dismay. But then of course he was a newcomer to this dangerous game and his absolute trust in her was pathetically apparent.

'You darling,' he laughed and pulled her to him, smothering her face with kisses. 'Don't worry. I'm perfectly capable of taking care of myself—and this.'

At the landing stage they boarded the powerful electric launch. Peter refused the services of the mechanic and having settled Tania on a pile of cushions in the stern took the controls himself. As he brought the lever over they shot out into the dark waters of the Bosphorus, and he turned the boat upstream.

She nestled down beside him, her head on his shoulder, striving to put out of her mind for a little while the terrible alternatives with which she was faced. The Eunuch had threatened—horrible things. Her mother had pleaded— and the prayers of the weak and helpless are doubly hard to resist; but she had decided nothing. All her life since she had left Russia as a small child, poverty, hardship, worry had been her lot. In recent years her better material circumstances had been more than offset by the hateful part she was compelled to play in the night life at the Grandpère. Only the Eunuch's protection, given on account of her work for him, saved her from the necessity of taking some man as her 'protector', a course which she knew only too well led finally to prostitution. And even as things were she was frequently compelled to submit to unpleasant familiarities, maudlin caresses, and loathsome pawings, in order to get sufficient material to satisfy the Eunuch's requirements.

Then, without warning, this tall fair, good-looking man had come into her grey and distasteful life. Treated her with sweet courtesy, charmed her imagination by his accounts of that sheltered and serene existence in the, to her, almost fabulously wealthy and powerful little island in the northern seas. Spoilt her for all other men in a few short days by his unfailing kindness and thought for her, by his chivalrous deference, as though, although he knew almost all the truth about her sordid life, he thought of her always as some beautiful princess. On top of all else she was physically attracted to him, and since that first night had felt the profound urge to give herself to him entirely. He had found his way to her mind by his lifting of her from the gutter to a pinnacle, to her heart by his gentle easy laughter, and to her body by his fevered response to her faintest caress. He loved her, genuinely, desperately, she had not a doubt, and she loved him, she had confessed it the previous night in those silent woods by utter abandonment to the divine fire that he lit in her veins. He trusted her implicitly. How then could be betray and ruin him.

They passed Ortakeuy where Swithin's Tobacco Depot, unseen, and unknown to either of them, now lay dark and silent, Bebek, Rumeli Hissar, and so came to the steps at Therapia.

'The great restaurant there, set in its lovely gardens, a favourite resort of the wealth and fashion of Constantinople, was brightly lighted. Many people had left the heat of the city this sultry August night to come out and dine on its luxuriously appointed terrace. A French *Maître d'hôtel* bowed them to a table, ordered their dishes and chose their wine. Neither of them could raise sufficient interest to do other than accept his tactful promptings.

When the food came, they hardly ate, but sat staring at each other across the table, both wrapped in the tragedy of their own thoughts. Tania smoked incessantly. Peter drank glass after glass of genuine unquestionably French Champagne from a magnum of Bollinger that he had ordered.

Half-way through the meal, he pushed his plate away. 'Oh what's the use!' he said abruptly. 'We were fools to come here. We have little enough time as it is. Shall we cut out the rest of dinner and go back to the launch?'

Tania nodded dumbly, she could not have swallowed another thing. All she wanted was to feel his arms gripped tight around her once again. She shuddered violently at the frightful thought that then she would be compelled to make her choice.

'Are you cold, dearest?' he asked with immediate concern.

'No,' she assured him. 'No, and if I were naked in a blizzard I would not be if I had you with me.'

'My sweet.' He grabbed her slim hand where it lay upon the damask table cloth, and gripped it till it hurt. Then he released it suddenly, called for his bill, sat staring at her while they fetched it, paid it without regard to change and, as she stood up, shepherded her from the terrace, down through the garden heavy with the scent of roses.

Back in the launch once more he steered it downstream a little way and tied it up again beneath a sheltered bank.

'Now,' he said huskily. 'Let's make ourselves comfortable.'

'Why not put the cushions inside the cabin,' she suggested, 'there is more room in there.'

Then she bit her thumb until her teeth dented its nail. Why had she said that, but even as she asked herself she knew. It was not that there was really much more room but it was pitch dark in there. Subconsciously her true purpose had prompted her and now she wanted to scream or weep hysterically.

With a few quick movements he arranged the pillows and a rug in the tiny cabin as she had suggested and, next moment, he seized her hand and drew her down beside him in the inky blackness.

She yielded without a murmur and felt herself half fainting in his embrace. Then she flung back her head, laced her arms about his neck and glued her mouth to his. A delicious trembling ran through all her limbs. She could feel his heart hammering beneath her breast as he pressed upon her. A passion of ecstasy thrilled through every nerve of her body.

This fiercely passionate onslaught was very different from their love making of the night before. Then he had been gentle, infinitely careful to give her emotions time to rise in concert with his own. But she preferred this almost brutal wooing and loved his rough handling of her. What did it matter if he crushed and hurt her. She was his to do what he would with in this glorious moment and tomorrow she would kiss every bruise that he had made upon the tender flesh of her arms and shoulders.

'Tomorrow!' That was now an appalling thought. 'He would be gone and she—where? In Istanbul, still the

Eunuch's pensioner for duties punctually performed, or under guard on her way to that devilish Kurd he had spoken of?'

'No!' Rather than face that she would kill herself—throw herself into the Bosphorus—that was the way out—but her mother. 'How could she leave that poor frail old woman to die in misery alone?'

Great tears welled up into her eyes and trickled out, running downwards to her ears. He was sighing heavily now but still kissing her on the face and neck. All at once his lips came into contact with the salty dampness and he drew back:

'Darling! You're crying! Have I hurt you? Oh, I've behaved like a great clumsy brute.'

'No,' she sobbed. 'I have been loving every moment of it. It is not that.'

'What is it then?' he asked with quick concern.

'That you—you do not *really* love me—you cannot.' She knew her accusation to be untrue but a thought had come to her when they had been seated staring at each other across the dinner table and now it had returned with redoubled force. How, if he cared as much for her as he appeared to do could he bear to leave her to the life he knew she led? Had their positions been reversed it would never have occurred to her that she could possibly go away unless he came too.

'Tania!' he exclaimed. 'I adore you—you know I do!'

'You say so,' she murmured bitterly. 'But it is so easy for a man to say things like that. You have probably said the same thing to other girls in Berlin, and Brussels, and Warsaw. You may mean it now perhaps, and for a week or so you will miss me, but after that you will find someone else and I shall be forgotten.'

'I'll never forget you—I swear it!' He bent to kiss her again but she turned her face away.

'If you love me how can you think to leave me. I will never go back to that horrible life at the Grandpère. I will kill myself.'

He groaned and raised himself a little. All his longing to have her with him always flooded back to him. He nearly —very nearly blurted: 'Tania come to England with me. I want you for my wife,' but those grey shapes that he had

278

seen in his nightmare seemed to be forming again, rising up out of the gently flowing waters and rearing their heads over the dark stern of the launch. Once more he heard their acid condemnation as clearly as if the shadows had spoken.

'An insult to us all!'

'He'll not have a penny from me!'

'Blood-red finger nails!'

'Cut him off!'

'Lust!'

'Tart!'

Beads of perspiration broke out on his forehead. He felt that he was suffocating in the hot sultry night and thrust a finger down his collar to ease his breathing, then he stammered miserably:

'I love you Tania—but I can't take you with me, there—there's my job.'

She shook back her soft dark hair, wiped the tears from her eyes and even managed a queer little laugh. 'I understand,' she gulped. 'Do not take any notice of the things I said. I did not mean them. I will be all right, but kiss me—love me again—love me again while there is time.'

He bent over her, no longer fiercely ardent as he had been before, but savouring her sweetness while his brain spun dizzily like a dying top.

Now was her time. She knew it. His passion was rising again quickly. He had not a thought in the world except for her. One small movement and she could slip her hand inside his coat. The little packet would pass from him to her without him having the faintest suspicion of it. In his overwrought state it was very improbable that he would discover his loss until after he had left her but believe that the thing had dropped from his pocket as he scrambled aboard the boat.

In her mind Tania pictured her mother, bent, tousle-headed, her lined face flushed to a hectic red from her weak heart, feebly protesting as she was thrust down into the hold of a cattle-boat—in which she would surely die, and then herself—yet that was not so terrible. Life had not been so good to her that she greatly feared to leave it; but her mother *must* be spared that final misery. Her hand moved up towards Peter's breast.

'When I think of you it won't be like this,' he murmured

softly, 'but as you were yesterday when we lay on the sands after our bathe. We were so divinely happy then.'

Her fingers slackened. She felt that she could *not* do it. Not even for her mother. This was love. Even if he did not love her as she loved him, that was not his fault. Men were different, incapable of the same depths of feeling as a woman. He loved her to the limits that nature had set for a man but her love was an infinite tenderness that transcended all other considerations. She could not mar that for anything or anybody. He would never know it but she would offer up herself, her mother, and all that was hers in order that he should not be ruined or disgraced. Very gently she withdrew her hand.

Then she recalled Kazdim's threat to kill him, if she failed to retain the packet, and saw that she must take it for his own protection. Not to do so was almost equivalent to handing him over to the executioner. The Eunuch's assassins were swift and deadly at their trade. They would fall on him with their long silent knives as he returned all unsuspecting to his bedroom at the *Pera*, and every trace of the crime would be removed before morning. He would just have disappeared as many another had before him in that cruel city of the Sultans. She moaned and shivered slightly.

'What is it my sweet?' He pressed her to him with renewed fervour.

'Oh nothing—nothing except that I am going so soon to lose you,' she whispered, but she was thinking rapidly. There was one way in which she still might save him without stealing the packet. She could warn him to go straight back to his Embassy and not leave it for a moment until it was time for him to set out on his journey—and then to have armed friends about him until the 'plane actually left the ground. It meant that she would have to give a convincing reason for her warning or else he would not take it. The only way she could do that was to confess herself a spy and an intending pickpocket. To tell him the truth—but how could she. That would shatter his love for her, and he would think of her ever afterwards as mean and vile. The thought was unbearable. And yet—what other course lay open. She must steel herself to do it, but not yet—not yet —not till they were on the very point of parting. Then she would tell him the whole truth and beg him to take immediate measures for his safety.

When she had once made that decision she had no regrets. She was supremely happy in the knowledge that she had not betrayed her love. A great calmness came over her and she responded to his renewed caresses, rather to give him pleasure than herself. For a little while she was the eternal mother who forever carries the male child in her arms.

At last he drew back, sat up and passed his hand over his eyes. Then he glanced at the luminous dial of his wrist watch and exclaimed:

'Darling! it's late—much later than I thought. It's nearing half past ten already so I must get you back at once. I'll start up the motor if you will collect the cushions and bring them out to the stern.'

As he got to his feet and scrambled from the cabin she began to straighten her clothes and gather up the pillows. Then, just as she was about to fold the rug, her fingers suddenly brushed over a small hard packet near the place where her shoulders had lain.

In a second she realised that it was the object of his journey. He had shown it to her only an hour and half before so, even in the darkness, she knew it again by its weight and size. Surely she thought, it was fate which had thrown this thing into her hands. If she kept it, this small flat packet, it meant life and security; if she gave it back, then death—for her mother and herself.

His voice came hoarse and disconsolate from outside the cabin where he sat by the rudder. 'Oh hell! I feel so awful about leaving you.'

'Do not worry, dearest,' she replied quietly. 'After to-morrow I shall be quite all right.'

She could not keep the packet. She knew that now. She must give it back to him and adhere to her decision. Shame herself by a full confession and implore him to guard his life.

Having no knowledge of the inner meaning of her words he was amazed and intensely hurt by her quiet acceptance of the situation. It stung him into an abrupt and bitter rejoinder:

'You're right I suppose. We'll both get over it. Everyone says that love never really lasts, and Lord knows we're young enough. Each of us will probably survive a dozen other love affairs before we die.'

Tania felt a sudden constriction in her breast. It was as though her heart had missed a beat. She clenched her fists until the sharp nails bit into the palms of her hands, and one of them held the little packet. 'So that was all he really felt,' the thought seared through her brain. 'Why then should she sacrifice herself and the helpless old lady who was dependent upon her.' Her quick Russian blood flamed to revolt. She had been mad ever to think of it. After all he was only like any other man and meant to take his pleasure in the future where he could, without a thought for her. She felt ashamed now, that she had loved him so much.

'Darling,' he called. 'You're being an awful time. What are you doing?'

'I'm coming,' she answered softly, and with quick efficient fingers she folded up the rug, carried it out to the stern beside him, and sat down upon it. The little packet was now reposing next to the bare skin of her thigh, wedged into the top of one of her long silk stockings.

The moon had risen. It lit the Bosphorus with a bluish pearl-grey light. The scene was one of indescribable loveliness as the launch sped southward past the great palaces and villas that fringed the waters, but neither of them gave it a single thought. They sat silent, both with a ghastly misery gnawing at their hearts.

By ten to eleven they were back at the Dolma Baghtche steps from which they had set out. A boatman relieved Peter of the launch, then they walked quickly up the hill, secured a roving taxi and headed for the street at which he had set her down after their previous evenings together.

In the taxi they clung to each other—still speechless. There seemed no adequate words with which to express their emotions, nothing that had not already been said, left to say.

All too soon the journey was accomplished. The cab pulled up on the corner they both knew so well. Peter got out. Tania followed him. He paid off the driver and turned towards her.

'This is goodbye,' she whispered.

'Not yet,' he shook his head. 'Tonight I mean to see you

to your door. I want the very last possible moment with you.'

Unprotesting, she turned, and they walked down the quiet, almost empty, thoroughfare. Peter noticed that both sides of it were lined with cheap, uninviting shops, nearly all of which were now in darkness. His depression deepened as he thought of her living in such a dismal neighbourhood.

They crossed the road and entered a side street. Grim little houses frowned down upon its broken pavements. In the dim light of the infrequent street lamps it seemed to stretch away to infinity. Occasionally a shuffling figure passed them.

At last they came to more shops, shuttered and silent, their fronts did not look as if they had received a coat of paint for two generations.

Tania turned again, into a narrower way, between more small houses—hovels almost; Peter saw that many of the windows were broken or boarded over. The stench of an overturned garbage tin, acrid and foul, caught his nostrils. Surely, he thought miserably, it isn't possible that she lives in this filthy slum.

In the last ten minutes Tania had suffered another revulsion of feeling and almost made up her mind to give him back the packet when they parted, but as they passed under an ancient rounded archway, dark and cavernous, she was thankful that she had kept it. This was just the sort of place where the Eunuch's men would lie in wait for him. If she gave it back what real use would any warning be. How could he hope to escape Kazdim who had boasted that very evening of having men even inside the British Embassy. Things were better as they were. She would keep it, hand it over to her employer when he arrived, and at least save three lives. Peter's, her mother's and her own.

They came out of the archway only to enter a narrow high walled alley, lit by a solitary jet of light from a grimy lamp fixed to the wall at its far end; turned the corner, and entered the fœtid court in which she dwelt.

As they halted before the baker's shop, she took out her key, thrust it in the lock, and pushed upon the narrow doorway; then she turned back to him.

In the bright moonlight Peter could see her face quite

283

clearly—and the row of small tumbledown houses. He was suddenly filled with an overwhelming certainty that he could not leave her to live out her life in these sordid surroundings. The fable that he had built up of her as a beautiful Princess enslaved by some malicious enchanter came back to him. For a second that grim line of family ghosts reared their heads in the moonbeams but he forced them out of his consciousness, seized her hands, and cried:

'Tania!—Tania! I meant to tell you before—ask you that is. I can't leave you like this. I want you to come back with me to England tomorrow.'

'No—no,' she shook her head and shrank away.

'Yes,' he insisted—'as my wife—once we're married you'll forget all this horror—just as though it had never been.'

'I—I cannot—*now*,' she stammered utterly overcome. How could she confess her theft—explain. The undreamed of had happened—but it had happened too late.

'You've got to,' he insisted. 'I shouldn't have sprung it on you like this, but I shall be back from Angora tomorrow by midday, and my train does not leave until three o'clock.'

A window was flung open above their heads. 'Tania!' called a wheezy voice. 'Is that you?'

She knew that it was her mother, but Peter glanced up and said: 'You must go now, dearest, but this is not goodbye. Make your arrangements in the morning and don't worry your sweet head about a single thing. I'll fix up for any money you want, and the tickets. and everything.' Then he added recklessly: 'Of course we'll take your mother too.'

'Tania,' came the wheezy voice again.

He leaned forward and kissed her lightly on the forehead. Incredibly relieved now that he had actually taken the plunge and absolutely determined to go through with the whole business. 'I'll be in the lounge of the *Pera* between half-past twelve and one. Up you go now. God bless you.'

Before she could find her voice, he had left her and his tall figure was disappearing into the dark alley. For a second she thought of running after him but her mother's voice came again from above. This time in a sharp whisper.

'Tania—have you got it?'

How she managed to stagger up the short, steep flight of stairs she did not know but next moment she was in the tiny sitting-room. Her mother was clawing at her with her fat useless hands and repeating the question. 'Have you got it—have you got it?'

Over her mother's shoulder, as in some awful nightmare, she saw the vast, still form of the Eunuch, overlapping the sides of the arm-chair, a great pile of cigarette ends making a small mountain in a brass ash tray beside him.

'Well!' he asked calmly. 'Where is it?'

Tania was white to the lips. She could only stare at him and shake her head dumbly.

'What!' he snarled, coming to his feet in one quick movement. 'By the Beard of the Prophet! Your mouth shall be filled with dust if my orders have proved of less account to you than this foreigner's kisses.'

'I could not get it,' she declared tremulously. 'I could not get it because you were wrong—he left it at his Embassy after all.'

'You swear that by your God and mine?'

'I swear it.'

Kazdim's great expanse of face had gone grey with fury.

'Oh mercy! mercy!' wailed the old Baroness, but he thrust her roughly aside and ran lightly toward the door.

'Wait!' cried Tania. She was seeking desperately in her bemused mind for some way to save Peter and yet return the packet to him. As the Eunuch paused with his hand upon the door a sudden inspiration came to her and she hurried on:

'What I have said is the truth. I only returned at this hour because you said I *must*. I made the excuse that my mother was ill and that I had to see her while he returned to the Embassy to collect the packet. Later we are to meet again. *Then* I shall be able to get it for you.'

The Eunuch's small dark eyes bored into hers. She prayed silently that he would believe her. If he did she could go out again, see Peter at the *Pera*, return the packet to him and make him take refuge with it in his Embassy.

Kazdim frowned. 'At what time will you be able to hand it to me?' he said at last.

'At two o'clock,' she lied. She dared not make it later in

285

case, if she left him too narrow a margin, he decided to employ his murderous alternative.

His cascade of chins creased in a slow acquiescent nod. 'Not a moment later,' he piped. 'I shall be waiting outside the hotel and if I find that you have lied to me you know well that a Wahabi would have less mercy for an Unbeliever than I for you.'

As the door banged behind her Tania sunk down on the divan. His small feet which so miraculously supported that huge body beat a tattoo of triumph in her topsy-turvy brain as he pattered down the stairs. Peter loved her—Peter loved her—*Loved her!* Just as she did him. That was all that mattered. She flung back her head and closed her tired eyes.

Then her mother came over and sat down beside her. 'Tania,' she whispered, 'my daughter, you will get it next time will you not? Otherwise the most terrible things will happen to us.'

Tania opened her eyes and looked at her mother in silence for a moment then she asked softly: 'Mother, were you ever really in love?'

The old woman raised her eyes and said simply: 'Yes, my dear—you were conceived in love.'

'I wonder if you will understand then. I am in love with Peter Carew, but that is not all. He also is in love with me—really in love. He wants me to marry him, mother.'

'To marry him, Tania!'

'Yes, and he wants to take us both back to England with him.'

'Have you—have you accepted?'

Tania shook her head. 'No. He did not ask me until after I had taken the packet, so I could not.'

'What! You have it here?'

'Yes, and I must go out again at once in order to return it to him. When he knows the truth about me he may not wish to marry me any more, but I must return it—all the same. Even if it costs my life and yours. Do you understand that, mother?'

The Baroness patted her daughter's shoulder. 'Yes, my dear,' she murmured. 'I understand. Whatever happens you must return it to him now.'

'Oh, mother!' Tania's head fell forward on the old

woman's shoulder. 'Forgive me if I have . . .'

The door crashed open. The Eunuch stood there, huge, triumphant, his little black eyes glinting, his tiny mouth twisted into an evil snarl. He had crept up the stairs again on tiptoe and, for the last two minutes had been listening with his ear placed against the crack of the flimsy door.

'I knew it,' he cried in a thin vindictive screech. 'You lied to me. I felt it in my bones.'

Then in three quick steps he was across the room. As Tania rose he seized her by the neck and flung her backwards across the divan. In his tremendously powerful grip she could do no more than twist and turn like a rabbit in a trap. He wasted no time asking her questions or searching her bag or fumbling at her breast. Kazdim Hari Bekar knew women and their ways better than any man West of Suez. With one swift movement of his flabby little hand he turned her skirt up to her chest, then ripped her silk stocking from thigh to knee, snatched the packet, and let her go.

The Baroness meanwhile was clawing at his back in a feeble endeavour to pull him off her daughter. As she saw the packet she snatched at it.

He swung round, raised his open hand and struck her with the cushion of it upon the side of her neck.

That one swift, vicious, cutting blow would have broken the arm of a child or the wrist of a man. Madam Vorontzoff's eyes started from her head and, with one gasp, she fell to the floor.

Tania screamed and flung herself upon her mother's body, but even as the door banged to and the patter of the Eunuch's tiny feet sounded upon the first stairs, she knew that her mother was dead, and that with him had gone that packet which, at the last, she had striven so desperately to protect.

25

The Plain Van

Peter did not discover his loss until he began to undress in his bedroom at the *Pera*. He hung his coat over the back of a chair and, meaning to put the packet under his pillow, thrust his hand into the breast pocket to get it.

For a good ten seconds he remained absolutely rigid, his tall figure slightly bent, his arm extended, his hand buried in the coat. Then, as though galvanised into action by an electric current, he began a frantic search through his other pockets although he knew already that it was useless.

The thing had been in his breast pocket and nowhere else. He had placed it there when Tyndall-Williams had handed it to him at the Embassy. He had put it back there after he had shown it to Tania in the taxi. He had not seen it since. But he had felt it. Once when he got out his note case to pay the bill after dinner, and again ten minutes later when, having tied up the launch below the restaurant at Therapia, he had taken Tania in his arms. It had pressed for a moment hard against his ribs from the force with which he had drawn her to him.

It must have fallen out of his pocket in the cabin then, and be on the floor still. The thought had no sooner come to him than he snatched up his coat and rushed out of the room.

Within seven minutes a taxi set him down again at the steps near the Mosque, just below the Dolma Baghtche Palace. To his intense relief the launch was still moored alongside. The boatman had only collected the rug and cushions, then left it at the place where they landed.

He jumped on board and dived into the little cabin, whipped out his matches and struck a couple. By their light he began a frantic hunt for the missing packet. It was nowhere in the centre of the floor. As the matches burnt out he struck others, devoutly thankful to find his box more than half full. Desperate with anxiety now he peered into shadowy corners and routed into lockers.

A rough voice hailed him in Turkish from the doorway. It was the boatman who, noticing the light in the cabin from his office-shed on shore had come on board to investigate.

Peter could speak no Turkish, but he had tipped the man lavishly before and, after making him understand what had happened in rough pantomime, used that universal language again to secure his assistance.

The man produced a torch. Together they searched every inch of the little cabin, the stern, and the short forward deck, then went ashore and examined the steps, the boatman's office, and the adjoining shed where the cushions were stored, without result.

When they had finished Peter stood for a few moments on the landing place, staring out with unseeing eyes across the moonlit waters of the Bosphorus. At nine o'clock he had treated that little packet so lightly, thinking of it only as the cause of a short but exceedingly annoying routine journey. Now, at twenty-past eleven, it had become an object of overwhelming importance.

He had no knowledge whatever of its contents, but that had no bearing on the matter. If they were only birthday greetings, or a piece of wedding cake, the fact remained that it had been entrusted to him as a King's Messenger for safe delivery to the British Chargé d'Affaires in Angora. He would have taken far more care of it had he not been so overwrought at the necessity of having to say goodbye to Tania. The thought of leaving her behind in Istanbul had driven everything else out of his mind, but he knew that, far from being able to offer that as an excuse for his negligence, his association with her would be an even more damning indictment against him when he had to give an account of his movements during the evening.

It meant instant dismissal. That was a certainty, and it was less than three months since he had been forced to resign from the Army. 'What a career!' he thought savagely, 'to be sacked from two services before reaching the age of twenty-three.'

The first affair had been sheer bad luck of course, but this was totally different. Peter knew that his name would be erased from the Foreign Office list with ignominy, which was virtually the same thing as being cashiered from one of the fighting services.

Suddenly he thought of Tania. Only half an hour before he had asked her to marry him, and promised to take her *and her mother* back to England on the following day. His bitter dejection became absolute panic.

He remembered now how hard Tyndall-Williams had pressed him to remain in the Embassy for the night, and he had refused because he was determined to have his last evening with Tania. When he was questioned he would have to disclose how long they had spent over dinner, and the much longer time they had spent making love in the launch.

The family would be certain to worm the inside story of his dismissal out of some member of the Foreign Office, and what would happen when the whole clan knew that he had had the audacity to bring home the innocent cause of his lapse from duty as his future wife? The loss of this packet was overwhelming. It spelt ruin to his plans and hopes on every side.

Having cudgelled his brains for any other place in which he could have dropped it, he decided that the taxi in which he had taken Tania home offered the only possibility. He must have it traced at once, but he had no idea of its number, so if he went to the police it would be impossible for them to get hold of the driver before they had circularised all the taxi garages in the morning—and that would be too late for him to proceed as though nothing had happened to Angora—even if they found it for him.

There was no alternative. He must go straight back to the British Embassy, report his loss, and face the music. With feet like lead, he walked over to his waiting taxi, gave the address, and was driven up the hill again.

When he arrived at the Embassy he found the Chancery locked up for the night, but on inquiring for Tyndall-Williams he was sent through to the residential portions of the building where an elderly butler informed him that the first secretary was in the garden.

'Is he alone?' asked Peter huskily.

'No, sir. Several other gentlemen are out there as well. Shall I take your name through to him?'

'Yes—no.' Peter hesitated and contradicted himself, funking the ordeal now that he was actually faced with it. He felt that he must have a few more minutes in which to pull himself together, so he added:

'I'll announce myself, thanks. You know who I am, don't you? I brought the bags from London last Tuesday and I called on Lady Cavendish the following afternoon, you may remember.'

'I remember you long before that, Mr. Peter, sir.' The elderly butler's face broke into a waggish smile. 'I was with Lady Waincourt, at Luke, when you used to stay with the young gentlemen there in the holidays. But that's a good few years back now.'

'Good Lord! yes,' Peter brightened. 'I was sure I knew your face when I called the other day. And your name's—now wait a moment, don't tell me—I know, Halket!'

'That's it, sir. Halket. Those were good days, Mr. Peter, although you did lead me a dance with your stink-bombs and booby traps.'

'Yes, we had great times at Luke, hadn't we?'

The old man smiled again, then his face went grave. 'I was most distressed, sir, if you'll forgive my mentioning it, most distressed to hear about that—er—unfortunate affair at Maidenhead.'

Peter winced. It brought him back with a horrid jolt to the far worse situation in which he was at the moment, but he managed to answer, 'So you even heard of that out here.'

'Why, yes, Mr. Peter. In these foreign places we have little to interest us except the news from home, and him being a Turk, it was the talk of the Embassy for a week or more. Of course, that Prince Ali deserved all he got. He comes to us here at times and he's no gentleman, not in the proper meaning of the word, but it was hard, very hard, on you and Captain Destime.'

'It was bad luck,' Peter agreed, then the elderly butler went on quietly:

'It's queer, isn't it, sir, the two of you both being here now on the same day.'

'Here! What on earth do you mean?'

'Why, Captain Destime arrived this morning, sir. In an awful state he was, and then he came rushing in on us again this afternoon. He's out there in the garden now.'

'Look here, Halket,' Peter spoke gruffly. 'Do something for me, will you. Get him away from the others and bring him in here to me without their knowing of it.'

'Certainly I will—if I can, Mr. Peter, but it won't be the other gentleman I'll have to get him away from. There's a lady in the case unless I'm much mistaken.'

'Never mind. Go and get him if you can. Say it's urgent —very urgent.' Peter had not the vaguest idea how Swithin could help him, but he was dreading his interview with Tyndall-Williams more than he feared the coming of Judgment Day, and the thought of a friend to whom he could pour out his trouble was irresistible.

As Halket left him, Peter sank into a chair in the hall and mopped his face with a handkerchief. He must be looking pretty grim, he thought, and wondered that the garrulous old chap had not commented on it.

On hearing footsteps, Peter stood up again. Swithin and Diana emerged from the garden arm in arm. Both had seraphically self-satisfied smiles on their faces. They greeted him simultaneously:

'Hallo, Peter!'

'How nice to see you here!'

'Thanks,' he said. 'It's nice to see you, too—and—er— together like this, I mean.'

Diana looked self-conscious for a moment and Swithin grinned. Then his bright eyes suddenly narrowed.

'What's the matter?' he asked abruptly. 'You're looking devilish queer.'

'I'm feeling it.' Peter flopped back into the chair. 'I've blotted my copy-book again—no, worse than that. I've spilt the whole bottle of ink over it this time.'

'You look as if you need a double brandy at the moment,' said Diana.

Halket had followed them in and Swithin glanced at him. 'Mr. Carew is not feeling too well, I'm afraid. D'you think you could get him something?'

'Certainly, sir. A double brandy, I think madam said.'

'What's bitten you, old chap?' Swithin asked kindly when the butler had disappeared.

Peter made a wry grimace. 'When I heard you were here, I asked to see you so that I could tell you about it before I go on the mat in front of Tyndall-Williams—and get myself hung.'

'What in the world have you been up to then?' Diana inquired. 'Spending all your journey money on chorus girls or making immoral suggestions to Lady Cavendish?'

'Good Lord, no! It's a thousand times worse than that. I've lost a blasted packet that Tyndall-Williams gave me to take to Angora.'

'What!' Swithin almost shouted.

'A double brandy, sir,' murmured Halket, appearing at his elbow.

'Thanks,' said Peter gratefully.

'You had better bring me one, too,' Swithin added grimly. 'Out in the garden if you don't mind. Come on, Peter. It's cooler out there and you can tell us about it without any likelihood of our being interrupted.'

Outside, they settled themselves on a semi-circular bench, hidden by a surrounding hedge of young cypresses from Tyndall-Williams and his friends, the murmur of whose voices came gently on the still night air from the place where they were seated some fifty yards away.

'Now,' said Swithin. 'Let's have it. You say you've lost the packet that Tyndall-Williams handed you this evening for transmission to Angora.'

'That's it,' Peter nodded miserably.

'Oh, Peter!' gasped Diana.

He gulped his brandy. 'I know. I deserve everything that's coming to me.'

Swithin shrugged his shoulders. 'You must forgive me being a bit sore, but I sweated blood over this business. However, that cuts no ice now, so let's get down to brass tacks. How did you come to lose it?'

'There was a girl—is, I mean,' Peter began.

'Go on, Peter,' urged Swithin. 'Is she a home product or an houri of this city?'

'She's a Russian—her name's Tania Vorontzoff.'

'Merciful heavens!' Diana groaned, 'you don't mean to say . . .'

'Your brandy, sir.' Halket appeared out of the darkness and proffered a glass on a salver.

Swithin took the glass and sighed profoundly: 'Thank you. God knows I need it.'

Diana glanced at the butler. 'I'm afraid it's very late, Halket, but I wonder if you could find me a drink, too.'

'By all means, madam. Would you care for a chicken sandwich with it perhaps?'

'That would be nice—if you are quite sure that we are not keeping you up?'

'Oh, no, madam. It is only twenty-five to twelve and I rarely go to bed before one.'

'So you fell for Tania, eh?' Swithin murmured as the butler turned away.

'You know her, then?' Peter exclaimed.

'Yes, we know her all right, and I suppose you realise that if you have been monkeying with her, you did not lose the packet, but that she *stole* it from you?'

'No,' Peter protested. 'No—it isn't possible, she wouldn't do a thing like that—she couldn't.'

'Believe me, she could. She is in the employ of Kazdim Hari Bekar.'

'Who's he?'

'Oh, he's a jolly little man. Great friend of mine. I've been seeing quite a lot of him lately. He's the Chief of the Secret Police here and about the biggest thug unhung.'

'You don't mean that Tania . . .'

'I do. I hate to hurt your feelings if you've really fallen for her badly, but the fact is she's a secret agent—a spy.'

'Good God!' Peter muttered miserably, 'and—and I've promised to marry her.'

'Peter, you haven't!' Diana suddenly sat bolt upright.

'She's not a spy—I don't believe it,' Peter choked out angrily.

Swithin shook his head. 'Both Diana and I know that she is, so it's useless for you to try and kid yourself, however much it hurts. Now be a good chap and tell us as clearly as you can just what did happen.'

With an effort Peter pulled himself together, and in less than two minutes he had given them an account of his stay in Constantinople, his affair with Tania, and its disastrous consequences. He had just finished when Halket appeared again.

As the butler set the tray down on the stone seat beside Diana, Swithin looked up at him and inquired, 'Is His Excellency's car in the garage?'

'No, sir. His Excellency went out just after dinner and he is not back yet.'

Diana nodded. 'That's right, Sir Francis told me that he was going down to see Daddy on the yacht for some special conference.'

'I see.' Swithin turned to Halket again. 'There must be other cars in the garage, though. I want to borrow one for half an hour—do you think you could arrange it for me?'

'Might I suggest that you—er—speak to Mr. Tyndall-Williams first, sir?'

'I'd rather not,' said Swithin frankly. 'I don't think he would mind by borrowing a car, but he's got the French Military Attaché with him at the moment, and as this is a private job I hardly like to disturb him about it now.'

'Quite so, sir.' Halket hesitated. 'Do you wish to drive yourself or would you require a chauffeur?'

'I must have a chauffeur, I'm afraid, and if there is any choice in the matter I'd prefer a closed car with side blinds. Otherwise I shall have to have myself driven out lying on the floor. Unfortunately the Turkish police are on the look-out for me, you see.'

'So I gathered sir. I happened to witness your arrival here this evening. A very fine performance, if I may be permitted to say so, sir.'

Swithin smiled. 'That's nice of you, Halket. Now will you be a real sportsman and try and fix up something for me. I'll leave a note for Mr. Tyndall-Williams with you which will exonerate you from all blame. If I don't manage to get back, he will be able to collect the car in the morning.'

'Very good, sir. I'm afraid that most of the chauffeurs are in bed by now—but I'll see what I can do.'

'Splendid—and the sooner I get off, the better. Then if all goes well, I'll be back by a quarter past twelve.'

'Darling! What *are* you going to do?' Diana cried the second Halket's back was turned.

'I'm going to have a cut at getting the darned thing back,' he declared.

'How can you,' she protested. 'We don't even know where it is.'

'We do, dearest. At least, I've got a pretty shrewd idea. Peter only left the girl at eleven o'clock. This thing is so important that she would never keep it till the morning. By the time he had got back to the *Pera*, she was on her way to Kazdim with it. He would not be at his office at this hour, so it's a hundred to one that she took it straight to his house. It's a wonder really, since he lives just behind the Mosque in the street leading down to the Dolma Baghtche steps, that Peter didn't run into her when he went back to search the launch.'

'Even if you're right—how can you possibly get hold of it?'

'By getting into Kazdim's house the way I came out. With all that's happened since, that seems days ago now, but it was really only the first thing this morning—so it's very unlikely that they've had the bars repaired yet.'

'Swithin! That would be sheer madness!'

'Why?' he countered. 'I should go in armed, so they won't have it all their own way this time if I do get caught, but if I'm lucky I'll find Kazdim on his own and get him in a corner. Then it will be my turn to laugh. The only thing is, Peter must come, too, and give me a leg up to that window—are you game, Peter?'

'Game? Good God, yes!' Peter shot out with almost frantic eagerness. The thought that there might still be a chance to repair his folly filled him with new life and he hurried on, 'I'll go anywhere with you—or without you. I'll do anything you tell me to. It's marvellous of you to . . .'

'Good lad!'

'Darling!' Diana's voice came hoarse and strained. 'There's not a hope of you succeeding. You're certain to get caught.'

'It's not like trying to break into a police station or a barracks,' he tried to reassure her. 'The place is only a private house, so Peter and I ought to be able to deal with the Eunuch and the one or two men he may have with him, between us, if we can only take him by surprise.'

'No, no. You must not even think of it.'

'Listen, my sweet.' Swithin took her hands and held them tightly in his own. 'In a little over an hour now, the Revolutionaries will be distributing the arms from their secret stores and unless we can stop it, the baloon goes up tomorrow at midnight. You *know* that the only chance lies in Kemal receiving the Kaka wafer before that, and anyhow

296

—for Peter's sake—we've simply got to get the darn thing back.'

'I know, I know,' Diana cried miserably. 'But, please, Swithin, think of me a little. I just can't bear that you should risk your life again.'

Peter put out a hand to stop her. 'That's all right. I wouldn't ask him to.'

She turned to him quickly. 'I'm terribly sorry, Peter. You've had the rottenest luck. I hate to stand in the way of what you must think is a chance to get out of your trouble, but honestly—to break into the Chief of Police's own house is absolute insanity.'

He nodded. 'I understand. Naturally you don't want Swithin to run such a big risk now you're—well, anyway, it's my show and I've got a gun in my bag at the *Pera*.'

'You can't go alone,' said Swithin firmly. 'You don't even know where the house is.'

'By the Dolma Baghtche, you said. You can describe it to me and I'll find it all right.'

Swithin shook his head. 'No, Peter. You're a good bit taller than I am, but you couldn't reach that window. This is a two-man job. It's quite useless for you to try and tackle it on your own.'

'Well, that's a pity—because I'm going to. If I do get shot or chucked into a Turkish prison, people won't think quite so badly of me as they would if I just crawled home with my tail between my legs. I should have been forced to take it lying down if you hadn't told me where the thing is likely to be at this moment, but since you have I've simply got to try and get it back—you must see that.'

'I do,' agreed Swithin, 'and I wish to God I hadn't told you now.'

For a moment they sat silent. Then Diana said very quietly, 'For one of you to go alone would be suicide, but two of you might stand some chance of getting away with it, so—so I give in.'

'No, it's not fair on you—I'll go alone,' Peter protested.

'You won't,' she said, with sudden sharpness, 'and if you try to, I shall walk straight over to Tyndall-Williams and tell him what you're up to. He'll see you don't leave the Embassy after that. Now, Swithin, tell me exactly what you intend to do.'

He lifted her hand and kissed it. 'If Halket can get us a car, we'll drive off in it to the street in which Kazdim has his house, leave it on the corner at the entrance of that alleyway I told you about, and get in at the window. The cell is only used very rarely, so it is unlikely to be occupied tonight and if that is so the door will not be locked. Then we'll go out through the passage to the garden and climb on to the balcony that runs the whole length of the house. The principal rooms are certain to open out on to that. We'll find Kazdim's study and as it's not yet midnight he'll probably be still at work. Then we break in, hold him up, get the locket, and make a dash with it back to the car.'

Diana shook her head. 'It's all very problematical, although, of course, that can't be helped, but the last part just won't do. He will almost certainly have a man on duty outside the street entrance who would question the driver of the car if it remains there while you're inside the house. Then your retreat will be cut off. And, in any case, you will never get away like that. He will be raising Cain down the telephone the second you've left him, and half the police in Pera will be out to stop you getting back to the Embassy. You'll never do it.'

'We can tie Kazdim up,' Swithin suggested.

She shook her head again. 'No, I don't like it. You must remember that the chances are you will be discovered and have to make a dash for it before you even get to him. It is essential that you should have a clear getaway.'

'You say this place is near the Dolma Baghtche steps,' Peter remarked. 'How about the launch. I expect it's still there. Couldn't we go in the car. Send it off directly it has dropped us, and then make off by water when we come out.'

'Now that *is* an idea,' Diana nodded. 'How far is the house from the steps, Swithin?'

'Not more than three hundred yards.'

'Good. Then immediately you reach the launch you will run out to the yacht in it. The whole thing is full of horrible uncertainties, but that is about the best arrangement we can make.'

'Right, darling.' Swithin stood up. 'I think we'd better go in then, and see if Halket's been able to get a car.'

Together they walked back to the entrance of the

Embassy. Halket met them in the doorway. A short, swarthy little man stood beside him.

'I've made an arrangement of which I hope you will approve, sir,' he said to Swithin. 'It occurred to me that since you said that you would prefer a closed car, the Embassy van might serve the purpose even better. It's a box Ford affair, and we collect the baggage in it from the station. A little uncomfortable, perhaps, but if you don't mind that, sir . . .'

'But that's marvellous!' exclaimed Swithin, 'we couldn't have anything better. How about a driver?'

The butler glanced at his companion. 'All the chauffeurs have gone for the night unfortunately, sir, but this is Murad. He is our electrician and does odd jobs about the house. I understand that he can drive a car, and he has volunteered to take you wherever you wish to go.'

'Splendid!' Swithin looked at the little electrician. 'And very kind of you, Mr. Murad. Am I right in thinking that you are not a Turk?'

Murad grinned and shook his head. 'No, I Syrian. Turks kill my father, mother, brothers, rape sister, all in big war against Eengleish—hate Turk.' He spat.

'I see.' Swithin turned back to Halket. 'One thing more. Several people in the Embassy must have pistols—do you think you could get a couple?'

'Really, sir, without permission I should hardly like . . .' the butler began uncomfortably, but Peter intervened.

'Come on, Halket. I'm in a mess and Captain Destime has very kindly offered to help me out, but where we're going we must have something to protect ourselves. Be a good chap and do your best for us.'

'Well, Mr. Peter, in that case . . .' Halket sighed heavily. 'I think that the Naval Attaché has one and he is sleeping out tonight. I'll go and see.'

'That's right,' Swithin encouraged him, 'and while you're gone I'll write that note for Mr. Tyndall-Williams which will let you out if we come up against any trouble.'

He sat down to the hall table and scribbled a brief line on a memo form, telling the first secretary that he had had to go out on an urgent private affair and had borrowed the Embassy van.

It was only just completed when Halket came downstairs

again gingerly carrying two pistols, one in each hand. They were a heavy Mark V. British Service revolver and a 9 mm. Webley and Scott automatic. He handed them over with extreme care and then produced a couple of handfuls of ammunition from his pockets.

'They are not loaded, sir,' he said to Swithin. 'But I've always thought them to be very dangerous things all the same.'

Swithin took them, passed the automatic to Peter, and began to load up. 'Well,' he smiled, 'I only hope we have no occasion to use them, but thank you for getting them all the same. Here is the note for Mr. Tyndall-Williams. You can give it to him if we fail to get back by one o'clock, but not before that, please.'

'Very good, sir. If you will come this way, I will show you to the van.'

They followed Halket out and walked after him round to the side of the Embassy. The canvas-covered Ford van had already been got out of the garage and stood there waiting for them. Swithin told Murad the corner at which they wished to be set down, then he climbed in and turned to say good-bye to Diana.

'Manners, my love, manners,' she said, scrambling after him into the low box back of the van. 'I do think you might have helped me up.'

'What the hell!' he exclaimed. 'Darling, you're not coming. Out you get!'

She shook her golden head. 'I only pray your luck holds, but what an amateur you are really, my sweet. Who do you think is going to make certain that the launch is still there— or have it got out again if it's not—unless I do. You have admitted yourself that it needs two of you to get into the house. Somebody has got to make certain that you have a clear getaway.'

'Diana, I won't have it,' he said sharply.

'I'm afraid you've got to.' She sat down on the floor-boards. 'Don't be a fool, darling, please. I'm not running the slightest risk. All I intend to do is to see that the launch is ready for you and sit in it until you come. If you don't turn up after you've been inside for half an hour, I shall go off to the yacht, stir up father and Sir Francis, who is probably still with him—and try and bring you help.'

'In that case . . .' he hesitated. 'But swear that you won't move a yard from the launch.'

'I swear. Come on, Peter. Hop in.'

Peter stepped up, and all three arranged themselves for the journey; then Murad closed the doors of the van, shutting them into a petrol-smelling darkness.

The Ford jolted and moved off. The hard floorboards were distinctly uncomfortable, but Diana leaned against Swithin and Peter leaned against the canvas side.

Murad was perhaps a better electrician than chauffeur, but after ten minutes's severe bumping the van halted. They all scrambled to their feet. Swithin put his hand upon the door to push it open, but as he did so the van suddenly moved forward again. They clutched at each other in the darkness and Peter fell. The other two pulled him to his feet, then the van stopped a second time.

Swithin put his arm round Diana and kissed her. 'We'll probably arrive in a hurry,' he said huskily, 'do be careful, sweet.'

'I'll be careful,' she whispered back, 'but what do you think I'm going to feel like waiting for you in that boat—I hate you for having let me in for this.'

'Not really?'

'Oh, of course not, you dear fool, but be as quick as you can, every moment is going to be an agony.'

Swithin pressed the door again. It did not give. 'Murad,' he called, realising that the van doors had a snap lock.

'Yes,' answered a voice. 'One moment, sir.'

They waited and then Swithin called again.

'We have arrived,' cried Murad, and he flung open the doors.

Swithin stepped out. Diana followed. For a moment their eyes were dazzled by bright lights, then they realised that they were standing in a courtyard.

'Where the devil are we?' exclaimed Peter, who had tumbled out after them.

'Welcome to my house,' piped a thin reedy voice, and as their eyes mastered the glare, they saw the Eunuch, vast, sardonic, chuckling, standing under the archway of a porch. Three soldiers stood on either side of him, their rifles levelled.

A moment later, Prince Ali walked out of the house, saluted, and bowed jerkily to Diana.

'It is a pleasure to see you here, Miss Duncannon,' he said quickly. 'When we have dealt with these gentlemen, you and I will be able to continue our conversation—from the point at which it was so rudely interrupted at Maidenhead.'

26

Two Go Home

In a second Diana realised what had happened. The self-satisfied smile on the face of the Turk-hating Mr. Murad told the whole story.

He was one of the Eunuch's men, of course, planted in the Embassy, and, she thought, in *what* a job for a secret agent. As the household electrician and handyman, he could listen in on telephones or, without arousing the least suspicion, visit every room in the place under the perfect cover of a little bag of tools.

He had probably been keeping an eye on them ever since Swithin's arrival that afternoon, and when Halket had gone along to arrange for a car had jumped at the chance of taking them all for a ride. How he must have laughed to himself when Swithin had named Kazdim's house as their destination, but instead of dropping them at the corner he had driven them right into the courtyard. That first halt had been when he was getting the gate open, and now they were in a pretty mess.

Diana's mind was naturally a quick one and these logical conclusions passed through it in less time than it took Prince Ali to speak his brief ironical greeting. Even before he had finished, her hands had shot out and grabbed Swithin and Peter each by an arm.

The soldiers were six men of Prince Ali's own regiment of Lazzes. Obviously his personal bodyguard, who had come with him on his visit to the Eunuch in the second of two large cars which stood a few feet from the van. She knew that at the least sign of resistance Swithin and Peter would be shot down. It would be instant death to fight or run. So she dug her fingers into the two men's arms and pulled them backwards with all her strength.

Prince Ali gave a sharp order. The soldiers closed in. Two of them remained with their rifles at the ready, while the other four seized Swithin and Peter, dragging them away from Diana. Both knew that the time for putting up a fight had passed. Her prompt action had prevented it.

With another jerky little bow, the Prince stepped forward and offered his arm to Diana. She placed her hand lightly on it and allowed him to lead her into the house. The Eunuch signed to the soldiers. They followed, pushing Swithin and Peter along in front of them. Kazdim and the other two brought up the rear.

They crossed a spacious tiled hall, with a gallery running round above it, and a fountain playing in a marble basin at its centre. Then passed into a small, comfortably furnished room, with book-lined shelves and one tall window. A great satinwood desk, from which a semi-circular portion had been cut to accommodate the stomach of its owner, and a specially made swivel chair of enormous proportions behind it, showed the room to be the Eunuch's special sanctum.

Prince Ali handed Diana to an armchair near the door and she sat down in it. She was very pale but her hands did not shake as she opened her bag, took out her case, and produced a cigarette. Ali lit it for her with a quick flick of his patent lighter.

Swithin and Peter were marched in, each held by two soldiers, and their party lined up against the wall. The Prince perched himself on the edge of the desk; he was obviously in an excellent humour for he nodded at the Eunuch and said, 'You may be seated, Kazdim.'

The elephantine Chef de Police bowed silently and sank into his special chair, as the Prince rapped out to the Lazzes, 'Search those two men for arms.'

Rough hands were run over Swithin and Peter. The Mark V. British Service revolver and the 9 mm. Webley and Scott automatic duly came to light and were placed upon the Eunuch's desk.

Diana was thinking quickly. Wondering what chance they had of escaping from this hornets' nest into which which they had been driven blindfold. She remembered the note that Swithin had left with Halket to be given to Tyndall-Williams at one o'clock. The first secretary would know then what had happened to them. But what would he do? What could he do, except see that Sir Francis registered an official protest against their detention in the proper quarter. It was hardly likely that any action would be taken on it before the morning and—so many things might happen between now and then. Diana stared at the carpet and drew very hard upon her cigarette.

Swithin was also thinking of that note and once more cursing his own stupidity. Feeling that it was not for him to give away Peter's calamity, he had said nothing of the loss of the packet containing the Kaka wafer or even where he meant to go—merely that he had borrowed the van for private purposes. When Tyndal-Williams received it and learned from Halket that Diana and Peter had gone out at the same time, he would doubtless be anxious enough about them all, but quite helpless to make a protest, since he would not have the faintest idea where they had gone—so they could not expect any help from that quarter. Swithin glanced at the tall window. It led on to the balcony; as he had guessed the Eunuch's room looked over the garden, but with the bodyguard of Lazzes in the house any attempt to break away and make a dash for it would be utterly futile, he and Peter would be shot down before they got five yards. He looked across at Diana and then quickly away again. She was taking it marvellously well—but . . . He swallowed hard and bit the inside of his lip.

'Out on the balcony,' snapped Ali to one of his men, and to another, 'you will remain outside the door. The rest of you can get back to the courtyard.'

With military precision they obeyed his order. There was a quick rattle of arms as five of them marched out of the room, and the sixth disappeared through the open window to commence pacing up and down the long balcony. The prisoners now remained alone with Ali and the Eunuch.

Peter stared at the two of them. It was through his folly that his friends had been landed in this grim situation, and he felt that it was up to him to make some sort of effort, however desperate, to get them out of it. Now that the guards had gone he weighed he chances of risking an attack. The Eunuch, having looked to see that it was loaded, was toying with the Webley Scott automatic behind his desk, a good fifteen feet away. Peter saw that he would almost certainly be shot before he could reach the desk and grab the service revolver, which still lay on it, but in the excitement Swithin and Diana might get away. They *might,* but how about the sentry who was pacing up and down the balcony—and the other one outside the door. Even if Swithin could tackle the first the chances were that he would be shot in the back by the second while lowering Diana over the balcony into the garden—and Prince Ali could hardly be expected to remain neutral. He had probably got a gun on him somewhere as well.

Concealing his thoughts was not one of Peter's strongest characteristics, and as his eyes switched from side to side the Prince divined his speculations.

'It is no use, Mr. Carew,' he said quietly. 'If you lift a finger you will be shot down like a rat. That will not make much difference to you of course as you are to be shot down quite soon in any case, but it would be a courtesy on your part to spare Miss Duncannon the unpleasantness of seeing your brains scattered on the carpet.'

'Shot,' stammered Peter. 'Why! What crime have I committed?'

'Your memory is a peculiarly short one,' the Prince remarked acidly. 'Obviously you have forgotten the last occasion on which you were in my presence.'

'No, I've only seen you once before—in England at the Boat Club Dance last June.'

'Well?—and it was you who was concerned with Captain Destime in that scandalous assault upon me.'

'Look here!' Peter protested hotly. 'You can't go and shoot people for a thing like that.'

'Can I not?' Ali slipped off the desk and drew himself up to his full height. 'I am a Prince of the Imperial House of Othman. Your offence was *lèse-majesté* in the first degree. Now you are on Turkish soil I intend to see that you receive the full and appropriate punishment for your act.'

Peter's mouth went sullen and he stuck out his chin angrily. 'You don't know what you're talking about. Turkey is a Republic. There is no such thing as *lèse-majesté* here now.'

'There are those who still adhere to the ancient laws and they will be happy to undertake your execution.'

'Execution!—murder you mean—I . . .'

'Your Highness.' Diana stood up. 'May I remind you that we are British subjects. Our presence here is known to our

306

Embassy. If any harm befalls us our Government will demand . . .'

'Do you think I care what they demand,' he cut her short quickly.

'The Gazi will care, she parried, 'and he will punish you as he has punished others. Your Royal blood will not save you from his anger.'

His teeth suddenly flashed in a quick smile. 'So you threaten me with the Gazi, eh? Why be so foolish when you know all about the Kaka. Within twenty-four hours he will be of as little account as the ash that falls from this cigarette. *I*, Ali Mahomet Bayezid Orchan shall be Caliph of Turkey and all the Faithful under Heaven.'

'The more reason then for Your Highness to avoid giving offence to Britain.' Diana's voice was very low but quite calm and clear. 'This arbitrary action that you speak of—the execution of these gentlemen without trial—would cause immense indignation throughout the whole English-speaking world. Surely you could hardly choose a more inauspicious manner in which to begin your reign.'

Ali walked over and stood in front of her. 'Do you think then that I am a complete fool,' he asked slowly. 'You say that your Embassy knows of your presence in this house. If they do—what then? They may have it searched to-morrow if they wish—but you will not be here. Since you already know of the coming revolution we can speak freely of it. Tomorrow night there is certain to be shooting in the streets. The dead bodies of all three of you will be left on some convenient street corner. When their discovery is reported to your Embassy my Foreign Minister will call in person on your Ambassador to offer our condolences that three of his nationals should have lost their lives through their own indiscretion. No Government can be held responsible for the safety of foreigners who chose to wander in public places during times of crisis.'

'You—Good God! you can't mean to kill her too,' Swithin burst out.

The Prince turned and looked at him. 'I find it regrettable myself, but what other course is open to me. As Miss Duncannon has so shrewdly pointed out, the British Government might bother me for explanations if they learned the true manner in which you two came to die, and

I have no desire to quarrel with them—yet. It would be a great stupidity then, on my part, to release her so that she could tell them that I had you shot. However, before she dies I wish to give her also a little lesson in humility.'

Diana saw the spark in Swithin's eyes. She knew that in another moment his control would snap, and that he would be shot down by the Eunuch as he launched himself on the Prince. She took a step forward and turned her back on him, placing herself so that she faced the desk and brought her body in the line of fire. By that small movement she had made it impossible for Swithin to spring at Ali without first thrusting her aside and she was certain that whatever happened he would not chance her being shot instead of himself.

Ali smiled as he noticed the manœuvre. It gave him enormous pleasure to be able to get under Swithin's skin. So he went on quietly. 'It will interest you to know, Miss Duncannon, that there is an ancient ritual when a Caliph summons a woman to his bed. I intend that you shall be the first to receive that honour during my Caliphate, or rather shall we say, since I anticipate by twenty-four hours, to receive it in the form of a dress rehearsal. The lady is bathed, perfumed, bejewelled, and robed in the most gorgeous garments by her envious companions who delight, by such servitude, to perfect the enjoyment of their lord; then she is led in procession to the Imperial chamber.'

Peter trembled with suppressed fury. He felt that he could not possibly allow this to go on any longer. He glanced at Swithin and saw that he obviously could do nothing; he was standing with his feet apart, his fists clenched, his eyeballs staring, while little beads of sweat had broken out on his forehead—but Diana stood between him and the Prince. Peter looked across the fifteen feet of bare carpet at the Eunuch. The distance seemed the length of a cricket pitch or more. Kazdim was watching him intently out of his little round black eyes; he smiled with devilish amusement and toyed with the big automatic. 'I shouldn't have a hope in hell,' Peter summed up the situation to himself in abject misery.

'The accompanying escort unrobes the lady garment by garment,' continued Ali, 'then retreats backwards with low obeisances, closing the doors and leaving the favoured one naked in the presence of her lord. He reclines at ease in the great bed of State inspecting this thing which is to be the instrument of his pleasure. She, overcome by the honour done her, falls upon her knees, touches the ground three times with her forehead and offers fervent prayers to Allah that, unworthy as she is, he may confer the inestimable blessing upon her of allowing her to conceive. Then with true humility she insinuates herself into the foot of the Imperial bed, creeps upwards little by little, until she can kiss the feet of the Descendant of the Prophet and receiving permission to advance, presses her lips to each of his legs in turn, inch by inch as she crawls forward on her belly . . .'

Diana fought to keep a hold over her intense cold anger. If she once let herself go and struck him she knew that Swithin, whose jerky breathing she could hear behind her, and Peter, glaring at the Prince with murderous hate three yards to her left, would come rushing forward, and that a second later the Eunuch would butcher them with his gun. Ali was perhaps even playing for that. She knew that it would give him an added pleasure to have them massacred in front of her eyes before having her carted off to the private apartments of his house. The blood had drained from her face, her mouth was parched and dry, but she said slowly, evenly, so that every word should sink in. 'Rather than let *Your Highness* touch me I would sleep with the filthiest *hamal* from the docks.'

The shot went home. From between her lowered eyelids she saw him wince, and knew that the lash of her tongue had caught his vanity on the raw. For a second he bared his teeth and she regretted her words fearing that he was going to strike her, but only because she knew that if he did it would be the sign for the massacre to begin. Then he recovered himself and smiled again as he threw a glance at Kazdim.

'Evidently you are not aware of the persuasive powers of Kazdim Pasha. He has had much experience of recalcitrant women, and as by tomorrow night he will rejoice in the title of His Highness the Chief Eunuch to the Commander of the Faithful, he too shall play his part in our dress rehearsal. When the escort has retired we will permit him to remain, in order that he may coax you through each separate stage of the ceremony.'

Kazdim chuckled in his many chins and his thin falsetto came queerly from the rose-bud mouth. 'To hear is to obey, Oh! Most Exalted One. May Allah bless the pleasures of the Illustrious Descendant of the Prophet. His servant is eager to show such small talents as he may possess in assuring the abject obedience of the slave that she may bring felicity to the Highest of all masters.'

There was a discreet rap on the door.

'Yes?' barked the Prince.

'It opened and Malik's head appeared. He salaamed to Ali, and then looked across at Kazdim.

'Agent 264 is here,' he announced, 'wishing to speak with you on a matter of great urgency and importance, but something is wrong with ...'

Next moment the door was pushed open, a cloaked figure thrust her way past him. It was Tania.

Her dark hair hung matted and dishevelled about her face, her eyes were glazed and staring, little flecks of foam showed at the corners of her red mouth. Her beautiful face was blank and stupid.

She looked wildly round. Peter saw no recognition in her glance as it swept over him. Her great dark eyes held the crazed look of a madwoman who has lost her wits from extreme suffering.

Suddenly her eyes came to rest upon the Eunuch. She screamed as though she had trodden on a white hot coal and, before Malik could stop her, pulled an old revolver from under her cloak.

As she fired the explosion seemed to shake the room. Kazdim had risen, his little mouth opened, a thin wail came from it. His black eyes started out from between their rolls of fat, a terrible agony seemed to shake his great body for a second, then he crashed forward on his desk, shot through the stomach.

Before Kazdim had fallen Peter flung himself on Malik from behind. With his much greater height and strength he swung the little Turk off his feet and brought his skull crashing against the woodwork of a bookcase.

'The door,' he yelled, as he smashed Malik's head into the wooden shelving, 'Lock the door!' but Diana needed no urging. She had slammed it shut behind the now gibbering Tania and turned the key.

As Diana moved from in front of Swithin his fist shot out. The blow caught Ali full in the mouth. Two of his front teeth gave under it and he went down in front of the desk. Swithin hurled himself on top of the prostrate Prince and, as he landed full upon his body driving every ounce of breath from it, he let out a shout.

'Peter—the man outside—for God's sake tackle him!'

Tania stood pointing at the great body of the Eunuch with the still smoking barrel of her gun. She was screaming wildly 'He killed my mother—he killed my mother!'

Diana snatched a heavy ledger from the Eunuch's desk and hurled it at the light. There was a crash of splintering glass.

Darkness blacked out the whole scene with startling suddenness, but Peter had already snatched up the Mark V. revolver from the desk, leaped across the struggling forms of Swithin and the Prince, and out on the balcony.

Swithin felt no scruples. With the ferocity of madness he smashed his fist into the prostrate Prince's face, kneed him in the stomach and then began to tear, with frantic fingers, at his collar.

It gave. He ripped away the linen shirt, thrust his hand inside, and grabbed the locket. One wrench and the new ribbon which held it snapped. He staggered to his feet and gasped out:

'Diana?'

'Here!' she cried from the balcony. 'Here—come on.'

As he turned there was another shattering report. The flash lit up the room as brightly as full daylight. The Eunuch, his withered apple cheeks sagging horribly, his face a grey distorted mask of pain—was firing from his desk. Tania stood opposite him, an imbecile smile upon her parted lips.

'Crash—crash—crash—crash.' The shots followed each other in rapid succession. By the light of the flashes, Swithin saw that Tania had a small round hole right in the centre of her forehead, and that there was a terrible gash just below her right eye. As the last shot reverberated through the room he saw her sag and collapse upon the floor.

'Swithin,' Diana was calling. 'Swithin—for God's sake come.'

Heavy blows were thudding on the door as the Lazz outside strove to break it in with the butt end of his rifle. Swithin dashed out on to the balcony. Diana was already astride the low balustrade. She dropped from sight as he appeared.

'Peter,' he yelled, as he slid over the balustrade and fell sprawling beside her. 'Peter—where are you?'

'Here,' came Peter's voice from above. 'Where's Tania?'

'Safe out of it—gone on ahead—come on, you fool,' Swithin shouted back as he picked himself up. Diana was running hard—already half-way across the garden.

Swithin pelted after her. The moon was sinking but it still gave them sufficient light to see a low arched doorway in the farther wall. As Diana reached it Swithin joined her.

Careless of their nails they both tore at it to get it open, but it was locked.

'Peter! Where the hell are you?' Swithin roared into the darkness.

'Coming——' came an answering shout and the sound of Peter's feet thudding as he fled across the garden.

As he came up Swithin snatched at his revolver. 'Give me that thing,' he panted. 'We'll be out of here in a second —did you manage that sentry?'

'Yes—hit him with the butt-end of the gun then chucked him head first over the balcony,' Peter gasped, 'but where is Tania?'

'Gone out a different way,' Swithin told him tersely, jamming the barrel of the revolver against the ancient lock.

A chorus of shouts went up from the balcony fifty yards behind them. The Prince's Lazz guard had broken through the door. A rifle cracked, and then another. A bullet flattened itself on the stonework above the door with a sharp smack. Swithin pressed the trigger of the revolver. Its bullet burst the lock and they wrenched the door open.

He seized Diana's arm. 'Run,' he urged her. 'Run.'

She shook herself free, snatched at the hem of her dress with both hands, pulled it up to her waist and, with her long silk-clad legs flickering in the waning moonlight, pelted down the hill.

As they shot round a bend in the street a hundred yards farther down, Peter, who was bringing up the rear, threw a glance over his shoulder. The soldiers were pouring out of the little door in the Eunuch's garden wall. One paused to fire. The bullet clicked on the cobbles, ricocheted with a loud whine and sung on into the wall of a house. Then the Lazzes started forward in pursuit.

Another moment and Swithin reached the Dolma Baghtche steps. With silent fervour he thanked the Gods of all mankind. The launch was still there. He grabbed the painter that secured it to a bollard.

Peter took a flying leap and landed in the stern. Diana tumbled after him, Swithin had loosed the rope.

'All clear,' he sang out as the soldiers came charging round the corner of the street. Peter pressed over the start-ing lever and the propeller churned the water. Swithin, kneeling in the bow, thrust off the nose of the launch with a boat-hook and they were speeding out into the Bosphorus.

Diana looked back. Dark figures were already running up and down the landing place in search of a boat with which to follow. Two of the figures stopped running. Then Swithin called sharply from the bow.

'Lie down!—they're going to fire.'

She dropped to her knees and scrambled into the low cabin. Peter flung himself flat beside the engine. Instantly after came the crack of rifles and the splintering of glass as the bullets crashed through the windows of the little deck-house where Diana was crouching.

Swithin crawled back from the bow. 'You all right?' he whispered anxiously.

'Yes,' she breathed. 'Yes.'

Then came Peter's voice. 'Tania!—where is she? Are you sure she got out the other way?'

There was another burst of firing from the shore. They cowered in the bottom of the launch as it raced through the water, then Swithin answered soberly. 'She saved us, Peter—but she went out the way we've all . . .'

'What!' Peter cut him short. 'You mean . . .?'

'That's it, old chap. Kazdim's dying now with a bullet in his guts, but he rallied after you dashed out to the bal-cony and put five shots into her at point blank range. One of them went clean through her head. She was quite dead, Peter, or else I wouldn't have left her.'

'Oh Hell!' moaned Peter. 'My dear . . . my dear!'

Diana stretched out a hand from the cabin to where he was crouching by the engine. 'Peter, you saw her. She had gone out of her mind. She was raving that Kazdim had killed her mother—poor girl, she must have been half-crazy with worry—torn between her love for you and the awful job she was forced to do. That last shock must have turned her brain.'

'That's it,' Swithin agreed slowly. 'The only clear thought she had left was to get the Eunuch—and she did.'

He lifted his head cautiously above the gunwale of the launch, wondering why the firing had stopped and muttered: 'They've managed to get a boat—they're after us.'

Diana peered up at him. 'Shall we be able to reach the *Golden Falcon* before they catch us do you think?'

'We ought to—I can see her anchor light already. More to the right, Peter—more to the right.'

Peter put over the wheel until Swithin checked him. He was so broken up by the thought of Tania—so young, so gay, so beautiful—lying dead where they had left her, that his actions were now like those of an automaton.

Swithin was thinking rapidly. If they succeeded in getting on board the yacht Prince Ali and his Lazzes would follow.

Diana, Peter and he would be arrested—and lugged ashore again to be butchered. Even if Sir Francis Cavendish were still on board, British Ambassador though he was, it was extremely unlikely that he would be able to protect them from the mad fury of the Prince. Still, there might be a chance to hide Diana if they could reach the yacht with a few moments grace.

The Lazzes began to fire again. A shot sang over the launch, another and another. Diana shut her eyes. Swithin swore profanely.

A hail sounded out of the semi-darkness ahead. It came from the after deck of the yacht. Peter risked a bullet and knelt, peering at the dark shape of the *Golden Falcon* as it loomed up before them. He gave the wheel a sharp twist and shut off the engine.

The crack of rifles still continued from the pursuing boat but the moon had slipped beneath the far horizon and now, in the darkness, the Lazzes were firing wild.

The launch turned, was caught in the current, swung for a moment, and scraped the yacht's gangway. Swithin had pulled Diana to her feet. Peter grabbed an iron stanchion.

'Now!' he cried. 'Jump!'

Swithin and Diana landed together on the narrow platform at the foot of the yacht's outboard ladder, staggered, and fell against the steep wooden stairs.

The racing tide sucked at the launch. It was torn from under Peter's feet and drifted away into the darkness. He clung to the stanchion, his legs dangling in the water, heaved himself up, and wriggled to safety as Swithin grabbed his arm.

Diana was already stumbling up the ladder as Peter scrambled to his feet. Swithin pushed him towards the stairs. 'After her!' he rasped, 'and tell them to hide her in the bunkers.' Then he pulled the revolver from his pocket.

'Ali's boat swept up alongside. There was a dark huddle of men in the middle of it. One of them stretched out a hand and grabbed the gangway. Swithin kicked it off. He felt that if only he could kill the Prince, Sir Francis or Sir George might be able to overawe the leaderless soldiers who would remain. In the half-light he could not distinguish which of the men was Ali so he fired right into the middle of the group.

There was a screech of pain, but one of the men had grabbed his leg and another was scrambling on to the platform. He kicked himself free and bolted up the ladder after Peter.

As he reached the lighted quarter-deck sailors seemed to be running in all directions. The shrill blast of a boatswain's whistle was calling 'All hands on deck.' The yacht's Captain came hurrying forward.

'What the hell's all this?' he thundered. Then he saw Diana.

Swithin grabbed his arm. 'For God's sake take her below, he urged breathlessly. As he spoke there came the sound of the Lazzes' feet pounding up the ladder. He turned and glimpsed Prince Ali at their head as they sprang on to the deck.

In the bright light Ali's face looked ghastly. It was covered with blood. His fine nose was twisted and broken where Swithin had smashed it in, blood trickled from his mouth and two of his front teeth were gone. His eyes were lit with the demoniacal glare of a maniac. He hurled himself on Swithin with the ferocity of a mad wolf. They crashed to the deck together.

The four Lazzes who had survived the fight, Servet, and another of the Eunuch's men, rushed forward ready to kill, but they could not strike at Swithin in that tumbling heap without risk of harming their Prince.

Peter and the Captain were endeavouring to drag Diana away, but she fought and struggled with them, determined to remain with Swithin.

Suddenly the door of the after deck-house swung open and a little group of men came out. Among them she recognised her father. 'Daddy,' she shrieked. 'Help, Daddy! Help!'

Sir George was in the middle of the group standing beside the British Ambassador, some of the others were in uniform, but alone and a little in front stood a slim grey-faced man in immaculate evening dress.

The bulk of the figures that Swithin had thought to be sailors drew together. Somebody barked an order. They sprang to attention, and then, like a whisper of the wind a murmur ran round the deck.

'The Gazi!—The Gazi!—The Gazi!'

Swithin wrenched himself free of Ali, rolled over and lurched to his feet. For a second he stood there staring at that almost legendary figure. Mustapha Kemal Pasha. The man who lives buried in the depths of Asia Minor. The man who had defied the might of the Victorious Allies, and with inferior forces driven the legions of the British Empire from Gallipoli into the sea. The greatest General of his age and the man who has welded the shattered remnants of an empire into a new nation.

Ali had also staggered to his feet. He stared round out of half-blinded eyes and a sudden horror spread over his blood-smeared face. But he ran forward pointing a shaking finger at Swithin.

'This man,' he stammered, 'is a secret agent—he has escaped from prison—he—he has shot two of my men!'

'So?' The Gazi's voice came harsh and cold. His tired, lined, bitter face expressed no emotion, but his great pale magnetic eyes bored through the Prince.

'Sir! Excellency!' Swithin gasped, thrusting his hand into his pocket and drawing out the locket. 'Judge—judge for yourself. Whatever I have done has been for your service.'

Kemal extended a long nervous hand and took the locket. Sir George, Sir Francis, Diana, Peter, the Prince, Swithin, the Gazi's entourage and the soldiers of the bodyguard did not make a single movement while he examined the inscription on the Kaka wafer. A hush like that of death fell upon the crowded deck.

Then in a clear incisive voice he read out the signatures upon it: 'Ali Mahomet Bayezid Orchan, Prince of the Ottoman Empire. Janik Lijje Azez, Prince of Kurdistan, Hassen ben Irrad, Emir of Kirkuk. Kazdim Hari Bekar, Chef de Police Secret. Waldo Nauenheimer, Direktor, Hartz Chemisch und Metallen Allgemein Gesellschaft.'

Swithin looked swiftly across the deck to where Diana, her hair all tumbled, her dress soiled and torn, stood now beside her father. She caught his glance, smiled, and then very rudely put her finger to her nose. Next moment he saw Arif and Jeanette standing side by side a few feet behind her and his heart leapt for joy to find that those two good friends of his were safe.

The Gazi was speaking again. 'Captain Destime. Turkey owes you much. Owing to your earlier work, which your Ambassador has reported to me, and that of your associates, the armament depots of these traitors are already in the hands of my trusted officers. We were not altogether unprepared and I have long suspected the loyalty of Azez and Ben Irrad. They are most carefully watched, and Nauenheimer was arrested by my orders this morning when about to leave the country. For this final proof against the ringleaders of the conspiracy which you have obtained I am grateful. I shall take an early opportunity of recognising your services in a fitting manner.'

He turned abruptly to one of his officers, and pointed at Prince Ali. 'Arrest that man. Take him ashore and hang him. He has proved disloyal to Turkey.'

As four members of the bodyguard closed round Prince Ali, Kemal was shaking hands with the Ambassador and Sir George Duncannon. Swithin caught the Gazi's last words to the latter.

'Tonight we have done much to reach a happy understanding. My Minister of Finance will work out the details with your brother.' Then with a quick stride he walked over to the gangway.

Three launches had come alongside. The Gazi left by the first, Ali between his guards in the second, and some minutes later the Ambassador prepared to depart in the third. Peter was standing dazed and silent at the ship's rail, staring down into the dark waters. As Sir Francis Cavendish was about to leave he took his arm, and said gently, 'I don't know what you've been up to, young man, and in the circumstances I don't intend to ask, but I think perhaps you had better come ashore with me.'

☙   ☙   ☙   ☙   ☙

Half an hour later Swithin stood in the stern of the yacht. Diana leaned against his shoulder. Underneath their feet the screws churned the water and a train of foam ran like a silver pathway from the ship's wake until it was hidden by the darkness. The twinkling lights of Stamboul were dimming in the distance as the *Golden Falcon* cleaved her way through the waters of the Bosphorus and out into the Marmara—carrying them home.

'Do you think you will enjoy this voyage better than our last?' she asked with a wicked smile.

'You little devil,' he laid his cheek against hers very gently, 'but why on earth didn't you tell about Waldo Nauenheimer?'

'I didn't know enough—to be certain. Only that he was an armament man—and going on to Constantinople after we reached Athens. You were terribly jealous weren't you —poor stupid. I was awfully sorry for you really—but you were so deep and intense that if I had displayed the least liking for you Waldo might have suspected that I was not quite as shallow as I seemed whereas my apparent passion for that nice idiot Cæsar Penton convinced him that I was perfectly harmless.'

Swithin grunted. 'I believe you liked the fellow really.'

'Of course I did,' she replied demurely—'otherwise I should have taken on Haddo Claydon-ffinch.'

'But think of all the hours we wasted, sweet—and you didn't succeed in getting anything out of Waldo anyway.'

'Really!' Diana exclaimed. 'The conceit of you amateurs. What do you think I've been up to these last two months. You dear fool, it was I who secured the information which enabled Kemal to arrest Waldo this morning.'

'Darling!'

'What?'

'Kiss and forgive me, sweet.'

As they drew apart for a moment someone turned on the radio in the deck-house. A clear harsh voice reverberated on the air.

'. . . and so to those who are members of the junior cells of the Kaka let the fate that has overtaken your leaders be a warning. I could trace you and hunt you down one by one if I would, but I prefer that you should come, of your own accord, to regard such attempts to wreck the sure foundation upon which I am building a new Turkey—with horror. For those . . .'

'It's the Gazi,' said Swithin, 'speaking to his people about the break up of the Kaka.'

'But they will all be in bed! It must be the middle of the night,' exclaimed Diana.

'No member of the Kaka will be asleep, darling—you forget, their arms were to be distributed tonight.'

The voice of Mustapha Kemal Pasha came again strong and vibrant, '. . . those followers of the Prophet who wish to continue the practice of their ancient faith are free to do so, as also are the Christians and the Jews. But let them beware how they attempt to tamper with the machinery of State. Religion and nationality are things apart. Men, and women alike, your proudest thought should be that each one of you is a Turk. As a nation we are second to none in our six centuries of history. Today we are healthier as a State than we have been for generations. Our ancient spirit grows to new manhood in a happier form. I am a Turk. I speak to all who have Turkish blood in their veins. Stand by me! Follow me! Obey my ordinances!—and for another six hundred years Turkey shall hold her place among the nations!'